NEWMAN

## Books by Roger Taylor

*The Call of the Sword*
*The Fall of Fyorlund*
*The Waking of Orthlund*
*Into Narsindal*
*Dream Finder*
*Farnor*
*Valderen*
*Whistler*
*Ibryen*
*Arash-Felloren*
*Caddoran*
*The Return of the Sword*
*The Keep*
*Travellers*
*Newman*
*Aikido–more than a martial art*

# NEWMAN

## Roger Taylor

*Published by*
**Bladud Books**

# Chapter 1

John Newman was a long time coming. "Like me," said his father. "A slow starter."

He had been officially due a fortnight earlier, and they had panicked calmly into hospital after a microscopic symptom on the due day. Subsequently however, John put his feet up and kept them up, sensing with the impeccable judgement of youth that his present billet was almost certainly superior to any other he was likely to get.

His father visited the hospital faithfully each day and gazed at his wife Ann with reproachful concern. After a week, the joke was palling. His "slow starter" slowly expired, as did his wife's "burnt the house down yet?" and each day, when all relevant instructions for the more or less efficient running of the house and the stocking of her hospital locker had been issued, they held hands and awaited the whim of their about-to-be firstborn.

Despite his underlying concern and his embarrassing incompetence at routine household tasks, Peter Newman quite enjoyed the limbo period of his wife's stay in hospital. The quiet, empty house, the solicitous concern of neighbours, the sense of impending events, gave a timeless quality of immediacy to his life and, business also being quiet, he engrossed himself in the minor tasks of his temporary bachelor existence.

Over the two weeks, the journey to the hospital, the long walk through confusing corridors, the identifying of significant personnel, etc, ran the gamut from hesitant strangeness through cheery ritual to unseeing familiarity. He was worldly-wise enough to corner the appropriate shamans and to persist pleasantly until his enquiries were answered. Technicalities aside, this boiled down to, "Stop worrying. It'll come when it's ready," and he reasoned, without solace, that if they were unconcerned, why should he be?

Contractions came and went, but showed no signs of attempting a long run until Ann had been in hospital for ten days and was about to be sent home after having been subjected to a variety of drips and potions in an attempt to galvanize her recalcitrant off-spring. It seemed, however, that the threat of being sent home un-separated, triggered mother and child's ancient genetic machinery more effectively than these several modern chemicals, and triggered also the hospital's far cruder machinery, which slowly re-focussed on Mrs. Newman, and started grinding into action.

It had been the intention of Peter Newman to remain with his wife to comfort and encourage her through the darker moments of her travail and, for quite a time, clammy hand held clammy hand while he uttered platitudes, though these were as much for his benefit as for hers. Inevitably it was not what either had expected. It was mundane, earthy, and hard work, although occasionally, as he looked down at his wife's red, sweat-stained face and sweat-dank hair, he felt a faint stirring of awe at what it was they were doing. She lay in the temporary wreck of her looks and dignity, and he in the temporary wreck of his domestic and business affairs, while forces outside their careful rationalizations inexorably prepared to sacrifice them for the continuation of their kind.

After an interminable period, Ann's eyes began to glaze with fatigue, and the tone in the delivery room altered.

"How long has this been going on now?"

"She's getting very tired..."

"Hm..."

A white coat put its hand across its mouth in thought and then, abruptly, the proceedings jerked into a new gear.

The force of this accelerated tenor of events deposited Peter Newman in a deserted waiting room across the corridor. He knew he had been professionally out-manoeuvred, but his instinctively polite reaction to a polite request—"Would you just wait here for a moment, Mr. Newman, while doctor..." etc etc—had carried him beyond the pale of a dignified return, so he sat and felt vaguely inadequate.

Fifteen minutes later, just as he had started prowling, a round cheerful nurse he had never seen before congratulated him on the birth of his son.

"Bloody hell," he said softly, as if winded, and sat down abruptly. For a few moments he gazed vacantly ahead, stunned like, many before him, by the advent of the unexpected emotions of father-hood. To his considerable surprise, he experienced and understood a feeling of humility, and saw the truth hidden in the clichés appropriate to such an occasion. All he could do was keep saying to him-self, "Welcome, little one, I'll do my best for you." Then, clenching and unclenching his hands in excitement, he got up and walked to the delivery room to examine the wrinkled red scream that all the fuss had been about.

# Chapter 2

Peter Newman ran his small business from his home—an attractive, rambling old house set in fertile, undulating countryside, near
enough to the city to give his family and business access to its benefits, but far enough to protect them from most of its less desirable
attributes such as the squalor and frenzy and violence.

John Newman's earliest memories were fringed with smoky autumn leaves and leaden winter skies over white clad landscapes, but
were mainly of grass and trees and sunlight, and images of his
father, white shirted and bare armed, gazing into the sky. Almost as
soon as he could walk he had been drawn into his father's lust for
life, and was marched and carried over miles of the surrounding
countryside.

Not all his memories were pleasant however, as he had an almost lethal mixture of inquisitiveness and persistence in his
makeup, and even under the supervision of his father, frequently
acquired cuts, bruises, stings, and other of the troubles to which
youthful flesh is heir. Also in his makeup was a reserve and a
strange deep sense of pride, and very seldom did he weep or even
cry out when hurt. Once he walked over three miles across fields,
through hedges and over ditches, sporting a huge gash in his leg
brought about by an unsuccessful vault over a barbed wire fence.
His black eyes watched the ensuing turmoil impassively as he stood
like a still centre, while a pool of blood expanded over the white
tiled kitchen floor. His mother turned alternately white then red,
and his father moved quietly, quickly and purposefully from telephone to first aid box, with panic and horror only just hidden behind concerned eyes. John Newman winced as the doctor stuck

needles into him and sewed up the wound, but though his lip trembled and he held his father's hand tightly, he volunteered no other reaction.

His father would look at him pensively at times. "Look at the lad," he would say. "He'd choke before he'd cry. It's not as if I've ever given him the 'big boys don't cry' rubbish. Where does it come from?"

"He's like your father," said Ann.

Peter sighed and put his hand to his forehead. "I hope not," he said. "But you could be right, he's certainly like him physically."

Ann looked at him in surprise. "You'd never noticed had you? He's exactly like your father. Same temperament, same looks, everything."

Peter did not reply immediately. His wife's remarks had brought about that strange mental metamorphosis which occurs when that which was obscure becomes, without changing, blindingly obvious. He quailed inwardly at the revelation and wondered how his wife could accept it so casually. But then, she only knew the surface layers of his father: those which he chose to expose. Peter knew the darker reaches, and sensed worse. He knew how that stern temperament could develop.

"Not absolutely everything, I hope. It looks as if I've surrounded myself after all," he said.

His wife put her arm around him. "Don't worry," she said. "You're away from the business now. The family ties are broken. Besides, you're not surrounded. There's quite a lot of your father in you, or you wouldn't have been able to do it. John will be all right."

Ironically, it was only because Peter carried his father's personality in some degree that John did indeed 'turn out all right'. Instinctively he treated the boy with openness and consistency and, where possible, fairness. But whenever John tested the limits of his emotional terrain, he found in his father an age-tempered implacability that he knew he could not yet match. He learned early that it was unwise to play one parent against the other. On the rare occasions he tried and succeeded, it was to face not a burst of his father's summary justice, but a sad wall of parental reproach more painful than anything that happened to him whenever he misjudged his father's mood during a 'debate'.

Peter learned too. He learned, as many had learned before, that though you may love your children, and they you, they can slip through your defences like water, and plunge a rasp across your nerve ends without mercy. He learned how easily a killing instinct could be invoked with the right key. Intellectually, he had always accepted that as part of his humanity he must be mainly predator: hunter and killer. But now he knew it emotionally, having felt a red-eyed demon surging in him, albeit briefly, for the first time since his own childhood. It shocked him a little at first, but being perceptive enough to see it, he was perceptive enough to accept rather than deny it, and thereby effectively tamed it.

As the need grew to accommodate John's increasingly vigorous personality, the vehicles for the more complex ground rules shifted away from direct force majeure, and became 'the deal'. Whenever Peter felt his son entrenching himself for a long siege, he would look at him, man to man, and say, "OK. Let's do a deal." And then, generally speaking, he would proceed to have most of his own way by virtue of higher reasoning power and lower cunning.

Peter's business ticked over steadily. It was sufficiently successful to protect them from the rigours of poverty, but would never make them rich. The work was spasmodic, and Peter worked as required, sometimes normal office hours, sometimes weekends and into the early hours of the morning. Then he would have days with nothing to do, either through lack of work, in which case he would make a nuisance of himself by prowling around the house fretfully, or because he had successfully passed all his immediate problems to someone else, in which case he would make a nuisance of himself by prowling around the house self-righteously. Ann would eventually tire of moving around him, and roar, "Have you nothing to do?" To which he would reply with a smirk, "No," and make a tennis stroke gesture to demonstrate his administrative expertise in delegation. "Only an idle man does not appreciate the value of leisure," he usually concluded.

So the three of them grew and thrived, their mildly chaotic lifestyle underlain by a continuity of affection, and made whole by an almost complete lack of concern for society's expectations of them. In many ways a complete and happy family.

# Chapter 3

Even in later years, John Newman could remember the black harbinger that brought the beginning of the end of that bright and happy time, a time in which life was normal and secure and everlasting in a way he was never to know again. It became like a clear distant picture—an image through the wrong end of a telescope.

He remembered the sledging with his friend Thomas-not-Tom.

Thomas was a little older, a little bigger, and much clumsier than John. He had untidy red hair, freckles, a wide turned-up nose, and thick lips. And John, in emulation of his apparent betters, had taken his outward appearance as the whole, and brutally classed him as a dimwit. One day however, in the schoolyard, they had raced for and reached 'the wall'—a small wall set a little in front of the main wall and on which they could stand, lean back, and overview the yard in splendid comfort. The taboos of the yard gave 'the wall' to whoever reached it first, and even seniors could not displace juniors. John was disappointed to have a dimwit for company but was in a condescending mood and conversed with Thomas as if he was an equal. Then talk eventually turned to the topic of pets, and Thomas described how he was looking after a young guinea pig.

"It keeps getting this sticky stuff over its eyes, so I wipe it off every morning with a soft cloth and warm water." He mimed the action.

"But they're so tiny, and they wriggle so much," said John.

Thomas smiled. "They're still enough if you're gentle with them," he said.

The words 'soft' and 'gentle' almost winded John and he felt scales fall from his eyes. The vision of this simple compassionate act formed in John's mind next to one of his mother cleaning out his own pet's hutch and muttering dire threats, while he stood looking down and shuffling his feet as if he were ankle deep in his own broken promises. He beamed at Thomas, instantly re-assessed him as distinctly superior to himself, and resolved to make a friend of him. He felt and accepted, with the clarity and honesty of youth, the cruel injustice of his earlier opinion, and was relieved that he had confined it to discreet avoidance and had never baited Thomas as was the practice of some of his peers. From that time they had been firm friends, spending most of their school holidays together, and generally terrorizing the neighbourhood. John's father was pleased with this friendship, as Thomas's quieter disposition tempered John's wilder and more alarming schemes, and softened a brutal streak that occasionally appeared.

On that pivotal day, they had been sledging all afternoon. The snow was thick, and it crunched underfoot into a hard layer with a surface as smooth as wet glass. The sky was leaden grey, with that uniformity of texture that only a snow-laden sky can have, and the air was tangibly still. Thomas and John had started the slope, but eventually there were seven or eight of them rending the winter quiet with their screams and shouts and laughter, the silver sounds dissipating over the muffled fields just as their steaming breaths disappeared into the air.

Henry Willis, the local shopkeeper's son, tried to take the icy slope standing on his sledge, then undeterred by that catastrophe attempted the same on two sledges. Two passing farm workers were snowballed and routed without returning fire, and for a little while they all shouted rude words at the tops of their voices. The penultimate event of the afternoon was 'Snot' Roberts, John's next door neighbour, travelling backwards down the slope and into a snow drift. This was executed with such aplomb that the whole group plunged into hysterical laughter which ended only when Dick Harrison pushed snow down someone's wellington. The ensuing snowball fight rounded off the afternoon perfectly, with John exhibiting his natural qualities of leadership by making an injudicious remark which resulted in Thomas and himself being bombarded by all the others.

On the way home, they were both silent as they lifted their heavy feet through the deep snow. There is a magic in walking through the quiet of a darkening winter day towards the yellow lights of home which must not be disturbed by words. They parted at John's gate with the merest nod, tomorrow's proceedings being determined by precedent and needing no comment.

Normally he entered the house via a swing on the gate and a series of special leaps and steps, but today the gate was untypically open, and his entry ritual could not be performed. A large black car parked in front of the house added further to this disturbed equilibrium. Although he could not have said why, the car seemed to John to have an aura of menace. His father's car was a beige coloured estate and not small, but this car felt bigger, more powerful, sitting patiently in the white glare of the porch light, the spiked snow chains on its tyres glinting like silver teeth. And it was clean, bearing only the slush of its latest journey, unlike his father's car which was very rarely cleaned, and always had a begrimed and bewildered appearance. He looked through the driver's window and the end of his nose made a wet line in the mist that immediately obscured his vision. He wiped it away with a gloved hand and saw that the interior too was immaculate. John knew little or nothing about cars, but he knew this one was both expensive and something special. It was already becoming the centrepiece of tomorrow's conversations, and he knew he would have to find out more.

Abruptly he shrugged off his unease and ran round to the back of the house and into the kitchen.

His ritual for entering here was unimpeded and his mother winced as he crashed in. The door was reprieved from too vigorous a slamming only by his rapid reading of her expression. "Mum. Whose is the car?"

"Oh, hello to you too," replied his mother, turning her attention back to her work. He walked over and put his arms around her. She looked down and smiled at him, putting her hand on his flushed cheek. "My, you are warm. What have you been doing?" she asked, knowing full well the answer.

"Oh. Nothing much. Just playing."

Ann pulled off his woollen cap and thrust it in his face. "Boots," she ordered.

Boots safely stored in their proper place and coat hung on its proper hook, he returned to his query. "Whose is the car, mum?"

11

He thought he felt a little tension in the way she was standing, but the answer was bland enough. "No-one special. Just one of daddy's clients."

"Most of my clients can't afford bicycles let alone cars," he mimicked.

His mother laughed. "Well, that's as may be. Don't be cheeky. Go and get yourself cleaned up; your dinner will be ready soon."

The car had quietly disappeared when he emerged for dinner and his father seemed preoccupied. Reading the signs, he judged it wise to defer questions to a more propitious time. However, that time never really came. His father vanished into his office after dinner and John did not see him again until he was going to bed.

"G'night dad," he said, putting his head round the office door.

"Come here John," said Peter, and held open his arms. John walked across the office and received a long embrace and a kiss on the head. He noticed there was nothing on the desk in front of his father.

"What are you doing dad?" he asked.

"Nothing special, son, just thinking about a problem that's cropped up."

"Oh," said John uncertainly.

His father kissed him again. "G'night son." It was final.

"G'night dad."

In the dark of his bedroom and the warmth of his bed it occurred to John that a prayer might not go amiss before descending into his current pink, white and mobile adventure involving his English teacher, and a bubbling new one involving a large black car and the performance of heroic deeds.

"Please God," he said. "Let it be a rich client for daddy."

# Chapter 4

From that day, a tension pervaded the house like a faint, unpleasant mist. There was no lessening of the small shows of affection that were the family's common currency, but both parents seemed to be preoccupied, and his father in particular seemed to be carrying a much shorter fuse than usual. On more than one occasion John had to beat a hasty retreat after some ill-judged remark. One day, at dinner, he stepped right over the edge. Bested by his father in a 'deal', he bridled and rebelled, disputing their established ground rules, even though he knew he was in the wrong. His father ignored the outburst and Ann tried briefly to intercede, but John persisted and turned on them both. Under normal circumstances his parents would have joined forces and laughed him out of his childish tantrum but, suddenly, Peter stood up, eyes blazing, and strode rapidly and purposefully around the table towards him, hand raised. As he reached John he paused as he felt the terrifying snarl of the angry dominant male filling his body and saw it reflected in the terror shining from his son's face and posture. He stopped, lowered his hand and, returning to his seat, sat down wearily. He beckoned John gently.

"Come here son." The boy went to him hesitantly and climbed onto his knee. "I'm sorry," said Peter. "I'm sorry I lost my temper and frightened you." His right hand idly turned a spoon over and his left arm embraced his son. There was a silence in the room. "I've got some difficult problems with work at the moment and they're worrying me." He looked into his son's face. "I wouldn't hurt you for the world. I love you. But sometimes you have to use your judgement. You know what I mean, don't you?"

The boy nodded. "I think so," he said.

"There are times for words and times for silence," continued his father. "Times when you must stand your ground and times when you must retreat. Judgement is knowing which. Don't be frightened of making mistakes, it's something you learn bit by bit." He put both arms around his son and kissed him. "Now go and help your mother with the washing up."

Later, when Thomas-not-Tom had lured John out into the twilight snow, Ann went up to her disconsolate husband and put her arms around him. "Don't worry so much. It'll turn out alright."

Peter in turn put his arms around her. "Maybe," he said, noncommittally. He looked around the room, taking in the familiar trivia of his life. The bits and pieces he could part with, but the whole they formed was imbued with a special quality and he would not lightly part with that.

The black car came again. John found it on his return from school. It glinted black in the porch-light like some powerful night predator. It made him uncomfortable again. It was like a deep sinister bass note presaging a change in the harmony of his life. Already developing his father's pragmatism in dealing with problems, he decided to forego his mother's evasive answers and to tackle the problem head on. After a moment's thought he unearthed an exercise book from his school bag. It contained a good mark for a maths test plus an adulatory comment from his teacher and would serve as an excuse to bend the house rules a little.

He knocked on the office door, called out "Dad" and pushed the door without waiting for a reply. The door opened a little and then bumped into something. He put his head through the gap to see what was in the way. The obstruction proved to be a large smartly dressed man who had been standing behind the door, most foolishly, as John thought, and who was now idly rubbing his leg where the doorknob had struck him. John looked up past the immaculate dark suit into a rugged oval face. Its expression was slightly puzzled and appeared to be waiting for instructions, but its eyes had a callous indifference in them that made John feel uneasy. The man gave John the impression of great size and strength: he drives that car, he thought.

The man did not move.

"What is it, John?" His father's voice cut quietly across the silence.

"I wanted to show you this," John replied, thrusting his book into the room.

"Come on then," said his father.

The big man received his instructions from somewhere, moved to one side and opened the door wide enough to admit the intruder. There was an atmosphere in the room that seemed to John to be the very essence of the atmosphere that had filled the house recently. His father was at his desk, turning slightly left and right on his swivel chair, and a third man was sitting in an armchair. The big man closed the door quietly and returned to his vigil. John took the book to his father and proudly displayed his work. Peter looked at it for a moment and then smiled.

"Very good," he said. "I told you that you'd begin to understand it soon."

"So this is John," came a voice. It was the man in the armchair, forestalling John's dismissal. His voice was warm and friendly and John looked at him intently. He too was wearing a dark suit though he seemed to carry it more easily than the big man. His hair was black but greying at the temples and his lean clean-shaven face framed a welcoming smile. He owns the car, thought John, and the man's gleaming teeth reminded him of the lamplit snow chains. The smile, however, revealed a gold filling which added a yellow distortion to the man's otherwise immaculate appearance, and made John feel uneasy again.

"Come here and let me have a look at you," he said. John looked at his father. Peter nodded, and John walked uncertainly round the desk to face the man. "May I look at your book?" John held it out without speaking. The man took it, thumbed carefully through it, pausing here and there, and then handed it back. "You're a neat worker," he said. "That's very good. You must ask your father when you don't understand something. Knowledge is important, and your father's a very clever and capable man. More so than many people imagine." John had the feeling that the words were not being addressed to him. Then the man seemed to start a little. He paused and looked at John thoughtfully. "You're very like your grandfather," he said. He glanced from Peter to John as if to confirm something, and then his face lit up in a smile again. "I'm very glad to have met you at last. I've heard a lot about you."

"Off you go now, John. You've seen what's going on and we're

15

rather busy." His father's voice interrupted, concluding his adventure. "Tell your mother I'll not be very long now."

Outside the office, John reflected that he had said nothing and learned nothing. He had not even asked about the car. Could he have a look inside? How fast did it go? How much did it cost? He pulled a wry face. The presence of the three adults, and someone else directing the conversation, had tongue-tied him. But the man with the bad tooth knew grandfather: his father's father, the mention of whose name would bring a shade over his father's face and a screen of evasiveness from both parents. He knew his grandad: his mother's father. He was great fun. But he had never even seen his grandfather, and always thought of him as a slightly sinister figure in the distance.

He decided he would draw himself to the attention of the visitors again in the hope of making good this setback. He would accidentally find himself playing some noisy game outside the office window.

A few minutes later he was in the garden, mittened and muffled and ready for action. He ran round to the side of the house where the light from the office window illuminated a rectangular patch of untrammelled snow. Before starting to make himself conspicuous, he hesitated, a cautionary note sounding in his mind. Standing well out of the light on a small wall, he peered through the office window. The three men were in the same positions. His father was twisting to and fro on the swivel chair in a more agitated manner and the seated man was leaning forward and emphasizing some point by gently prodding the palm of his left hand with his right forefinger. Suddenly Peter slammed his hand on the desk and said something angrily. The seated man slumped back into his chair and rested his forehead in his left hand as if in some despair. Then the man by the door spoke briefly, his face becoming red and angry. He finished with a gesture, pointing his finger at Peter. The seated man looked up during the outburst and raised his left hand slightly in discreet remonstrance.

Then a strange thing happened. Standing on the snow-covered wall, hypnotised by this window picture glowing like a great television screen, John felt a chilly silence emanating from the scene. Everyone in the room was motionless. His father sat staring straight ahead. The man by the door was still pointing and the seated man had his hand still raised slightly. The television show had turned into a vivid still-life. Very slowly Peter turned and faced the man by the door. He had his back to the window and John could not see his face, nor could he hear anything being said, but the big man seemed to shrink visibly. John felt fear mingling in the chill. It was the big man's fear. Momentarily John felt the man's urge to turn and run. Then, rock still in his chair, Peter turned back slowly and looked at the seated man.

John jumped down from the wall and ran back into the warm familiarity of the house.

The two men left shortly afterwards. John heard no farewells at the door, but he felt the rumble of the car as it crunched quietly through the snow.

His father was very cheerful that evening, but instinct curbed John's curiosity about the men, and on several occasions he looked up to find his father staring at him.

# Chapter 5

Over the next few months the atmosphere in the house lightened a little, even though circumstances militated against it somewhat. The weather also seemed loathe to acknowledge the change of the seasons. The winter, having arrived early, continued its guise as unwelcome visitor by staying late and weighing heavily on its host. Snow fell everywhere, and remained everywhere. Then more fell. Then the frost came and illuminated the country with its bitter gaze. Bright white sunny days and clear night skies such as none had seen for generations.

Those who could unclench themselves from their wintry stoops and gaze upwards saw the glory of the Milky Way poured across the sky and the countless eyes of the Universe gazing indifferently back, inviting a revised sense of perspective. Earthbound souls, however, suffered earthbound pangs, and there was the usual crop of grotesqueries to demonstrate the complete unpreparedness of the Englishman to acknowledge the existence of winter, and his asinine surprise that it should keep returning each year. People died alone in their rooms. People died in steely tangles when the warm isolation of their cars lulled them into misjudging the true nature of the outside world. People died only yards from home for the same reason when white-out, drift and blizzard transformed the familiar scenery. Insurance companies worked overtime. Honest plumbers worked overtime and made money; dishonest plumbers worked overtime and made money and enemies. Most roads, railways and airports were blocked from time to time.

In fairness, it was a particularly severe winter. Some rivers froze. In certain areas, even the sea froze, and some of the snow in the mountains was destined to be there still when the next winter came. And in fairness also, most of the population adjusted quickly, and life returned to its routines after a little while, but clad in large boots, woolly socks and matching ensemble. When the temperature rose to freezing point, conversations started with, "Warm today isn't it?" The Englishman's peculiar genius for not seeing things coming is amply compensated for by his ability to adapt fairly quickly to changed circumstances, but which is cause and which is effect remains undecided.

The brutal winter left in an unpleasant and flooding thaw, leaving a few more dead, and leading to a damp reluctant spring. This in turn gave way to a short and storm-troubled summer.

Through it all the Newman nest remained warm and cosy. Somewhat to his surprise, Peter found his business expanding. Two new and large clients presented themselves unexpectedly.

"We've seen the work you've done for one of our customers, Mr. Newman, and are very impressed. We've a scheme we'd like you to look at." He mimicked a telephone conversation to Ann, thrusting thumbs into imaginary braces and then rubbing his hands in delight.

The scheme proved to be bigger than anything he had ever tackled, but it was interesting and within both his capability and the capacity of his business, so he tackled it with relish. The client, as usual, altered various items abruptly and forgot important pieces of information, so quite frequently Peter had to dump work into his wastepaper basket and extend busy days into long evenings and weekends. However the client paid promptly and was better behaved than average, so he pleaded exigencies of the service whenever Ann, disturbed at 3 a.m. by his slumping into bed, would sit up, blearily focus on the clock and mutter less than ladylike imprecations into the hallowed stillness of their nuptial chamber.

This improvement in his father's worldly conditions largely passed over John's head, as Peter knew that the growth of his son was not an event to be missed and always made time available for being with him. Added to this, both he and Ann took what John considered to be a wholly unwarranted and embarrassing interest in his education, and would patiently and regularly wade through his schoolwork, interrogating him with mock or real severity depending on the circumstances. He never dared to enquire, but he was sure none of his friends at school suffered such an indignity.

John at this stage was showing a marked aptitude for maths and such elementary science as he was being taught, and would spend hours poring over popular technical magazines and books. He built eccentric and original structures with a construction kit, seeming to delight in using pieces to fulfil functions for which they had not been intended, and he developed an almost lethal interest in chemistry. This was soon put under direct and rigorous parental control by a wild-eyed Ann following a series of incidents that started with the ruin of various kitchen utensils, went on to the permanent staining of her stove, and the filling of the kitchen with an evil smelling smoke, and culminated in a venture that left John with singed hair, black face, temporary deafness and very shaky knees.

"He didn't cry though."

Peter's business was only small, but it was prospering. His wife filled the house with a comforting radiance and his son regularly cut a swathe through any vestige of tranquility that might inadvertently settle on the proceedings. He valued his family life above all things, and was sensitive to anything that might disrupt this harmony. He thus had very mixed feelings when he was approached by the second large company to undertake work for them. Their scheme was also big, and he knew he could not handle it alone with his present commitments. And yet it could not sensibly be refused.

After a great deal of thought, an unusually serious debate with his wife, and a typically serious debate with his bank manager, he hired two assistants. It was only the feeling of permanent change invoked by formal employment that made Peter feel uneasy. He had no qualms about the quality of his two employees, as they had both done freelance work for him in the past, and both were personable and conscientious. It was fortuitous for him that both had fallen on hard times recently and were only too happy to accept employment. The three of them could just manage in his office, although the necessary removal of a desk and files into the hallway caused some rumbling from Ann.

Matthew Vance was tall and thin. He had a pale, rather drawn face, and walked with a slight stoop. He seemed to be permanently absorbed in solving a perplexing problem, and his introspective manner made him appear rather slow and foolish. He was neither. He would plod away at the most intractable problems, turning over and examining the pieces in meticulous detail, and relentlessly placing them where they belonged to form a final picture. Occasionally he would forget where he was going and spend hours descending into ever diminishing minutiae, but eventually he would slowly raise his head, push his left hand into his hair, scratch his head, click his tongue disapprovingly and drop his papers into the waste bin with an audible sigh. Then he would sit staring into space for a few minutes with his elbows on the desk and resting his chin in his hands.

Mark Donnell was almost the complete opposite. Medium height and with a fidgety disposition, he was careful but he lacked Matthew's meticulous attention to detail and was apt to make intuitive leaps when tackling awkward problems: sometimes accurately, other times less so.

Peter was pleased they worked together well, as their combined talents covered a wide area, and they balanced each other's excesses: Matthew's tendency to indolence and defeatism, Mark's tendency to greed and ambition.

Inevitably their names earned them the soubriquet of the Two Apostles from Ann, but Peter was a little touchy about his new charges and tried not to smile when she floated it across the dinner table. Ann smiled back at his unsuccessful and narrow-eyed attempt, but John would turn his smile into a twitch at an admonitory gesture from his father's forefinger. Life, he knew, was not fair. And what was sauce for the goose was quite frequently not sauce for the gosling.

The new order worked smoothly for quite a time. In fact it worked with considerable efficiency, and the two major schemes proceeded well and without detriment to the needs of the smaller clients. After a while however, there was a slow, almost imperceptible deterioration in the previously harmonious relations that Peter had had with his two new clients.

It started when his invoices began to be settled less promptly. The business had in the past been quite successful, and with Peter having basically simple tastes, he had been able to operate on Mr. Micawber's principle that expenditure should not exceed income, and he was thus not without assets. He had ensured that the increased outlay involved in paying his two employees and contending with the other expenses involved in dealing with the larger contracts before his own invoices were paid, could be covered for three months from his own resources and were backed for a further period by his bank. He had an instinctive mistrust of debt, but such as he might incur should be limited, reasonable and well covered. The clients were, after all, both reputable and buoyant, and his contracts were good.

Like many before him when they have encountered this difficulty for the first time, Peter was slow and reluctant to pursue his money. He let several weeks slip by before somewhat awkwardly picking up the telephone and contacting the accounts office.

"I'm awfully sorry, Mr. Newman, we've had a new girl in the invoice department, and she's misfiled a whole batch of invoices. We've just about got it sorted out now. You've no idea. I'm afraid it's got to go through the computer, but I'll mark yours urgent and we should be able to get something to you shortly."

"I'm awfully sorry, Mr. Newman. There's no problem of course, but the auditors have been looking at the overall financing of this scheme, and Mr. Jones had yours and some others in his file when he went to see them."

He could do no more than make polite noises in reply to these excuses, but they left him feeling distinctly uncomfortable. He felt a faint concern at his vulnerability should either of these large organisations let him down, but reflected that he had no real cause for concern, and he was still looking after his smaller clients quite satisfactorily. If the worst came to the worst, he could survive comfortably with these and he was sure he could do a deal with Matthew and Mark to revert to their original relationship in gradual stages. He was pleased he had made no wild promises when he had employed them.

However, things did not work out so conveniently. Slowly but surely the payments slipped further into arrears until they were several months behind. There was little he could do. Payments were still regular, albeit slow, so he could not reasonably do any desk banging, and, in any event, his desk banging would be unlikely to have any effect on these particular clients. Also his occasional enquiries would be met with polite and reasonable if somewhat vague apologies from junior members of staff and the odd cheque would arrive with a brief hand-written apology appended by a more senior employee.

More seriously, both firms became involved in mergers and

takeovers which resulted not only in further delays in payments, but also in extensive staff changes. It was some time before Peter found out which new departments were looking after the schemes, and who was in charge of them. Then, of course, came 'major policy changes', endless discussion about what had been done and why, what ought to be done and how, and inevitably more and more delays.

"One of these companies playing silly beggars would be too much," he blazed at Ann one day, after a particularly trying interview with a new manager. "But both of them. Bloody hell. And as for that fatuous oaf who's just wasted my entire day..." He rarely swore in front of his wife and she sat quietly looking at him through this fairly considerable outburst, searching for a way to help. She knew a display of affection could provoke an uneasy response in his present mood and lead to tensions which would only add to his problems.

"Well now," she said, looking at him with her eyes wide in mock horror. "You should let your feelings out more. Don't pen them up so, it's bad for you."

He chuckled and waved a dismissive left hand at her. The solidity of his domestic life protected him from himself many times, but it could not protect him from what was actually happening.

The constant chopping and changing of the schemes was affecting not only his financial position, but also his own will to continue working conscientiously for clients who, apparently, did not seem to care to listen to his advice or gain from his experience. Matthew and Mark were also beginning to feel the strain, seeing weeks and weeks of work discarded and third rate ideas insisted upon.

"What annoys me, Peter," said Mark, "is that when this damn thing doesn't work properly, we'll be blamed for it, not the clown who authorized it." Matthew nodded in agreement.

"I know," said Peter. "But there's nothing we can do. We've given them our advice in writing, fortunately, so there's that. It's a great shame. Both these schemes started so well and could have been so good. Now they'll be tenth rate at best, and God knows what at worst." He looked out of the window into a wet late afternoon and capped his troubles with incongruity. "And it's been a bloody awful summer as well."

# Chapter 6

Harry was a lucky boy. Six weeks he had been in this job—his first job. Times generally were hard and it was difficult for school-leavers to find employment, but on an impulse he had walked through the gates of the factory yard and straight up to a prefabricated cabin that served as an office. Inside was a dusty smelling foyer a few feet square. The decor was fly-specked off-yellow. To his right a narrow window ledge sported a rusty washer and two screws, while to his left was a battered door and a frosted glass window bearing a faded notice fastened on with crackling sticky tape and announcing 'Enquiries'.

Harry knocked on the window. The noise of typing emanating from behind the door continued unchecked, so he knocked again, louder. The typing stopped, a chair scuffed back and a blurred blonde head appeared behind the window. There was a brief struggle and the window reluctantly slid back. A round, sulky face surrounded by a frizz of blonde hair stared out at him. It wore too much makeup and was chewing gum. Evaluating Harry at a glance it spoke.

"Yes. What d'you want?"

"Er," he stuttered. "Have you got any jobs?"

There was no hesitation. "No. Sorry, love."

He had not really expected anything else, but the brief interchange had dented the fragile confidence that had impelled him in there, and the day went a little dimmer.

"Will you be having any soon?" he asked. She was about to reply when the door opened and a large grey-haired man stepped in.

"Sort these out will you, Mary," he said, pushing a wad of papers through the open window. "And give me that last batch of drawings."

Mary disappeared from the window and could be heard scuttling about the office. The man leaned on the wall and looked at Harry.

"What do you want, son?" he asked. His voice was not particularly loud, but it contained authority. To Harry he was probably 'the Boss'.

"I'm looking for a job mister," he replied.

A brief look of sympathy came into the man's eyes.

"You and a few others. Who sent you?" he asked.

Harry shrugged. "No-one, I just... er... walked in. Thought I'd try."

"It's always worth a try, son, but there's nothing here for you, sorry."

Mary's face appeared at the window again.

"Johnny's off again, Charley. The flu."

This announcement, with its knowingly accented coda, provoked a response out of all proportion to its apparent import. The man swore.

"Flu, my backside. He's a lazy little sod. I'm fed up with that kid, he's nothing but a blasted nuisance." Adding, as an afterthought, "And he's useless." He looked at Harry sternly. "You. Can you make tea?"

"Yes sir." The "sir" came automatically.

"Can you get here at eight o'clock prompt every day?"

Harry caught the mood and anticipated.

"Yes sir. Just show me what to do and I'll do it."

"We'll see," said the man. "You're hired. Mary. Fix him up."

He turned and left abruptly. Harry turned to the girl. The sulky face broke into a smile and the right eye closed in a monumental wink.

So Harry became a tea boy and general dogsbody for the site. He enjoyed the job and became proficient in the necessary skills such as remembering who took what and how much in his tea, and memorizing complicated orders to be collected from the nearby cafe. He also demonstrated a considerable aptitude for mental arithmetic as a result of such errands, an aptitude that would have been greeted with blatant disbelief by his maths teacher over the last few years. Following a prolonged haggle during which he reeled off the orders and cash received from each of some eight people and then the prices and change due, one of the gangers eyed him warily, but with surprised respect.

"I think we'll have you for bonus clerk, lad," he said. Charley, the foreman, watched him also and mentally noted him for chain lad when opportunity arose; it was difficult to find people who were prepared to use their heads. Harry was a lucky boy.

He was thinking about asking a girl from the wages office for a date when he went into the kitchen in the main site office to start the tea for the morning break. Automatically flicking on the gas switch, he reached for the matches on the shelf. They were gone. He looked quickly into the adjacent office but there was no-one there.

"Damn. The tea's going to be late. I wish people would put things back," he muttered to himself as he went to the outer door and looked for someone from whom he could borrow a light.

He was not normally careless, but a pleasant preoccupation with his would-be date, a slight disturbance in his routine and a cold to destroy his sense of smell, all conspired against him today. He clicked the borrowed lighter once, then twice. It lit. And so did the office. The resultant explosion set the timber structure ablaze, detonated a series of gas cylinders and spread to the adjacent office block, doing extensive damage. As for Harry, the blast threw him against the outer door which fortunately yielded under the impact. Lying on the door, he travelled through the air and along the road some twenty yards before coming to rest. He was found unconscious by his workmates, and amid cries of "Don't move him," he was covered with a donkey jacket, lifted on his impromptu stretcher, deposited on a truck and driven to hospital. Subsequently he awoke there, slightly singed and very sore but otherwise uninjured. Harry was a lucky boy.

Peter Newman was less lucky. The office damaged in the fire belonged to one of his two major clients. The area worst damaged was the administrative department and a great many irreplaceable records were destroyed—at least that is what he was told. On first hearing the news, he felt a wave of suspicion lapping round the fringes of his mind. He knew the building. Those records were not kept there. Yes, true, they weren't normally kept there, but they'd been moved there temporarily while alterations were being made and to help so-and-so collate various bits of information. There was also, he found later, a little hesitancy on the part of the insurance company before they finally paid. Still, he reasoned, what benefit would anyone gain from destroying all this information. It was only going to make life more difficult for everyone.

And difficult it became. The difficulties he had experienced over the past months dwindled into insignificance when compared with subsequent developments. Alterations abounded. His client's staff came and went with alarming frequency, each creating swirls of confusion. Parts of schemes already completed were, as predicted, failing to work properly, but...

"Dear Mr. Newman, I regret we can find no record of the letter you refer to, but in any event, we are advised..." etc etc. Payments were stopped and disputed. "I'm very sorry, Mr. Newman, Mr. Jenkins isn't with us any more and everything to do with this scheme is being handled at Board level." etc etc.

John and Ann had known Peter only as a relaxed and happy man, delighting in simple pleasures and intuitively rejecting the more transient irritations of life. But under the mounting pressure he was changing. His face seemed to be permanently lined, and he moved like a fretful caged animal. Ann felt the strain also and tried to let it pass over her, but she was not always successful and they had some bitter quarrels. Their relationship was strong enough to handle them and, indeed, they seemed to ease the strains to some extent by eventually enabling Ann to offer such gentle solace as she could, and Peter to receive it without fear or resentment. But both knew that the situation could not continue without terrible and sad things happening.

Peter loved and leaned on his wife more than she ever knew and resolves darkened in him when he saw the pain he was causing her. Ann in her turn noted an enigmatic and strangely primitive trait forming in her husband's character, although sometimes she wondered if it was actually forming or simply being uncovered.

One day, Mark Donnell asked to speak to Peter privately. He seemed a little sheepish.

"I've had this offer, Peter," he said.

"Offer?"

"Yes, it came out of the blue. Their technical director just rang up and said he'd seen my work and would I come round for a chat."

Peter sat down and folded his arms but said nothing.

"I went. Just out of curiosity, and then this. Out of the blue," he repeated as he handed a letter to Peter. Peter looked at the prestigious letterhead and then read the letter slowly. He whistled quietly.

"Some offer, Mark. Salary, benefits, holidays I couldn't begin to offer. And promotional prospects I'll never be able to offer."

"I didn't tout for this, Peter," said Mark, earnestly. "I wouldn't do that, not with things here in the state they are. But it's a marvellous job. I don't know what to do. My leaving could finish you."

"I know you didn't go looking for this, Mark," said Peter gently. "You can't refuse it. You'll never get another chance like it, believe me. This mess here is none of your making, so get clear of it and don't worry. I'll get through to the end of it one way or another."

They talked for some time, and Peter was surprised at the genuine conflict between Mark's loyalty and his ambition. But he saw no benefit in leaving Mark with a conscience more bruised than it was, and eventually persuaded him to accept the offer. When Mark had left the room, Peter could not forbear a smile as the self-righteous glow of his magnanimity dimmed somewhat when he thought, *anyway, where he's going, he may end up as a good client.*

Later that same day he received a letter from his bank manager. It was not the first, and it was not altogether unexpected, but its tone showed a change from concern to mild truculence, and it was quite apparent that matters were nearing a conclusion. Peter's stomach turned, and then he set about drafting a reply and chasing his clients for money again.

With Mark gone, there was little Peter and Matthew could do but keep baling in an attempt not so much to improve things as simply to prevent their deteriorating any faster.

Matthew looked up from his desk and caught Peter staring at him. Peter flushed slightly. "I'm sorry Matthew. I was just thinking about something."

Matthew smiled. "Don't worry, I don't think I'll be having any unexpected offers. Not enough pizzazz. Don't shine in the dark like Mark."

"I'm not too sure about that, Matthew," replied Peter. "You undersell yourself. You're certainly a fair mind reader."

That was not in fact what he had been thinking about. He had been shuffling random thoughts and ideas that had been swirling around in his mind for some time and which seemed to be on the verge of coalescing into a coherent picture, but Matthew's interruption had scattered them again.

He became more and more pensive and preoccupied, effectively giving up all attempts to progress the two offending schemes. He would sit staring into the fire, resting his head on his hands. There was no defeat in his posture, and Ann more than once felt she was in the presence of a complete stranger. She explained to John his father's preoccupation, as well as she could, but she dared not speak to Peter until he came out of his sombre reveries.

He was trapped, he was totally vulnerable to two clients who seemed to be verging on the insane. If they did not pay him he could do nothing. Nothing, that is, of any immediate practical value. The English legal system was infinitely slow and would be a lottery in such a complicated technical matter. In fact his clients could and probably would sue him, even though all the confusion and consequent error was of their own making. His bank had at last run out of patience and would soon shed its bland exterior. Everything he owned, everything he had worked for was now at risk.

He got up and went to the telephone. He would have to let Matthew go while he could still pay him, and then handle the consequences alone.

Matthew's mother answered the telephone. "Could I speak to Matthew, Mrs Vance? It's Peter Newman."

The reply was distraught. "Oh Mr. Newman, I was going to ring you tomorrow. Something awful's happened."

Matthew had been attacked. Neighbours had found him lying on the pavement near his home, unconscious and savagely beaten. No-one had seen or heard anything, but he had two broken ribs, a broken arm and a variety of cuts and extensive bruising. His wallet and watch had been taken, so presumably the motive had been robbery, but he himself remembered little. He thought perhaps there had been a car behind him, and he was fairly certain that more than one man had attacked him, but otherwise nothing.

Peter muttered consolatory remarks into the phone and slowly replaced the receiver. He was shocked, and the thought of Matthew under pounding, senseless fists angered him. For a while his own concerns dispersed, but they soon returned. Matthew would not be fit for work for several weeks, and he did not have several weeks left. Now he really was on his own. The thought stuck in his mind. Alone. His last practical, technical help gone. Matthew did not live in the city, nor in one of its rougher suburbs. He lived in a quiet, ordinary suburban street of Saturday-polished cars and Sunday-cut lawns. And who would attack someone like Matthew? He did not look like a person who might be carrying a lot of money, not that that was necessarily a protection. Also he was tall. To a casual thief he could have looked like quite a powerful man. A thief might possibly attack a shabby person, but he would be unlikely to attack anyone who might offer resistance.

The incident jarred. A picture formed in his mind abruptly. It's not possible, he thought. I'm going paranoid. All this expense, this planning, it can't be true, it just can't be. But if it was, all he had to do was wait.

A few days later he sat at his desk looking at three letters. One from each of his clients and one from his bank. The coup de grâce, he thought. The picture in his mind had not wavered. The *why* bewildered him, and the *how* stunned him, but all he had to do now was wait.

He looked out of the window. It had been an unusually cold day for September, and the sky had a characteristic hue. Even as he looked, thick snowflakes started to fall and settle on the cold ground. *Ye gods,* he thought, *snow in September, and after another miserable summer.*

"Dad. It's snowing." John burst in unannounced. Peter did not reply, but remained staring out of the window at the whitening landscape. The telephone rang, its noise rending the grey stillness. Peter started.

Without turning he said, "Answer it for me please, John."

John picked up the receiver purposefully and spoke the number.

"May I speak to Mr. Newman please?" said a voice. It sounded old, but powerful and commanding and it sent a chill down John's back.

"Who shall I say is calling?" he replied nervously.

"That's little Johnny isn't it?" said the voice.

"John, sir," he answered in a slightly injured tone.

There was a slight chuckle down the phone. "John it is, young man," came the reply.

31

Mollified, John asked again who was calling, and carefully noted the reply. He held the receiver out to his father.

"He says he's grandfather."

# Chapter 7

The door of the old family house was opened by a man of about Peter's own age. He had straight, dark brown hair, an open, square face and large innocent brown eyes.

"Mr. Newman is expecting you, sir," he said in a quiet voice before Peter could speak. The man's whole attitude was quiet and deferential but without any trace of sycophancy, and his movements had a relaxed economy and grace which Peter recognised.

"Welcome home sir," he said, unexpectedly helping Peter to remove his coat. "Mr. Newman would like you to go straight in. I believe you know where the office is."

Peter nodded. He certainly knew where it was. It was the only place forbidden to him when he was a child, and he had fantasized endlessly about what was in there and what his father did. He walked slowly up the wide stairs and along a familiar corridor towards the office.

He stood for a moment looking at the door pensively, all fantasies and childish memories, he noted, crushed under a grim present reality. He heard a remote-control lock click open and a familiar voice said, "Come in, Peter," through a speaker that he could not see.

The room was quite large, sparsely furnished and simply decorated. His father was sitting upright in a high winged armchair, his head turned sideways to look out through a window. He turned to his son and without speaking gestured towards a chair opposite. Peter sat down and returned his father's gaze.

"Why?" he asked after a while. His father looked down briefly.

"There's a piece of music by Charles Ives called 'The Unanswered Question' in which the would-be answerer gets more and more frantic and eventually has only silence to offer while the universe hums gently on in the background through it all."

"I know the piece," said Peter with some impatience, but he would never have dreamt that his father knew it—more uneasy ground under his feet. His father continued as if uninterrupted.

"Don't you find, even at your age, that motivation is irrelevant? I find that when I do something, it is for one apparent reason then, if I think about it a little, a few more possible reasons occur to me. Then, perhaps unbidden, another reason or two will appear spontaneously, and I wonder what's bubbling on down there in the murky depths of my subconscious. Perhaps your question is unanswerable."

Peter glowered at him malevolently. "You're wasting my time," he said angrily. "You didn't concoct this... this Byzantine extravaganza on some zen-like whim. What the devil do you want?" He had raised his voice and emphasised his question by banging his hands on the chair arms.

His father's face showed mild amusement.

"Wasted your time? What are you going to do with time now?"

Peter knew it had been a foolish thing to say as soon as he had said it, and that it was equally foolish to lose his temper with his father. In frustration he looked down and pressed his fingertips to his forehead while his father looked on impassively.

"You know the answer to your question, don't you?" his father said, eventually.

Peter replied without looking up. "You want me to join the business."

"Not quite," said his father, shifting a little in his seat. Peter looked up, surprised, and met his father's strange gaze. "It is *necessary* that you join the business."

"Necessary for whom?" asked Peter.

"For you, for your family, for countless others."

"And?" Peter looked at his father significantly.

The old man nodded and moved his right hand in a small gesture of concession. "Yes, and for me, son," he said gently.

*Damn,* thought Peter, *the old bugger's playing me like a violin.*

"I can see my need, and my family's," he said. "They're painfully obvious thanks to your machinations, but *you* never needed anyone. And as for countless others..." He shrugged in disbelief.

"Your need and that of the others are the same. Your present problems are nothing compared with the reality of your situation," replied his father with a dismissive flick of his hand. "My own need is admittedly different and personal, but I've no real escape from it."

There was a sincere regret in his voice that could not be denied.

"Father," said Peter. "I know what the business is. It's foul. I don't want anything to do with it. In any case, it's huge. You have your fingers in every conceivable pie. I could be of no earthly use to you. I'm a small businessman not a corporate executive. Ye gods, I'm not even moderately successful any more."

His father's tone became more matter of fact. "You misjudge yourself, Peter. You took a lot of nailing. Your little firm handled itself extremely well, especially as you didn't know what was happening. I was impressed. Genes will out. If it hadn't been for the opportunities provided by that fire, you'd probably still be struggling on, costing me a fortune. The exercise was not intended to take so long by any means. Bastard I might be, but I'm not a sadist."

"Well, I'm hogtied now," replied Peter with some vehemence. "But I'm damned if I'll work for you."

There was a flash of anger across his father's face. "Now you're wasting *my* time Peter. You'll do as you're bloody well told." Briefly, Peter felt eight years old again under his father's tone. "You know it. You've absolutely no alternative, I've made sure of that. You can do nothing. You can, however, spare me the whining about your inability. You are the only person I can trust for this job and, thank God, you're capable of it. What you don't know I'll soon teach you. Besides, you've learned quite a lot recently haven't you?" Peter did not reply. "I know what you think of the business," continued his father more quietly. "And there's worse than you know. But there's also better, and you have no conception of its size and importance, none at all." His tone became gentle. "Peter, what I've done to you has been regrettable, to say the least, but I've had no alternative. You're my child and I love you. I'd have given almost anything to avoid hurting you, but it wasn't to be. You have to be part of the business. You were born to it. I let you go when you were younger hoping you might come back of your own accord. When you didn't and time began pressing, I tried to persuade you, unsuccessfully. So I've had to force you." He paused. "Now we come to it. I will not release you. I can't. Far too much is at stake for me to consider anything else.

But please trust me. You're not the only one who is trapped. You know how you feel about little Johnny, do you think I'd bind you so if I had any alternative? You've been trapped all your life. All I've done is show you the bars. They cage us both."

Peter never decided whether his father was a brilliant and loving man trapped by circumstances beyond his control, or a megalomaniac caught in a web of his own intriguing. Probably both, he would conclude, in his more reflective moments.

Later they walked together in the garden—two dark coated figures idly scarring the new snow with their footprints. The air was quiet and still and calm, and the sun was a watery yellow, glimmering through thin cloud. Peter was still assimilating the discussion with his father and reconciling himself to the position in which he found himself. The muffled quiet of the garden suited him. He could not deny the victim's gratitude to the torturer when the pain stopped, and for all the shock of his father's treatment of him, his nett reaction was one of relief. All the tangle of his business commitments could disappear overnight and both he and his family could be made financially secure for the rest of their lives.

He was a pragmatic person and reasoned that the price he would have to pay would be eased greatly by this knowledge, and he saw no reason why he should not hold part of himself aloof to cherish his family and to savour the few comparatively simple pleasures he valued. The two men were silent as they walked, both rapt in thought. Peter's thoughts about his father were necessarily complex, and the intensity of the day's encounter following years of silence whirled them out of all semblance of consistency. His father had even shown him the master plan for the destruction of his business and his consequent enthralment.

"Look. You'll be interested in this," he had said, pressing a button on the console by his desk. A wall panel slid back to reveal a large, highly detailed chart. His father pressed another button and the chart was illuminated in the wintry gloom that was beginning to pervade the room. "Go and look," he said. "It's a bit old-fashioned, but it gives me a nice overall view and I like to be able to see the whole of a picture at once, don't you?"

Peter got up and walked over to the chart.

"Most of the detail I did on the computer, of course. You'll see the references. And I've left the lower probability branches as open tails. No point in being too fussy is there?" continued his father. But Peter did not hear. The meaning of the chart was sinking in. He saw in coloured lines and symbols and his father's neat hand the entire route he had travelled since his father's last attempt at persuasion had failed. It was a rationalization of his own garbled hindsight. His father came and stood beside him and began to lead him through the chart. Peter's brain reeled as he listened and watched, carried along by his father's enthusiasm, part horrified at the intrinsic callousness of it, part fascinated by the deep insight it demonstrated and the incredible management expertise it represented—relishing the points where his own efforts to maintain his equilibrium had tangled and re-directed the plan, and admiring its adaptability in taking advantage of random chance such as the office fire. In spite of what it was, he was too professional to be other than awed. And the cost! Ye gods. His father seemed to read his thoughts.

"No, you didn't come cheap, Peter, but you're worth it," he said.

Peter looked down at his feet, warm in their black boots, crunching the snow, then around at the garden with its bushes and trees and snow-covered flower beds and lawns. He stared at a thin sapling nearby, bound to a stout stake and protected by a wire cage. Why had his father shown him that chart? Was it a whim, an impulse? Was it to demonstrate his prowess as a manipulator, or to let Peter know how much he was wanted? Was it simply to make him think, to realise what skills and assets were his for the taking, or to show that he was trusted and nothing would be hidden from him, or to show he could not hide anything from his father? Or was it to complete the destruction of his own view of himself and of his father? He shook his head and looked at his father standing a few feet away watching a bird hopping across the snow. His father nodded slowly and grunted as if he too had reached the end of a train of thought.

He turned and looked at Peter. He was a large impressive man, like a kindly feudal lord, a rugged symbol of life in the chilling garden.

"You will join me, Peter?" he said, halfway between question and statement. He paused. "I'll release you from your obligations whether you do or not."

Peter breathed out. Was this a loving father pleading with his son for help, or a consummate actor delivering his pivotal line? Either way, Peter knew he had only one answer.

37

# Chapter 8

So an ambivalent Peter joined his father's business. He never knew whether his father had lured or compelled him, and he grew to agree with his father's assessment of motivation—at best, an intriguing exercise, at worst a distracting irrelevance. It dawned on him that same day when he was driving back from his father's house that the only real motive is probably survival. That was why his father had done what he had done, that was why he was going to do what he was going to do—to survive. He thought of himself as a humane, perhaps even civilized man, and he cringed inwardly at his conclusion and its implications. Even taking care to avoid pain to others as I survive is only for my own long-term security, he thought. I can't even grace that with the guise of humanity, of disinterested caring. Then again, is it such an ignoble conclusion?

He brushed the thoughts from his mind.

"Sod it," he said out loud. "I'll be lucky if I survive the journey home in this lot."

The snow was melting, but it had been thick and well compacted in the day and now, lubricated by the thaw, it was very treacherous. Having already had two slight skids, he was maintaining a considerable distance from the car in front and was relieved to see the car behind doing likewise. Peter was not trained to think that way, so he never noticed that the car behind had been following him since he had left his father's house.

At home that night he found he could not tell Ann everything. His pride would not let him tell her he had been a pawn in a grotesque game, and he could not face rejecting the various arguments she would raise to enable them to settle their affairs and live happily, if poorly, ever after. So he lied, or more correctly, omitted much of the truth. It was the first time he had kept anything from her and he felt a little wretched. He knew he would have to keep more and more things from her in the future, but he resolved to keep what he considered to be his real self for her alone.

Though he was assailed by doubts about his decision, a little reflection reminded him that he could never work at his own business again, even if only because he would never know which jobs were bait containing his father's hook. And, he realized, the professional in him was looking forward to working with his father. Also, his own business now seemed very small and distant.

So he told Ann, quite simply, "My father heard about the difficulties I'm in. He's offered me a good job and he's going to do what he can with the bank and both companies—which will probably be a lot."

Ann was both delighted and concerned. Delighted because this terrible burden she felt unable to help with would be lifted from her husband, but concerned because she knew of Peter's dislike for his father and his business.

"I think I'll have to reassess my father," he said quite genuinely, and also in an attempt to forestall his wife's concern. "It's been a shaking day. I've learned a lot of things, about me and about him. Please don't worry, I'm sure I'll be able to cope with everything alright. In fact, in some ways I'm rather excited. And it'll be such a relief to be free of those terrible schemes."

He had agreed with his father to spend a few days relaxing with his family and winding down his remaining business commitments, so he spent the next day pottering about his office, sorting out paper and files, speaking on the telephone to old clients and generally tying up loose ends. Almost all of his clients were personal friends and he was touched by the unanimity of their congratulations and their regrets at his closing his company. He was not an excessively sentimental man, and the frenzy of the recent months had effectively destroyed the small sense of pride and affection that used to be enshrined in the paraphernalia of his office, but it was a little more harrowing than he had envisaged and he was pleased when he had finished. He knew he must try to maintain this sense of caring for apparently inconsequential items, but he felt that as time passed he must inevitably become a harsher and more callous man.

Two days later, another three letters lay on his desk. One was from his bank thanking him for the substantial payment and regretting they had twisted his arm, and hoping they could be of further service in the future, etc etc. Peter looked at the statement which had accompanied the letter. The payment had cancelled his overdraft and left a credit balance equal to as much as he would make in two successful years. The other two were from his erstwhile clients. Sorry about all the confusion, changes of staff and policy, unforeseen circumstances, schemes regretfully cancelled, no fault of yours, happy to use you again, herewith cheque to cover extra work hitherto disputed and loss of fees due to abandonment etc etc. Both contained cheques for amounts far in excess of what he could reasonably have earned, and both were virtually identical. He had never read such ridiculous letters in his entire career, and he recognised his father's finishing touch in their deliberate clumsiness. I've got the message, Father; the exclamation mark wasn't really necessary, he thought. Still, the prospect of not having to worry about money for a few years was very pleasant.

# Chapter 9

The change in his father's circumstances, yet again, had little effect on John. In fact, his father seemed to be more meticulous than ever in keeping contact with him. The main difference was that Peter had to be away from home during the day and evening more than before, and the time at home, being less, became much more organized. As far as John understood the matter, his father had once upon a time quarrelled with his grandfather and they were now friends again. Not only that, his grandfather had given his father a job, and they were now quite well off. In fact, John suspected they were beginning to be quite rich. It was, however, a sore point with him that this new-found affluence manifested itself in shoes and shirts and other such irrelevancies and a relatively small amount, in his opinion, was added to his pocket money. He tried to negotiate with his father, but found him singularly unwilling to deal. He also tried a little stamping and screaming, but it was not really in character, and being either ignored or laughed at, he soon abandoned that as a possible avenue to wealth.

He noticed that his father was much more cheerful than he had been for a long time, but he sensed a sadness in him that he could not understand. No-one could analyse Peter Newman's feelings, least of all a child. But a child could feel them, and John would offer greater balm than he could ever know by occasionally going to his father unbidden and embracing him.

After a few months of the new regime, the house was plunged into chaos by the arrival of builders. Peter's father had wanted him to move to a 'better designed' house, nearer to his own property on the other side of the city.

"Yours is too difficult to secure and you're having to do too much travelling. You're too vulnerable," he had said. But he had eventually yielded a small victory to his son. Peter was unequivocal and uncompromising. John's life was not to be disrupted in any way, and while not approving of what he considered to be excessive sentimentality—"Good grief Peter, he'll take a change like that in his stride at his age"—his father conceded, rather than risk contact with that in Peter's soul which stared through his eyes when business matters impinged in any way on his son. He had seen it flash briefly once or twice and remembered Carlo returning from an earlier interview with his son.

Carlo was an old employee with a long and dark history in the business. He was a hard man by any definition and not one who could be intimidated, but he was visibly shaken by something that had happened at the meeting. "He's your son, Mr. Newman. I think he'll take a lot of punishment himself without turning, but if anything threatens his family, particularly his son..." He shrugged significantly. "I can say this to you Mr. Newman because you've known me a long time. We've fought together. You know what I'm worth. He looked at me and..." He drew in a breath sharply through pursed lips then, hesitantly, "With all due respect to your judgement, I think it would not be a beneficial approach."

"Thank you, Carlo, you've done well. I'll respect your judgement in this matter," he had replied. And so he had. All pressure on Peter from that point was direct. Interesting, thought the old man subsequently. If I push on your family I will push you away. If I push on you, it will be your concern for their concern about you that will make you accessible. Interesting.

"They're very thoughtful and tidy," said Ann, tiptoeing over covered carpets between carefully stacked heaps of building materials, about a week after the builders moved in. Had she been more familiar with the building industry, she would have been astonished at their efficiency, and quite probably suspicious. The 'surveyors', as she called them, who appeared from time to time and pottered round, taking measurements and staring significantly at walls and ceilings, and talking to the workmen were, along with the workmen, part of a team of leading security specialists, who were installing a very sophisticated security system under the guise of household improvements.

The new double-glazed windows and doors were, unbeknown to Ann, bulletproof. The door and window locks and the alarm system protecting not only the house, but also the boundary walls, were considerably more than the 'standard insurance requirement for company executives'. The modest landscaping of the garden surreptitiously cleared certain important sight lines, the self-contained CHP system and the extended freezers, ostensibly to cut household expenses, made them capable of many weeks self-sufficiency, and so on.

When the mayhem had finished, everyone was pleased. Ann had had all her modest household fantasies realized, and Peter had turned the house into a substantial fortress without Ann knowing. Even Peter's father grudgingly agreed. "Well you're not a bad designer. It's on the right lines, I suppose."

John, having been carefully consulted about the decor, had tolerated decorators in his own room and had ruefully accepted the domesticating of various other rooms which had previously been wild and empty. But by far the most exciting development for him was the conversion of the basement into a shooting range.

For almost as long as he could remember, Peter had been interested in firearms. It had been an interest covertly fostered by his father, and subsequently openly encouraged when it had taken root. Having received top class tuition, he had become an excellent target shooter with rifle and pistol, but had drifted away from it when he quarrelled with his father and his marriage and his business began to occupy more of his time. Now his father advised him to spend some time regaining his old skills.

"It'll relax you in more ways than one," he said. "Teach young John while you're at it. He'll love it."

Peter was beginning to learn enough about the business to realize that there could be occasions when his personal safety might be at risk, although he could accept it only in academic terms—his stomach told him nothing. Still, he reasoned, it will do no harm to get my eye back in, and it's high time John was taught anyway.

So John was introduced to the world of firearms. There was no demur from Ann. She was country born and free from the more grotesque obsessions that cloud most women's judgements when dealing with firearms. In fact she was that rare being, a naturally good shot. Once she had been shown how a particular weapon worked, she would pick it up, load it, and assume some strange firing position, all in a manner guaranteed to make Peter wince, and then shoot a group similar to or even better than he had been able to achieve after extensive practice.

"I don't know how you do it," he used to say.

"Just point it and pull the trigger," she would reply. "How do you do it?"

He had never been able to answer that. All he could do was whimper and clench his teeth. He had, of course, always been pleased about her ability and accepted her superiority over him with what he considered to be quiet dignity, although it was not always easy, especially if she felt provocative and, looking at his target, would click her tongue and shake her head sadly. What did bewilder him slightly was that although she was such a good shot, she was utterly indifferent to shooting as a sport. Now, however, he was simply pleased that she could pick up a gun and use it competently. It ticked off one item on a long contingency list that was developing as his knowledge of the business grew.

Unlike his mother, John was not a natural, but he was intelligent and attentive, and after some initial over-excitement he soon began to make progress. Peter would have preferred to teach him with an air pistol or possibly a .22 single shot, but the only ones he had were heavy and bulky and far too awkward for a child's hand, so he opted for a small .22 automatic pistol. John was only too keen to practice every day, and soon became quite competent with either hand. Peter never allowed him to join a club, so it was a long time before he realized that target shooting did not normally involve shooting one target right-handed and then one target left-handed. Once he was consistently placing ten shots in a four-inch group at twenty yards, Peter surreptitiously eased him into a more advanced programme of training. Bringing the gun up from its rest position and, as quickly as possible firing one shot, then raising the gun and firing two shots, then raising it and firing at a target that appeared only for two seconds, then one and a half seconds, then one second. Eventually John could put four shots on two targets in under two seconds, using either hand.

Peter was pleased with the boy's progress and introduced him to his .357 Magnum. It was a small framed revolver, which he preferred to the bulkier models, being less awkward to carry all day in a holster, and John could handle it reasonably comfortably. Using light .38 special target loads, the recoil was not severe and John had no difficulty in eventually shooting groups comparable with those from his .22. He didn't have the strength in his hands to fire the revolver double action, but his father taught him the combat stance, with its tensioned double-handed grip to control the recoil, and also how to draw a gun from a holster.

Peter also used his son's training to recapture some of his own pleasure in the sport, and they ran all manner of competitions to amuse themselves. They had a great deal of scope. The range would have been the envy of even the most sophisticated clubs, not to mention most police training ranges. It had turning targets, targets that could move across or up and down the range, variable lighting, an elaborate falling plate shoot that Peter had designed himself, a sound controlled projection system and a computer to ring any number of changes from any piece of equipment. Their favourite game was one of the simplest. On a given signal, both drew their guns and shot at a pair of square metal plates. These were hinged, and the first shooter to knock down his pair was the winner. Peter had insisted on two plates each, as he and his .357 revolver were no match for John with his younger reflexes and the rate of fire he could get from his .22 automatic.

After a few months John's enthusiasm waned gradually and Peter eased off his secret training programme. He was well satisfied. The boy had a very high awareness of gun safety and could handle both rifle and pistol extremely well in a wide range of disciplines. He would have a hobby he would enjoy for years and possibly a skill that might one day save his life. He ticked off another item on his contingency list.

He was also well satisfied with his own progress. Keeping up with John had been hard work and he had enjoyed honing his own rusty technique.

Over that period, while Peter was teaching John, so his father had been teaching Peter. His knowledge of the business widened and deepened. Some of the things he learned frightened him and he was not too surprised or alarmed when one day the two teaching lines crossed, and his father advised him that it would be a good idea if he wore his gun when he was not in the office.

"Father, this is England," he offered as a token remonstrance.

"Peter, don't be naive," was the only reply.

He was also not surprised when he was granted legal permission to carry the gun loaded and at any time. The ostensible reason, to be heavily buried in the official records, was that "Mr. Newman is occasionally obliged, on very short notice, to carry valuables, cash and sensitive documents in areas where there is a high risk of serious personal attack, and where a conspicuous police presence would be counter-productive." The real reason was that his father had pulled a tiny string and the city's Chief Constable had jumped to.

# Chapter 10

Peter was alternately appalled and fascinated by the business and by his father. The size of the business and its known subsidiaries was staggering. Then there were the unknown subsidiaries. In his less buoyant moods, he thought that there was no business on earth in which he was not involved in some way. And the links by which these many pieces were joined and authority vested in one man were bewildering in the extreme. Every day his view of the whole increased under his father's guidance, and every day his view of his father increased.

The man's intellect and knowledge and experience were truly formidable, and Peter stood in some awe, very uncertain that he could even begin to replace his father when the time came. But paradoxically, along with the man's perceptiveness, his psychological insight, human understanding and true humility, rode cunning deviousness, treachery, a ruthless callousness and a monumental ego. Both his father and the business reminded him of the Chinese yin-yang symbol: part black, part white, with some white in the black and some black in the white, and the whole perfectly symmetrical. Except, he thought, there was no clear-cut border between black and white. Just a varying grey penumbra, no clear lines anywhere, no certainty, and a feeling that the symbol was really three dimensional and mobile, not flat and static. What distressed Peter was the knowledge that the dark needed the light and vice versa. He knew enough to know that not only could the dark not be eliminated, but it was arguable that it should be. It was a reflection of human nature. The destruction of the dark would unbalance and shatter the whole and who could even guess at what repercussions would follow the consequent oscillations. It was a moral dilemma which was probably insoluble in principle. Perhaps all he could ever do was clarify the grey area and ease the friction between the two. He began to feel the pressure of the trap that held his father and now him. When your vehicle goes out of control you concentrate on steering, not where your destination is—you concentrate on travelling hopefully, not arriving. And yet the trap was, at least in part, of his father's own making.

"One of the reasons I didn't attend to you as I'd have liked when you were young, was that I was fighting for my life, sometimes literally," said his father one day in a rare moment of nostalgia. "My father greatly stabilized and consolidated this business, and he was a bloody-handed old devil." He paused reflectively. "But he left some pretty lethal tail-ends for me to cut off I can tell you. Anyway, they're dealt with long ago and you'll take over the organization larger and more efficient than it's ever been, thanks to me."

"But it's too big, father. I had no idea. Isn't it possible to start slowly trimming it down?"

His father looked at him slowly. "You'll learn. You should know already we need this size if we're to have the flexibility to avoid the constraints that some would put on us. We can't afford the luxury of dancing to the tune of politicians and public officials. That would be the tail wagging the dog."

Peter did not press his point. He was not sure enough of his ground and he sensed it was a very dangerous area to tread against his father. He felt the rightness of his suggestion, even from his limited knowledge of the business, but he could not deny the practical validity of his father's last remark. He wondered if the business was organic enough to heal itself if portions were broken off, or would it fragment into chaos beyond a certain point, or would other organizations form spontaneously and lead to the internecine disputes that had cost so dear in the past? And all this power in one pair of hands, or was it power? Perhaps, after all, he was being handed the reins of a runaway stagecoach full of passengers. But underneath all his emotional and intellectual toing and froing, he knew that an imbalance was developing. The dark side of his symbol was expanding, becoming more dominant. The nett total of human suffering was growing. He did not debate this with his father, as he knew he would not, perhaps could not, listen. But a tiny hesitant seed of resolve formed within him. I've no choice but to take these reins, I'm the only person here, and I and my family will be destroyed if I do not, either directly or as a result of the destruction of others. I must take them if only for my own sake, but I will lead them my way.

Peter stretched out and rubbed his eyes. "Yes," said his father, getting up from his desk. "I'm tired too. It's been a long day. But good, mind you, good."

Peter looked uncertainly at the papers in front of him. "Well," he said. "I'm not too sure. Your proposal for implementing your will is of course impeccable. A classic unobtrusive abuse of power, and yet another object lesson for me."

His father inclined his head in acknowledgement and smiled slightly.

"But the decision itself, I don't know. That was very difficult."

His father walked over to the fireplace and, checking his watch, carefully adjusted the fingers of the large chiming clock. He looked at his son in the mirror which hung above the clock. "No Peter. That decision was easy."

"How can you say that, father? When those mines close, that region will become derelict. There's nothing else there."

"I don't dispute that. But I've spent all day going over the facts with you. Even though the miners are, in reality, underpaid, the mines haven't made any profit for years, their equipment is antiquated, they're nearly worked out, they're intrinsically dangerous because of their geological structure, and now to cap it all there have been earth tremors in the same region."

Peter waited. His father turned round. "The decision to close is easy. There's really no alternative. If I bail them out by arranging for some form of financial aid, it will simply be throwing good money after bad, and merely postpone the inevitable. More importantly, that money could be better used elsewhere in the region. And how would you feel if we kept the mines open artificially, and the miners had to move into those deeper strata, the unstable ones?" He pointed vaguely to a folder on his desk. "There could be a massive tragedy. No, the decision wasn't difficult, it was simply unpleasant and sad. You'll know a hard decision when you get one to make. This one has been unusually simple. More typically you'll have to choose between two evils when there's precious few good points on either side and the bad points are equally balanced. Those are the hard decisions."

"Yes, I accept your reasoning," replied Peter. "But it's just that I feel that in manipulating this situation as we're intending to, we ought similarly to arrange something for the people most directly affected."

His father smiled. "I agree. Even though they don't even know we exist, there's no point gratuitously making enemies when a little ingenuity will gain friends."

"That's not quite what I meant and you know it," said Peter.

"But it's true isn't it, Peter? I've told you before. Don't be so concerned with motivation. It's futile. You must always have options in mind, contingency plans. Bread on the water, my boy," he said in a mock Jewish accent. The unexpected flash of humour made Peter laugh and wave his hand dismissively. "Anyway," continued his father. "You're the conservationist. I'd have thought you'd have worked it out for yourself."

"What do you mean?"

His father became thoughtful. He stroked his nose with his forefinger. "I think I'll let you handle the details yourself, but think about this. That area used to be farming land, quite an old and stable rural economy. It's very debatable whether the finding of those minerals in that area served the best interests of the natives one jot. Most of the miners are from farming stock, so some at least may want to return to the land. If my memory serves me correctly, we have agencies which could be arranged to fund a scheme to encourage the redevelopment of farming and give advice on appropriate technology. Yes," he mused. "That's an interesting idea. I'll set you on it tomorrow. See what you can do."

Peter looked at his father suspiciously. "You've had this set up all the time," he said.

"No, no," protested his father. "In all conscience Peter, it really only just occurred to me." Peter grunted non-committally.

The old man looked down into the fire. "I'm glad you're settling in, Peter," he said. "You're good for me. You argue with me. Few people can do that. Few people *dare* do that. We'll do well for the business together. It's a long way from being all bad, isn't it?

Peter nodded and smiled, but did not answer. He got up slowly and took his coat from the chair. "Anyway, I'm off," he said, gathering some papers from his desk. "I'll read these again tonight and get started tomorrow. Cheerio."

He walked towards the door.

"Peter." The tone was stern. Peter caught his father's eye. He was looking at the desk. On it lay his belt and the holster containing his revolver. Peter sighed. He put down his briefcase, picked up the belt and manoeuvred it through the loops on his trousers, his father watching him.

"I know what you're thinking, Peter," he said. "This is England. It's ridiculous walking around like Wyatt Earp, etc etc."

Peter smiled at the mimicry in spite of himself, but his father continued. "You're not in England any more. You're in a world where local customs and normal ground rules don't apply. Take my advice. Get used to carrying it. It's only an option you might need, but it's like swimming. You may only need it once in your life, but then you'll *really* need it."

Peter nodded. "I understand. It's just..." He searched for a word. "Culture shock, I suppose you'd call it. To be honest, I feel like a prune, not Wyatt Earp."

"Too bad." His father's tone and expression squashed the levity. "Wear it, and don't forget it again. I've let you get away with murder and it's got to stop. It's company rules and no-one's exempt."

Peter looked at him seriously. "You do realize that I've no idea whether I could use it in self-defence. Against people. I've got years of range safety procedures in my bones."

"None of us knows the answer to that until it happens, but my bet is that you would if you had to. Genes will out. Anyway, if you keep your eyes open and don't let the local cover fool you, you'll probably never have to use it. But..."

He raised an admonitory finger.

"I know, I know. Contingencies."

Peter pulled out the gun, instinctively checked it and dropped it into the pocket of his overcoat. His father nodded approvingly.

"How's John getting on with his martial arts classes?" he asked casually, as Peter fastened his coat. Peter looked up and smiled.

"Oh, he loves it. More than I ever did. He's really taken..." He stopped. "How did you know?" he asked suspiciously. His father looked at him in innocent bewilderment. Peter stuttered. "It's only a bit of sport for him."

His father raised his eyebrows. "Oh, sport. I see. Very good for young people, sport," he nodded, allowing his amused knowledge of the truth to show through.

Peter fumbled for words again. "Well... well..." Then, abruptly. "Well, hell. I don't know why I should explain to you. It's, it's..."

"Contingency planning?" offered his father with a broad laugh. Peter became quiet and gentle.

"Yes, of course it is. Even outside this." He swept his arm round the room. "Life seems to be getting harsher, more violent. As you say, if he ever needs it, he'll really need it. But he does enjoy it and it'll do him a lot of good—teach him a lot of discipline."

Peter moved to the door again. "Oh, by the way," he said, turning round in the doorway and pointing his index finger at his father and raising his thumb. "He shoots good, too."

"I know," said his father with another broad smile and a wink.

Peter closed the door quietly.

"And so do you," said the old man to himself, his face now solemn and pensive. "You're doing well. Keep it up."

# Chapter 11

Peter walked round the outside of the house to the garage, instead of using the inside door. It was a dark autumn evening with a damp gusty wind blowing, and a fine drizzle turning the crackling leaves into a treacherous slither. Peter took a deep cold breath and reflected that being alive was wonderful and that for all his concerns, he was a lucky and fortunate individual.

As he approached the garage, the doors slid back, activated, he knew, by one of his father's assistants who would have been watching on the closed-circuit television. He gave an acknowledging wave to one of the visible cameras, and a wink to one of the hidden ones he had eventually located.

In a room in the centre of the house, the assistant in question watched impassively as the car moved slowly out of the garage and down the drive. His left hand flicked a switch to close the garage doors, and another to open the main gates. On the monitor screen the car's brake lights shone bright for a moment, reflecting in the wet road surface, as Peter prepared to pull out into the road. Then the car moved out of sight. The left hand pressed the switch back to close the gates and then reached out for a telephone handset on the control panel. Holding the handset, the hand tapped out a number with its forefinger. There was an almost immediate click as the call was received, but there was no voice.

"He just left," said the assistant. There was no reply—just another click. The assistant slowly hung the handset back in its cradle, and then leaned back in his chair and continued his observation of the monitor screens in front of him.

Peter enjoyed his new car. To all outward appearances it was just another fairly expensive estate car, one grade up from his previous one and quite commensurate with his new job, as advertised to friends and neighbours. It's most conspicuous feature was that it was invariably clean and polished, and this fact alone produced more raised eyebrows than the car itself. The cleanliness was of course a minor perquisite of the job and no tribute to any change of heart by Peter. He had only ever bowed a most cursory knee to the more fatuous fripperies of social convention, and now he adopted them purely as disguise while he moved around in his father's brave old world. Underneath the gloss, however, the car was very different. Its engine belonged to a far more powerful vehicle, and the braking system and suspension had been adjusted accordingly. The body had been discreetly strengthened. It had a security system which amongst other things made it virtually impossible for anyone to break in or even tamper with it, and transmitted a radio signal to Peter to let him know if anything was amiss. Of course, the whole vehicle, tyres included, was bulletproof.

As he changed down and accelerated to pass a lorry, he relished the ease with which the car surged forward and pushed him in the back. It was quite seductive, like the business itself—powerful, well-tuned, disciplined.

"And dangerous," he said out loud, changing back into top gear. Looking in his mirror he saw a van overtake the lorry and settle in behind him.

Thinking about the business turned his mind to his parting conversation with his father. It had never occurred to him that his father would be interested in what John was doing. Peter had done some martial arts when he was young, and while he had acquired some useful knowledge, no spark had ever been struck, and his father was too preoccupied to hold his nose to the grindstone for long. He had, however, done enough to realize the value of such training, and determined that John would benefit from such a study.

He had used one of his father's motley praetorian guard as the prime source of information. The man was a great burly Australian who looked like a farmer but was in fact an expert on international finance, and a karateka whose speed and strength had to be seen to be believed. His awesome reputation amongst his peers was totally belied by his gentle demeanour and his fund of tall tales. After discreetly checking the advice, in the manner of his father, he was able to put John in two martial art classes where he would be taught properly and not be distracted by the sporting element that diluted the value of many others.

"Talk about sport to these people, digger," said his informant, grinning as he drove a great fist into the palm of his other hand, "and you'll go home in a paper bag."

Peter accepted the advice with a nod and a smile and reflected that tomorrow this same man would probably be using those hands as sensitively as a ballet dancer while he was making some inordinately complex point about off-shore tax law.

John had taken immediately to karate, but a certain pressure had been necessary with the aikido, with its very strict discipline and the apparent irrelevancy of much of its training. However, he had eventually settled down and progressed well in both.

"And you knew all the time, didn't you, you old bugger?" Peter said out loud again. He knew it was of no consequence, but all the same, he wondered whether his father had found out by accident or through some routine report on his behaviour.

He slowed down as he entered a narrow length of road which twisted steeply downhill. He quite enjoyed this short section, as around one particular bend a break in the trees revealed the suburbs below, and at night he always thought the lights had a magical quality appearing as they did, very suddenly, through the trees. He noticed in his mirror that the van was still behind him, and driving rather too close. The unnecessary headlights annoyed him and he missed the anticipated view while he was swearing. At the bottom of the hill, the road straightened out so he accelerated and left the van some way behind.

He began to mull over his next day's work. He could make a start on the farming project his father had mentioned. Returning the disrupted community back to agricultural self-sufficiency using high technology thinking to improve low technology practices was to learn from and respect tradition while removing the more onerous appendages it had acquired through the years. It appealed to him enormously, as his father must have known. With all its ambiguities, it was what the business could do well. Could do, should do, and in so far as he was able to affect matters, would do. He would tackle the scheme with relish and also use it to practice weaving the delicate nets of manipulations that his father used so well to effect his will.

The van was back. Headlights in his mirror so that he could get no indication of who was driving or what other traffic lay behind.

"Damn," he muttered. He had no desire to hurry and no intention of being pressured so he signalled a left turn and eased into a layby to let the van pass. He watched it as it passed but it was travelling fast and the streetlights illuminated only a dirty window, so he could not see the driver. He pulled out again as the van disappeared round a bend in the road ahead.

The drizzle had stopped, but the road was very wet and a little treacherous in places due to the autumn leaves, so he was glad the road was empty and he could pursue his own steady pace. He was looking forward to a quiet evening at home with Ann and John and he was feeling very relaxed.

The relaxation faded a little when he looked in his mirror again and saw the van pulling out from a gateway behind him. Reason told him that it had probably been making a delivery, but a sixth sense made him uncomfortable and his hands clenched and unclenched the steering wheel unconsciously. It dawned on him slowly that the van had been behind him for a long way, and the route from his father's house to his own was not one which many drivers would have to take, skimming as it did the outskirts of the city in a ragged line of minor roads. He peered into his mirror to look for the driver, but the headlights obscured everything, and he began to feel alarmed. Get a grip, he thought. You're being silly. All the same, it was a lonely stretch of road he was approaching, cutting through a section of woodland, and he decided it would be advisable to check on his persistent companion.

He thought about the road ahead and made his decision. A few hundred yards further on he took his foot off the accelerator and watched the van coming nearer as he gradually slowed down. Then, without signalling, he swung the car hard right into a side road. The van followed. The last consoling threads of coincidence were slipping from him. Now we'll see, he thought, as he approached a roundabout and, again without signalling, he drove right round and headed back the way he had come. His stomach tightened and he felt suddenly cold as he looked in his mirror and saw the van's headlights swinging round after him.

That was it. He slammed the car into third gear and pushed his right foot down onto the floor. The tyres screamed and he was thrown back harshly against his seat as the powerful engine responded. Approaching the junction with the main road, he realized he was going too fast, but he had sufficient command left to pump his brake pedal to avoid skidding on the wet road.

"Calm down," he said to himself. "Calm down."

Even so, he overshot the junction slightly and was more than relieved that the main road was clear. He realized that, quite ridiculously, he was signalling a right turn, and also that he was beginning to panic.

"Calm down," he repeated, but the headlights were turning into the main road after him and he stopped listening to himself. He had to get away, and the car's power was his only hope. Panic took over. Fortunately, he had many years' experience of reasonably careful driving imbued in his frame, and his body refused to match the headlong race of his mind. It preserved him for quite a way, although he had never taken a fast bend or controlled a real skid in his life. But eventually the forces of disorder won the day and with unerring accuracy he picked exactly the wrong moment to brake when taking a sharp right-hand bend in the middle of the woods.

It is debatable whether he could have taken the bend safely in good weather at the speed he was travelling, but the wet surface and the leaves clinched it, and the car spun round and round, temporarily relieving its occupant of the burden of responsibility for control. When it stopped, the back was almost touching a stone wall running along the edge of the road, and the front was jutting out into the road. Peter was trembling—childish terror and adult experience fighting for control.

The van came screamed round the bend, headlights menacing.

"No, no, no."

The words were almost a whimper and their strange, pathetic sound seemed to resolve the conflict, as if the child had fled with them. Simultaneously he heard his father say, "You're not in England any more," and himself telling John, "You must keep at it, you mustn't quit."

The one pointed up the loneliness he was learning, the other touched the ties of love that bound him to life and, peculiarly, a sense of both pride and responsibility. He must not let John down.

The almost hysterical terror was turning slowly into anger and he realized who he was again. A tiny, objective part of his mind reminded him that his trembling was a natural response to danger; to prepare the body for movement, not paralysis.

The van pulled up with its front wheels in front of his own.

"You're not in England any more."

He fumbled for the gun in his pocket. The door of the van slid open and a figure was illuminated by the car's headlights. It was a man wearing a balaclava mask and dressed in a bulky car coat. As he turned to step out of the van, Peter saw he was carrying a shotgun. Familiar as he was with the sight of firearms, the sight of one that might be used against him had a strange effect on him.

All the clattering pandemonium in his mind and body disappeared instantly. Not a sudden draining, but instantly. He was in another world. One with no past and no future, no memories or anticipations, no awareness of self, nothing. Only a universal and vivid certainty which needed no name and to which all was dedicated. Following the predestined course of this universe his door opened with dreamlike ease, a sight picture appeared sharp and still in front of him, hands rested on the most perfect and comfortable rest imaginable, a trigger was pulled three times with a flawless smoothness.

Then the universe vanished and the pandemonium returned. There was a cry from the figure as it fell back inside the van, a frenzied screeching of tyres, and the van was gone.

Peter sat there, half out of his car, his hands resting on the junction between the door and the car body, his ears ringing with the concussion of his .357 and his body trembling uncontrollably. He looked blankly at the revolver, aware that he should feel grateful but unable to remember how. The intense vividness of the last few seconds hung like an afterglow in his mind. He leaned out of the car and vomited.

Slowly, some semblance of normality started to return and his hot flushed face felt the damp night air. He got out of the car, walked over to the wall and touched its mossy surface for no apparent reason. Then he leaned his forehead against it and waited for his breathing and heartbeat to slow down. Turning round he looked into the forest shadows illuminated by the car headlights, and identified the noise that had been puzzling him as his car engine.

It came to him that although he was weak and shaky, the worst reaction had passed, because in its wake came questions. Worse than the questions was his growing assessment of his own conduct. He would need to think about that. He returned to the car and stepping gingerly round the mess he had made, dropped gratefully into the driver's seat, quietly closed the door and started off for home again.

"Take it easy," he said to himself. "You're in shock. Nice and steady does it."

The thought occurred to him that the van might return, but he rejected it. He had killed the man with the shotgun without a doubt. Killed. He felt the word should have had more effect on him. That's some social barrier you just broke, my boy, he thought. You're not in England any more. But there was nothing. Nothing could pass the oldest rule of gun handling. The man had been about to point a gun at him. That was a direct threat to his life and offered no time for calm reflection, so he had shot at him until the threat had gone—his only legitimate response. The man had died as a result. That was his own fault. No moral ambiguity. His fault. Amen.

As he drove home, he made no effort to stop himself reliving the incident and noting the questions that arose. He was old enough to realize that benefits can be had from anything, and that, for his own sake, he must analyse and criticise his own behaviour as objectively as possible. Also the constant replaying of the film was a necessary therapy. As with grief, certain things had to come out, sooner or later, and sooner was far better than later.

By the time he reached home he was fully recovered from the outward physical signs of the incident so it was comparatively easy to convince Ann that his preoccupation that evening was due to business problems—a fact that he felt could be true, which is why she smelt no lie on his breath. He realized he could no more tell her the truth than slash her face with a razor.

He did not ring his father. He did not want to speak to him until his thoughts were much clearer and the incident further away. He had a fitful and uneasy night.

"So Peter," his father said next day. "Your questions are why didn't I see them sooner, why didn't I use my car radio, and why did I get out of the car, which was bulletproof, instead of using it as a weapon?" His father had listened with complete impassivity as Peter, feeling a profound sense of unreality, had recounted his tale. Now he spoke in a matter-of-fact manner which caught Peter off-guard.

"There are other questions of course, which I'm sure you've considered," he continued. "Such as why? Who? And..." He leaned forward and spoke with a tone of mixed concern and frustration. "Why didn't you ring me as soon as you reached home?"

Peter fidgeted a little. "That was probably a mistake," he said. "I was probably shocked, but I felt I needed to think. I'm sorry."

His father breathed out noisily and slapped his hand on the desk. "Sorry," he said in some irritation. "My men could have been out in minutes looking for that van. Saints, Peter. There could be a body out there with three of your very identifiable bullets in it." He caught the change in Peter's face. "Yes," he said. "I thought you'd missed that little gem in your philosophical considerations."

"What shall I do then? I need your advice," Peter said quietly. His father stared down at the floor thoughtfully, rubbing his upper lip with his forefinger.

"At the moment," he said eventually. "Nothing. There's nothing you can do anyway. I'll make enquiries to see if anything's turned up and, as you said, we can always plead shock to account for the delay in reporting the matter if things go wrong."

Peter sighed. "I've messed it all up haven't I, Father?" he said apologetically. His father looked at him, inclining his head sideways.

"No," he said. "As a matter of fact you didn't. You made a lot of serious mistakes, but that's partly my fault. I hadn't envisaged this and I've neglected some of your basic training. Been too lax with the company rules. We've been lucky to get away with it. Still, having dug yourself into a hole, you pulled yourself out with some style. You did well. Any repercussions we should be able to handle, and it seems to me that all we need to do with you is teach you to drive properly."

Then he leaned forward and spoke very quietly and seriously. "I've had people try to kill me Peter, in many ways. There's no other feeling remotely like it. It's not something you could get used to, but now it's happened to you, you'll have no trouble in learning the little tricks of observation that can usually keep you out of trouble.

It's only a matter of developing a few new habits and this will concentrate your mind wonderfully."

"And how do I deal with having killed someone?" asked Peter.

His father leaned back and shrugged carelessly.

"No problem, Peter. You didn't kill him. He killed himself, you know that. Anybody who waves a gun about like that is asking to be shot. He would be alive now if he hadn't chased you and pointed a gun at you, wouldn't he? He did it of his own accord. He could have killed you. You have neither legal nor moral responsibility for him. Forget it."

"But..."

"But nothing. Feel sadness if you must. Nothing more. It's no different than if he'd thrown himself in front of your car."

"I know you're right father, but I can't help feeling..."

His father slapped the desk again, hard and angrily. "Peter, enough," he said. "You've survived, that's all that matters. We've only two concerns. Firstly, deal with any outside complications that might arise. Secondly, ensure that you are better trained to avoid or at least escape anything similar in future. Even sitting where you sit now you'll make decisions affecting thousands of people. Some of them will be destroyed in one way or another by your action. Some day, almost inevitably, you'll have to arrange for some perfectly innocent individual to be killed because he is in the way."

"For the greater good. The ends justify the means," said Peter with some distaste. His father sighed and his anger vanished. For the briefest instant, Peter saw a tired old man sitting in front of him.

"Peter," said his father. "There are no ends, no real ends. There are only means. Nothing ever ends. Directions change, that's all. And yes, it will be for the greater good, and you'll be the arbiter of it whether you like it or not. You'll have no choice."

Peter stood up and walked to the window. He looked out at the trees losing their last leaves and at the gardener patiently sweeping them up. He knew that part of him was being calloused over, like a fighter's knuckles or a guitarist's fingers. He even knew that his own lack of regret about it was a measure of it. He nodded and raised his hand to acknowledge that he had no reply.

"I'll go and have a work-out. It'll disentangle me. I'll be alright shortly."

"I know you will Peter. You go on down to the gym. I want a word with Joey for a few minutes then I'll send him down to kick you around a bit."

He pressed a button on his desk. As Peter reached the door, his father spoke again. "Do some shooting while you're down there. Get your nerve back."

Peter nodded and almost collided with Joey arriving in answer to his father's summons.

The household establishment comprised cooks and bottle washers, secretarial staff, technical assistants, security staff, and so on, in common with other large houses that doubled as homes and company headquarters. But Newman's staff were a little different. They came and went after varying periods, but all came from a pool he had brought together over many years, after much careful sifting and weeding. They were all very rich people, but each had also some personal reason for unswerving loyalty to his employer. And an unusual feature was that while they were all considerable experts in their respective callings, each could do the other's jobs to some extent if necessary, and yet each was sufficient master of his own to ensure that the group was free from the petty frictions common to other similar groups. It amused Peter to think of this egalitarian assortment of souls flourishing under his father's absolute despotism, but he knew it was an inevitable consequence of his father's intolerance of inefficiency or incompetence, especially that inefficiency that developed if people were allowed the luxury of personal animosity.

Joey was primarily in charge of security arrangements, for the company as a whole and also for the house in particular. He was in his mid-fifties, medium height but with a stocky solid build, red faced and with black curly hair. Like everyone else in the household he dressed soberly, without any affectation. Peter noticed that there were not even any beards or moustaches in the house. Not by any arbitrary edict of his father, but simply because no-one could be bothered with unnecessary decorative features.

"Sit down Joey," said Mr. Newman when Peter had left. The man sat down rather carefully. "How are the ribs?"

Joey smiled ruefully. "Pretty sore, Mr. Newman," he said. "It was quite a job getting up this morning. But it's only bruising, it'll ease in a day or two."

"They're not cracked?"

Joey shook his head dismissively. "No. I've been kicked worse in bed."

"Fair enough. Now, business. You've had a chance to think since last night. Is there anything you'd like to add? Any new light shone on the event?"

"No, nothing. We followed him as arranged. He didn't spot us for miles, which was bad. When he did spot us he flushed us out quite nicely, but then he panicked. And he drives like a dog, Mr. Newman. We've got to do something about that. He frightened me to death when he spun into that bend. I thought we'd killed him." Joey's voice contained genuine concern. "Then he doesn't ram me off the road when I deliberately parked in front of him. But..."

He emphasised the word with an extended forefinger and his tone changed from concern to triumph. "When I started out of the door with the shotgun, he didn't hesitate. He was out like greased lightning and the next thing I remember is coming to sprawled across the seat sore as hell and thinking, 'I'm dead', with Ron going for the land speed record and yelling 'Jeezus Christ, Jeezus Christ.'"

Joey burst out laughing at the memory and then clamped his hand to his side. He grimaced at the pain and then continued more quietly. "I'll tell you though, Mr. Newman. When he came out of that car, there was no question about who was going to win. The very look of him froze me, and no-one's ever done that before, no-one. He's your son beyond a doubt. I'd stand back to back with him any day."

Newman nodded in acknowledgement of the compliment. Joey's loyalty passing to his son would be important later on.

"How well did he shoot?" he asked. Joey reached into his pocket and pulled out three mutilated bullets. Getting up as carefully as he had sat down, he put them on the desk. "They made a two-inch group in my coat, and if it took him half a second to pull them off I'll eat them. I'm glad he didn't try a head shot. The jacket was bulletproof but the balaclava sure as hell wasn't."

There was a slight unease in his voice and Newman pitched his reply very carefully. "I know how my son shoots. There was never any question of a head shot."

His manner was casual but very confident with just a touch of hurt in it that Joey could think he would have put him at risk. Then he picked up the bullets and smiled. "Two inches, eh? Very impressive. Wadcutters too."

"Yes, nice touch that. A flat-nosed target bullet for appearances sake, and a great hairy combat load behind it."

Newman nodded again. His assurance seemed to have worked.

"Very good, Joey. In fact, excellent. I'm more than pleased. The whole thing was most successful. You did a damn good job."

He became pensive. "It was a hard thing to do for both of us. But he had to be tested. He hasn't come up through the mill like everyone else. Now we've got another measure of his mettle. With a little sharpening he'll do fine. What I'd like you to do now is take his driving in hand and generally teach him about defensive living. Take whatever time you need, but he'll be in a very receptive mood right now so I suggest you push him hard."

"What are you going to tell him about the attack?"

Newman shrugged. "He's in the gym now. Go and tell him we've made some enquiries. It was a couple of street thieves who thought he was someone else. Someone carrying money. We've located the body and dealt with it and the driver is still running—you know the sort of thing."

Joey nodded and moved to the door.

"Oh, and while you're down there, kick him around a bit. It's his first and he's feeling a bit confused. Some violent physical exercise will help sort him out."

When Joey had gone, Newman leaned back in his chair, closed his eyes and breathed out a long breath. He had had to test Peter, to establish his credibility with himself and with the immediate staff, but it had nearly been a disaster. He hadn't anticipated his son's massive response, and while he was pleased, he was also troubled because his own misjudgement nearly cost him one of his best men and, worse, had put a dangerous sliver of doubt into the man's mind which he may or may not have successfully removed. You should have known you were too close to him to make such fine calculations, he thought. You made a monumental mistake. He realized now that if Peter had been a little calmer, he would indeed have made a head shot. It was his style. Only his residual panic made him fire at the first vital target his sights encountered. His son was a very dangerous man. Genes will out, he thought.

He sat for a long time with his head back and his eyes closed.

# Chapter 12

Hugh and Minna were siblings. They shared the same mother. Hugh was the elder by just over a year. He was named after his father, Hugh Byrne, a drunken lout whose behaviour eventually led to his wife killing him.

Hugh Byrne's wife, Sarah, was a beautiful woman. Tall and straight and dignified, with long hair, black as night, framing a high cheek-boned face and bright piercing eyes. The sole detraction from this face was its nose, which was a little too narrow, and twisted slightly to one side. It was a face that life could turn shrewish and peevish, or powerful and commanding. In Sarah's case it would be the latter. She contained a deep silence, like a great motionless lake that would drown anyone who disturbed it, and life's petty features left her unmoved.

She was married at twenty to her first boyfriend, leaving a loving family quietly distraught. "You're too young really," was the only admonition that her parents dared offer. And that gently. Both knew that more vigorous opposition would not stem the flood of life welling through their daughter, but would only tear and scar the bonds of affection that should be gently eased and lengthened. So they loved her, kept their darker forebodings to themselves and resolved to make the best of it. They had to admit that, after due allowance for their thorn-tinted spectacles, the son they were about to gain was not too bad. A little immature perhaps—he tried to be a masculine man as advertised on television, and was thus inclined to drink too much. And as such he was a little too coarse in his ways for their daughter. Generally speaking, however, he was polite enough to them and he had a good steady job.

Sarah saw some of his faults, but assumed they would fade with time and marriage and, implicitly, her influence. But of course she was wrong. He was a tragically flawed vessel. He had passed nature's more rigorous tests in the womb, but he carried internal stresses that would eventually crack him wide open.

His work as a building inspector with the local authority brought him constantly into contact with people who were only too willing to buy him drinks, pat him on the back, call him a good fellow, do odd little jobs for him or provide materials, and as a good fellow, he occasionally turned a blind eye, thereby laying a minefield for himself. Nothing too serious, of course, no money ever changed hands, but there was an area in which spurious friendships outweighed his duty to his employer, and he knew this area was too large. In struggling to reassert his authority he would become arbitrary and heavy handed which would lead to complaints to his employer which he could not subsequently justify, or else some minor executive, with great politeness and reasonableness, and professions of sincerity and conscientiousness would lure him off the straight and narrow again. And from this vantage point he would be able to sense the hidden scorn of the site workers when they bought his drinks and treated him as 'one of the boys'.

His employers were not unaware of his problems, and his inadequacy began to cause problems for them also. Thus he began to carry an increasing burden which he could not share with his wife, either because he was too inarticulate, or too ashamed, or perhaps even because he could not recognize it. Sarah, for her part, gave him what love and affection she could, but stinking of drink he was deeply unlovable and it was difficult. And she herself was soon carrying a burden of her own in the form of their son-to-be.

The announcement of the pregnancy was celebrated by Hugh getting drunk and being brought home unconscious. Sarah lay awake next to him for a long time, and began for the first time to see some of the different paths that lay ahead of her. She turned her head to whisper an endearment to her sleeping husband, as a pledge to a more hopeful future, but at the same time he turned over to face her and she recoiled as a wave of dank beer-fouled breath hit her full in the face. She turned her back on him guiltily and, unconsciously putting her hand on her abdomen, she said a quiet sad prayer to fortune.

Her pregnancy was a little worse than average, with wearying backaches, indigestion and sickness, and it was not helped by the long cold winter which made walking and driving so much more of an effort. But she was basically of a stoical disposition and refused to be downed by these inconveniences, unpleasant though they were. She was, however, increasingly distressed by the accelerating deterioration of her husband. Whether he turned more to drink because of her increasing absorption with her unborn child, or she looked more to her child because of his drinking, or whether it was a relentless march of each treading one foot in front of the other, is of no real concern. The nett effect was that the child, their joint creation, which should have brought them closer, split them apart. With all her senses heightened by the miraculous chemistry working within her, she began to find him physically repulsive when he was drunk where previously she had found him rather funny or just a little pathetic. One night she pushed him away violently, unable to accept his fetid embrace. He swore in his hurt and struck her. The next day he did not apologize, because he did not remember. Nor did he ask her why her arm was bruised purple, torn as he was between his little boy's pain and his brutish man's anger. She began to think, when the baby's born, we'll be alright again. But it was not to be.

The child was born one wintry Wednesday afternoon, and Hugh wet the baby's head with a vengeance. Partly because it was expected of him and he had to receive the plaudits of his drinking cronies, and partly because he wanted to forget all about the 'damn kid'. Later that night in a fit of maudlin sentimentality he tried to visit his wife in hospital, but during the course of a garbled conversation with a duty nurse he abruptly stood up, said "Excuse me," and crashed to the floor. Having banged his head rather severely, he was kept in overnight for observation, a fact which caused much harmless jocularity among the nurses tending Sarah, but which made her stomach go tight. The next morning saw him fragile and full of remorse, promising a new life, renouncing drink for ever, and Sarah, cradling her new son in her arm, reached out her free hand and laid it on her husband's cheek. He put his hand over it and pressed it hard into his face. "I'm sorry Sarah," he said. "I don't know what's happened to me. I don't mean to do what I do." It was a rare and fleeting perceptiveness, and it was the last intimate conversation they had.

The presence of the baby at home and the inevitable disruption of every aspect of their domestic life seemed to aggravate him more and more, his personality fragmenting almost visibly. He took to hitting Sarah regularly. A childish viciousness appeared, and it became so that he could not speak to her without pinching her or gripping her and digging in his fingers or punching her in the back. What affection Sarah still had for her husband was rapidly transferred to her son, and the emotional vacuum was filled by fear.

Eventually, in despair, she sought the advice of her parents. "You'll have to get away from him, for the baby's sake," was the consensus. "Perhaps he'll come to his senses when you're not there and he sees what he's done." It was agreed after a great deal of hand wringing and tears, but Sarah made a mistake. She would talk it out with him tonight—one last effort—reason with him, explain that a temporary separation would be the best for all of them.

Hugh, however, was long past reason, and was in a peculiarly malevolent mood on his return that night.

"What the fuck's this?" he snarled as soon as he saw her case in the hall. There was a note in his voice so savage that Sarah's carefully thought-out speech vanished immediately.

"I've had enough, Hugh. I'm going to mum and dad's for a bit," she stammered. "Until we can sort things out."

He swayed on his feet and screwed up his eyes. "Fucking great. Piss off then, you cow. I'll be glad to see the back of you, and that scrawking brat."

His voice was so hate-laden she felt the control slipping away from him, so she offered no comment. The less said the better. Words would be grist to the mill of his torment. Discussion would have to wait.

As she went into the front room to pick up the baby, she heard him muttering further obscenities. The baby was fast asleep in his carrycot. He had pulled his arms from under the blankets and they were resting on the pillow above his head. As she picked up the cot, the door was slammed with appalling force. The baby jumped, woke up and started a loud complaint. Sarah turned round angrily.

"Now look what you've done..."

Her voice faded when she saw her husband. He was leaning on the door and his face was livid. She put the cot down gently and reached out a hand to her husband.

"Hugh..."

He took two long strides across the room, seized her by the lapels with one hand and pushed her hard against the wall. He leaned his whole weight on her and squashed his mouth over hers. She could not breathe. Eventually he drew his head back and she turned her head away, spitting as she did so and trying to raise her hand to wipe her mouth. He gripped her face with his free hand and jerked it round to face him.

"You'll go when I fucking well say so, and you'll go when I've had what I want. You can go upstairs or you can do it here, suit yourself," and he crushed her harder against the wall. She felt as if she were somewhere else and that this was a grotesque dream.

"No, Hugh, you can't..."

He squeezed her face painfully and pushed her head into the wall.

"I can and I will and you'll fucking enjoy it or you'll get this."

He pushed the knuckles of his fist info her face. The baby's cry rose louder and filled the room. Hugh's voice followed it up in a hysterical crescendo.

"For fuck's sake shut that damn kid up."

"He's frightened, Hugh. I'll try..."

Her husband's voice went very quiet, and she felt a terrible trembling tension in him as he let her go. "I'll shut the little bugger up," he said through clenched teeth. He picked up the cot and glowered into it. "Shut up," he screamed into the baby's face. The baby's voice rose even louder into a shriek of terror. Hugh laid the cot down and raised his clenched fist back to deliver a blow.

"No," cried Sarah, an ancient instinct overriding all other considerations. She hurled herself forward and crashed into her husband. She heard the sound of breaking glass and a strange gurgling sound as she scrambled to her feet and snatched up the baby, but she ignored them.

Hugh Byrne died as a result of the severing of major blood vessels in his throat when he collapsed under the influence of drink and fell through a French window. The coroner expressed his sympathy to the widow and assured her that though it may not appear so at the moment, time would ease the pain and, being young and attractive she would doubtless eventually marry again and live a full and happy life. He was a very nice, thoughtful old man.

71

The investigating officer was Graham Adrin. He it was who came in answer to Sarah's eventual 999 call, and he it was who became Sarah's second victim that night. When he arrived, she had calmed the baby and put it to bed and she was sitting on the stairs sobbing. He cast a professional eye over the scene in the front room, grimaced, made a brief speech into his radio and came back into the hall, closing the door quietly behind him. He took off his helmet and crouched down by the bereaved in order to administer a little emotional first aid.

Putting his arm around her shoulders he said gently, but professionally, "Come on love." Sarah looked up briefly into his face without stopping her weeping, and Graham Adrin fell into that lake never to be seen again. Even disfigured by tears and shock, Sarah's face was for him. It tightened his chest and jellied his legs and he knew he was lost.

When his sergeant arrived, they were still sitting on the stairs. She still crying on his shoulder and he with his arm around her feeling very strange indeed. The sergeant looked at his bewildered underling over imaginary spectacles.

"Right Adrin," he said significantly. "The woman constable will take over now."

Three months later, Sarah became Sarah Adrin at a quiet Registry Office ceremony. Both knew it was probably too soon, but Graham's passion was combined with gentleness, and his almost pathetic patience and vulnerability eased away Sarah's concerns. She had lost most of her sense of guilt and made most of her way to a deeper understanding in a period of almost continuous weeping over some six days. She knew in some way she was responsible for Hugh's decline and that she would always bear the scar, but on reflection she doubted she could ever have stopped it. Strangely, she never felt any guilt for his death. Love of her child came first, that was bedrock, and in the interests of preserving her life with her child she decided it would be advisable not to mention that she had pushed her husband on that fateful night. The bottom of the lake was very hard.

Ten months later a daughter was born.

"Call her Minna," said Sarah, and Minna it was, sister to Hugh. The two children were very quiet. They watched everything and said little. Their mother had stamped her genetic code on them powerfully, as if the fathers were irrelevant. The children looked almost like twins with their black hair, thin handsome faces and bright eyes. They also inherited their mother's stillness, and over the years they learned to communicate with one another by imperceptible signs and gestures. It was almost as if they were really one person.

When Hugh moved to his secondary school, Sarah worried in case Minna would be upset at the parting, but she had forgotten the primordial culture of the schoolyard. They were of different ages and in different classes and thus had nothing to do with one another at school. Apart from arriving in the morning and leaving in the afternoon, any schooltime meeting was adventitious and of no consequence. Thus as the primary and secondary schools were quite close and the travelling remained virtually the same, neither appeared to miss the other. Had Sarah been able to see deeper into her children, she would have seen they had a closeness that could never be affected by distance.

Hugh being normally a quiet boy, Sarah barely noticed that he was quieter than usual after starting his new school. What little difference she did notice she attributed to the effects of the change, and tiredness, and presumed they would pass. Questions such as "What have you done today," merely elicited the response, "Oh, nothing much," and even his stepfather, who considered himself quite a skilled interrogator, could get precious little more. Parents have no business interfering in the real world.

Sadly, Hugh's silence was a symptom of a more serious problem. He was being bullied. Not that the problem was his alone. A large part of the school was held in terror by one of the older pupils, a burly youth called Nash. He was neither the biggest nor the strongest boy in the school, but his aggressive temperament had made him master of his own school year on arrival and thus of all the intakes that followed. His natural flair for leadership had gathered a small cohort around him, but his brutal instincts ensured that this comprised sadists and fawners of equal nastiness but lesser vigour, who were only too ready to act as intermediaries in the implementing of his will.

When Hugh arrived with the other new pupils, all clean and shining and nervous, Nash's venture was extortion. He had reached a stage in life when his earthly desires needed to be financed, so he extemporized on a theme he had picked up from the television. He even used some of the dialogue, suitably modified.

"Look upon it as insurance, kid," he would say to some hapless victim. "It'll insure you don't get your head thumped." Upon which, for the further entertainment of his court, he would issue a receipt for the premium in the form of a brutally twisted ear or similar.

Many a neat blazer and satchel was scuffed, many cherished pencil sets smashed. Bright hearts were scarred by loss of innocence and knowledge of fear and injustice under his baleful influence. And, unfortunately, Nash had sufficient wit to pitch his demands at a level he knew would not attract parental attention, so the only glimmer of hope the children had was that he would eventually leave. Hugh, in common with most of his peers, was no match for this, and after a terrifying initiation into the system, dutifully paid his premiums.

He despised some of his new companions for turning into toadies for this ogre, but despised himself equally for being too frightened to do what he knew he should. His nightly thoughts became filled with schemes involving the total obliteration of this schoolyard terror, but morning brought only a little wrench of despair.

Only one person in Hugh's class had stood up to Nash and refused to pay one of the collectors. This obduracy was duly reported and Nash prepared himself for one of his set piece demonstrations. He was not too concerned, there was always one who needed to be shown the error of his ways, and it served as a useful example to any others who might be feeling brave. It also reinforced his own position amongst his peers.

During the break, he had the offender pointed out to him and sent two of his group to advise him what was about to happen. Like most bullies, Nash was very sensitive in his understanding and use of fear. Then came the formal approach, a bold straight stride, the thin end of a menacing wedge moving across the playground. The wedge stopped and spread into a semi-circle. He looked down at the offending boy and noted that his determination was just mastering his fear. That was good, the demonstration could proceed.

"The money, kid."

The boy looked around, but saw neither escape nor rescue.

"No, it's mine," he said.

"Not any more it isn't," said Nash with a smile for his appreciative audience. He reached forward quickly, put his hand behind the boy's head and pulled viciously at his hair.

The boy's head went back and he grimaced in pain, but he did not cry out, except to say, "No."

Nash was not given to prolonged negotiations. He yanked the hair even harder and, thrusting his hand into the boy's pockets, took out what money he could find. "You can pay extra in future, 'til you learn not to be such a cheeky little sod."

With this exclamation, he released the boy and pushed him back hard into the wall. Abruptly the boy cried out.

"That's mine," and surged forward, arms flailing. The onslaught took his tormentor back apace, but height and weight were against the attacker and he finished lying on the ground squashed under Nash's bulk. Nash banged the boy's head on the floor a couple of times before he got up, by way of a finishing touch. Walking away from the scene he accepted the adulation of his court, but surreptitiously, as if straightening his coat, he rubbed his stomach. That kid had hurt—lucky punch I suppose. Still, he resolved deep inside, leave him alone unless it becomes absolutely necessary.

The boy remained sitting on the ground, his knees pulled up to his chest and his face buried in them. His hands were pressing the back of his head as his classmates stood around not knowing what to do. Hugh's heart went out to this hero, this boy who had done what he had wanted to do but had feared just this outcome. He crouched down by him.

"Are you alright?" he asked.

"Yes, thanks," came a muffled reply.

"You'd better come and clean yourself up. The bell'll be going in a minute."

The boy got up slowly, still rubbing his head, and Hugh escorted him to the cloakroom.

They sat alone for a few minutes on the hard wooden benches, inhaling the miasma of wet raincoats and floor cleaner. Hugh looked at the boy.

"Which one are you?" he asked, thinking of the list of names read out by their teacher each day. The boy cocked his head on one side and looked puzzled. "What's your name?" amplified Hugh. "I'm Hugh Byrne."

The black-eyed boy had stopped rubbing his head and was leaning back into someone's coat. "I'm John Newman," he said.

# Chapter 13

John was dismayed by his encounter with Nash and bitterly resentful. Like Hugh, his mind fomented with schemes of vengeance, and many a time he plunged Nash and his crew into oblivion. But at school he paid his weregild as demanded, in expiation of his crime of failure.

He and Hugh became good friends, and though Hugh was the follower, the admirer, he was without servility. He would talk to Minna about his new friend, and what a marvellous thing he had done, and Minna demanded to have him pointed out one day as she met her brother after school. John had seen the dark-haired little girl waiting outside school and was particularly pleased when he found she was Hugh's sister. He decided that when she was a little older, he would have her as a girlfriend, she was very pretty. Minna was not pretty in fact. She was like her mother—striking. Men's eyes turned to her automatically.

John had not reported the bullying to his parents. He had lied about the torn pockets, saying it had been done in a game, and he had lied about the cost of his school meals. The first did not bother him, but the second did. Peter, however, was suspicious, and in the end put it to him directly.

"Are you being bullied at school?"

John mishandled the matter completely.

"No," he said, not looking at his father and walking out of the room. Peter had his limits and John had just passed one. His name rang through the house in a tone that was quite unequivocal. Ann closed her eyes and made herself small in her chair. John returned at as reluctant a pace as he dared risk.

"Come here, John," said his father, more gently, in response to his wife's silent plea. "Don't walk away from me when I'm talking to you. I wouldn't do it to you and I don't expect you to do it to me." John's face was impassive. "Now, I'll ask you again. Are you being bullied at school?"

John looked down and shuffled his feet, but did not answer. Peter looked at him thoughtfully. The silence gave him the answer he needed, but what was he to do about it?

"John, bullies have to be tackled head-on, but sometimes, most times, it's very difficult and people need help. Please tell me what's happening and I might be able to help. I won't do anything with the school without discussing it with you, ok?"

John was tempted, father was dealing. But no, it was against his instincts, parents do not belong in the schoolyard. He shook his head. His father was about to speak again when he looked up.

"I'll deal with it, dad," he said.

Peter looked at him again. "Can you?" he asked.

"I think so," muttered John in reply. Peter realized that only harm would come from smashing down John's taboos, so he played his only card.

"I'm not too sure, John. Everyone needs help sometimes. I'll not press you because you've got your own reasons for staying silent and I'll trust your judgement, but promise me this: if it gets any worse or if you find you can't handle it, come and tell me. We'll talk again." Then, as an afterthought. "And if I can't help you now, then at least discuss it with your sensei. Is that fair?"

John nodded and made a relieved escape.

Peter and Ann discussed the problem, but in the end decided that in the absence of names and incidents they would have to wait and see what happened.

"You see him more than I do," said Peter in conclusion. "Just keep an extra eye open for any unusual wear and tear, or funny moods. If John's spending too much money, he may be paying protection to some enterprising young yob in the fourth or fifth year, and sooner or later he'll have to learn the error of his ways."

Ann nodded agreement, but later she realized the statement had been equivocal. Was it John or the enterprising young yob who would have to learn the error of his ways? And why had Peter's voice faded away and his face become hard and withdrawn as he said it.

***

Peter made only one more reference to this conversation, and that, apparently fleeting. It was as he was dropping John off at his karate class one evening. "Don't forget," he said as John was getting out of the car. "Have a word with sensei about your problem at school."

John gave a little nod as he closed the door, but said nothing. He gave a wave as the car moved away and then turned and walked through the thawing sludge and damp dripping night towards the entrance of the sports hall. He knew that his father would return to the topic again after he considered sufficient time had elapsed for John to do something, and part of him resented it. He was not going to discuss it with his karate sensei, because to John he was not a very approachable person and would probably only advise him on various techniques which, John knew, would be useless against the superior strength and weight of Nash. In addition, the class was large and he was very much the youngest, and it was unlikely that an opportunity would present itself. As he pushed open the glass door he decided that if the worst came to the worst, he would tell his father the truth. It usually saved complications.

Actually, the instructor was fond and proud of his young pupil, but ironically was a little reserved in discussing the philosophical side of his art with a child. He had put John in the senior class because Peter closely monitored his progress and had intimated that he wanted his son to be familiar with tackling people larger and stronger than himself as soon as he had mastered sufficient basic technique to prevent him hindering the class. The instructor found that Mr. Newman's suggestions possessed a peculiar force, but the boy was in any event a good pupil so he raised no objection. Routinely he advised Peter that the subject of bullying had not been raised that evening.

John, however, did intend to discuss it with his aikido instructor. He liked both the arts, but they were very different at his level of understanding. The aikido class with its very wide range of ages, and its almost equal division of men and women, seemed rarely to mention combat and violence, and used terms such as harmony and non-violence and spiritual energy—terms which he could not understand, but which he felt referred to things of importance. And yet, in contrast, there was the enormous physical effort which this gentle art could require. The murderous pain of the most delicately applied wrist locks, and above all its marvellous swirling spherical throws. It was indisputably a powerful fighting art, but it was also more. Karate he practiced, aikido he practiced and thought about. The essence of both was in fact paradox, and John was dabbling, unknowingly, at the edges of a great sea of knowledge and experience. A sea that could only be navigated by the mind, body and intuition being one.

When, days later, he mentioned bullying to his aikido instructor, he was a little surprised by the response. The instructor handed the class to an assistant and took John off the tatami and over to a corner of the dojo. John, shrewdly and correctly, suspected a paternal influence, but said nothing.

"Tell me what has happened," said the instructor simply. John had hovered between presenting a hypothetical case and presenting a case on behalf of an unnamed friend, but in the end he told the truth. The instructor listened intently. When John had finished, he asked, "Have you told your parents or your teachers about this?"

John shook his head. "No, but my dad suspects something and suggested I talk to you."

"What do you think I can do to help?" asked the instructor.

John did not answer immediately. "I don't know," he said eventually. "It's my problem and I'll have to deal with it. I think maybe he thought you'd be able to show me some special techniques, but that wouldn't be any good, would it? I forgot all my training when the fight started."

The instructor smiled. "No you didn't, John, not really. Your attitude was sound. You stood your ground for a right cause. You will have strengthened some of your friends a little and weakened the bully a little. That's good. You're simply not experienced enough to use your techniques in a fight with someone much bigger and stronger than you. You've done enough training to get some idea of how much more you have to do before your aikido or your karate can become really effective." John nodded. "Your father told me he suspected you were being bullied, and paying money for the privilege."

The sudden openness thrilled John.

"He wanted me to discuss it with you if you raised the subject, not so that I could teach you any special techniques which, as you said, would be nonsense, but so that perhaps you could get your own thoughts straight. Do you understand?" John nodded again. "I can't tell you what to do, but I'll tell you this, although it's very hard to accept. Bullies have to be faced and fought whatever the cost. Be they children, adults, organizations, even governments and countries. If they are not fought, they become bigger and bigger and worse and worse, and eventually the price of their defeat becomes terrible. Look what a gang your Nash has to do his dirty work, and that's all because he's had no opposition for several years."

The conversation was beginning to alarm John. Daydreams were one thing, but real life had hard edges. "I can't fight him, sensei," he blurted out.

"You already have," came the reply without pause.

"Yes, and got hurt." John was reproachful.

The instructor chuckled. "Come off it, John. You've been hurt by experts, by me and the others. But I understand. When I hurt you with *nikkyo*," a particularly excruciating wrist lock, "you fear the pain, but not me. You know everything is controlled and that you can stop the pain when you've had enough. But when Nash hurt you, there was no control, and there was viciousness wasn't there? You could feel it, I'm sure, and it was a new and nasty experience. But it was experience."

"I can't fight him, sensei," John repeated.

"I wouldn't suggest that you do John, but think about what I've said. Just think about it. There's no shame in fear. But get your mind clear about what you're frightened of. Never deceive yourself."

John spat out his last thoughts, faintly embarrassed. "What should I do if I forget my techniques again?"

The instructor made no comment about the shift from 'can't fight' to 'how to fight'. He judged this last comment to be John's assessment of the heart of the problem. He looked at him seriously. "John. If you're confronted. If all avenues of escape, *all* of them, have been closed, either by others or because they're inacceptable, and only you can judge that, then you will have to fight. The choice won't be yours. Once you have that clear in your mind, then forget all your techniques. Those that you know well enough for them to be effective, you'll use without thinking. The others will clutter your mind and trip you up. Think only 'I am right' and rely on your instinct to protect you. You'll find your fear can turn into anger very quickly once you commit yourself wholeheartedly. But, John." He raised a cautionary finger and looked straight at him. "Be absolutely sure you are right. Do you understand?"

"Hai, sensei."

The instructor looked at him for a moment. "Good boy," he said. "Off you go. Rejoin the class."

The instructor sat in the corner of the dojo for some time after they had finished talking. He remembered being bullied at school, and being unable to do anything about it, and he wondered how he would have responded to such a conversation. Not well, he suspected. He sent John Newman a silent but huge good luck cry across the dojo and the years.

Peter was late home that night, but made his regular visit to his son's bedroom. Quietly he opened the door, but as the landing light cut into the room, John sat up abruptly, suddenly wide awake.

"I'm sorry, John. I didn't mean to wake you."

"It's alright, dad," said John, lying down again. Peter moved over to the bed to adjust the dishevelled blankets. His son nestled down in the pillow. "I spoke to sensei dad."

"Yes, I know. I called in on the way home."

"I still don't know what to do."

"Sleep on it, John. Think about it, but don't worry. You can't do anything about it now, and anyway it's not the kind of thing you can lay plans for."

"You won't tell anyone at school will you?" said John in some alarm as he realized the secrets he had shed along with part of his burden.

"No," said Peter. "I won't go to the school until you tell me it's getting out of hand."

He bent down and kissed the boy.

"G'night dad."

"G'night son."

Thereafter, John took from his mother only the money he needed for his meals. The money for Nash he took from his own savings and spending money. That at least was one part of his shame he could deal with.

At school he enjoyed most of the lessons, and apart from the constant shadow of Nash, felt secure both in his new friends and the old ones who had come with him—'Snot', Dick, Henry, Thomas not Tom, and others. He developed further his ability to avoid difficulties and became known as a highly skilled dodger. In the playground he would play football and cricket and whatever else was in vogue with relish and skill, using the considerable aptitude for physical activity that his father's surreptitious but intense training had developed. But in the gym and on the sports field he was inept, incompetent and sluggish. Not to such an extent that he would be punished, but sufficiently to ensure he was not selected for any of the school sports or athletics teams. That too was his father's influence, but this time unwitting. He could never remember the context, or even if the remark had been addressed to him, but he remembered his father's pained face and bitter exclamation.

"There's all the competition you need in real life, and no damn rules—and no bloody referee."

He was liked by most of his classmates because he did not seek their favour nor despise their differences. He attracted loyalty and he offered it in return. But Nash still unsettled him. His father seemed to have dropped the matter, but John knew from experience that he was merely waiting. John was afraid of Nash, and could see no way of escape. He took some solace, as did everyone else, in the fact that Nash would eventually leave, but days in that kind of shadow are too long and hopeless, and while his fear and his anger buttressed one another to form a great arch with his own self-esteem as the keystone, a small black and venomous pool bubbled menacingly, deep inside him—an unchildlike and atavistic thing.

Every Monday, Nash's swaggering aides would visit their class, and every Monday he would hand over his money. *His* money. The pool bubbled. But his face remained neutral, the fear in him keeping him from attracting attention in any way. Nash however, remembered him and discreetly watched him whenever he could. He would rub his stomach reflectively, nobody had ever hit him and hurt him like that before and he'd fix him yet. He too was building up an edifice of hate and fear, and also envy. He could see the affection and loyalty John commanded from his friends, and he reflected bitterly on the quality of his own followers whom, for the most part he regarded with contempt. He took John's laughter and popularity as a personal insult, and his constant disappearing from sight as a deliberate provocation. It was not, of course, it was merely

John realizing he had made himself conspicuous and using the natural cover to avoid further observation. But Nash's mind had slipped into an obsessive notch, and like a ratchet it would go only one way. Every sight of John pushed it further on.

Some wispy caution prevented him from making a direct assault, so he started on Hugh, and for several weeks he entertained his court with regular torments and humiliations of the boy. John watched in dismay as Hugh would be snatched struggling from his friends, to return soaking wet or bruised and tear-stained, his jacket or trousers torn, or his small possessions smashed, and worst of all, trembling.

"You'll have to tell your parents," John whispered to him, his mind crying out *Coward, you tell yours*.

But Hugh would only shake his head.

One day it was particularly bad and John sat with him in the cloakroom while he washed himself and dried his clothes on the radiators.

"Look at this," he said, huskily. "Look what that bastard's done."

He held out a red fountain pen for John's inspection. It was broken beyond repair. "Shoved the nib into the wall and then stamped on it, the bastard."

He looked at it, his face creasing. "Minna gave me this," he burst out furiously. "What am I going to tell her?"

Then came tears. Miserable, long pent-up tears. John could not look at him, his own arch of fear and anger was still solid, and a tiny part of him said, *Well it could be me*.

He hated that more than he hated his fear and helplessness.

That afternoon they left school together as usual, and Minna stepped quietly out of the shade to meet them. She took Hugh's hand and looked into his face. They did not speak, but a tear formed in her eyes.

"Well, look here. Byrne's got a little girlfriend."

Nash's voice crashed through the hubbub of departing children. John felt Hugh stiffen and, in spite of himself, stepped in front of his friend.

"Piss off, Nash, leave him alone. You've done enough."

He heard the words coming out of his mouth, but his mind was a long way inside staring out in disbelief. Nash's hand seized his lapels and dragged him forward until their faces were inches apart.

"What did you say, Pewman?" he whispered loudly through clenched teeth. The witticism brought a few sniggers from his colleagues, who were gathering round in anticipation of further entertainment. John could not speak.

"What did you say?" repeated Nash with a snarl and a savage shake.

"Leave him alone," came an unfamiliar voice. Minna had entered the fray and swung her satchel at Nash. He pushed John away viciously, and turned his attention to this new prospect. John fell several feet away in a pile of snow, and lay there gazing through the wintry dark at the scene being enacted in the light spread by the lamp over the school gate. Minna stood staring up at Nash, defiant and unafraid. Nash reached behind her and, applying his favourite device, seized the hair at the back of her head and yanked it. Minna arched her back and let out a pitiful scream. John heard it and watched as Hugh stepped forward to intervene. Nash pushed him away with an oath and he went sprawling into the snow out of the lamplight. Minna cried out again. John heard something cry out in reply. It was a primeval howl from within himself. His arch had tumbled. Fear fell before anger and the black pool frothed over and filled his eyes.

Nash turned at the noise and automatically released the girl. He noticed the circle of his followers widen at the same time as he noticed the charging junior.

For a bully, being tall and heavy has certain distinct advantages. However, like most things in life, height is also not without disadvantages. One of these is that if you are charged by a much smaller person, head down, then that head could be at a most inconvenient level. Certainly it was in this case, and Nash measured the extent of the disadvantage to a nicety when the top of John Newman's head drove into his testicles. He gasped and staggered back against the school wall and, unwittingly, John delivered a merciless coup de grâce using those same appendages to cushion the top of his head from impact with the brickwork. Nash's eyes started out and his mouth opened but he slumped down noiselessly and fell over on his back with John clambering over him and pounding him relentlessly.

It took two teachers to prise the screaming boy from his unconscious prey. One of Nash's bolder friends had tried but had received an elbow where his leader had received a head and he had passed rapidly from the proceedings. Nash's court reverted to being a group of excited and bewildered schoolboys as the teachers ministered to the downed tyrant, and John stood in the snow shaking with battle fatigue. He felt empty and sick, but he knew that a shadow had gone, and that he would be alright soon. Everything would be alright soon.

After a moment he stooped and picked up his case. Turning round he saw Hugh and Minna staring at him in a way he could not understand. They came one either side of him and, taking his arms, led him quietly into the wintry gloom, away from the group buzzing under the light. John reached out for something normal.

"I'm sorry about your pen, Hugh."

"You knocked him out, John. Right out," said Hugh with awe. Minna just stared at him.

No serious consequences arose from the destruction of Nash. Primus being gone, his cohort disbanded and, released into the light, a horde of now vindictive avengers disclosed in full all his fund-raising activities to the school authorities. The time of Nash's leaving had arrived prematurely and to great rejoicing, and increased vigilance by staff ensured that no similar entrepreneur would arise for a long time.


Peter discreetly picked up post-mortem details from various sources, and related them to Ann with some delight. She was uncertain. She was pleased her son had dealt with his problem, but unhappy about the manner. She could not conceive her child having such violence in him.

"It's all this karate and stuff," she said sourly.

"No it's not, love," replied Peter. "They'll help him control and channel any violence in him."

Ann shrugged, unbelieving. She had heard it before.

"Couldn't you have seen the teachers?" she asked.

"What could I have told them," he replied. "John wouldn't tell me anything, and even I don't have contacts in the playground. Besides, John has to learn to make his own way. We did a deal. He'd have come to me if it got too bad."

Ann was still not convinced. She was becoming unhappy with the way Peter was directing their son, but she could not find the words to explain her unhappiness. Peter's love for John was patent.

That night at dinner, Peter raised the subject casually.

"I hear you fixed Nash up, John."

John looked up and stopped chewing. He nodded.

"Any problems?" asked his father. John shook his head. Peter knew that this was the full extent of any explanation he would receive. He was pleased John had not boasted.

"After dinner, we'll go down in the basement. I think it's time you had a go with my .357. Do you fancy that?"

"Yes, very much," said Ann, before John could nod again. She pushed her chair back and stood up. Looking at the two surprised males she made a dismissive gesture.

"Come down when you've washed up. I'll wipe the socks off the pair of you."

Peter and John looked at one another then finished their meal in silence.

# Chapter 14

Grandfather was dead.

John did not know quite what he should do. It was his first experience of death at close hand, and he was rather surprised at his own indifference. The only feeling he noted was a slight tinge of excitement at the prospect of attending his first funeral, and he realized that this was not really proper. In fairness, his reaction was not untypical for a young boy, and he had not known his paternal grandfather very well. Peter's father had only visited them once or twice a year, and while such visits were entertaining, John rarely spoke to him alone. He always regarded him as a distant and dominating figure, although he often had the feeling that the old man was watching him.

And now he was dead, and John was sitting on the fringe of a small group of black whispering figures, feeling very unusual. His black shoes shone, and his dark suit and tie were immaculate. It was only the most indignant of stares that had prevented his mother from combing his hair for him. Death meant nothing to him but he could certainly feel the presence of forces that would brook no opposition.

He got up quietly and walked into an adjacent room where a table was being laid for the mourners to return to. Sarah Adrin and Thomas not Tom's mother had undertaken the task of feeding this modest group, and were pursuing it with quiet efficiency. Ann was flapping a little and was eventually ushered out. John stared at the spread. Far more than the group could eat, even allowing for his own personal greed, and he wondered why on earth people who were supposed to be sad would want to eat anything.

"What do you want, John?" asked Thomas's mother, cutting into his reverie and easing him out of her way while she manipulated more food onto the apparently full table.

"I came to see if you wanted any help," he lied. He had really come to look at Sarah Adrin, with whom he was deeply, truly and everlastingly in love.

"No, there's nothing you can do, thank you," came the reply. "Besides, you're in your best suit."

Sarah Adrin came in bearing yet more food. She looked at John. "You look very smart John, very handsome," she said. John blushed, partly because of the compliment and partly because the sight of his beloved was doing things to him for which a dark suit and a funeral seemed most inappropriate. He stammered a 'thank you' and backed out of the room. Even such brief proximity to his loved one would fuel the fires of heroic and sacrificial deeds for nights to come, but it made his feelings about his first funeral even more confused.

He returned to the room where the mourners were waiting and went over to sit by his father. Peter patted his hand and smiled.

"Who are these people?" whispered John.

"They work for your grandfather, but they're also some of his oldest friends," whispered Peter in reply.

John looked round at the waiting figures. For the most part they seemed to be staff from the house, which he had visited once or twice.

"Who's guarding his house?" he asked. Under his father's tuition, which in turn stemmed from his grandfather's, John automatically lived defensively and he was puzzled and concerned at this lapse in security. Peter was not surprised and he answered routinely.

"The automatic system's on, John. We'll hear if anything happens."

In fact, his calm was not quite genuine. The automatic system was good, but severe, with little flexibility for coping with human vagueness or uncertainty. If a thief attempted to enter the house, there was a fair probability he would be killed, and that would add complications which he could well do without. The last thing he wanted was time-consuming police enquiries—any hint of an interregnum in the business could have profound consequences.

As it was, something important was still missing. His father had told him many times that on his death he would receive a key which would reveal to him the totality of the business and his father's plans for its future development, but nothing had appeared so far and a preliminary search of his father's effects had yielded nothing.

"Dad," whispered John.

Peter looked up and turned in the direction that John was indicating. Through the French windows he could see the black funeral cars turning into the drive.

John did nothing except keep quiet and watch through the ceremony. It was simple and short. He felt nothing, but noticed one or two of the women shedding a few tears and, to his horror, some of the men looked a little tight-lipped. His father too was stone faced. To beguile the time and to ease the discomfort of the hard wooden seats, he looked up at the intricate beams and arches above his head, and leaping from one to the next he nimbly rescued Sarah Adrin several times. He did not know from what, but his rescues were stylish.

After the ceremony, the vicar stood by the door and shook hands with everyone as they left.

"Oh, Mr. Newman," he said as Peter offered his hand. "Your father asked me to give you this."

He fussed from one pocket to another and eventually produced a battered manilla envelope. "I'm afraid it's rather crumpled," he said apologetically, smiling nervously and fidgeting.

"My father?" said Peter, unable to keep the surprise out of his voice.

"Oh yes," said the vicar. "He would often come round for a chat. A very interesting and clever man. And very generous to us, very generous."

Peter muttered his thanks. Pondering this strange revelation about his father, he started towards the waiting cars. He tore open the envelope carefully, and pulled out a piece of paper. On it was written a long list of numbers. It was the key he had been waiting for. He looked round at the snow-covered cemetery glinting in the bright sunlight, and tried to read his father's mind. Why should he entrust this most precious item to this vicar? Was it his bizarre sense of humour?—blessed are the meek, for they shall inherit the earth—or was it part of some deep loneliness, a lack of real trust in anyone he knew, even his son, or was it just one of his 'quiet' security techniques. He had known him to send millions of pounds worth of diamonds by ordinary mail.

"You alright, Peter?"

It was Joey. Peter started.

"Yes thanks, Joey. Just got caught by a little memory."

Joey nodded and patted him on the arm. "We're all behind you, Peter, all of us, you know that."

Peter nodded thoughtfully and then looked again at the paper in his hand. Its value was beyond measure. If it was lost, the consequences would be unthinkable. Very slowly and carefully he placed it deep into his inside pocket. When he got into the car, his hands were shaking.

Later that evening Peter sat in his office at home. In front of him was the computer terminal that linked him to the computer at his father's house. He tapped in the number from the paper and followed the subsequent instructions. After a series of elaborately coded procedures to further confirm his identity, a simple message appeared on the screen.

"Peter, I presume I must be dead now. I love you. Thank you for the happiness you have given me and please forgive me for what I have had to do to you. I think by now you probably understand why, but you most definitely will very shortly. You know a lot about the business, but it is far bigger than you think. You are the only person who can handle it. Look at my plans for the future. They're good. They'll strengthen us even further and with care and energy you'll hand on an even larger business to John. Too many people depend on us for anything other than our complete dedication. Do not be daunted by the size. I'll not burden you with more than you can bear. Keep your wife by you Peter, she is good and true and will anchor you."

Peter stared at this message for a long time, then he reached forward and pressed a key. The screen flickered.

Two hours later, John knocked gently on the door and opened it.

"Dad," he called softly. No reply. "Dad."

The room was dark except for the light of a flickering candle. John knew the sign, he had seen it once before, just before his father went to work for his grandfather. Some crisis was near and Peter needed stillness and the soft primitive light to quieten himself. John started to close the door gently.

"Come in, John. You're not disturbing me."

His father's voice came from the dark shadow in the chair behind the desk.

"Did you just come to say goodnight, or was it something special?"

John shook his head. "No, just goodnight." He hesitated. "Are you alright dad?"

"Yes, I'm fine. I've just had to make a difficult decision that's all. But it's made now."

"You'll miss grandad helping you, won't you?"

The shadow nodded. "Hm. I will."

"I'll help you one day dad."

"I know you will, son."

The candle flickered and danced shadows around the room. John bent forward into the deep shadow and embraced his father.

When John had gone, Peter sat a little longer, thinking. He remembered his father's words from long ago. "The decision was not difficult, it was simply unpleasant and sad."

He looked at the sharp clear shadows cast by the candle and the yin/yang symbol floated and bubbled into his mind. Not the slightly blurred one he had seen when he was learning about the business and was enthralled by its power and its technical elegance, but a grotesque shifting distortion, the black corroding the white into a deathly grey. *Maybe I can bear it father. I've no alternative but to try. But it's too big and too black and too wrong. Maybe in a lifetime I can balance it, but I'll not expand it.*

# Chapter 15

John's remaining years at school were uneventful. His battle with Nash brought him the adulation of his own year, and the grudging respect of senior years. It carried his name across the yearly tribal lines, and even some of the sixth formers sought him out and said 'well done'. It was a heady time, but his father's acid humour kept his true self etched out clearly, and gradually the deed passed into playground folklore leaving him unscathed.

From the box of clichés that is the source of the average school report, 'works well, pleasant, co-operative, conscientious,' were the most commonly drawn. Indeed, they fairly summarized the boy. Only the physical education teachers dissented somewhat. They knew he was not pulling his weight, and suspected, rightly, that this was wilful. They rather resented this free spirit who could play their games but would not, and who laughed at their rules. They suspected him as a domesticated animal suspects a wild one, but as he never actually said anything overtly heretical, they had to content themselves with secret sighs, and draw 'fair, could do better,' from the box.

All through John's schooling Peter was implementing an intense and complementary course of education, and by the time he was due to leave, John was a skilful driver and competent pilot, he could swim and rock-climb and ski to quite a reasonable standard, and he had learnt how to survive on his own in the mountains of Scotland and Wales. Peter organized the development of his son as ruthlessly as any other project the business handled. He used its power and resources to obtain the finest instruction, thereby ensuring that John would not only be taught effectively, but quickly. Experts, real experts, are such because they understand the heart of their subjects and explain directly and simply. Perhaps even more importantly they teach humility by judging themselves by the extent of their failings rather than the extent of their successes. Peter used the business to bring these instructors subtly into John's ken through local organizations, and judicious subsidies ensured that on any course several of his friends would be there also. Thus John never far outdistanced his friends in any particular subject, and certainly never felt superior. He and his friends achieved excellence without thinking about it because Peter ensured it was the only standard set. Only in later years did John realize the full value of his early training.

Hugh and Minna followed him through school as fast and firm friends. The strange solid relationship between the siblings opened and closed around John after his fight with Nash, and never opened again. Each had their own friends and separate lives, but these were spokes on the wheel of which Hugh, Minna and John formed the hub. Sometimes Minna would just sit and stare at John, as if waiting for a command. If he caught her at it, he would smile and she would return the smile and keep on staring. Any other boy of John's age could not have withstood Minna's bright penetrating gaze. If any of their friends saw her do it, some ribald comment could be expected.

"Ho ho John, look out, Minna's thinking rude thoughts again."

Minna would turn her gaze onto the offender, narrow her eyes and offer a mock menacing fist, usually with such style and timing as to destroy the watchers with laughter, but she was never disconcerted or embarrassed by such remarks.

"Deep, that one," Peter would say. "Like her mother. They're nice kids, both of them, but I can't make either of them out."

Strangely, although John's unbridled and adolescent lust for Sarah Adrin inevitably dwindled to form part of his youthful landscape, it never transferred itself to Minna, even though she developed her mother's handsome features and poise.

Time separated them. John and Hugh left to go to university, and Minna was left alone to plough a solitary but self-assured furrow through her final school year. When she too left for university, the furrow was full of the remains of broken and unrequited swains.

John had been torn between studying science or history at university, and had discussed it seriously and at length with his father before deciding. Peter wanted him to study science, but brought no heavy guns to bear, nor any devious cunning. It was important to him that John made his own decision—any lack in his education when he joined the business could always be made good subsequently.

"History is more important than many people allow, John. Personally, I'd make it a compulsory subject right through school. But it's a subject you can study anytime. Maths, physics and the like, you can't. You need instruction and the special environment. You have an aptitude for scientific thinking and vision, and it will be invaluable to you if you join the business," summarized Peter's attitude and he was relieved when John opted for a science course.

The choice made, other aspects of John's further education could not be left to chance, and he found himself accepted for the local university which had excellent scientific departments. It also avoided his having to leave home and thus made Peter's supervision easier and more comprehensive.

His first week was a whirl of new faces and new places, filling in this form, filling in that form, navigating around elaborate and lethally polished corridors and stairways, mistaking students for lecturers and vice versa, repelling the blandishments of the many and varied societies, studying notice boards, buying books, destructive testing of the venomous table d'hote of the cafeteria, and on and on.

"You'll be alright when you've found the toilets and where to hang your coat," said his father ironically as his son slumped into a chair after one particularly hectic day.

"Father," replied the son. "You are a tower of strength, and an unfailing support to me. A fount of advice that I can only describe as utterly useless. I'd call that place a zoo run by lunatics, but it would be an insult to the average animal and the average lunatic. I'm awarding myself the order of the feet up. Please do not disturb me until I have attained Nirvana."

Gradually the clashing mass of shining new students quietened as each found his new routine, and John's initial excitement turned into a glowing enthusiasm for where he was and what he was doing. He was far from impressed by some of the lecturers, but he was not temperamentally inclined to sulk and fume, so he simply found the knowledge they failed to impart from some other source.

By the end of the first term, his schooldays seemed a million miles away. Quite tall, like his grandfather, quite handsome—"In a weird kind of a way," offered Minna—confident and assured in his posture and manner, he was thriving and he knew it and revelled in it. He was rather sobered by the state of some of the students with whom he had started. Some, like himself, had adjusted to the strange new conditions and were prospering. Some were still adjusting, but were battling on, but others were falling by the wayside. What upset him, and at the same time, in spite of himself, disgusted him, was watching these others fall from innocence. There was the look on the face of one pretty girl who shyly trusted and ended pregnant and infected. He could scarcely bear to look at her pain. There were those he called 'the hearties', whose idea of maturity was drinking and vomiting and lying about exploits with women, and the even weaker sparks who trailed in their wake. Then there were those who looked to drugs to protect them from reality, and there was a host of other intermediate follies.

At home, no-one drank, no-one smoked, and medicines were never taken except when prescribed by a doctor, and then with a very poor grace.

When he, or anyone else in the household acquired some ailment, Peter would say, "It'll pass, shut up moaning." His theory was that any symptoms would either disappear, in which case treatment was irrelevant, or get worse, in which case proper advice could be sought. The family generally suffered from psychosomatic good health.

These were not matters given any great weight, but John inevitably acquired Peter's prejudices towards certain social habits, if only from his comments on TV commercials. Harassed businessmen and housewives taking refuge in headache and cold cures were classified as 'junkies', and drinkers, especially beer drinkers, were 'mindless oafs'. Having had his attention drawn to the similarity between the smell of beer and the smell of a urinal, John was not disposed to argue.

Only once had a really serious attitude appeared and that was when John had been in his third year at school. One of the sixth formers had given him and several others a white powder together with some very explicit instructions on its use. "It'll give you a really great feeling, really great," he said. Unaware of anything sinister, John showed the powder to his parents. His father went quiet, and John did likewise—he recognised his father's rare but savage anger near the surface, and hoped it was not to be directed at him.

"This is a drug John," he said quietly and gently, and John relaxed. The missiles were to pass overhead on their way to some other target. "They give it away free, and at first it makes you feel good. Then after a while you have to take it because if you don't you'll be in pain. Then they start charging you for it. The price goes up and up and you need more and more just to escape the pain."

Peter's voice was far away and his face was grim and drawn. "In the end, you'll do anything for it, anything. It'll be all you can think of. Believe me John. I know about drugs." There was a long silence and Peter stared at the small package. Then he sighed. "Who gave this to you and who else did he give it to?"

The voice was more matter-of-fact, but still serious, and John gave the names without hesitation. Schoolboy loyalty was one thing, but his father in this quiet mood was quite another.

"Good boy," said his father when he had finished. "I'll attend to this."

John looked alarmed. "I'll keep your name out of it, don't worry," said his father, smiling at last. "This is very serious John. If anything remotely like it happens again, you tell me immediately."

"He said it would make us feel great, dad," John said in mitigation.

His father's face became sad again. "He'd say anything, John," he replied. "He's almost certainly addicted himself and is having to make more customers just to pay for his own habit. Trust me, John. I've never lied to you. Some experiences you take for granted. You don't stick your hand in boiling water or your finger in a light socket to see what it's like. You take other people's word that it's dangerous. Well this." He tapped the package. "This is at least as dangerous as either of those." Then, more cheerfully. "Besides, you usually feel great, don't you?"

In the playground the next day, all his friends reported mysterious telephone calls and subsequent confiscation of their gifts. The sixth former never returned to school, and rumour had it that he had had some kind of an accident and would be in hospital for a long time.

So while John had an active social life at university, and sufficient wit and compassion when looking at his fellow students to realize that there but for the grace of his father went he, he did not know his own inner strength, and was apt to be harsh in some of his judgements. He could not totally chase from his mind the idea that the sooner these souls died out, the sooner they would stop breeding and perpetuating their weaknesses. He was not proud of the thought, nor particularly convinced by it, but it was there and had to be acknowledged.

By the end of his first year, he considered himself to be very grown up. His organizing nature, and the background atmosphere covertly prepared by his father, ensured that he not only knew what he was supposed to know, but actually understood most of it, and his exam results were very creditable. Pursuing his own inexorable policy, Peter found him a job with a small energy consultancy for his long summer vacation. "It's a good little firm, John, and it's going places. We helped with their early financing, and still have a small interest. Brian Gerard says he can find a spot for you, and I'm sure you'll enjoy working for him. It'll also get you out from under your mother's feet."

In actual fact, the business had founded the consultancy and owned it lock stock and barrel, but Brian Gerard, its apparent owner, knew nothing of this, and Peter saw no reason why John should know either, hence his pretence that the appointment was simply an application of the Old Pals Act.

Before he started his new job, John spent a couple of weeks walking in the Welsh mountains. He was fortunate, the weather was bright and sunny, an increasingly rare occurrence, and he walked at a leisurely pace along rocky paths and grassy ridges, up shaley slopes and across sheets of broken rocks, up leg-screaming grass slopes and down alarming stream beds. He paddled his glowing feet in icy lakes and watched deep reflections tremble and ripple. He saw sunrises and sunsets and even one spectacular moonrise. The great bright disc peeped suddenly over the shoulder of a mountain and then, far larger than when at its height, it rose slowly but inexorably to fill the cwm where he had camped with a wash of pale light and plunge the crags and crannies into blackest night. He would look up at peaks and ridges looming huge and majestic above him, then he would climb them and look back into the beautiful valley he had left, and all around at the rolling, softened remains of the ancient ice-smashed ranges.

He felt no loneliness, but was very much at one with the great stillness of the mountains, and he discreetly avoided any other wanderers he saw. The great soaring ravens and purposeful kestrels and all the other wildlife seemed to harmonize. Even the thunderous roar of jet fighters bursting occasionally through the valleys did not seem wrong or out of proportion—it was the human contribution. But people felt like chattering apes and he wanted none of them. So few people did he in fact meet that his voice sounded strange in his own ears when he actually spoke to anyone.

One evening he pitched his tent in a small sheltered nook high above a valley. He had walked a long way and was very tired, and after eating a rather primitive meal he sat down with his back against a warm, dry rock and watched the sun sink behind distant peaks. In spite of himself, the drowsiness in his legs spread rapidly upwards and he fell asleep. Then, quite suddenly, he was looking over a white snow-covered landscape, bright in the dazzling moonlight. It was beautiful and he felt a great peace and calm within him, although there seemed to be the residue of a terrible shivering. All around him, ringing in his ears and filling the sky and the whole Universe, was a great baying song, rising and falling. Something was by his side but he could not turn to look at it. He was formulating questions in his mind when he awoke. The distant sky was dark red, and his little camp was quiet and still, and though the air felt warm, he shivered a little and made hastily for his sleeping bag.

A few days after his return, he was sitting staring thoughtfully into the flickering fire. His mother was asleep with an open book on her lap, and his father was sitting awake but with his eyes closed after having shown particular interest in a television news programme. Their old clock ticked its unhurried way through the hours, pausing now and then to make some lugubrious horological clunk.

"Dad?"

"Yes."

"Are you busy?"

His father opened his eyes and smiled.

"No," he said. "I was just mulling over an unexpected problem at work. What do you want?"

101

John scratched his leg and then stretched both legs straight out in front of him.

"I was thinking in Wales. I really haven't the faintest idea what I want to do."

Peter turned down the sound on the television set.

"What do you mean?" he asked.

"Well, when I leave university, I don't know what I want to do for a living. Thinking back, I seem simply to have drifted into this course without any real thought." He laughed awkwardly. "I thought I'd thought about it, but really I hadn't. I suppose I just wanted to keep on doing science like at school. I never thought about a job."

His father relaxed back into his chair.

"Don't worry about it, John. I never encouraged you to think in those terms, because I can always find a job for you in the business."

John looked across at him sharply and opened his mouth to speak. Peter raised his hand to forestall the interruption.

"You'll get no job in the business you're not fit for, and you won't displace more suitable candidates simply because you're my son, so don't worry on that score."

John looked down at his hands and then across at his father again.

"I don't know anything about your business, dad. Neither you nor mum ever talk about it."

Peter shrugged. "It's no big secret," he lied. "I prefer to leave what I can at the office, and your mother isn't remotely interested."

"It's a finance house or something isn't it? I can't see me taking to economics."

Peter smiled and tapped his mouth with the edge of his forefinger. He was smiling at the memory of his father. One of his favourite tricks was to manipulate economic advisers to governments to obtain the decisions he wanted. He remembered finding him one day laughing, with tears running down his face.

"I know you shouldn't laugh at dumb brutes Peter, but just look at this."

It was a recent report by some government advisory committee, and they had responded exactly as Peter's father had arranged through his manipulation of various financial institutions and the news media.

"Oh dear," he said, wiping his eyes. "They are a bunch of fatuous asses, but life would be greyer without them. Who said circus was dead?"

"It's alright, John," said Peter, laughing involuntarily as he briefly recaptured his father's amusement. "I can't see you joining the halt and the blind either. We're not just a finance house, although we do a lot of financing. Really we're a sort of holding company. We have controlling interests in many areas of commerce and industry, so I'm concerned mainly with various kinds of strategic planning, resource allocation, and so on."

"Still sounds dull," said John reluctantly.

"It's my explanation that's dull, John," said Peter. "Not the business. It's too big to summarize."

He leaned forward and spoke quietly and very seriously.

"We're a powerful and wealthy group John. With power and wealth you can shape many of your own ends. Sometimes they have to be bad ends, it can't always be helped, but many more good things can be achieved and that's never dull. For now, you can, and you must, go your own way, but one day the business will attract you back. It's in your blood. If I were a poet, I'd say it was your destiny."

John was puzzled by this unexpected seriousness, and looked quizzically at his father. Peter sat back and smiled again. "And we've got a computer set-up you wouldn't begin to believe."

Here, John was confident his father was in error. He was even inclined to be contemptuous. Waving his hand airily, he said, "Commercial jobs. Just filing and accounts. If you want to see a real computer, I'll show you the one at the university."

Peter could not resist a party trick. He reached into his pocket and pulled out what appeared to be another remote controller for the television.

"Watch," he said, pointing to the television. He pressed a few buttons on the controller. The television screen flickered and the name of the university computer appeared.

Tap, tap, tap. The screen changed. John started forward. "Confidential Student Report. John Newman. John Newman is a..."

Tap, tap, tap. The screen reverted back to its television programme.

"Bloody hell!" John exclaimed. "That was my personal file.

They're supposed to be protected by all manner of encryption. How the devil...?"

Peter shrugged. "I can't tell you that, can I? It's confidential, isn't it? Still, it's not a bad little machine you've got there. How many batteries does it take?"

John was having difficulty forming words.

His father suddenly stood up. "I've got one or two things to sort out in the office," he said. Then bending down he put his hand on John's shoulder and spoke gently but very seriously again, looking straight into his eyes. "It's a big computer John, state of the art would be the trendy expression, and it's a big business. But remember, all business matters are like family matters. Not to be repeated anywhere—anywhere! You understand?"

"Yes dad, of course."

"Good boy."

Peter patted his son's shoulder and walked out of the room.

That night in bed, Peter lay awake for a little while. He knew, as his father had known, that John would have to inherit the business one day. The consequences of his not doing so would be appalling. But he felt guilty. He did not think he had it in him to trap John the way he had been trapped, but John had to be lured in. At least he had been given more auspicious circumstances to lay the groundwork than his own father had when he was young and literally fighting to consolidate the business. All the same, he could not avoid a twinge of guilt and resentment at the bait he had just floated in front of his son.

# Chapter 16

Brian Gerard was a fat, red-faced man, short and bouncy, and never still. He got up from behind his desk and marched briskly forward, hand extended, when John was shown into his office. His grip was not hard, but his handshake was vigorous as he led John to a chair.

"Nice to meet you John," he said. "Very nice. I hope you'll enjoy your little stay with us." John opened his mouth to reply, but Brian continued.

"We're quite a small firm at the moment, so we're pretty informal and have very little problem with who does what etc. You'll find that my assistants normally follow a job through from the beginning to the end, so you get a good overall picture and can really get involved. It gives a sense of progress and achievement. That's important, don't you think?"

John made as if to answer again, but Brian was using the question simply to change into top gear.

"We do an important job here, John. The future's here." He tapped his desk. "Right here. And we're amongst the first people to greet it..." The telephone rang. He picked it up and had a brief conversation with someone who was obviously a client. A small spasm of irritation passed over his face as he put the phone down.

"John. I'm very sorry. I'll have to postpone our little chat. A flap has broken out with one of our more fragile clients, and I'll have to attend to it immediately."

John stood up and found himself being briskly led by the arm to the door.

"Ours is a specialised business, John," continued Brian, still in top gear. "I'll try and arrange for you to get some field and design experience, but for now I think you'll be best employed in research. Freddy!" he shouted. John started. Brian Gerard invariably used his voice in lieu of an intercom.

"Yes, Mr. Gerard." The quiet reply came from a fair-haired girl just entering the room.

"Freddy dear, take Mr. Newman down to Ronny, please. I've got to dash off and see whatsisname. I'll probably be back about eleven."

And with that he was gone. John looked at his escort, bewildered.

"Yes," she said. "He *is* always like that. You'll get used to him. Now, if you'll just give me one minute, I'll find out which whatsisname he's going to see and then I'll look after you."

She disappeared into another office, leaving John alone looking around at the little reception office. His father had spoken highly of this company and yet here it was in one of the older office blocks in the city. A small unprepossessing office for its manager, and an even smaller one for his secretary. Further, all the office equipment seemed to be at least secondhand, except, he noticed, for a very sophisticated computer terminal. It really did not give the feeling of a company cutting a swathe into the future.

Freddy reappeared.

"Right!" she said briskly. "That's him sorted out. Now for you." She held out her hand. "First of all, welcome to the asylum."

He took the offered hand gently. It felt cool and soft and he wondered whether he should hold it a little too long and say something complimentary and sophisticated, but wiser counsel prevailed. He decided he would probably only make himself look ridiculous, so he released the hand and chose to appear a little shy and reserved.

"Thank you, miss...?"

"Just call me Freddy like everyone else," she said.

"Freddy?"

"Yes. You're John aren't you?" she replied, leaving the unspoken query unanswered.

"Yes," he said, not daring to ask.

"Come on. I'll take you down to Ronny."

He followed her down a small flight of stone steps guarded by an old wooden banister with an iron balustrade, and along an ill-lit wooden-floored corridor, past office doors which someone had attempted to enliven with some amateurish paintings. If it had not been for the lively noises permeating into the corridor from these offices, John felt he might have been dropped into a novel by Dickens or Kafka. Freddy half turned and looked up at him.

"You'll like Ronny," she said. "He's nice. And very clever. Here we are."

They stopped outside a door bearing the handwritten sign "Research?". She put her hand out to push it open.

"Just a minute, miss... er, Freddy. Could you show me the other way out?" said John.

"Other way out?" she echoed, her voice and face puzzled. "What do you mean?"

He shrugged. "There's another way out isn't there?"

"Well yes," she said. "Just follow this corridor round the corner, and then down the stairs."

"I'll just have a look," he said, and walked briskly down the corridor. When he returned a few seconds later, she was smiling but uncertain.

"Satisfied?" she asked.

"Perfectly," he replied with a laugh to reassure her.

"I think you're going to fit in here very well. You're obviously potty. What do you do? Collect exits?"

He winked and pushed the door open for her.

The office was bright and airy but unbelievably untidy, and again apparently furnished exclusively with well-abused equipment. A grey-haired man with his glasses up on his forehead was sitting at a desk, and a woman was conferring with another man at a drawing board. The woman looked up briefly and nudged the man.

"Haha," he said. "The new boy."

"New man, actually," said Freddy. "Ronny, this is John Newman, the student. Remember? He'll be with us through the summer."

The grey-haired man pulled his glasses down onto his nose and then looked over the top of them at John.

"Ah, yes," he said, standing up. "Pleased to meet you John. Sit down, sit down."

He lifted a bundle of documents off a chair and after searching round for a space, put them on the floor.

"I'll probably see you later, John," said Freddy as she backed out of the room.

"Oh, thank you," he said, half raising himself from the chair.

"Well," said Ronny. "I suppose we'll have to find something for you to do. What is it you've been studying at the university?"

"It's the new general science course, with maths and physics as specializations."

"That's handy," said Ronny. "It'll be nice to have someone in the office who can count," he said loudly, obviously for ears other than John's. The woman at the drawing board examined her fingernails, and the man cleared his throat and peered attentively at the paper in front of him. "Which reminds me," continued Ronny, standing up. "Let me introduce you to your colleagues-to-be. June Morris, George Niven—John Newman."

The introduction was shouted across the office and the two people came over and shook hands.

"John here," said Ronny, looking from one to the other. "Is studying maths, which, as I said, means he's probably capable of counting to well in excess of ten, which will be a marked improvement for this office, won't it? If you've any trouble, go and ask him."

John would have been embarrassed by this exchange had it not been obviously some kind of office joke and not directed at him.

"Anyway," said Ronny. "We'd better find something for you to get started on."

He stroked his chin then looked at his watch.

"How's your practical chemistry?" he asked. John was taken aback slightly.

"Reasonable," he stuttered eventually.

"Good, good," said Ronny sitting down at his desk again. "George, show John were the tea things are and give him our individual prescriptions."

Over the summer months, John settled into his temporary job. He found that the untidiness was only an overspill from creativity, and that his three colleagues, for all their casualness and banter, were both talented and practical.

"Flexibility is what I want, John," his father had said more than once. "Every kind of flexibility. That is what a good education will give you. Don't you forget it. Don't be frightened to reject your own ideas. They're like plants. They don't die, they break down and provide humus and nourishment for new growth."

And this office is certainly full of humus, he thought, every time he looked round. He also learned about the various temperaments he was closeted with and soon found out when to speak and when not. Once or twice there were blistering rows during which he tried to make himself part of the furniture. Then abruptly they would all be laughing and the charged atmosphere would disappear as if by magic.

His initial chagrin at being made tea boy soon disappeared when he realized that any of them would do the job without giving it a second thought. Within a few days he had been given the job of tidying up the office and sorting out the filing system. He was pleased with this because it gave him an opportunity to read many of the documents and to develop an overall view of the research department. From this, he realized that the function of the department was not in fact research, but really collation and the creative assessment and interpretation of the latest findings in the field. Energy and resource conservation began to excite him.

Everyone was pleased with John's filing system, although he could not escape the feeling that their enthusiasm contained a certain amount of amused tolerance. He carefully explained it to everyone in turn and became quite proprietorial, if not dictatorial, in his attitude towards it. A place for everything and everything in its place, he thought to himself, but he had wits enough not to say it out loud. It was, in fact, a good system. Simple to use, flexible, well cross-referenced and with plenty of spare room for expansion, and the office's appreciation was quite genuine. The office was tidier than it had been for a long time, and quite a lot of time was saved that was previously spent digging through mounds of papers. He was beginning to get the impression that a working life could really be quite smooth and ordered, and that he was an undeniable boon to these capable but disorganized individuals. He saw himself as a central administrator, co-ordinating schemes, issuing guidance and instructions to his underlings, making grandiose strategic decisions for the greater good of all, which, of course, he alone could see, and receiving due respect and gratitude in return.

Unfortunately, a draught blew into his daydream and toppled his house of cards. Brian Gerard entered the office one morning and stood gazing round in surprise.

"Well, well. Who's responsible for all this order and tidiness?"

June pointed a thumb towards John.

"Well done, John," said Brian. "It does these three no harm at all to be tidy every now and then, no harm at all."

John smiled cautiously. He was not too happy with the phrase "every now and then".

"Anyway, Ronny." Brian pulled up a chair and sat alongside Ronny at his desk. "We've hit a snag on this Midlands industrial complex."

And with that he signalled the end of John Newman's first and last illusions about working for a living. The snag referred to was in fact a major and serious problem, and faced with it, John's three colleagues simply reverted back to their traditional working practices.

There was little or nothing John could do. He spent the next few weeks making tea and coffee, running out for meals, crunching numbers out on his desk calculator and occasionally the computer, preparing sketch plans one day and throwing them in the bin the next, and generally acting as powder monkey.

"Ah well, looks like muddy boots, then," concluded George one day after he and June and Ronny had had their heads together for some time over one particularly intractable problem, and John found himself clad in waterproofs and hard hat, wandering round a vast building site. After two or three days of climbing ladders, walking endlessly back and forth across the site, holding tape measures with spiked ends specially designed to gouge cold finger ends, and vainly trying to keep his notebook dry in the pouring rain, he began to enjoy it and to think that the building industry might usefully benefit from him. His wellington-booted legs developed the longer and more purposeful stride which befitted this notion. However, he was not too distressed for the industry when he returned to the comparative sanity of his Research Office. His few days on site had been hard and had not enabled him to obtain any real idea of what was happening. His overwhelming impression was of noise and chaos and communication problems between the various people on site that seemed to be in principle insoluble.

And then abruptly the panic was over. One last frenzy of plan folding and letter writing and then it stopped. John stared ruefully at the remains of his filing system, and at the debris scattered around the office. June was sympathetic.

"Don't be upset, John, you did a good job with the filing and you've been a great help over the last few weeks. Get this lot mopped up and we'll use it. Promise."

John knitted his brows. "Jesus, June, why on earth don't you use the computer for all this?"

June looked thoughtful. "I'm not sure really. This..." she waved her arm across the office, "is the way that seems to suit us. We do make a good team, and it's results that matter in the end. A lot of the stuff we use is on computer, but these loose ends are difficult to incorporate effectively. Tidy up what you've got and see what you think."

He agreed, somewhat reluctantly, but still spent a large part of his remaining time with the company trying to further rationalize the office.

The inertia of established practice was, however, too much for him. They had accepted his old-fashioned filing system without demur—in fact with some relief, but they put up a substantial and vitriolic resistance when he tried tentatively to introduce a computerized version. In the end he gave up and George took pity on him.

"Don't be discouraged. Life in industry is very different from life at university. You stagger from compromise to compromise. It can't be helped."

"I suppose so," John replied. "But it just seems to me there are so many little things that could be tidied up that would speed things up. Make life easier."

George nodded and repeated June's message. "Yes. You're right and you're wrong, John. There are a lot of small things that could be changed, but they don't really slow us down, they form part of the rhythm of our working. What's most important is that we work well as a group and produce the required results. It's overall efficiency that counts. Not every part of a machine works at its peak efficiency, even though the machine as a whole might work at peak efficiency. Right?"

John nodded.

"You've not been here long enough to really understand how this office works, let alone how the firm as a whole works, but what you've done, you've done well, and you've been a great help. Don't get too upset when you see your plans and ideas being flushed down the pan. That's the fate of most ideas round here."

"You sound like my father," said John.

"Clever fellow is he, then, your dad?" came the reply.

John found George interesting and likable, and had many intriguing conversations with him. June on the other hand, while being pleasant and willing to answer questions, did not indulge in idle chatter or speculative conversation, and if he caught her in the wrong mood she could be icily sarcastic. Ronny spoke hardly at all, but when he did it was usually to considerable effect. With his grey hair, his glasses pushed up on his forehead and his generally shuffling gait, he looked like the stereotype of an absent-minded professor, but he ran the office with a kind of benign ruthlessness, gently pointing out loose ends and inconsistencies in the work of the others, and ensuring that everything that left the office warranted serious attention from whoever it was destined for. Only once did John see him look agitated.

Brian Gerard had made one of his brief, staccato visits to the office and temporarily upended it.

"What on earth does he do apart from mess everyone around?" John asked Ronny in some exasperation.

Ronny blew out a noisy breath, dropped his glasses onto his nose and peered over them. "He's the boss. Yours not to reason why," he said quietly after a moment. It was a typically gentle rebuke and John began a discreet retreat.

"John," said Ronny in an unusually firm voice. John looked at him. "Brian Gerard is an exceptional man. He leads, we follow. He's totally dedicated to resource conservation and he has the ability to transform ideals into commercial realities and sell them to hardbitten businessmen. That's what he does."

John sat down, surprised at this outburst, mild though it was. Ronny leaned forward and put his elbows on the desk, his face alive and serious. He entwined his fingers and emphasized his words by tapping the edges of his hands on the desk.

"For years we've destroyed resources and poisoned the environment, John. Years. A double betrayal of the future. We're supposed to be trustees, but what will our kids get? A poisoned world plundered of any resources that might help them put it right." His face tightened. "Brian Gerard is one of the few people who could prevent it, or at least lessen it. His kind of dedication is rare, and even rarer is his ability to sell ideas. He abhors any kind of waste, and he goes for it like a wild animal. Clients like him because he saves them thousands, eventually, and he gives them a feeling of moral superiority. Look at this desk. Fifty years old if it's a day. Look at all our routine office furniture. Three things in common—old, secondhand, and perfectly adequate for their jobs. When they outlive their usefulness, which will not be for a long time, he'll sell them to someone of like mind, or break them into other useful components. He'd find a market for the squeak on a pig." He smiled and picked up a piece of paper from his desk. "Even our paper is recycled endlessly. We write on every square inch of it that's blank, then send it for recycling again. Tiny things John, but important. They're symptoms of an attitude, a caring. A caring for balance, for the future." He pointed vaguely upwards. "Those heat exchangers and solar cells upstairs are as sophisticated as any in the world. Like those in your house. But even in them a lot of the components are secondhand."

Ronny sat back and rested his hands on his stomach.

"Don't take Brian at face value. He's deep and clever, and very concerned. You can be sure your father would have had nothing to do with him had he not been."

John was taken aback by this unexpected eulogy, and intrigued by its concluding remark.

"You know my father?" he asked.

"Oh yes. Very clever man. Helped us a great deal when we were starting up. Financed us and designed our computer system."

"Did he indeed?" said John, looking at the nearby terminal and thinking uncharitably that his father probably had access to everything in it.

"Yes, and he's sent a great many clients to us as well."

"Is that why I got the job?" said John before he could stop himself.

Ronny looked straight at him. "It's why you got an interview and a start. If you'd been no good, it would have been a toss-up as to who threw you out first—us or your father."

*That* had a distinct ring of truth about it.

The job ended with the summer vacation and John decided he would like to return the following year. Peter was pleased with his son, and at his developing maturity.

"It's an interesting business and a good firm," he said. "It's certainly got a big future. We'll probably be moving in on it ourselves soon. We can give Brian the funds he needs for further expansion and development work. It's one possible string for your bow, isn't it, John? Mull it over, but concentrate on your university work. Learn there while you can, you'll never get as good an opportunity again."

# Chapter 17

In keeping with the cloistered academic calm of a university, the first year's study had weeded out the more immature and incompetent with a ruthlessness that many a dictator would have envied, and John felt a greater personal confidence and stability when he returned after the summer vacation.

His brief sojourn with Brian Gerard's company had taught him a great deal and he was becoming increasingly intrigued by his father's business. But these distractions he put to one side, to germinate in the quieter reaches of his mind while he took his father's advice and made the most of the university.

He enjoyed the student life without being lured into its more inane excesses. He loved to argue and debate, no matter what the outcome. To see his own ideas either sharpened or destroyed was a constant delight to him, but he gradually became aware that his contact with the real world, assiduously maintained by his father, was colouring his arguments, and he would sit and think about this in the dark of his own room during the still hours of the morning. A conflict arose between his aesthetic appreciation of the clarity of logical reasoning, mathematics and science generally, and his more emotional appreciation of matters practical. He was sufficiently analytical to realize that it was happening, and to note the pull between "knowledge for its own sake" and "what earthly use is that?"

After a while, however, he reconciled them by accepting both as being valid viewpoints. The family blood was asserting itself and he was turning into one of those rare individuals whose sharp and appreciative academic mind runs in harness with an instinctive and more predatory grasp of realities. Later on, as he became involved in the bizarre, almost mystical reaches of atomic physics, he was amused to see that logic and intuition were not after all very different from one another.

His remaining years at university, punctuated by spells with Brian Gerard, developed even further both his academic and his worldly characteristics, and while he had many and good friends, he felt himself set apart a little from his fellow students. More correctly, he set himself apart, finding no desire within himself for deep personal commitments to other people. Ironically, the other family trait of leadership developed in him also and drew people towards him. He was quiet and polite and attentive which made him attractive to older students and members of staff, and he had a confident and modest sureness which drew his own age group to him. He did little or nothing to encourage this, but people gravitated towards him and clustered like electrons round a nucleus, at once drawn and held at a distance.

He had a few girlfriends, but he tended to stand outside and make due note of the effect of his own passions, and his girlfriends eventually drifted away, baffled and frustrated by his self-sufficiency.

Inside himself he began to note a strange sensation, a feeling of something impending, a feeling that he could and would do great things, and that this was why he was different from his fellows. After a while he named the feeling his destiny, using his father's word, and then he felt vaguely embarrassed. He never spoke of it to anyone, but it grew steadily and he began to realize that thanks to his father he had mental and physical disciplines beyond his age and that in his father's enigmatic business was some huge instrument of fate.

Once or twice each year he would disappear into the Welsh mountains for a few weeks, and return hairy and primitive. As he splashed his solitary way across the hills he felt this strange drive within him and he would think about the great forces of nature that had formed the country around him, and about the great forces of man that had formed human society. He knew that certain individuals had in the past welded disparate peoples into great nations, and he wondered what it must be like to be such a person. There was much turmoil and horror in the present world. Was he destined to do something about that? He knew also that empires crumbled as emperors died and he wondered if those dying giants had known the future, and if so could they have done anything to ease the death throes of their own creation, or were their own egos such that they considered the end of the world the only fitting tribute to their own passing—Götterdämmerung. Then his mother would survey him on his return and say with resignation, "I'm surprised you don't get arrested for frightening the sheep looking like that," or "Oh, it's not *the* Owain Glyndwr is it?" and dreams of empire, fluttering flags and eagle-browed leadership vanished like smoke in the wind. But the deeper glow persisted.

Years before, Peter's father had tested him by ordeal to ascertain the nature of his son and possible successor. Peter never knew that that panic-stricken drive and its culmination in a stand against death had been contrived, but he knew it marked for him the real passing from one world to another—a metamorphosis. Now, in his turn, he watched John growing and developing and nearing the time when he too would have to know himself. And he saw within him a strange restlessness that could not find utterance. Was it a struggle within the chrysalis? He knew that John must be the right man to help him control the business and to take over in due course, but...? More slowly than his own father, he formed the question: could he, or should he, place John in some extremity so that this unease could take form? More perceptively than his father, he knew he was too close to his son to be objective in his judgement. He wavered painfully. Fate, however, was kinder to Peter than it had been to his father, and the decision was taken from his hands.

One year, John took a trip to Wales in December. Winter had again arrived early, and many of the mountains were covered in snow. In summer he would wander footloose and fancy free, his physical stamina plus good equipment and a knowledge of the terrain being sufficient to protect him from the rains and mists that often celebrated around the hilltops. An inadvertent dowsing or a missed path in summer would mean a few hours of damp discomfort and fatigue, but in winter it was different—a missed path or a slip could mean death. Wind and cold would tear away the body's heat, deaden the stoutest limbs and addle the sharpest brains very quickly. John was adventurous, but not foolhardy. He planned his routes carefully, checked his equipment and food, and studied the weather forecasts thoroughly before setting out up a winter hill.

Today it read cold but clear, visibility would be good and there would be little or no wind. The views would be spectacular and, without the wind to blast the cold into his face it would be an exhilarating walk. A day of high promise.

He planned out a walk which was predominantly along a well-established path that would bring him back to his car, tucked away in a small car park just off the main road. He was amused to note that the van he parked next to bore the legend of a Youth Club from near his own home, one which Hugh and Minna and his other friends had attended. He patted it affectionately as he walked past.

Occasionally, as he trudged up the winding pathway, he heard children's voices rising and falling in the distance. Coming to the crown of a small rise, he saw a group of five children on the other side of the river that tumbled down out of the vast cwm which dominated the scene. They were accompanied by a man who had a large dog on a lead. John smiled at this tiny eruption of colour threading its way up the tree covered slope. He was surprised to see them where they were, as it was the route he intended to take and was off the main footpath. Sometimes the presence of people on the mountain irritated him, but the sound of their woodwind voices over the snow evoked the feeling of a pleasant memory and he quite looked forward to catching up with the little group. However, they were well ahead of him, and as he had set out early purposely to allow himself as leisurely a walk as the temperature would allow, he judged they would near the top ridge before he reached then.

He reached the point at which he had to leave the path, and slithered carefully down the slope to the small footbridge at the bottom of the little valley that the river had cut. He stood for a few minutes looking down into the main sunlit valley he was leaving, and then up at the mountains, sharp against the blue sky. Then he gazed into the icy turmoil of the waterfall just upstream.

He walked up through the trees and eventually reached a gap in a stone wall. A mass of footprints in the snow indicated the passage of the children and their dog earlier. He looked up to the ridge ahead. Usually a hill walk involved walking up to one skyline only to be greeted by yet another rise. But here, the skyline was the top, and the way to it, he knew, was much further than it appeared to be. It was a long, long, grassy slope, broken by rocky outcrops. Way ahead he saw the colourful little dots, and they reminded him of the scale of the scene he was looking at.

Some considerable time later, about three quarters of the way up the slope, and closing with the group, he paused to catch his breath and rest his legs.

"Bit too fast," he said out loud, as he sat down on a rock and rubbed his legs, reproaching himself for not pacing the walk better. He reached down to adjust the laces on his boots and a large snowflake settled slowly on the back of his hand. He stared at it and a cold settled on his heart. He looked up. The air was suddenly full of snow. Turning, he looked down into the valley, but it was gone, hidden by a dense grey mass of cloud. Then the wind started to blow.

Reflexively he threw up the hood of his waterproof, fastened the zips on his several cardigans and waterproof and pulled on his gloves. His first feeling after that was almost panic, and he had to fight an urge to run back downhill towards the comfort and safety of his waiting car. However, he was not without experience of bad weather walking, and calmer counsels prevailed almost immediately. It was the suddenness and unexpectedness of the onslaught that had taken him unawares. He staggered as a violent gust of wind hit him, and he had to turn his face away from the stinging snow. Visibility was down to a few yards, and he was beginning to feel uneasy. The weather was supposed to have been fine and clear, a cold frosty day, and now this. That it was a freak storm was obvious, but a surge of bitterness ran through him when he thought of the weather forecast he had so carefully studied, and he clenched his teeth and swore. Then, as if released by the oath, an urgent but quieter voice said, *find cover fast, this may be here for hours.*

He looked at his compass and then slowly, carefully, peering desperately into the swirling haze, he moved forward up the hill towards where he had noted a large rocky outcrop just before he had stopped. He felt the ground before each step, and took slow deep breaths to keep his mind steady. It was not easy. The battering of the wind and the rattle of snowflakes on his waterproof, and the great difficulty he was having in focussing and judging distance, were very disorienting. He slipped and fell on all fours several times, but eventually he reached the outcrop and collapsed in a small sheltered cranny between two rocks.

Freed from the wind, he paused to assess his situation. His compass and his watch were intact, as was his pack with the map, clothes and food, and he had his emergency kit in his pocket. It was not too late in the day, so he could sit tight for an hour or so before running the risk of being benighted. He decided that as the weather was unexpected, so it might be short lived, and to wait would be the best policy.

He sat and stared into the grey mass of snow streaking horizontally past the rocks that sheltered him, and wondered where the bright clear winter's day of a few minutes ago had gone. This probably looks like a quiet grey cloud from the valley, he thought. In fact, he was wrong. The freak storm had hit the whole area, and badly. And he was wrong about the duration of the storm. It was set in for a long time. He looked anxiously at his watch as it neared his deadline and the weather showed no signs of abating. When the deadline arrived and the weather was, if anything, worse, he felt there was no way he could safely venture out into the storm and struggle down the hill. He reluctantly reached the conclusion that he was there for the night, and he started to pile up a snow wall at the entrance to his impromptu shelter. Sterner disciplines were beginning to take over.

He had never built a snow wall before, but the entrance was small and he eventually succeeded in sealing himself in except for a small air opening. He settled back against the rock, feeling fairly snug and very smug. He had worked cautiously to avoid sweating and he was rather cold and stiff, but he assessed his advantages. He was uninjured, he was not too cold, he was dry and he had plenty of food. In addition, he knew on the map almost exactly where he was. He could survive a night of discomfort even though he might not enjoy it, and when the light returned, even if the storm was still blowing, he could cautiously navigate his way back down. All in all, it should prove quite an interesting experience. He could always keep it up his sleeve as a quiet boast in case it came in handy at the University.

Picnic time, he thought.

"Our first meal in our new house," he said out loud as he reached into his pack for a box of sandwiches. As he pulled it out he felt his chest go leaden. The plastic box was bright blue with a bright orange lid. The sight of it in the light of his torch reminded him instantly of the group of children he had been following. A thin straggly line of brightly coloured beads high above him on the hillside.

"Oh God," he whispered. "No. Tiny dots of coloured confetti blowing in this wind."

He pushed the box back into his pack unopened, and leaned back against the rock with a sigh. What should he do? What *could* he do? This wind was strong enough to unbalance a grown man. It would lift a child like a kite and when he saw them last they had been very nearly at the ridge, where the wind would be at its worst and where the long grassy slope ended in crags and sheer rock faces tumbling into the far cwm. Was the man leading them an experienced winter walker? He thought probably yes. Inexperienced walkers generally avoided snow, preferring to be killed by carelessness in the summer. But on the other hand, he doubted that many walkers had ever experienced such unexpected conditions. He certainly hadn't. If he left his present nook, what chance was there that he would find them? It was probable that he would be injured in the howling conditions outside, yet could he sit there safe all night when there was a possibility that children only a few hundred yards away might be dying? This last thought clinched the matter for him. If the worst came to the worst he could always find another hole, and if he did not start soon what light there was would be gone. He checked his boots and clothes to make sure he was as weathertight as he could be, then he wrestled his pack onto his back and, bracing himself, crawled forward out of his shelter.

The blast of the wind staggered him as he tried to stand, but he did not fall. Involuntarily hunching his shoulders against the wind, he stood for a moment studying his compass. The children had been straight ahead of him up the slope. Following a route north west should take him past where they had been and would lead directly to the ridge, then along and down until eventually it joined the footpath. He moved forward cautiously, testing the ground carefully as he went. The wind was as strong as ever, and the snow was drifting. Twice he found himself walking into deeper and deeper snow, and had to retreat carefully—he would have given much for a long stick. He had no idea how far from the top he was as his progress was painfully slow, and the wind with its noise and buffeting seemed to be beating all reason from him. He started to feel cold and he noticed that the pale grey swirling around him was darkening. The cold started him shivering, and fear took over. You must be insane, he thought. Find a rock and dig a hole. Not yet, not yet, it's not such a big hill, it can't be far to the top and they might be there.

People die here, John. Die. Real life death.

Not me, I'm fit and strong, I've got good equipment and food, I'm alright for a while.

You're losing heat, John, and your wits, you've got the night to get through.

I mustn't stop now.

Suppose you slip and injure yourself.

I'll manage somehow. Piss off, I won't slip if I concentrate.

The wind seemed to be increasing and the ground was becoming very uneven. He judged he was walking over snow covered rocks. No sooner had he reached this conclusion than his feet went unexpectedly through the snow and he stumbled forward with a cry. A burning pain shot up his leg and momentarily suffused his whole body. He rolled over and lay clenching and unclenching his hands in the snow as fear and self-recrimination took charge and the wind blew snow into his eyes and mouth and his nose.

You're going to die, John, in the snow. This wind will take your heat away well before morning, especially as you're injured, and you'll be just another mountain statistic.

Some destiny.

Another faint voice spoke within him.

Get up, straight away. As soon as you hit the floor, get up, make it a habit, a reflex.

GET UP!

He gritted his teeth, rolled again and curled up his knees until he was on all fours. He rotated his injured ankle carefully. It was painful, but not broken, he decided, if he was able to move it so much. It was probably a sprain, an overstretched muscle, but he realized that no matter what had happened, no matter how much it hurt, he had no alternative but to move on. He had done what he could for the children and now he would have to find shelter, dig in for the night and try to relax the pain from his damaged foot. It was getting dark and he knew he was too bewildered to undertake any kind of a search.

He took off his pack and with fumbling, chilled fingers, managed to open it, and pull out his torch. Its bright beam revealed nothing but snowflakes streaming purposefully away from him. He started to crawl forward, too frightened to risk his injured foot by walking on the treacherous ground. He proceeded by crawling a little and then shining his torch briefly into the darkness before crawling again. He knew there must be a suitable rock nearby and that he would find it if he did not lose heart.

Resting on his elbows, he clicked the torch on again and peered into its streaked beam. The wind screamed around him, filling everything with noise, and suddenly, as if lured by the light, two baleful green eyes and a dark shape came out of the darkness towards him. Something deep inside him lurched and curled his insides in primitive terror. His heart was thundering, but the range of his torch was only a few feet and he had no time to think or reason his terror away before he found himself muzzle to muzzle with a large Alsatian. He closed his eyes and breathed out in relief.

"Christ, dog, you frightened the wits out of me," he said.

The dog sniffed him indifferently and then turned and walked away. It was the children's dog. He crawled on all fours after it.

"Hello," he shouted. "Is anyone there?"

But he could hardly hear himself over the noise of the wind. The dog was soon out of range of the torch, but it had made deep footprints in the snow so he followed them in the hope that it was moving to shelter.

Then they disappeared off sharply to the left, onto a small patch of bare rock. Shelter, he thought, and shone his torch into the darkness. It illuminated five children huddled together in a dip under an inclined rock, their eyes wide in terror.

"It's alright, kids," he said, as he crawled over to them. "I've been looking for you."

"Are you the rescue people?" asked one.

"No, it's that fellow who was behind us," answered another before John could speak.

"That's right," he said. "I was behind you. I'm afraid I'm not the mountain rescue."

"What are we going to do, mister?" asked the first child, a girl of about twelve, wearing an orange waterproof.

John eased himself against the rock and sagged. It was an indescribable relief to be out of the wind. "Nothing," he said eventually. "Just stay here and do our best to keep warm."

"I'm cold and I want to go home, I'm frightened," wailed another voice in the dark. The torch picked out a tear-stained face huddling against the girl in the orange waterproof.

"What's your name," asked John.

"John," came the reply.

John smiled. "That's my name too. Listen, John, we're all cold and frightened, but we'll be alright if we keep calm and think carefully about things. Now, you've picked a good spot here, and..." He shone his torch over the children. "You've all got good warm clothes. Has anyone got any food?"

There was some nodding. "We were just going to eat it when it started snowing."

"Good," said John. "Then we're definitely going to be alright, but it's not going to be very nice, so try not to get too upset. We're all in it together, alright?"

His namesake nodded.

"Now, we've got a job to do, and then we can cuddle up and keep warm all together."

The children stared at him vacantly.

"Come on," he said, and set them to work building a snow wall.

He crawled out of the shelter of the rock and pushed snow in towards them, showing them where and how to lay it. Gradually it turned into a game for them as the wall slowly rose. The only problem was the dog, which was wandering up and down fretfully and kept knocking sections of the wall down as it jumped in and out. Eventually, the girl in the orange waterproof seized its collar and forced it to lie down out of the way.

John finally patted the top section hard against the rock and then crawled in on his stomach. The wall had taken longer than he had imagined, and he was tired. Inside, the noise of the wind was considerably reduced and the freedom from eddies and swirls of wind and snow made it feel almost pleasant. He was in the process of blocking up the opening with his pack when the dog nosed it out of the way and crawled in. It blundered round for a few moments in the torchlit shadows and received much abuse from the children until it eventually circled and flopped down between two of them. John finished closing the opening and almost immediately the dog got up and went over and started scratching at the pack and whimpering.

"He wants to go out," said one of the children.

"I can see that," replied John rather tartly. "What's his name?"

"Fred," came the answer.

What a name for such a fine dog, he thought.

"Sit down, Fred," he said in his most commanding tone. The dog ignored him and continued scratching and whimpering.

"You'll have to let him out."

"What's the matter with him, anyway?" asked John.

"He's looking for Cap," said someone.

"Cap?" John queried.

Then he remembered the man who had been with the children. His concern with his own journey and his injury and his concern to shelter both himself and the children had filled his mind completely.

"The man who was with you," he said. "Where is he?"

Surely he'd not wandered off and left the children to fend for themselves. He remembered his own near panic. There was no reply.

"Where is he?" he asked again.

"He fell off," said the girl in orange.

"What do you mean, fell off?"

The girl's voice was flat. "Fell off. The wind blew him over the edge."

"Edge? Where are we?"

"We're on the top, I thought you knew."

There was a reproach in her voice and she was near to tears.

"It's alright," he said as gently as he could. "I wasn't exactly sure where I was. I couldn't see where I was going when I found you. Now tell me what happened."

The girl fumbled with the string of her hood.

"When it started to snow, we were walking along the path. Along the top. Cap put us here and told us to wait. He only went up there." She pointed. "Only a few yards. He stood on some rocks. I think he was trying to see how far he could see. And the wind blew him over."

Only the muffled sound of the wind and the dog's whimpering could be heard in the little shelter. The girl spoke again. "I was too frightened to go and see what had happened. I said everyone had to stay here."

John reached out and took her hand. "You did right, love," he said. "You've probably saved everyone's life doing that. The wind's very strong and very dangerous. You wouldn't have been able to do anything."

Then, very softly, she said. "I thought I heard him calling after he'd fallen."

The dog's whimpering rose again and for a timeless moment John became the dog. Smelt the myriad scents of the shelter, felt the pain and frustration of inability, remembered hearing the faint voice of his master, felt the aching need to search. Then it passed and he felt a chill pass over him, deeper by far than the cold of the mountain and the weather.

"Where was he standing?" he asked.

The girl pointed again. John heard himself say, "I'll go and look for him."

"Don't leave us, mister," said the girl.

He squeezed her hand gently.

"What's your name?" he asked.

"Sally," she said.

"Sally, I *have* to go and look. I won't be very long, and I'll leave my rope laid out so that I can follow it back."

The girl looked very uncertain.

He gave her his compass, and spent some time explaining how she must get down from the mountain as soon as the snow stopped and it was light enough.

"Block up the opening with my pack when I've gone," he said. "Just leave enough space for air to get in, then cuddle together and try and go to sleep. Alright?"

Then he pulled his pack away from the opening, and moved to one side as the dog scurried out. He crawled after it and waited until the children had blocked the opening, before heading off in the direction the girl had pointed. If he was on the ridge path, then the rocky edge could only be a few feet away, and in confirmation, the ground rose up suddenly in front of him. The wind was screaming and hammering at him, the snow hurtling past him, and his ankle was throbbing painfully.

What on earth am I doing? he thought. If he's gone over the edge, he's long dead. But some compulsion pushed him on up the little knoll until his torch beam shone into black space and the ground under his hand curved sharply down and away from him. He felt a

126

twinge of vertigo as the wind seemed to blow under him and lift him. He flattened himself and waited for his heart to steady.

Cautiously, he shone the torch from left to right, looking for a vantage point that would enable him to look down the rock face he knew he had now reached. To his left, a little higher, stood a crag, defining the edge more clearly than the snow streaked grass slope he was lying on. He crawled across to it, and still lying down, poked his head over the edge and shone the torch down.

The snow in its beam was moving in all directions, including upwards, as the wind swirled and eddied over the ridge and was released into the void of the cwm below. Guided by who can guess what instinct, the light fell full on an upturned face several feet down from the top. It was largely hidden in a balaclava helmet, but John saw its eyes move as the light struck them.

Like his father before him, but for a different reason, John found himself in another place. One where only a single certainty could be allowed. Reason knew that in that howling blackness could be a long, clattering, and fearful death, but that was not here. Here there could only be that same certainty. He unwound the rest of his rope, fastened a solid and elegant knot with fluid fingers around a stout spur of rock, and swung himself over the edge. The small cleft that had caught the man felt infinitely wide, and the man feather light as he gathered him up and put him on his shoulder. Then there was a childlike climb back up the rope along great steppingstone projections, and the two tumbled back over the edge into the wind and snow and this world.

John's ankle had been glowing gold and comforting, but now it burned hot and agonizing, and his mind was filled with horror at what he had just done. The figure by him stirred in the dark.

"Come on," John shouted urgently, and shone the torch to find his guide rope.

He dragged the man back to the shelter, crawled in, and unceremoniously pulled the man in after him. The dog rushed in from nowhere before he could seal the opening and his enthusiasm threatened to destroy the shelter until his barely conscious master managed to restrain him. After some tears and clamour, the group gradually fell silent and they each drifted into sleep.

John's ankle throbbed unmercifully, and he took a stern grip of his breathing so that he could relax properly and not waste his energy in fruitlessly fighting the pain. As he floated into the twilight before sleep, when the mind is freed, he watched himself travel time and again over the strange golden road he had taken down the cwm face to rescue the stranded man.

That he should have done such a thing defied reason, but it had been indisputably the only way forward, a strange harmony that could not, in principle, be analysed, because it was a single whole. The feeling he had called his destiny came on him. He *was* different.

Alone, but not lonely.

Somewhere, sometime, there was something important for him to do—other golden roads to travel.

Unclear images shone in his mind, and slowly the muffled roar of the wind mingled in his head with the sound of his breathing and the breathing of the others, and he drifted into a deep exhausted sleep.

Consciousness came back painfully. He felt like one huge ache and it was quite a time before he realized where he was and remembered what had happened. Slowly and carefully he moved his hands and his feet, then his arms and legs. His conscious mind was telling him he was just stiff through sleeping on rock in cramped and none too warm conditions, but for a while his body was fairly convinced he was dying, if not already dead.

It did not seem as dark in the shelter as it had before he went to sleep. He looked around. A little daylight was seeping around his pack wedged into the entrance. He fumbled for his torch and shone it on his watch. It was morning.

He smiled. They had survived the night and had several hours of light ahead, but what happened next would depend on the weather. He could not hear the wind, but it could still be snowing, or it could be dense cloud, or both. He pulled his pack away from the entrance and, screwing up his eyes against the light that surged in, wriggled out on his stomach.

He forced his reluctant body to stand up. His ankle was painful, but could take some weight, he found. That's a relief, he thought, turning round and opening his eyes fully. As he straightened up, the scene thundered into his head like a massive organ chord in a great cathedral, and he heard himself gasp.

All around, as far as the eye could see, were dazzling white mountains, clear and sharp, shining in the bright sunlight against the vivid blue sky. He stood very still, fearing to do anything that would disturb this vision. He felt he could almost see himself from far above, a small black spellbound speck in a vast landscape of wintry perfection.

Profane noises, however, soon brought him back to earth. The children, disturbed by his movement and by the light in the shelter, were waking and disentangling themselves. Cries of pain, indignation and reproach rose from the opening in the snow wall, then a unified chorus of vilification arose and the dog scrambled out, tongue lolling, ears up, tail wagging, quite unabashed by the tone of the leave-taking. One by one the children followed, wearing varying degrees of self-pity, and finally came Cap, moving with that caution which betokens the lowered pain threshold of the newly wakened. John stretched out his hand.

"Come on," he said. "You'll loosen up in a minute."

Cap stood up and looked at his redeemer. He started visibly.

"John?" came a muffled note of disbelief from behind the balaclava. John looked puzzled and peered into the man's face. Cap pulled off the balaclava.

"My God," exclaimed John. "Hugh."

The two men stared at one another.

"I don't know what to say," said John.

Hugh's face looked tormented, as if he needed to weep but could not.

"John, I don't know what to say either."

His voice was hoarse, and he looked as if he was about to collapse. John took his arm and supported him. "I remember staring for ever into blackness, with the cold all around, and an eternal pit below, and demons screaming and tormenting me. I didn't know whether I was mad or dead and in the outer reaches of hell. I was just waiting."

John felt his friend's horror and put his arms around him. This embrace was all he could offer. Words could shine no light into that darkness.

"Then a bright light shone through it all, like a door into another world, and a great force drew me into it."

He looked up abruptly and stared at John strangely. "I'm sorry for the strange talk, John, it's probably shock, but I can see things clearly that are normally hidden. You're a special person. I've known it since we first met. Very special."

John grimaced at this eulogy, although it was brief and without affectation, but part of him understood it as Hugh's oath of fealty, and that part of him accepted it. He slapped his friend on the arm.

"Come on, Hugh. We're all alive. That's the main thing. Let's get these kids off the hill."

The journey down was long and hard. They had deep drifts to contend with. John's ankle troubled him and Hugh found movement difficult due to the bruising he had received from his fall. But they were in good spirits. John had insisted that they eat half of their food while at the top, and that alone put life back into them.

"Quarter of an hour's not going to make any difference. We need this food, and we've earned this view, Hugh. We'll probably never see its like again," he said, gazing round at the snow-covered peaks.

"Nor taste food as good," said Hugh chewing a sorry looking sandwich. "Here, take this."

He pulled a piece off the sandwich he was eating and, breaking it in half, offered John one portion and threw the other into the air.

"A gift to the mountain," he said.

# Chapter 18

One evening, some months after the incident on the mountain, John and his father were sitting quietly reading. John put down his book and stared for several minutes into the fire.

"Something strange happened to me on that mountain, dad," he said.

Peter looked up.

"Strange?" he echoed.

"Yes, I can't explain it."

"I don't understand, John. Strange—how?"

John made a wry face and shrugged. Peter was tempted to be brusque with his son but something in John's manner cautioned him that an inappropriate action would frighten away the timid spirit that was struggling to appear. He closed his book softly and laid it on the floor, then he leaned back in his chair.

"Strange is a strange word to use, John," he said with a slight smile. "Frightening I could understand, perhaps even exhilarating, but strange?"

John still seemed to be fumbling for words—something needed to be said. Peter leaned forward. "John, we don't normally talk about these things. Family is family. A lot is taken for granted. Words are often irrelevant. One loves one's children almost no matter what. But I've always been proud of the way you behaved. You have a sure touch. What you did on that mountain made me more than proud. It made me feel..." Now it was his turn to search for a word. "I don't know. Honoured. Privileged to have had anything to do with you. Everyone is given some opportunity to measure himself in some way, and you can take some pride in your achievement.

Mind you." He sat back and became more matter of fact. "I wouldn't have thought it was like you to take chances with those odds."

"That's the thing, dad," said John quietly. "The risk. When I came out of my first shelter, I weighed the risks. I weighed them against my conscience, against a responsibility I felt for those kids, even though I didn't know them. That was a calculated decision. But when that torch beam went straight to Hugh's face... straight to it, dad. No wavering, no searching. The question of a decision somehow didn't exist."

He tried to explain to his father the strange otherworldliness, the shining certainty he had experienced in his rescue of Hugh.

"It seems to dominate my life even now, that rightness, that perfection. It sounds ridiculous really."

Both sat without speaking for some time. Part of the fire collapsed in a small flurry of sparks.

"It's not ridiculous, John," said Peter. "I do understand. I've had a similar experience, only in my case it involved saving my own life, not someone else's."

John looked at him.

"I can't tell you about it yet. One day I will. But a day doesn't pass in which it doesn't occur to me, and it will be the same with you. It'll add a lot to your life—insight, call it what you will."

John wanted to tell his father about the feeling he had that he would do great things, of the strange deep relationship he had developed with Hugh and Minna, but they seemed somehow to be darker forces, and were even harder to find words for.

He remembered Minna greeting them when they returned to the nearby village with part of one of the many search parties that were scouring the hills and that they had met halfway down. Minna embraced Hugh with tears and relief, and John with surprise and delight. A church hall had been turned into a temporary rescue centre and John sat down thankfully on a wooden chair as if it had been a luxurious armchair.

The hall was decorated for Christmas and he stared at the coloured streamers curving in and out of the great timber roof beams, the children's pictures around the walls, and the tinselled Christmas tree topped with its silver star. He smelt the warm and savoury odours of cooking mixed with those of gas and paraffin heaters, he heard the melodious Welsh language rising and falling across the hall, and he felt that special communion of people which occurs when great need arises.

Not all was light and joy though. Like the original Christmas, there were many miraculous rescues and many tragic deaths in those two days. One man struggled three miles with a broken leg and collapsed to freeze to death within a few feet of a house. Another, like Hugh, was blown off a ridge but, unlike Hugh, fell two hundred feet to land uninjured in a snow drift. The impact carried him several feet into the drift, and when he had recovered his wits he dug himself a snow cave and sat out the storm. Now, however, for John, there was warmth and respite and some semblance of normality.

He noticed Hugh and Minna talking together on the other side of the hall. Hugh was talking quietly, without excitement or agitation, and the two were staring at one another in that strange way of theirs. Almost as if she felt his gaze across the room, Minna turned and looked straight at John. She came across and sat beside him, her bright eyes staring at him, unblinking.

"Hugh told me what you did," she said flatly.

John shrugged a little, but before he could speak she put her arms around him and held him. Not with any exaggerated emotion or passionate release, but just a simple embrace that he could not have broken with his greatest effort. He felt a deep commitment from her as he had from Hugh. It was beyond words and beyond his control. They had bound themselves to him more than ever before and part of him understood.

After that evening, Peter gave John small items of work to do in connection with the business. It was all done with apparent casualness, but in reality it was carefully calculated to give John some insight into the extent and nature of the business. John, under the impression he was simply helping with the occasional office bottleneck, did the work diligently and paid little conscious heed to the implications of what he was doing. His main interest was his university work during term time, and his work with Brian Gerard in the summer.

Brian's business was booming. Diminishing resources aggravated by instability in most underdeveloped countries, plus increasingly longer and colder winters worldwide, had effected a major change in public opinion, and commerce and industry were also facing new realities. Massive economies had always been available to those who used recycling and energy conservation techniques, but the change in public opinion had made the use of irreplaceable fuels almost a heresy, and Brian's consultancy found the workload increasing at an incredible rate. Unfortunately, having pushed so hard against the inertia of public indifference for so long, Brian continued pushing when the resistance had gone, and found himself running almost out of control. This was all too apparent to his staff who watched in helpless dismay as their employer showed every indication of working himself into a complete collapse.

"You needn't worry too much, John," said his father one day. "I've managed to fix up some extra finance and management assistance for Brian. He'll be able to get more staff and upgrade his computer systems. It should ease the load on him considerably."

John was not hopeful.

"I doubt that," he replied. "I don't think Brian can stop. The bigger his business gets, the harder he'll work."

His father patted him on the shoulder. "No, no. I can't afford the risk, he's too valuable a man to lose. I'll be talking to him seriously soon. I'll do a deal with him. I'm sure he'll accept my guidance."

And accept it he did. The next time John went to work there he found the staff drastically increased and every conceivable type of computer aid in use to minimize effort. But Brian himself was almost serene.

"Persuasive man, your father, John," was all he would say.

Most of the new staff, including two very senior assistants, had, John discovered, come from a rival practice which had collapsed when its financial backers had suddenly withdrawn their support and the principal and a large sum of money had mysteriously disappeared. He was pleased to find, however, that the atmosphere of the place was largely unchanged.

The research department still bore its equivocal paper notice, and although it contained more people, it was still a dump.

"Batten down the hatches," George would say when John arrived each year. "The new broom's back. Polish your paperclips."

Freddy was still Brian's secretary and still worked in the same little office. John found, to his surprise, that he was becoming drawn to her, although she was not the prettiest girl he had ever known. He found her company enjoyable and relaxing and he felt at ease with her, although she had a deflating wit not dissimilar to his mother's. More surprising still, he noticed a strong twinge of jealousy when he learned she had a boyfriend. He had imagined himself well above that kind of thing.

Back at the university his academic enthusiasm coupled with his increasing awareness of matters practical was cutting a swathe through his work. He obtained his Bachelor's and his Master's degrees with an ease that slightly disconcerted some of his more staid colleagues, and then he turned his attention to the possibility of a PhD.

This proved to be much harder than he had envisaged. There would be no problem with funds, nor any problem in finding a university to take him. In fact, his own was prepared to set aside its usual practice of advising graduates to move elsewhere to obtain their doctorates. The problem, quite simply, was what to do? John was universally curious. He had no overwhelming desire to pursue any particular speciality and the work for a PhD was necessarily very specialized.

"I find it very difficult to advise you, John," said his father. "Perhaps if you consider the matter from the point of view of which project will provide the happiest working conditions for you."

John looked askance. Peter threw up his hands.

"It's only a suggestion. It seems to me you don't really give a toss what you do so long as you do something, so you may as well do something that involves working in a way you enjoy. Think about it."

John did think about it. His father's comments had been rather simplistic, but they were not altogether unfair. On reflection he realized he did not want to play a small part in a vast long-term research project, emerging as a sort of production line PhD. Nor did he want to be involved in what he called a tea clipper project—one which was effectively being duplicated by others elsewhere and the primary object of which was to "be there first". Nor did he want anything that would bring him into serious contact with the vicious in-fighting that underlay the university's outward academic calm. That was one aspect of university life that he both disliked and despised—in part because it frightened him. He had seen people jockeying for position at Brian Gerard's, and he was beginning to learn that his father was no mean operator, but all this was for

135

understandable motives, greed or power, and was conducted in the main within the restraints that operated in packs of predatory animals. The academics on the other hand seemed to fight with bitter personal acrimony, all restraints being thrown to the winds. It was as if living on rarefied academic planes had blunted their natural instinct to constrain their fighting in the interests of the greater good. He wanted none of that. It was diseased.

Untypically, his father started to nag.

"For crying out loud, John. You're behaving like a prima donna. Pick something and get on with it, or I'll pick something for you."

This concentrated John's mind wonderfully. He could go several rounds with his father, but nowhere near the full distance. A deadline had been set.

During a quiet spell at work some days after that remark, he was sitting with his head resting on his hands, idly watching a shadow move across his drawing board as the sun shone briefly into the well of the building and directly through his window. He was startled out of his reverie by a magazine landing on his desk.

"You're interested in history aren't you, John? Here's a comic for you."

It was George. "I found it at the bottom of an old drawer at home. Thought it might be of interest to you. Bung it in the filing system when you've finished."

He grinned and winked and pointed to the wastepaper basket. John looked at the magazine. It was several years old and was one of a series of ecology/self- sufficiency magazines that had flourished briefly and then faded away leaving only two or three influential and rather stuffy periodicals to mark their passing.

He thumbed through it. There were articles on house insulation, heat recycling, solar energy, wind and wave power, mixed in with articles on humane farming, pesticide-free gardening and all manner of political polemic inveighing against the then government for its secrecy and incompetence and a variety of other sins. He smiled. Times don't change, he thought. We'd be lost without the clowns we ask to govern us. Then, briefly, like a distant rumbling, came to him the knowledge that one day he too would order the fates of others. It passed as quickly as it had come and he let it go.

He was intrigued by the technical articles. Most of the ideas had become irrelevant because of changes in technology and materials, but some of them could legitimately be regarded as the fountain head of certain modern conservation techniques, and were very interesting.

Towards the end he encountered a letters page. One was headed "Heat Storage Breakthrough?" It was a peculiar letter, and the editor's heading was partly ironic. The writer was a university lecturer, and he was bemoaning the fact that his research project had been cancelled following a serious accident. He had been working on a chemical heat storage system of some promise, but during tests it had become unstable and exploded, doing considerable damage, including sending one piece of apparatus through two partition walls and a very large plate glass window. No-one had been hurt, thundered the writer, so what was all the fuss about? Just a slight imbalance, the discovery of the century, and so on. John judged that quite a lot of the letter had been edited out, and from the style of the remainder came to the conclusion that the project had been cancelled not only because of the accident, but also, and probably principally, because its author was a prick of some magnitude. However, one sentence contained an outline of the process, and this caught John's attention. He was cautious about new ideas that flared suddenly, apparently illuminating all. He had had quite a few himself, only to see them fade into nothingness on close scrutiny. But this was interesting.

"Where can I find out about this magazine?" he called across to George. George did not move other than to lift his left arm and point to the computer console.

"Thanks."

John spent the rest of that day sat at the console. He obtained earlier copies of the magazine and also its contemporaries. The man had written to them all, constantly, and was obviously regarded as the court jester. His early letters outlined his ideas on heat storage, but their presentation portrayed the writer as a crank, and this disguised their intrinsic worth. The later letters were all in the same vein as the one John had read originally—reproachful and defensive. From his writing, John considered it was a miracle he had ever been given the opportunity to mount a research project, however small. He obviously had a flare for irritating people, and being unsackable, had been fobbed off by the university authorities for the sake of a quiet life. What happened to him after the accident was harder to trace. The university records simply showed he had left, and gave no indication of where he had gone.

John stared at the screen and tapped his thumb nail against his teeth. Where on earth could he look next? The university might possibly have the man's old research papers, but he thought that unlikely, and most of the staff who knew him would certainly be retired or dead by now. Dead end indeed. Then a glimmer came into his mind. He carefully placed the printouts and his notes, together with the magazine, into his case and walked out of the office. He felt quite excited as he clattered down the stairs three at a time.

As the glass doors of the building hissed together behind him and he walked across the sunlit square, he noted reflexively that it was the third consecutive day he had left using that exit.

"Dad, I wonder if you could help me?"

There was some embarrassment in the question, and Peter looked sideways at his son through narrowed eyes.

"Depends," he replied.

"I think I might have found something for my PhD research."

Peter's face changed from mock suspicion to mock indignation. "About time too," he said. "What's your problem?"

John described his day's work and its inconclusive end.

"And?" asked his father finally.

"Well, I thought it might be possible for you to trace him for me. I need to know what happened to him and his research notes."

"How am I supposed to do that John? I'm not a detective."

John cleared his throat and curled his thumb towards the computer console. Peter raised his eyebrows.

"You mean look into the public records?" He drew in a breath. "That's illegal John, you know that. And they'll be code protected."

"Come on Dad," said John, trying to end the charade. "Stop messing about. You were into my confidential university record fast enough with your fancy computer."

It took them longer than they expected. The records were old and incomplete, and the man had moved around a great deal after leaving the university. Eventually they finished with a coroner's report, a small provincial newspaper article about a newly arrived resident tragically killed in a mysterious explosion in his workshop, and the name and address of a surviving young sister.

# Chapter 19

John wrote several times to the sister, but received no replies.

"She's still alive, John," said his father. "At least, she's still drawing a pension so it's a reasonable assumption she is."

The time for making a decision on his PhD was too close to indulge in any further delay so John decided he had no alternative but to go and see the lady personally.

It was a long rambling journey with little opportunity for using his car's powerful engine to make rapid progress, so he ambled along at a relatively sedate pace, except for the odd occasion when he could not resist leaving some ostensibly more powerful car standing. It was early autumn, and away from the frenzy of the motorways and trunk roads the countryside was peaceful and still. Twice John stopped just to gaze at the landscape, and to breathe in the autumn air. Its scents bore memories of times that seemed long gone. Thomas-not-Tom and his other friends, misty mouthed in the autumn evening, collecting wood for their bonfire, tying ropes around lopped branches and hauling them across fields in triumph. Walking with his mother and father through the woods, kicking dead leaves noisily. Watching red sunset nights darken, and scarves and boots begin to appear. His mother did not like autumn very much.

"Everything's dying," she would say, but he enjoyed it for what it was.

The countryside had the feeling of just starting to be drowsy prior to a long warm sleep. But he enjoyed climbing back into his car and driving in its sophisticated warmth and comfort along unfamiliar twisting roads, identifying villages and towns and even getting lost once or twice.

It was late afternoon when he reached his destination. Although it was only a small village, he managed to find a room at the one and only public house.

"We're not really residential," said the landlord confidingly. "But we've a nice spare room you can use if you like. It used to be our boy's, so we keep it for him and for occasional visitors like yourself, although we're not exactly a tourist centre."

The man was short and stocky and had a slight stoop. He also had a strong local accent which John found irresistible. He took John's small bag and led him upstairs, regaling him pleasantly with oddments of family and local history, and pausing only to shout down the hallway, "Mother, we've got a visitor."

Mother was also short, and fatter than was good for her judging by the way she puffed. But she fitted perfectly, bustling out of her kitchen, grey hair pulled back into a bun, round shiny face with happy eyes, and big practical hands smoothing down her blue patterned apron.

"The room will be lovely," said John looking round at the neat little bedroom with its traces of occasional occupation. The wooden floor had been stained and a small, slightly frayed runner of carpet was placed to protect unwary feet. The ceiling sloped down over the bed, following the line of the roof to the eaves, and there was a small window in the wall next to the bed.

He wondered how many hours had been spent by the room's original occupant, kneeling on that bed and, head on hands, gazing out through the window across the fields to the woods in the distance.

"Hang your coat in the hall, and come in the parlour when you're ready," said the landlord, backing out of the door.

Downstairs, John looked at the parlour door standing ajar, and then walked into the kitchen. He noted the backdoor and its bolt and mortice lock with a key in it.

"Sorry," he said to the landlord's wife with a smile. "Got lost."

"In here, Mr...?" the landlord's voice rolled along the hall.

"Newman, John Newman," said John as he entered the parlour.

The landlord was sitting in an armchair by the fireplace. He gestured John to the seat opposite.

"You're just in time for tea," he said. John looked concerned.

"No, really. I can't impose on you like this." But he was interrupted.

"Oh, it's no trouble, we've always got plenty in, and Mother likes cooking for three. It's just a little something to tide you over until supper time."

And tide him over it did. The little something proved to be a substantial three course meal, after which John returned to his armchair to ponder words like "bountiful" and "replete". He was quite relieved that his offer to help with the kitchen chores had been rejected, as he had reservations about his ability to stand for too long.

"That's what's called country fare, is it?" he asked the landlord.

The landlord grinned. "Mother enjoyed that," he said. Then, confidentially, "She misses the lad, you know. Likes to have someone to feed."

They talked for a little while about nothing in particular until the landlord stood up and excused himself.

"I'll have to get things ready for opening now," he said. John made as if to stand up, but the landlord laid a hand on his shoulder. "Sit yourself down, there's nothing you can do, but thanks for offering. You sit and rest, you've come a long way. You must be tired. Watch the telly if you like, and there's newspapers here." He lifted a cushion at the end of the couch.

John was not disposed to argue. He was certainly tired, and he felt as if he had eaten enough to last a week or more. He picked up the paper, a local one, and looked at the TV programmes. There was nothing of any interest so he browsed idly through the weddings and fetes and the misdoings of the local worthies. The chair was comfortable and the room was warm and peaceful, with a vague hum of familiar activity elsewhere in the house.

A hand shook his arm gently. "I've made you a little something for supper."

John woke up abruptly. It was the landlord's wife. He sat up in the chair, feeling rather awkward.

"Good Lord," he said. "I must have nodded off. What time is it?"

She pointed to the clock. He had been asleep for over three hours.

"I've never done that before in my life. Sleeping the evening in an armchair." His tone was one of surprise, and he still felt bewildered and slightly embarrassed. "I'm awfully sorry. It was very rude of me."

"Nonsense," beamed the woman. "You were grand company."

"Company?"

"Yes. There was nothing on the telly, so I sat and talked to you while I was knitting." He could not help but laugh.

"Oh," he managed.

"Talk to father for hours I do," she went on. "When he's asleep. Get a good programme on the telly, and he's out like a light. Then I can have a good talk to him." Then, more knowingly, "Don't talk to him much when he's awake though. Too much trouble repeating things and explaining. And him not listening anyway." Then she laughed—a high bubbling laugh that lit the room. "Besides, you were tired, and country air's a bit too much for most townsfolk. Let him sleep, I thought, do him good."

John patted his stomach. "I don't think it was your country air, I think it was your country cooking."

"Would you like a little . . .?" She indicated a huge plate of sandwiches.

"Bless you, no thank you," he said. "That was such a splendid tea you made, I'm still full."

The woman seemed about to pursue her recommendation, but further pressure on his digestive system was avoided by the entry of the landlord.

"Quiet tonight," he said. "Still, can't grumble. It keeps me away from loose women."

He delivered a massive wink to John as he said this.

"You're embarrassing the lad, father," said his wife. "Sit down and eat your supper. You sure you don't want anything, Mr. Newman?"

"I'm certain, thank you very much," said John, raising his hand.

"Down here on business or pleasure, Mr. Newman?" asked the landlord, chewing a large sandwich.

"A little bit of both actually," replied John. "Perhaps you can help me. I'm trying to find a Miss Jennifer Jenkins."

The landlord screwed up his mouth pensively. "Jenkins, Jenkins. I don't think... Oh. Yes. It'll be old Miss Jenny he wants, mother. Miss Jenny at Ash Cottage."

"That's it," said John. "Ash Cottage."

"Nice old dear Miss Jenny, but funny you know," said the landlord. "Not been here long. Keeps herself to herself."

His wife snorted quietly. "She's been here over twelve years father, and seeing as she's strict Methodist she wouldn't have anything much to say to you would she?"

"No, I suppose not," conceded the landlord, and retreated behind his paper with yet another wink to John.

"Are you a relative of Miss Jenny?" asked the woman, clicking her knitting needles steadily but looking straight at John. His immediate reaction was to think, family business, say nothing, but there was a solid comfort to this room and this couple which reminded him of his own childhood.

"No, I'm not a relative," he said. "In fact, I don't even know her. I want to see her about some work her brother was doing."

"Oh. I didn't know she had a brother."

"She hasn't now, unfortunately. I'm afraid he was killed in an accident."

"Oh dear," sighed the woman, and lowered her knitting into her lap.

"It was a long time ago," said John to reassure her. I don't really think she'll be able to help, but she might know some of his old friends and I might be able to get what I want from them."

Eventually the knitting started again, but John decided not to re-open the conversation and glanced down idly at the papers on his lap. The woman caught his attention with a little cough. He looked up. She nodded towards her husband and smiled. He was sound asleep and the arms holding the newspaper were slowly sinking onto the arms of the chair.

Later, John lay in bed and looked up at the pink curtains covering the window by his bed, and at the ceiling sloping down towards him. They were illuminated by a small battery powered night light which was sitting on a bedside table and which he had turned on at a whim. He felt the presence of the previous occupant looking at this view with young eyes, and smelling the distinctive scents of the room, and it reminded him of the comfort and stability of his own boyhood. The whole world should be like this all the time, he thought—all the time. He reached out and clicked off the little light and, turning onto his side, closed his eyes and drifted back in time to his own childhood bedroom.

He had arranged with the landlord to be wakened when the rest of the house awoke, and the first thing he did was draw the small curtains and spend a few minutes gazing around the room in the pale morning light. Then he knelt on the bed and opened the window, and gazed out over the misty fields. Autumn smells, cold and wet but not unpleasant, assailed him. Running his hand along the edge of the windowsill, he felt the room's comfort around him and wondered again about the ghost of the boy who had once been here.

More prosaic matters, however, were about to overtake him for, as he dressed and shaved and packed his few belongings, the room filled with rare aromas. Although he was far from certain that his digestive system had finished with the previous day's meal, he went downstairs and surrendered again, with only the merest flicker of guilt, to the sin of overindulgence, by devouring a huge three course English breakfast.

The words 'conspicuous consumption', 'unbridled greed' and similar chimed in his head later as he walked at a leisurely pace along the village street, pride overcoming discomfort and forbidding him to take his belt out by a notch.

"Ash Cottage is just along the road. First turning on the left outside the village. You won't need your car, it's only a few minutes walk," said the landlord, and John had welcomed the prospect of a brief walk to ease his surfeit. However, the countryman's 'few minutes walk' is not the same as the townsman's, and John was beginning to think he had missed the turning when he came at last to the entrance to Ash Cottage, some three quarters of a mile from the end of the village. He struggled with the gate and made his way along a narrow path to the front door. The garden was old, but well kept, not manicured like some of the new ones he had seen in the village, and there were signs of improvised repairs to a rainwater pipe and one or two other items indicating that Miss Jenny was at least mobile and in some command of the situation.

He knocked firmly but not too loudly on the brass knocker, and then stepped back and stood slightly to one side.

"Coming," came a high-pitched sing-song voice from some way behind the door, and after some confused rattling a tiny elfin figure appeared.

"Yes?" it said.

"Miss Jenkins?" asked John.

"Yes," it smiled.

"My name is John Newman, Miss Jenkins. I wrote to you about

your brother..." Before he could go on, Miss Jenny covered her mouth with her hand, like a schoolgirl who had forgotten her homework.

"Oh dear, dear, dear me," she said, bustling forward and taking hold of his arm. "I'm awfully sorry. And you coming all this way. Oh dear, dear, come in, come in."

She fired the commands with great rapidity, at the same time leading John into the house.

"Mind your head," she ordered as she ushered him into the cottage's small front room. John ducked just in time to avoid a low beam.

"These places weren't built for big people like you," she said.

Settling him into an armchair, she left the room to return a few minutes later clutching several letters and envelopes. She stood opposite him with her head cocked on one side, not much taller standing than he was sitting, and he found it hard not to smile.

"I'm a naughty girl, aren't I?" she said. John was about to reply, but she continued. "They were very nice letters, and I've been meaning to reply, but I keep forgetting. There's always something else to do isn't there?"

"It's not important, Miss Jenkins, not now that I'm here anyway. It's just that I wanted to have a word with you about your brother, if it's convenient."

"Would you like a cup of tea?" she said.

"Er, no thank you," he protested faintly. "I've just had something at the pub."

"And biscuits?" she continued regardless.

It dawned on John that he would have to pursue his enquiry at her pace if he was going to make any progress and, shortly afterwards he was nursing a large cup of tea and slowly nibbling a biscuit.

She was sitting opposite him with her hands crossed in her lap, again looking like a schoolgirl.

"So you want to know about Sammy?" she said. "All this way for Sammy."

"Sammy?" John queried. "Oh, of course, your brother. I'm sorry, I'd forgotten his Christian name."

To John's dismay a large tear ran down her cheek. He looked round desperately for somewhere to put his cup so that he could unearth a handkerchief, but she had wiped the tear away in a trice and was smiling again.

"Dear me. Don't mind my silliness, Mr. Newton. I always have a little weep when I think of Sammy. He was my big brother you know, much older than me. I loved him. Thought he was wonderful. But he was such a silly boy," she said, crossly smacking her tiny right fist into her left hand as if to chase away the ghostly memories forming around her. "Such a silly boy," she repeated. "He got so angry with things, and with himself, and with other people. And, of course, they got angry with him in turn. Well, people do, don't they?"

John nodded. "What did he get so angry about?" he asked.

"Oh, this silly invention of his. He wanted to be a famous scientist. 'Jennikins, I'll save the world,' he used to say. 'I'll be the most famous scientist ever.' Then he blew up the university."

She giggled infectiously. "The professor was so angry," she said guiltily, and then she giggled again. "And Sammy didn't care, you know. He was just cross because his precious experiment had to stop. Oh dear me, dear me." And the handkerchief removed this time a tear of laughter.

John thought he could risk a question.

"What your brother was doing, Miss Jenkins, could have been as important as he said, and I'd like to find out more about it. The university have nothing. Do you by any chance have any of his old notes?"

She clasped her hands in her lap again and screwed up her face intently.

"It's such a long time ago. Let me see now." John waited. "I hadn't the heart to throw his stuff out when I moved here. Poor Sammy. Silly boy. So there might be something in the loft."

Two hours later, John was driving home. On the passenger seat beside him was a cardboard box full of exercise books and loose-leaf papers. When he had eventually manipulated an ancient and shaky pair of step ladders through the house and succeeded in struggling into the loft, he had banged his head on a purlin, torn his jacket on a nail that had been left projecting from that same purlin for that specific purpose, and nearly put his foot through the ceiling before he came across the box, covered in dust and lying amongst other relics of previous lifestyles. A quick glance had shown the contents to be research notes that Jenkins had been using before the accident at the university, and when he had shown them to Miss Jenny, she had thrust them into his arms.

"You take them, you take them," she chimed. "They're no use to me. I don't want to save the world. I'm surprised the mice haven't eaten them. But mind..." She raised a finger. "You see my Sammy gets any credit if they're any use. Poor Boy."

Assurances given, his last sight of her was a little schoolgirl wave and a large smile as she stood by her garden gate until she disappeared from view as he walked round a bend, back towards the village. What a strange, happy little soul, he thought.

Back at the pub he made his farewells to the landlord and his wife, but had to exercise his every diplomatic skill to avoid being lured in for 'a little snack' to help him on his way.

Peter sat in his father's old office, looking at the paper in front of him. It was John's summary of Jenkins' work, and his assessment of its worth and its potential. He pressed a button on the telephone.

"Joey. Have the boys scrape John up, hose him down and send him in, please."

There was a chuckle from the other end.

"Right boss."

A few minutes later John entered the office. Peter was writing and waved him to a chair.

"Won't be a minute, John."

John sat down very slowly. When Peter had finished his writing, he looked up at his son and grinned. John's face was flushed from effort, his hair was wet and plastered down, his bottom lip was swollen, giving him a slightly sulky look and he was sitting in a way which indicated a fairly uniform spread of discomfort. Peter's grin turned into a laugh.

"Enjoy your work-out?" he asked.

John glowered at him. "Where on earth did you find those people, dad?"

"They're all faithful old family retainers, John, and don't you forget it," replied his father. "They're a good bunch aren't they? In fact they're the best."

"Best what?" asked John.

Peter looked at him. "Best Head Office staff, of course."

It was, in fact, John's first visit to his father's office since he was a child, and he was both impressed and puzzled. He noticed immediately that the security in the place was massive, albeit discreet, and he presumed there was much more which could not be seen. There were a few offices, and he encountered and was introduced to various members of staff, but it was not the crowded busy hive he had imagined. In addition, everyone had a certain physical presence which he could feel but not define, and they all, men and women, dressed similarly. Dark discreet suits, not a vestige of ostentation, no rings or any form of decoration or jewellery. It was a very strange place and he decided it was rather frightening. Even his father seemed to be a different person in that spartan, tidy office —a colder, more aloof man than the one he knew at home. John had occasionally felt the power emanating from his father, and something deep within him resonated in sympathy.

The aloofness was, however, gone for the moment, vanished in laughter. John continued in mock reproach.

"You said, 'Come along. I'll have a look at your proposals and you can have a little work-out with some of the boys in the gym.'—your words. Little, you said. Boys, you said. You didn't mention the girls, did you? Look at me now. One long bruise, and every bone in my body broken."

"Don't say that please John, not that, not every bone. I'll have to pay them a bonus for that."

"Very droll dad, very droll."

"Still," said Peter, more seriously. "You've never had such a good work-out have you?"

"No, that's true," said John resignedly. "I haven't trained much over the last few years, but I didn't think I was that rusty."

"You're not all that rusty John, although we'll have to sharpen you up a little. It's just that all my staff are very good. They have to be. Men and women."

John nodded ruefully and touched his swollen mouth.

"Why, dad?"

Peter leaned back in his chair and swivelled it from side to side as he looked at his son.

"It's just company policy John," he said.

John grimaced at the avoidance.

"But why, dad? What's the point? If you have people who are very important to you, you can hire protection."

Peter raised his eyebrows and sighed a little. "John, don't be dense. Protection that can be hired by one party can be bought by another. That's an ancient lesson. I shouldn't have to tell you that. You're the historian. This business arose out of blood and mayhem, treachery and corruption. Even today there are aspects of it that involve considerable personal risk to individuals. Over the years, countless officers have been killed by their own guards who have been suborned. In the ultimate analysis, our executives have to be able to defend themselves against anything, be it attack from their colleagues or the random misfortune of the streets. Anything else is too risky."

He put his arms on the desk and spoke quietly and steadily, looking straight at his son.

"When I say they are the best, it's not a fatuous euphemism for very good, or even excellent. It's a simple statement of fact. No company wields Occam's razor like we do. Our employees are winnowed out of thousands—thousands, John. The people you've just been working out with are not clerks and typists. One of them is an expert in international finance, another in international law. There's a political assessor, one of the finest seismologists in the world, and a strategic weapons specialist who lets the U.S. Government think it employs him. If you think you've been trampled on physically, you should see what they can do to you intellectually."

John was taken aback completely by this sudden revelation. He had never known his father discuss the business other than in the vaguest terms, and then only when politeness dictated. His mind buzzed with questions, but his father gave him no opportunity to ask them. He had picked up the paper from his desk and was looking at it thoughtfully.

"I've discussed this assessment of yours with some of our chemical consultants, and with Brian Gerard. Their conclusions are similar to yours. The actual experimentation is risky, and we'll have to lay out a lot on the safety aspects if we don't want you to go the same way as Mr. Jenkins. But everyone feels the project will yield at worst some useful information and at best could hit a considerable jackpot. So, we'll go ahead."

"We?" queried John. "Who's this we?"

"The business, of course, John."

John shook his head as if to waken himself.

"I must have missed something," he said. "How'd the business get into this? This was just an idea for a PhD thesis. You were going to advise me on my presentation to the university. You know, full stops, commas and things. Now you're talking as if you intend to do the project yourself."

Peter dropped the paper back onto the desk and leaned back in his chair.

"I'm sorry, John. I should have explained more carefully, but in all honesty I've only made up my own mind this morning."

He started swivelling his chair from side to side again.

"Just think about this for a minute. If I'm any judge of you, you're not really an academic. You've got a couple of good degrees, which you earned, and you enjoy solving intellectual problems. You have an aesthetic appreciation of maths and science, but really you'd prefer to be participating in something that could yield a good practical result, something that would be of use to people in their ordinary lives."

"Today's pure research is tomorrow's applied, Dad," defended John.

"I accept that, John. We sponsor a great deal of pure research, but just bear with me for a moment. Am I not right in my assessment of your interest?"

John ignored the question.

"Get to the deal Dad, I'm listening," he said knowingly. Peter smiled, but ignored the comment.

"I've been watching you look for a project. You could have done any one of a dozen potty research schemes, but you didn't really start to move yourself until you came across one with some immediate practical value. On balance I'd say you were more interested in today's applied than tomorrow's, for all your vaunted indifference."

"So?"

"So, I concluded that the PhD as such is not really of any interest to you. It's just a piece of paper expressing the opinion of people whose opinion you're not really interested in. Is that true?"

John was quiet for a moment.

"I suppose it is," he said reluctantly. "I'd never really considered it in those terms, but I'm afraid you might be right."

"Good," said Peter. "Then this is what I have in mind."

Peter explained his proposals in detail. He thought the project could yield substantial commercial and social benefits, so he did not want John bogged down with academic duties, or hampered by petty financial restrictions. Perhaps most of all, however, he did not want any unnecessary complications with the ownership and the security of the project. Ownership could always be adjusted with money if there was an argument, but security was security—ideas, once out, could not be put back again. A special research group would be set up with Brian Gerard in charge of management and John in charge of the research programme, assisted by four scientists seconded from various other companies. More importantly, the group would have access to specialists in many other technical fields, and to a vast amount of computerized data. The proposals were far in excess of what could have been done at the university, and gave John an almost completely free hand. He sat enthralled as his father unfurled the details, and any attractions the university might have held for him faded into nothingness in the glare of the vision they offered. Like his father before him, he felt the power and resource of the business, and they seduced him utterly.

# Chapter 20

John was less sorry at leaving university than he would have imagined. It left in him a host of memories, mainly good, that would be released spontaneously from time to time by some random stimulus—a smell, a colour, a sound—and which he could take some delight in. But on the whole he parted from his university life like a fruit will part from a tree. It had done its job faithfully and well but could now no longer be of service. Coming as it did, at the right time, the parting was natural and painless. He looked forward to his new job with considerable excitement. His father had been right. On reflection, he realized his main interest lay in today's problems, not tomorrow's possibilities, and he was becoming increasingly interested in his father's business.

In reality he was following a carefully laid bait. Peter's conscience had long since stopped troubling him. His sole concern now was to ensure that John was up to the job, and could be led into it with as little pressure as possible.

John's first view of the new laboratory dampened his enthusiasm somewhat. In the family tradition of maintaining 'quiet' security, the building was old and down at heel, although it bore all the signs of a new enthusiastic company moving in. Fresh paint, new doors and windows, and a general newly-brushed appearance. A small nameplate by the main gate declaimed 'Brijon Trading Co. Ltd.' Stepping out of Brian Gerard's car to open the gate, John looked at the sign and winced visibly. He looked at Brian, who shrugged a disclaimer from behind the steering wheel and then drove the car through the gate and straight into a parking place. John looked at the modest fence around the building, and then dropped the gate's bolt into its housing, leaving the gate wide open.

"Turn your car round, Brian," he said casually, circling his left hand horizontally as he walked towards the entrance to the building. Brian was in the process of locking the car and seemed inclined to demur, but John was beginning to develop the characteristics of his father, and casual though the remark had appeared it had a gentle force which made it difficult to deny. He looked at John for a moment, then got back into his car and turned it round so that it faced away from the building. John watched him in amusement as he locked the car and walked across to the entrance. He looked like the nervous and fussy Brian Gerard he had seen when he first met him. He recognized the symptoms.

"Well, say it," he said.

"Say what?" replied Brian.

"You know damn well what," said John.

Brian snorted. "You're getting as bad as your father with your potty ways, young John."

John smiled broadly and winked at him. "There now. You feel much better for that don't you?" he said. Brian snorted again.

"Who thought up the Brijon Trading Co, Brian?" asked John as they walked along a corridor.

"Your father."

"Jesus Christ, what for?"

Brian stopped and looked at him in surprise. "Well, well. I see you're not totally lost then."

"What do you mean?"

"Security John, security. No-one's going to be interested in some new tinpot little company, especially with a name like that. If we put up Gerard International Research Division, we'd be up to our eyes in thieves, industrial spies, publicity and god knows what else."

John nodded. "Brijon it is then, Bri."

Brian Gerard glowered at him. It was his least favourite diminutive.

John examined the building in detail and noted his father's handiwork everywhere. It was a rectangular two storey block with clear space all round. The walls were brick and the floors and roof concrete. The windows were protected by wire cages, and John knew that although they looked ordinary they would be made of a special steel alloy, and the wall anchors would be correspondingly robust. Behind them the windows would be bulletproof and also mounted in well secured frames. It would be easier to break through the brickwork than the windows, although that would be equally futile as the building had been lined internally and, as usual, the alarm system was far more sophisticated than it appeared. Routinely for one of Brian's buildings it was self-sufficient in heat, electrical power and waste disposal, and had water supply to last for several weeks. Like his own home, it was an inconspicuous fortress, and John was well pleased with it. He knew that the tour of inspection was irrelevant. All aspects of security, including the selection of the staff, would have been attended to meticulously by his father. Nonetheless, his own training made it necessary for him to check the place, and he quite enjoyed attempting to devise methods that could breach his father's systems, even though he rarely succeeded.

The real purpose of the visit was an introductory staff meeting. Peter had provided John with a dossier on each member of the small team, and he had been studying them carefully. George Niven he already knew. Matthew Vance he remembered from his childhood—one of the two apostles. He smiled. There were two scientists he did not know but who had impressive records and, for administration, Freddy. He was very pleased about that, although he had to admit his interest was less than professional. Everything seemed to be in order, but as the time for the meeting approached he became progressively more concerned about the fact that though he was supposed to be in charge, he was the youngest of the group, and in many ways the least experienced. Brian Gerard did not help matters by introducing him *very* briefly before handing the meeting over to him.

"He did very well," said Brian later to Peter, as they sat in a restaurant high above the city.

"Good," replied Peter in a tone which meant continue.

"You know, I'd never noticed before, but he has a remarkable way with people, a sort of polite authority. It was only a little get-together, but without any awkwardness at all he took charge and dealt with all the points that had to be dealt with, chop, chop, chop. Who does what and when. Security. He was very good on that. It's always a touchy business telling people like that they can't take work home.

Making arrangements for regular progress meetings, all informal, but important." He paused as a waiter appeared and lowered a plate in front of him. "I was frankly impressed. I knew he was a bright lad, but that was a surprise. You know, Peter, what I think it is? He opens people up, and he listens." He emphasized the point with a shake of his fork. "He listens."

"Good," said Peter, this time finally.

Brian Gerard attended to his meal and wondered, not for the first time, about Peter Newman. He had known him and been friendly with him for a long time but, equally, he did not know him at all. He did not even know what his job was, except that it was to do with finance. He did not work for the institutions that had financed his company, but it was indisputably his influence that had arranged the finance. Then again, he seemed to have contacts in so many other fields—computers, building, security and all manners of engineering and service industries. And yet here he was, presumably a very rich man, but frugal and simple in everything. His quiet dark suit, his unpretentious car, this reasonable but far from lavish restaurant. Strange man. When all the facts were considered, he was really a distant and shadowy figure. Brian looked at him sitting there quietly eating. For an instant, he had an impression that he was sitting opposite a roaring irresistible vortex of power, like a wild and powerful animal, capable of anything both physically and morally, something demonic and primeval.

He felt his pulse start to race, and he caught his breath.

Peter heard the faint gasp and looked up, concerned. "You alright, Brian?" he asked.

The voice blew away part of the mist of Brian's vision.

"Fine," he said, patting his chest. "Bit went down the wrong way."

Peter smiled and blew away the remainder of the vision. "That's a relief. I don't want you choking to death. I'm relying on you to keep John in order."

I must have been working too hard again, thought Brian as he finished his meal. Peter's a good friend even if I don't know much about him. He's just a private person. I'd be nowhere without him, and he's never asked anything unreasonable in return.

The meal ended in inconsequential chatter, and they parted outside the building. Brian watched Peter walking off to the car park, just another dark suited cypher. Even so, he thought, he's a most unusual man. I wonder who you really are, Peter Newman—and your son?

Sam Jenkins' heat store had consisted of two chemicals which absorbed heat as they slowly combined at any temperature above minus fifteen degrees Celsius. The unusual feature of his finding was that with the addition of a catalyst, the resultant compound could be easily dissociated into its original components with a consequent release of heat. The unfortunate, and for Sammy, fatal feature of his finding was that the reaction was extremely difficult to control. Injudicious release of the stored heat caused reactions which released all the stored energy explosively. It was one such release that blew poor Sammy out of the coils of academe, and another that blew him off this mortal coil completely.

His research notes were good, free as they were from the rhetoric of his public utterances. He had been a gifted and capable scientist who would have made a major contribution to scientific progress had he not been blessed with the ability to consistently enrage those that life brought him into contact with. As it was, his contribution consisted of giving a future and more mellow team a head start.

John, as leader of the team, had been given a quite clear and unequivocal design brief from his father.

"Don't bother me with details, John," he said. "What Joe public wants is a box he can leave in the sun, or somewhere warm, and then plug it into his water system and draw off water at whatever temperature he sets it to. Amen. It's your job to bridge the gap between Sam Jenkins' notes and that box. Just keep me up to date on your general progress, ok?"

John looked a little pained. "Dad, it's not that easy. This stuff's dangerous if it forms unstable compounds..."

Peter continued as if John had not spoken, his voice a little frosty. "Furthermore, this box must be quite safe, even if some loony throws it out of the window or puts it on the fire, ok?"

John began to take in the deep martyred breath of the misunderstood technician, but Peter slammed his hand on the desk before he could speak and a brief flash of anger in his eyes made John sit up and decide he could dispense with the play-acting.

"John, I'm very busy and very tired. I've told you what to do and given you a first-class team and damn near unlimited resources. I'll say this once and I don't want you to forget it. I'm not interested in the thousand and one reasons why an idea won't work. I'm only interested in the one reason that makes it work. You can do it and you will. Just be thorough, professional and careful. You know I'll help you all I can, just don't forget where you're going."

The project proceeded comfortably, if unspectacularly, and John became more and more involved as their results accumulated over the next few months.

"It can be so irritating," he said one day to Brian. "It feels like a word on the tip of my tongue that won't come out."

Brian was not much help. "Go and have a few days off," he said. "You're hitting a stale patch, digging yourself into a rut."

"But I need to know, Dad," he said to his father later that same day. "I can't let go of it."

Peter looked at him thoughtfully. "Why don't you do what Brian says? The project won't go away. It'll be here when you get back. Have a few days off." John was still reluctant. "John, you're banging your head against a wall. It may be that the solution is in there waiting to come out when you've finished hammering. In any event, you'll get no intuitive flashes while you're tired and irritable. Or would you like a work-out with the boys and girls at the office?"

John's eyes widened and he drew in an audible breath through pursed lips. "No thanks, Dad. I'll pass on that, I think. I can always hurl myself off a cliff if I feel in need of extensive internal damage and broken limbs."

John eventually followed his father's advice and wandered off in his car for a few days, sleeping rough and looking at quite ordinary places made unique simply because he had not seen them before. No great inspiration came to him, but much of the buzz and clatter in his mind faded away and he returned much relaxed and suffused with an enthusiasm which won him some sidelong glances from his colleagues.

He did not, however, take his father's fairly brusque advice on the matter of his budding romance with Freddy.

"Don't go screwing the staff, John. You may have to sack her one day."

Peter was not normally insensitive, but he had not noticed the real nature of the burgeoning relationship and his flippant remark genuinely hurt John. He realized this almost the instant the words were out, and he apologized after placating his wife who was glaring at him balefully and was obviously looking for the sharpest instrument in her very cutting vocabulary.

"Even so, John," he concluded. "Take care. You're in an ambivalent position. Don't spoil anything. She's both a nice girl and a valuable employee."

And a major security risk if things get fouled up, he thought.

Contingencies, contingencies, he could hear his father say. The split between Peter the family man and Peter the businessman was now habitual and did not distress him as it had at first. But he knew that only his wife and family anchored him in wild seas of megalomania, and enabled him to see the rightness of the course he was charting.

# Chapter 21

The major problem with the heat storage system was the difficulty in controlling the reaction that released the heat. Maths, physics, chemistry and mechanical engineering combined forces and assaulted it vigorously, but a solution continued to elude the team. They did succeed in modifying the compound so that it was less prone to break down into unstable components, but Peter's 'box' seemed as far away as ever. John's feeling that the solution was on the tip of his tongue faded slowly, and this enabled him to stop thrashing about mentally and to apply himself methodically and patiently. But all avenues of endeavour seemed to reach the same dead end. There were times when John became very dispirited and he had difficulty in keeping it from the others. Brian Gerard could usually be counted on to bounce him out of it.

"Come on John, it's not so bad. We do have a very efficient heat storage system that can be made commercially. That will recoup the cost of the project in no time, and it's a hell of a breakthrough."

John agreed reluctantly. "Yes, but it's too elaborate, Brian. Separators and diffusers and coolers. Too many mechanical parts. Too much maintenance needed. Anybody neglects a job or if there's a pump failure or a current failure at the wrong time, and bingo. And the size of it... Until we lick this basic instability, we're going nowhere."

"It'll still make a good practical unit for commercial and industrial concerns. Don't knock it," insisted Brian.

"Alright, Brian. Your chronic optimism must be contagious. But even my father's beginning to rumble."

Peter's rumbling was in fact only routine progress chasing. The cost of the project was miniscule compared with its possible bene-fits, and Brian was correct when he pointed out that the progress to date could be used to make commercially successful equipment which would recover all the outlay.

One evening, John was sitting in his office looking over the res-ults of a recent test run. He was working late because he was anxious to finish a batch of tests before they closed down the pro-ject for a while in the hope that a few weeks away would enable everyone to stand back and obtain a different perspective on the whole venture. Safety procedures were automated, and when sensors detected too rapid a change in temperature in too small an area, the system automatically switched in an emergency cooling unit and started to shut the experiment down. Nevertheless, as ex-plosion was a real possibility, it was a house rule that certain exper-iments were not to be left unattended so that the shut-down procedure could be done manually if the automatic system failed and set off audible warnings.

John had volunteered to stay with the experiment as he had high hopes that it would yield some new data, and most of the others had families to go home to. However, nothing new was being pro-duced—merely confirmation of what they already knew. He yawned and leaned back in his chair and stretched.

"Bugger this," he said out loud, throwing the file onto his desk.

Everyone had been working too hard. A few weeks off would do *him* good as well.

He smiled at the prospect of walking through Wales. Two weeks peace and quiet. Freddy had demurred when he invited her.

"You're not getting me in a tent halfway up a wet Welsh hillside," she had said, and his protestations had fallen on deaf ears. "I've heard about your great traverses from your mother and father, seven league booting it from ridge to ridge. I probably couldn't even keep up with you."

There was a large germ of truth in this, but he sat down and donned his little boy lost look as a last ditch effort. She looked up at him over the console she was working at, and relented a little.

"John. I won't come. I've done some hill walking, but I couldn't keep up with you and you know it. You travel alone and you need to be alone. You'd get angry with me holding you back all the time and neither of us would want that."

John admitted defeat. His communion with the hills was indeed for him alone, and while he did not hurry, he was fit, strong and agile, and did cover a lot of ground when he got going. He did not know what it would be like with someone else, even Freddy, but he had to concede it could be a sad affair. Reflexively, however, he opened his mouth for a parting shot.

"*Ewch allan,*" said Freddy before he could speak.

"What?" said John, his mouth remaining open in surprise.

"*Ewch allan,*" she repeated. "It's Welsh, boyo," she said in a sing song accent. "It means clear off I'm busy." He looked at her suspiciously. She raised her left hand from the console and without looking up pointed to the door. As he was leaving the room, he turned.

"I bet it doesn't mean anything of the kind," he said. "You don't know any Welsh. You've read it somewhere. It probably means Gents Toilet."

He closed the door gently but quickly and beat a hasty retreat to his own office.

His reverie was broken by the lights blazing momentarily and then going out.

"Damn!"

It was a dispute by power supply workers, an inter-union quarrel that had been brewing for some time. Probably most of the city would be in darkness. He tapped his fingers impatiently on the table through the brief interval until the lab's own generators cut in. Then he spent a few minutes tidying his desk and working out the best route home to avoid the city centre which would soon be crowded with traffic as motorists tried to negotiate major junctions with their headlights blazing to obscure everyone else's view and with no traffic signals working. He looked at his watch. Half an hour at the most and the experiment would be finished and he could leave.

Walking along the corridor to the main lab, he looked out into the inky darkness. All he could see was his own reflection in the window. It made him feel peculiarly exposed. An island of light in that great sea of darkness.

As soon as he opened the lab door he knew something was wrong. Everything was quiet and there was a faint but unmistakable smell in the air. It was the smell that emanated from the heat storage unit when it was on the verge of becoming unstable. And the silence told him the pumps were not working. He took in the temperature gauge reading across the room. It was too high. His mind raced.

Why hadn't the alarm sounded?

Why hadn't shut-down begun?

Why had the pumps stopped working?

Something to do with that sudden glare of light before the power cut. Something had happened just when the experiment had passed the final fail-safe point. Without thinking, he started to run over to the test bench, swinging his left hand mightily into a large red emergency alarm button as he went. His senses were so heightened that it seemed an eternity before the siren started to wail. In one of those timeless instants that shock can induce, he viewed a thousand thoughts. He saw the fire and ambulance services leaving their depots, alerted by the link that was activated at the same time as the siren. He remembered the engineer he had discussed it with. He saw himself blown to pieces and he saw his own funeral. What would they say about him? What a pity he'd never made the heat store work properly. He was angry that the knowledge would elude him. Then he saw alternatives. He agonized with regret as his entire married life with Freddy passed by, his succession to his father's business, and his own success, his children growing up and taking over from him, his dignified and quiet old age surrounded by loved ones, and so much else that life held for him.

Then he was by the equipment. The sound of the siren hemmed him in. It was solid and it filled the Universe, and he could see that he was too late. Manual shutdown was impossible, the experiment was going to explode.

Fast though his mind was working, his body moved ahead of it. He felt his powerful leg muscles unwind of their own accord and his body twist and arch as he floated through the siren's sound over a nearby bench to land curled up like a ball on the far side. His body automatically used the momentum of the roll to bring him upright. Then he saw his own shadow black in a bright light on the doors ahead as a great hand struck him in the back and hurled him towards them. He saw the doors beginning to open just as he reached them. He noted cracks slowly working their way across the glass panels, and thought it was beautiful—like a spider's web.

It was a long time before the colour dappled darkness knew it was John Newman, and even then it relinquished the knowledge from time to time. Noises echoed in it and pains and trembling and many things it knew were bad.

"Lucky," said one noise.

"Strong," said another.

"Serious," said another.

"John," said many. Its creator spoke.

"John, you must fight. I know you can hear me and understand. You must fight. You can do it. I'll help."

And the darkness tried to fight towards the light. Then another voice spoke, without noise.

"Go to the quiet place within you and be made whole," and everything became quiet floating darkness.

More and more the darkness knew it was John Newman, until eventually there was just John Newman, lying in pain and defeat, in darkness, but not of it. He tried to speak but his throat was dry and burning and all he made was a peculiar croaking sound.

A familiar voice said, "Nurse, nurse, he's coming round."

Then many confusing things happened in the darkness. His body convulsed and his throat burned again as he felt poisons pumping up through him and out of his mouth. A cool hand took his head and held it, and then gently wiped his clammy face, then tiny drops of cold water ran into his parched mouth and he felt a soft pillow under his head.

"He'll probably sleep a while now."

He had little or no sense of time and little or no sense of curiosity. Drifting in darkness from one state to another, he began gradually to recognize when he was dreaming and when he was awake, by the clarity of the noises and the vigour of the manhandlings he received. He could not identify specific pains, they seemed to be all over him, but when he remembered, he followed the inner voice and went to the quiet place within him, deeply relaxed and filled with warmth. He was collecting enough of his wits to realize he had been badly hurt and that the quickest way out was to assist his body in curing itself.

Then he woke and a new sensation impinged on him.

Light.

It took him quite a long time to realize what it was, and that the images should be in focus. His brain scrambled desperately with vague, familiar ideas and then a shining silver curtain rail came out of the mist and stood sharp and clear against a white ceiling. With it came many other sensations. He had his body back—arms, legs, hands, feet, everything. He was in bed in hospital. What the devil was he doing here? He turned his head to look at the room and a pain jarred through his neck and shoulders and made him grunt. He swore and closed his eyes. The pain was bad, but it felt like bad stiffness and muscle strain rather than damaged tissue, so breathing very slowly and deeply, and relaxing as much as he could, he slowly moved his head from side to side and up and down, testing the limits of the pain. He remembered that waking is always the worst time following an injury—the body is stiff from lack of movement, and the mind is not alert enough to control proceedings.

Well, we're awake now, he thought, and opening his eyes he slowly gazed round the room. Something was vaguely wrong with what he was seeing, but he could not pinpoint what it was. To his right was a large window through which he could see a blue sky and white clouds. He looked at this scene for a long time thinking it was probably the loveliest sight he had ever seen, then he returned to his slow and cautious examination of the rest of the room.

It was like a modest hotel room—neat, clean, sparsely but adequately furnished, and decorated in a colour obviously carefully chosen to soothe the sick without lulling them into lethargy. He resented that. The room felt claustrophobic. Christ, he didn't want to be here.

"Hello," he croaked. "Is anyone there?"

He felt ridiculous. A nurse appeared in the doorway—red-haired, freckle-faced, with professional eyes and a large smiling mouth.

"Welcome to the land of the living, Mr. Newman," she said, walking across to him and fussing his sheets and his pillows straight. "How are you feeling now?"

It was obvious from her tone and manner that she knew him quite well and that they had apparently spoken together previously. He could remember no such familiarity and he felt mildly indignant. He looked at her suspiciously.

"I'm fine now," he managed. "I'll be going home in a little while."

To his horror she laughed, then leaning forward she took his face in her hands and kissed him on the forehead. "You're a lovely boy," she said, patting his cheek. "Just let me call doctor and you can have a little chat before you go."

And with that she was gone. He would have a word or two to say to someone about that, being manhandled like a baby by a stranger. And laughing at him as well. Or should it be baby-handled? He couldn't make up his mind about that immediately. Then a tall white-coated man appeared. He had greying black hair and a stern but friendly face. John decided he would put up with the nurse if this man had sent her, but she really should not be so familiar.

The doctor took his wrist and looked at his watch. He must be in a hurry, thought John. Then he laid an icy hand on his forehead and nodded. John realized he was drifting away again.

"What happened to me, doctor?" he said in a brief moment of lucidity.

"You had an argument with an explosion, a fire, a glass door and a large part of the rest of the building. You're lucky to be alive."

Then, more urgently, "Nurse!"

John muttered that he never argued, he did deals, then he fell into a deep nowhere. He was buffeted and pushed. He stood naked and shivering in a screaming blizzard arguing with a green-eyed dog about where his clothes were, but the blizzard was in Miss Jenny's loft, and moving to a clinching point in his argument he slid between the joists into a black well swirling with snow and filled with a wailing sound. Hugh's face looked down at him, getting smaller and smaller. Then Minna was there, holding his hand as they watched his grandfather being buried, and his father turned round and stared at all the people around the grave and they shrank and dwindled away and his father reached out and seizing a tombstone shook the whole planet.

Occasionally he was aware of being in the real world and of being moved, and people talking to him, but the boundary between unreality and reality was not clear to him. He seized Matthew Vance's arm and whispered urgently.

"Get a molecular biologist, Matthew. OK? A molecular biologist. A geneticist. OK?" Matthew would understand.

Then Freddy was looking down at him and holding his hand.

He smiled. "I knew a dog called Fred once. Good Wales for place, dog's is," he said seriously, then, with a feeling that something was not quite right about that, he skimmed the world handing out black boxes to grateful millions, but everywhere was filled with the flapping of great black wings, and he opened his eyes to see Hugh and Minna looking at him. Hugh had his hand on the curtain.

"Is the light troubling you, John?" he said, while Minna just sat and looked deep into him, willing him whole again with her entire being. He lifted his right hand in acknowledgement then wrote an indignant letter to his MP about over-familiar nurses, but decided to read it out personally in the House of Commons.

Opening his eyes suddenly, he looked up at the white ceiling. Remembering his sore neck and shoulders, he slowly looked round the room. Something was still not quite right with the view, but it looked familiar and ordinary, and he felt exhausted. The red-haired nurse appeared in the doorway and smiled.

"Welcome back again, Mr. Newman. Are you going to stay this time?"

He nodded carefully. "If you'll have me," he said.

She smiled again. "I'll get the doctor."

John turned his head and looked out of the window. It was another fine sunny day. The doctor came in and sat beside the bed. "I'm afraid you're missing rather a nice summer," he said. John nodded. "How are you feeling?"

"Battered," John replied.

"A very apt description," said the doctor. "Do you remember what happened to you?"

John's forehead wrinkled. "No. I can remember a power cut in the office. And waiting for the generator to cut in. Then nothing until now. What the devil happened?"

The doctor was matter of fact. "I don't know the gory details— your father can probably give you those—but apparently an experiment you were doing went wrong and blew up. You were blown through a glass door and into some metal lockers. They fell on top of you and actually protected you from part of the roof that the explosion brought down."

"I'm glad I can't remember that," said John. "What's the sum total of the damage?"

The doctor looked at him thoughtfully.

"When you came in, I didn't think you'd have a whole bone in your body. But somehow, miraculously, you'd broken nothing, save some cracked ribs. However, you'd dislocated a few things, were massively bruised, somewhat scorched, concussed, lacerated and bleeding internally. We've spent the past few weeks putting you together again, and nursing you through a rather nasty secondary infection that seemed hell-bent on killing you, and now here you are. A shadow of your former self, but thanks to your considerable fitness, alive and reasonably whole."

John caught the hesitant inflection in the doctor's voice.

"Reasonably whole?" he queried.

The man looked straight at him.

"You're a strong man, John, inside and out. I can't say this to you gently." He paused very briefly and took a breath. "Your left eye was badly damaged when you went through the glass door. We've had to remove it."

John raised his hand to his left eye. There were bandages there. He'd never noticed them. He shuddered. Strangely, his first thought was not pain at the loss of his eye and the disfigurement, but horror at the manner of its loss.

"Thank God I can't remember," he repeated earnestly. "Anything else?"

"No John, nothing permanent. You'll be in a lot of discomfort for quite a time, but like I said, you're strong and fit. You'll be back to normal quite soon if you make the effort."

He stood as if to leave and then sat down again. "I'm sorry about your eye, John. We did what we could, but it was useless, there was just too much damage."

Like any doctor, giving bad news was the thing he hated above all else, and it was not always made easier when the patient took it passively. "Do you want to ask me anything about it?"

John still had his hand to his bandaged eye. He shook his head.

"You may find it helpful to scream and shout," said the doctor. John took his hand from his eye and laid it on the doctor's arm.

"It's alright, doctor, I understand. I'll scream and shout if I need to, don't worry. Right now I'm beginning to realize that thanks to good fortune and the efforts of yourself and your people I'm alive and that's... truly marvellous. Thank you."

The doctor did not reply directly. He stood up.

"We'll talk about the practicalities before you go, but for now, just ring for the nurse and ask for me if you want to talk. Any time."

John nodded.

When the doctor had gone, John lay back and looked out into the blue sky through the window. His stomach had turned into lead just before the doctor made his announcement. Visions of paralysis and worse had floated into his mind, and the actual disclosure had come almost as a relief. He was surprised at his own lack of response. Perhaps I'm in shock, he thought, but he doubted it. He had told the doctor the truth. He was alive. He felt alive, and he was glad to be alive. Look at that sky, and those clouds, he thought. He knew strength could be restored to his beaten frame and, thinking it was time to get back into training anyway, he dozed off.

Over the next few weeks, John's strength returned rapidly, largely because his own determination was determined to outdo that of his physiotherapist. Their relationship was lively. Within the first ten minutes of their meeting he had inquired whether they had met in a previous incarnation in some dungeon or other, and had received an acid congratulation on being the first adult to make that remark today.

And his repetition of, "You're a hard man," did not go down too well either, she being a most attractive young lady.

"You do realize, Mr. Newman," she said one day, after he had been particularly bumptious. "That I have to encourage people to extend their limits? Occasionally to tolerate quite a lot of pain and discomfort for their own good."

He looked at her suspiciously. She bent forward towards him and, six inches from his face, flashed him a winning smile.

"Well," she continued. "There's nothing in my book of professional ethics that says I mustn't enjoy it."

John cried pax. She reminded him of his father, and he could recognize an indefensible position when he was in it.

The loss of his eye seemed to trouble him less than his friends and the doctors had imagined. Initially he was too weak to indulge in excessive self-pity, and the first time he looked in a mirror he was more shocked by his drawn, bruised and tired face than by the neatly closed eye.

"Good God," he said. "What a mess."

He leaned forward and peered closely into the glass.

"I can't believe it," he said, fingering his face. "I look like fifty hangovers, and I don't even drink."

"You never were much to look at," said Freddy, putting her arms around him. He kissed her hair.

"Bless you," he said. "It's summer inside as well as out with you here. I'll get myself into shape as quickly as I can."

By the time he was fit again, he was reasonably used to his one-eyed condition. The details of the accident he discovered from his father. A surge of electricity just before the power cut had blown the fuses in the lab when the experiment was just passing its last fail-safe point.

"A coincidence," said his father. "A thousand to one shot."

John had been pulled out by the fire brigade who arrived within minutes of the explosion.

That was all Peter said, but he casually left a newspaper on the bed when he left. Browsing through it, John came across a gory photograph in the middle pages. The associated article explained that the authorities believed that militant workers had deliberately caused the surge before cutting off the power. Three people had died as a result of this action and several other serious accidents had occurred, so their two leaders had been arrested, to much public acclaim. They were, however, released within days because of legal technicalities, and had left the magistrate's court in high humour, surrounded by several members of the private army they used to maintain 'democratic' control of their union. The police had been reluctantly obliged to restrain a large and very angry crowd of citizens, whose general demeanour was not improved by the rhetoric they were receiving from the two men and their group.

As they reached the foot of the courthouse steps, a taxi pulled up. The back door opened and the two men were cut down by a thunderous blast of large gauge shot. The gun and a couple of smoke canisters were thrown onto the pavement and the taxi was driven smoothly and quietly away.

Estimated time of execution approximately two and a half seconds.

Local CCTV was off-line for service.

The reporter had added an interesting footnote. The police were reticent about the gun used in the incident, but he had reason to believe that it was one stolen recently from a police armoury. The use of a stolen police weapon in a spectacular public killing was, some may recall, a characteristic feature of a spate of gangland killings that had plagued the country some years ago.

John looked at the photographs again and felt strangely uneasy. His father did not normally carry newspapers around.

# Chapter 22

John was quite anxious to return to the project. He had mulled over some ideas while in hospital and he wanted to discuss them with the rest of the team. His father, however, had other ideas.

"You can have your discussion," he said. "And you can keep in touch and advise on the project, but I'm taking you off it full-time. I want you to help me more directly in future."

John was angry. "Christ dad, what for? I'm good at that job and it's really starting to take shape now. We're a good team. We work well. I don't want to be some kind of pin-striped administrator." He rose to his theme. "In fact, I'm not going to be! I'll do what I bloody well want."

The memory of his young son throwing one of his occasional tantrums floated before Peter as John's outburst went over the top, and he found it hard not to smile. He raised his hands and sank back in his chair.

"I'm sorry, John. I put it badly. Just bear with me while I explain." John grunted non-committally. "The position is this. The project was beginning to stick in a rut. We all knew that. That's why you were having a break." John nodded. "During the break it was my intention to discuss with Brian the possibility of an injection of new blood in the hope that this might shake things loose. You, however, rearranged everything, literally. We now have to rebuild the lab as well as re-examine our strategy, so I've fixed a meeting for tomorrow, of the whole team, plus a couple of others as you suggested."

"As *I* suggested?" said John in surprise.

"Don't you remember? In the hospital?" John shook his head. "It was when you were feverish. Matthew was sitting with you. You came round suddenly, grabbed him and said, "get a molecular biologist, and a geneticist" and then you drifted off again."

John looked blank. His father shrugged and continued. "Well, you know Matthew. Anyone else would have dismissed it along with the other stuff you were rambling on about. But he chewed it over and over and then took it to the others and they agreed it was an interesting idea."

"Good Lord," said John, unable to think of anything else.

"So tomorrow you can have a good heavy session. Work out what you want in the way of new lab equipment, and lay the ground for a new start."

"But why can't I stay with the project? I can handle it," John said, more conciliatory.

"I'm well aware of that, John," replied his father. "But... your involvement was really only intended to be short-term. You've been there far longer than a normal PhD project would have taken, and it's my estimation that you've probably contributed as much as you can."

He paused to see how his son would react to this, half expecting another outburst. But John sat quietly in his chair, staring down at his hands.

I wonder when you stop feeling for them, thought Peter. He wanted to put his arms around him as he had when John was a little boy.

John looked up. "That's a bit of a facer, Dad," he said quietly.

"I'm sorry, John. I understand how you feel, and I'd rather not have had to say it, but I think you realize I'm right. You know it's no reflection on your work, it's just that sometimes, in fact, most times, things have to be handed over to others to maintain progress. It's highly probable that the team that finishes this project will be totally different from the one that started it."

John looked as if he was being convinced. "You're sure it's not because I blew the place up?" he said in an injured and suspicious voice. His tone was such that Peter could not avoid laughing this time.

"No, no. I should've expected that really, based on your past record. You always were wild without Thomas to control you." He became more serious again. "To be honest, I'm not being totally objective or professional by any means. You damn near died in that explosion. And in the hospital. You're too old for me to protect you from life's vagaries, but I'll be a much happier man when you're well away from that stuff. I won't embarrass you with a lot of sentiment John, but I don't want another episode like that ever again." Then, more lightheartedly, "And your mother. Wow." He pursed his lips and shook both hands.

This time John laughed. "So what do I do next?" he asked.

"Tomorrow you go to this meeting—I don't intend you to lose touch by any means. Then you get in your car, you pick up Freddy and you shove off somewhere for a few weeks. Do nothing. Only an idle man doesn't appreciate the value of leisure. Make the most of this weather. God knows, the sun seems to have been a rarity these last few years. Then we'll talk again about you helping me, ok?"

John nodded. "Alright, Dad. You're the boss."

His father had, as usual, presented his arguments in such a manner that no other reply was really possible. John thought though, as he sat and watched his father, that there was a tiredness in him showing through occasionally. He felt a little lonely. He too felt like reaching out and saying, "Let me help you, Dad. Just show me how."

When he returned from his holiday, John was full of good intentions. To shake the cobwebs from his joints he took up his martial arts training again, coupled with a graduated exercise routine that would eventually bring him to an alarming state of good health. He also took to using the basement range almost every day, and while the good weather lasted he spent some time on the company's outdoor range. He enjoyed the quiet intense concentration of long range rifle shooting, his prone body in almost total contact with the earth, the smell of grass inches below his face, the sun falling warm on his back, while its heat caused the target to wobble and distort. And there were usually larks twittering high above, invisible in the blue sky, their songs undisturbed by the occasional crack of his rifle, and the swish of the bullet making its long journey to the target.

Peter watched his son carefully, and slowly eased him into the business. The introduction was much slower than in his own case, because John was younger than he had been, and did not have any real experience in business matters. In addition, Peter felt that John might baulk at many of the business's interests. He had to be well

175

and truly aware of the business's positive values before he learned about its negative ones. Peter could not bring himself to think the word "trapped", but the image in his mind was clear enough. He himself was feeling increasingly weary.

Over the years, he had managed to stop or redirect his father's schemes for expansion, but it had been a pitilessly hard task. The illegal activities the business was involved in had fewer constraints on them than the legal ones, and because of this they had a greater tendency to expand, particularly when governments resorted to panic measures to stop them and passed wholly impractical laws or, in over-reacting, lost much of the support of the people.

As a result, the business had a massive momentum towards increased illegality, and dealing with this taxed him heartily. It was a painstaking and wretched job, but he knew it had to be done, and he knew he was the only one who could do it. That circumstances not of his choosing had placed him where he was, as they would in turn place John, was his sole justification.

In this situation, which was the greater immorality? To turn away, knowing that the business would then grow uncontrollably, becoming darker and more corrupting and more corrosive of the very societies it was embedded in, or to accept the sceptre in his hand and attempt to control it, even though it meant committing almost every known deceit and treachery. He could not accept that the ends should justify the means, but often he had no choice.

These paradoxical considerations rarely bothered him seriously. He could not afford the luxury. Everything was for him paradoxical. He lived both in the world and out of it. Out of it by virtue of his activities being above all moral and statute law, yet in it because these activities had to touch deep into the everyday lives of people, businesses and governments. Out of it because his time was spent coldly manipulating the fortunes of millions, and in it because his time was spent loving his wife and son and enjoying his few simple pleasures. Out of it because he must sentence his son to the same, and in it because in his heart he still stood by his cradle waiting silently in the dark for his quiet breathing to reassure him he was still alive. His sole criterion became, which action will, in the long term, cause the least pain to the least number, and his growing fear was that although he had effectively stopped the business expanding, it being an organic structure, it would start again spontaneously, unless he could train John properly. Worse, it could all fall into the hands of anyone who had the wit to see the reins flying loose, and it was an instrument of terrible power.

# Chapter 23

John was reluctantly obliged to agree that the business was not quite as dull as he had imagined. His father was an excellent teacher, and seduced his son just as he had been seduced—by technical elegance, by excellence, by shining schemes, tinged only slightly with black.

He was lured into Peter's world slowly but surely.

If a politician or a bureaucrat stood in the way of a scheme, the question was not the rights and wrongs of his position, it was, simply, how do we get rid of him? Bribery? Once assured of the worth of the scheme, John did not object too strongly to bribery, or a scandal in the local paper, or a little blackmail, or a little of everything. John would work it out, for the greater good, without immoderate distaste, and then he would use the power of the business with relish to implement it. Unlike Peter, and to Peter's surprise, John had very few moral qualms about some of the more unsavoury aspects of the business that he was allowed to see, and he also began to show a streak of harshness and impatience. It came to Peter that maybe John was too young, too unused to his own weaknesses to come too soon towards the centre of such a power, but alternatively, perhaps John had in fact been born out of the world. He looked back in time to his father, and then forward to his son, and saw little difference. Genes will out, he thought and, ironically, that thought spurred him and some of his weariness fell away. Here was someone destined for his role. He, Peter, was just the regent, the caretaker, the sweeper. John would take his burden with willing hands, as his birthright, not standing tall until he could bear it fully. Peter would part with it with relief, and fade into bumbling obscurity holding his wife's hand. But equally, the boy must not snatch the burden, he must not oust the pack leader in combat, he must receive it as a bounty, and he must not receive it until he was truly ready. Peter's last task was to teach John who was the dominant male of the pack, and then to step back when he longer was.

"You're looking very happy and relaxed tonight," said Ann.

Peter smiled. "Yes. John's doing very well. He's beginning to help quite a lot. For the first time in ages I'm really looking forward to tomorrow. It's very good. He'll knock into shape very well."

John had wanted to bring Freddy into the business, but Peter rejected the idea unequivocally.

"No. Quite definitely not," he said.

"Why? She's a very capable administrator."

"I'm aware of that, but you're going to marry her and you can't have your wife involved in the business."

John did not know whether to be bewildered or indignant.

"Who said I'm going to marry her? It's the first I've heard of it."

Peter did not look up from his writing. "You surprise me, John. Everyone else knows, except perhaps Freddy."

Then he looked up and put his hand to his mouth in mock dismay. "I say, I haven't spoilt a surprise have I?"

John made a peculiar noise and bent to his work again.

"I'll tell you who we will have in the business though," continued Peter, looking up again. John met his gaze defensively, and waited.

"Hugh and Minna."

"Hugh and Minna?" echoed John, a strange bell resonating deep within him. "Why?"

Peter laid down his pen carefully, leaned back and started to swivel to and fro hypnotically. "It's difficult to put into words, John. I think it's to do with loyalty. They both have an extraordinary attachment to you. They're the kind of people who would guard your back at any cost to themselves. They feel right. They'd fit in, and they'd be right for you."

John did not know how to respond. His father was not normally given to vagueness, but somehow he understood. Hugh and Minna *were* a strange self-sufficient couple, needing no-one but, at their choosing, he was tied to them and they to him in some unfathomable way, and his father had sensed it. The idea had the feeling of both a surprise and an inevitable conclusion.

"Whatever you say, Dad," he conceded. "I trust your judgement. I'm not sure what they're both doing these days, but I'll ring them tonight and talk it over."

"Hugh is a management trainee with a chemical engineering company, and Minna is working for some computer firm. Neither are hysterically happy in their jobs."

Peter threw two folders onto his desk. This time John was genuinely surprised. He walked across the room and picked them up. It took him only a couple of minutes to flick through them both as he sat on the corner of his father's desk. He whistled softly as he put them down.

"Wow. You're a hard man, Dad. How long did it take you to put that lot together?"

"Not long," replied his father. "Marvellous thing, technology."

He pointed to the computer console.

"Brief, accurate and to the point. And very professional," said John, thumbing through the top folder idly. "Wait a minute," he said suddenly. "What the devil's this?" He picked up the folder and read one page in some agitation. Dropping it, he picked up the second folder and did the same. At the back of each folder was an appendix, outlining a variety of ways in which Hugh and Minna could effectively be coerced into the business.

"Hell," he said loudly. "I don't mind all the facts and figures, even this character assessment crap, but I'm damned if I'm going to let any of this happen. They're my friends."

His father did not look up during this outburst.

"John," he said icily. "Please pay more attention to details. You skim through the reports and miss the appendices, then you don't read them properly when you find them. They refer to contingency plans, do they not?"

John did not move or speak. His father continued. "They're also clearly marked as having a low probability, are they not?" John gritted his teeth and stuck his chin out sulkily. "Go and read both reports again. And this time properly. I think you'll find that a straightforward business offer will be jumped at by both of them, particularly as it will involve working with you. But..." he paused and looked straight at his son. "If we decide. We, John. You and I.

181

If we decide that it's in our best interests to have them working for us, then we will do whatever we have to to achieve that end. Do you understand?"

John still looked surly, but he nodded and turned his face away from his father's gaze. Picking up the folders he went back to his desk. Peter spun his chair right round, and affected to be looking out into the brown autumn twilight. He smiled to himself. You're still a pup John, he thought. You'll have to learn to growl better than that.

Peter was correct, as usual, thought John rather grudgingly. A telephone call brought both Hugh and Minna round to the house that evening.

"Approach it quietly," advised his father before they arrived. "Be circumspect."

"Don't worry, Dad. I've seen you operate. I know what to do. I can handle it. I can be very subtle," he said pointedly. A light appeared on the security monitor and two dark figures flickered into view on the closed-circuit television. John got up and was walking along the hallway as the bell rang.

Peter sat listening to the babble of greetings coming through the half open door. He heard John's voice rising to quieten the noise.

"Listen, listen, listen," he said excitedly. "How would you two like to dump those half-baked jobs you've got and come and work with me in Dad's business?"

Peter screwed up his face in a pained expression and rested his forehead in his left hand. Ann failed to suppress a laugh, and he opened one eye and glowered at her.

"Oh yes," she said. "He's seen you operate, quite definitely. Very subtle."

Any further interchange was forestalled by Hugh and Minna coming into the room dragging John behind them. Minna relinquished John's hand and walked over to Peter. She knelt down by him and stared up at him. Peter always found her gaze disconcerting.

"We'd love to work with John, Mr. Newman," she said. "Both of us."

"Yes, Mr. Newman," said Hugh, more prosaically. "It's very good of you to think of us."

Peter succeeded in pulling himself free of Minna's gaze.

"But you haven't even asked what the jobs are, or what salary."

Hugh and Minna exchanged a brief glance, and then they spoke simultaneously.

"It doesn't matter," they said.

"John'll look after us," said Hugh.

"We belong to him," said Minna.

Peter knew he did not begin to understand these two. Belong to him! What on earth did that mean? He knew also that he had been right to suggest their employment. But the other world was encroaching on his home—he dismissed it sharply.

"I haven't the faintest idea what you're talking about, Minna," he laughed, kissing her on the forehead. "John needs two good personal assistants, and I couldn't think of anyone who he'd like to work with more. There's quite a lot of initial training to get you into our ways, but I'm sure you'll make the grade, and I think you'll find that your salaries will be more than adequate." He winked broadly. He felt again, very strongly, that the future was opening out and that capable hands were available to shape it.

They spent the evening at a restaurant in the city. It turned into one of those occasions that can only arise spontaneously. When all moods are in harmony, and memory recalls it as glowing silver with laughter and warmth and perfection.

Hugh and Minna were admittedly surprised at their basic training. They had imagined brash pep talks and shrewd-eyed advice from PR men working on automatic pilot.

"What the hell do I need to learn to shoot for, and all this self-defence stuff?" muttered Hugh. "It's years since we used to do it."

"It's company policy, Hugh," repeated John. "I've explained why. It's just contingency planning. You'll become a valuable and important asset to the business. You have to develop the art of defensive living. The whole business is geared to it. We assess probabilities and prepare contingency plans. One probability is that our top men, having to move around quite a lot, and being important, could become kidnap victims, or just fall foul of routine street violence, any kind of violence. You must know how to handle yourself, Hugh. A lot of bad situations can be avoided simply by observation and instinct, if you train properly. It's no hardship and in fact it'll probably make you feel much more relaxed and secure."

Hugh was still doubtful. "Why don't you get bodyguards to look after your top men. I feel ridiculous wearing this thing," he said, hitching up his trousers.

Deja vu, thought Peter, casually overhearing this exchange and remembering his own conversations with his father.

"You know damn well why," said John. "Don't you?" Then he looked at his friend's waistline and laughed. "I'm not surprised you feel ridiculous wearing it like that," he said. He undid Hugh's belt and made various adjustments to the strap and holster.

"Bodyguards are corruptible, conspicuous, breed a false sense of security, double your logistical problems and generally make life too inflexible," intoned Hugh dutifully.

John was still fiddling with the recalcitrant belt. "Top of the class, Hugh," he said. "Well done."

He patted the holster. "That's better. At least you should reach the range without your trousers falling down."

Hugh smiled, but John could see he was still only partly convinced. He looked at him. "Hey, Hugh. Trust me. This business is the culmination of years, generations even, of some pretty hard experience. We never do anything that isn't absolutely necessary. Things happen here that I don't begin to understand, so I just trust my father's judgement. If you can't see the logic of a procedure you can at least accept that you probably don't have all the facts and you have to accept that the business's experience exceeds yours by quite a margin."

Hugh shrugged regretfully. "I don't mean to be awkward. It's just that this place is so incredible, so unconventional. I feel like I'm in another age, another world."

John nodded. "I know how you feel. It quite frequently catches me unawares as well. Stick with it. It'll make more sense as you get more familiar with everything."

Later, Peter asked John how the two new recruits were getting on.

"Pretty good," replied John. "Hugh likes to have things explained, but he always did. When he argues with you, Dad, listen to him. He's never deliberately obtuse. He's either trying to clarify something in his own mind, or make you look at something in a new way. Don't just shut him up, he's got a lot to offer."

Peter smiled. "OK. You're the boss. But...?" he said, anticipating John's query.

"Minna," said John. "I think you should look at these reports."

Peter was swaying to and fro in his chair again as he pondered Minna's file.

"Hm," he said. "I hadn't anticipated this. It's remarkable. The boys and girls are not given to casual praise, but this is exceptional."

"Should we do anything about it? Is there any special job she can do?" asked John.

Peter shook his head slowly. "There's only one thing we can do, John. We must look after her. She's a natural, a most gifted girl. Shooting, driving, flying, and all those fighting arts. Good heavens, I've never seen anything like it. Little Minna. Really remarkable. We must just ensure that these considerable talents are developed to their fullest. It's a good job her loyalty to you is total."

"Or?" queried John.

Peter did not answer, affecting not to hear the question, and John felt he should not pursue the matter.

"You don't think there'll be any jealousy between them do you?" continued Peter.

John shook his head. "No," he said. "They don't know the meaning of the word. Hugh's as pleased as punch with his little sister. He's encouraging her, and she's helping him. There'll be no problems like that."

"Good," said his father, handing back the two files and walking over to the window.

"Good," he repeated idly to himself as he stared out across the snow-covered garden. Hugh was well above average, and Minna was quite unique. If they fulfilled their initial promise, John would have all the support he needed in the future. The weather might be getting colder and colder, but the future of the business was looking rosier and rosier.

# Chapter 24

The winter was long, howling and bleak, but John passed through it in a heady glow, ignited by two events on one day.

"We've done it, we've bloody done it," came Brian Gerard's near hysterical voice over the telephone. John's involvement in the business was growing steadily and he had been able to keep only a most cursory interest in the work at 'the store', which was what he and his father had christened the Brijon Trading Co. He had no idea what Brian was babbling about.

"Slowly Brian," he pleaded. "Take it slowly. What have you done?"

"It, John. It. We've stabilized it. We've licked it. It works."

Understanding dawned, but he could hardly believe it. He tried to quell Brian.

"How stable is it?" he asked suspiciously. Brian was too high in the air to be offended. "Completely, John. It's absolutely loony-proof. You come and see. We've got a test running right now."

Then he rang off.

"Brian. Wait," roared John, too late. "Bloody typical," he said, gazing down at the buzzing handset. "I suppose he'll talk to himself for ten minutes before he realizes he's hung up."

But the news was rippling his facade of calm. The project had been going on for a long time, painstakingly plodding away, seemingly asymptotic—always getting nearer, but never quite making it—and he had long ago foregone the delights of speculating on how the heat store could be used. But now, triggered by Brian Gerard's frenzy, the old fantasies began to stir again.

He put down the telephone and started struggling into his outdoor clothes. As he was leaving the office he bumped into his father.

"I'm going to the store. Brian says they've cracked it. They're running a test now," he called, as he ran along the corridor to the top of the stairs.

Peter paused to assimilate the message, then shouted to him to wait even as he heard the door closing.

"Blast," he said. "He'll get his fool head blown off again."

As he reached the head of the stairs he saw Hugh and Minna dashing after John. Minna turned and looked up at him before he could speak. She gave a smile and a hand signal. Everything will be ok, it said.

He walked down the stairs and opened the front door. Outside, the winter cold hit him immediately, and he hunched his shoulders. John's car was well down the driveway with Minna in the passenger seat, but he raised an acknowledging hand as Hugh drove past in the back-up car.

"You worry too much about him."

It was Joey. Peter turned to him and he shrugged.

"John needs back-up like a shark in a swimming pool," he said.

Peter smiled. "Yes, I know," he said resignedly. "I can't help it. I suppose you never stop feeling concern for your children."

He stared after the receding clouds of steam trailing behind the cars and hanging briefly in the still air. "I sit and look at him sometimes, with that damned patch over his eye, and I feel like weeping."

Joey nodded sympathetically, but said nothing. He had learned that Peter was more expressive and confiding than his father, or his son, but he had learned also that it made no difference when hard things had to be done. They were done as efficiently and ruthlessly as ever.

"Still," said Peter, abruptly dispelling the mood. "We're moving into a new age. John's going to have important things to do and he's going to need those two. It's our job..." he took the older man's arm and turned him back to the door, "...to make sure he can operate both solo and in a team. Right?" Joey nodded again and opened the door.

"Funny couple though, those two," he said.

Peter felt the unease in the remark. "I know what you mean," he said. "You're an old soldier, Joey. You're not too happy about anyone who hasn't come up through the ranks are you?"

Joey had not expected this immediate thrust to the heart of his concern. He looked uncomfortable and shrugged vaguely. Peter moved towards the stairs and gestured him to follow.

"I didn't come up through the ranks, did I, Joey?" Peter said.

The act of walking up the stairs had dispelled Joey's awkwardness. "You did, actually," he replied, reverting slightly to his elder statesman role. "In a way. Your father beat the shit out of you before you joined us. Not many could have handled that the way you did. You backed Carlo down. Ye gods. Then you put that thief away." Unconsciously he put his hand on his ribcage. "Your father was pleased and proud of everything you did. You're family. It's been in you from the cradle."

Peter nodded reflectively. "It's in John doubly, Joey," he said.

"I know," said Joey. "But those two. I just feel... Our ways are not for nothing, Peter. Suppose they turn. Hugh's more than a match for most, and Minna's unbelievably dangerous—she frightens me. We couldn't stop them."

Peter looked at him. "They won't turn," he said with authority. "I understand your feeling, Joey, and I've always made note of your concerns, but trust me—trust the family—they won't turn. It's difficult to explain. I don't pretend to understand it, but those two will look after John better than we could."

He knew he had not convinced Joey, but that would be no bad thing. The most important thing was that the matter had been aired. It had been rumbling for some time, but at least now it would not fester unseen and break out as something worse at some more critical time.

There was only one car in the yard when John reached 'the store'. It was Brian's. There was, however, evidence that several had left recently. Minna glanced at the tracks in the snow.

"Nothing untoward here," she said, lightly. "Just park the car. I'll check who's inside."

She was out of the car and moving across the snow before John could reply. He smiled to himself as he watched her disappear into the building, then he reversed the car into a convenient position. Almost immediately, Minna reappeared in the doorway and signalled to him and to Hugh waiting in the other car across the road.

Brian greeted them effusively as they entered the laboratory. John eyed him warily.

189

"Brian, you're pissed," he said.

Brian grinned. "Just a little, maybe," he said. "But come and look. You'll get drunk just looking at it."

As they walked over to the equipment, John felt a muscle twitch in his dead eye, and a slight coldness pass over him.

"Here it is," announced Brian proudly. Then, melodramatically. "The future."

John looked at the equipment. It was only marginally different from the arrangement that had nearly killed him, but he saw immediately that all the safety devices had been disconnected. He stared at it in silence for some time.

"It's really happened, Brian?" he asked eventually.

"It's really happened, John. It's stable. We've got a million and one tiny technical problems to solve to get the best commercial unit, but the big problem's solved."

"Incredible," said John. "After all this time."

"Where is everyone?" asked Minna.

"They're out celebrating," said Brian.

"Having started here, presumably," said John looking at mugs and cups strewn on a nearby bench and bottles in a waste bin. Minna looked at him.

"Security will be alright, Minna," he said. "They're company people and they're on profit sharing. They haven't worked so hard for so long to jeopardise everything at the last moment. Brian, you said this was foolproof. What did you mean exactly?"

"Exactly? Exactly that," said Brian. "These materials cannot be made unstable. Look."

He walked over to a bank of small storage bins, reached into one and scooped out a handful of powder.

"Here's our end product," he said, spreading it on a fireproof sheet. "And here," reaching into a second bin with his other hand. "Is the catalyst."

He dropped it onto the other powder and mixed the two with his pencil. John jumped involuntarily and started back. He felt Minna pick up his alarm and reflexively reached out to catch her arm as it was drawing her gun.

"It's alright," he whispered urgently. "It's alright."

Brian, unaware that the angel of death had just passed over, stood back from the bench proprietorially.

"There," he said. The powder slowly changed colour, then it started to glow until the whole mass was incandescent. "It'll glow like that for quite some time," he said.

"Good grief," said John reverently, moving closer to the glowing mass. "It wasn't much more than that that demolished half the lab."

"We've got to check it out for aging, fatigue deterioration, any bizarre light or humidity effects di da di da," said Brian. "But that's all routine. We've licked it John. Licked it."

John was still bent over staring, as though hypnotized, at the glowing powder.

"So all the complicated separation systems, they've all gone?"

"Yes," said Brian. "We picked up what you said in hospital, stopped messing about with external control systems and got inside the molecules themselves. Let them do the controlling."

John let out a soft breath of appreciation. "And the cost?"

"Well, as I said, some to-ing and fro-ing, but so far looking good."

John straightened up and smiled. He held out his hand. "Congratulations, Brian. Keep the pressure up. Get all the i's dotted and the t's crossed, and then we'll start thinking commercially. I'll call Dad and tell him what's happened, then we'll track down the rest of your colleagues and join the celebrations."

Later that evening, John walked through the snow, orange in the light of the street lamps, with Freddy by his side. The city street was quiet. She was linking his arm with both of hers and leaning on him more heavily than usual. He looked down at her and laughed.

"You're drunk," he said. "Everybody's drunk tonight. Brian's drunk in charge of a laboratory, and you're drunk in charge of a one-eyed bandit."

She returned his gaze. "I most certainly am not drunk," she said. "Relaxed, certainly. Happy, certainly." She rubbed her cheek on his shoulder and squeezed his arm. "But drunk, never."

"I notice you daren't let go of my arm."

"I might be somewhat replete with good food," Freddy conceded. "That, plus a long day, has fatigued me, hence my need for a little support, but to the charge of drunkenness I still plead not guilty."

"Well, in view of your past good character, I'll accept your plea, but I can't do the same for your colleagues in crime."

"I should think not," she said, then she laughed. They had all become noisier and noisier as the evening progressed, except Matthew

Vance, who became quieter and quieter and then fell over. The reminder of Matthew's quiet and dignified sinking below the table made them both giggle.

"It's been a lovely night, John," she said.

"Yes, but I don't think it's done much for productivity at the store tomorrow. It'll have more corpses in it than the morgue."

"You won't be one of them though, will you?" she said in a more subdued tone.

"One of what?" he asked.

"One of the corpses."

"I don't understand you."

"Oh. I don't know. You seem to be joining in and enjoying yourself, but I can't help feeling that part of you is standing aloof."

He put his arm around her. "I do join in and enjoy myself, but part of me wants to be alone. Needs to be alone. It's not a bad thing. It's just the way I am. It hurts no-one, least of all me."

"Will that part of you always be alone?" she said softly.

He nodded. "Yes always. It has to be."

Freddy did not reply, and they walked on a little way. John cleared his throat awkwardly.

"But the rest of me won't be alone. The rest of me is going to marry you so that the alone part won't become a lonely part, and there'll always be plenty of light."

They stopped walking and looked at one another. Dark silhouettes casting darker shadows on the silent orange-lit snow.

"Please," he said quietly.

A tear ran down Freddy's cheek. "You are a one-eyed bandit, aren't you?" she said gently.

John nodded and bent forward and kissed her.

# Chapter 25

Richard Gwilier's mother, though well-intentioned, was weak and incompetent, and quite genuinely ill-used by life. His overall memory of his father was of several brief appearances, each being terminated by the arrival of the police. Only two memories of his father were highlighted in his mind. One was of a day in the park when they had played football and chased around the trees, and then slithered down the slide together. His father had pushed him high and squealing on the swings, and a sun had shone unexpectedly in his life.

The other was more ambivalent. His father had caught him playing truant and dragged him roughly through the streets to home. His father's moods being unpredictable, Richard made no small effort to escape, but all to no avail. At home he was thrown equally roughly onto the living room couch and he had curled up covering his head with his arms in anticipation of a thrashing. Whether his father had intended to beat him and had simply lost the energy with the struggle home, or whether he had intended the lecture that ensued, Richard never discovered. But he was not beaten. When he had peeped out, his father was sitting in the armchair opposite, his elbows on his knees and his face buried in his hands. He sat like that for a long time, and Richard's urge to make a dash for the door was slowly overcome by curiosity.

His father looked up and caught his eye. Richard, for all his youth, was powerfully struck by the look of pain on his father's face.

"Listen, Dickie," he said, hesitantly. "I'm sorry I'm such a piss awful father to you. I don't seem to be able to help myself. I start off getting things sorted out, and then I do something stupid and it's all wasted. I don't know what it is, whether it's my fault or what. I follow people, Dickie. Then I find myself in trouble, and they're gone."

Richard sat wide-eyed.

"Listen Dickie. I want you to learn one thing off me, just one thing. You mustn't do what I've done. You must make your own way. Don't follow anyone. Have them follow you."

Then he became vicious in his despair and pointed a menacing finger. "And don't bloody well scow off school again, d'ye hear me?"

He got out of his chair and came and crouched in front of his son. "Look kid. I've been in jail a lot. More in than out, I suppose. Well I've learnt something at last. Something I should've seen years ago. They're all stupid in there. Thick and useless and little, Dickie. They're all little people, pathetic little people. The real thieves are out there." He pointed to the window. "Big cars, flash suits, fancy offices, girls. You know why?"

He waited, but Richard just sat staring. "I'll tell you why. Because they use their heads, that's why. They get other people to take the risks. That's what you've got to do. I know you're not stupid, I've seen some of your school work. You learn every damn thing you can, and then, when you're older, you'll be the one in the big car and the flash suit. And you'll be the one telling people like me what to do."

He prodded himself contemptuously in the chest.

"Ok," Richard risked cautiously after an awkward silence. His father nodded then jerked his head to indicate he could leave. As he was going through the door, his father spoke again.

"Think on now. If I find you've been playing hooky again I'll really leather you. Take no notice of your mates. They're jail fodder, thick and stupid. Go your own way. It won't be easy, but you look after number one."

Richard rarely took any notice of his father, but something in his manner that day struck a chord deep inside him and from then on he walked along a lonely path of ambition haunted by it. He became a kind of model pupil, but his teachers did not know quite what to make of him. He was assiduous and persistent in the subjects he thought were useful, or happened to like, and he was sulkily competent in all the others.

"He never says anything, or does anything naughty," said his art teacher one day. "And his work is quite good, but he seems to radiate a... um... withering contempt?"

He took a great shine to history, taking a particular interest in famous leaders and fighters. In the playground, his friends soon found it was a foolish thing to provoke him about his new-found intellectual interests.

"Too scared to play hooky. Chicken, chicken," jeered one boy exasperated at the lack of response to some fairly vigorous teasing. Richard rounded on him.

"Sod off," he said. "You're the stupid chicken. You're the one who'll get his stupid head cut off and be too stupid to know it's gone."

The other boy stopped his impromptu dance, elbows akimbo, and the immediate circle of children went quiet with expectation. Then he charged, arms flailing. Richard, almost without thinking, thrust out his right hand, and caught his opponent squarely in the face. The boy dropped to his knees, blood streaming from his nose and top lip. Richard stood and looked at him, uncertain what to do next. There were mounting whispers of admiration and awe from the onlookers. Blood had been drawn, real blood.

"Hit him. With his fist. Right in the mouth. Wow!"

Richard felt himself the focus of attention and he enjoyed it. His hand was desperately sore and his knees were shaking, but he determined to give no indication to anyone. Then his father's words came to him, bright in the confusion.

"Get them to follow you."

And he knew how it was to be done. It was in his history books. He extended his hand to his still kneeling opponent. "Come on, let's get you cleaned up, the bell'll be going in a minute."

From that day, Richard Gwilier followed few men. Such as he did follow were those from whom he could learn, and always he kept his vision on where they were going, as well as where they had been.

Shortly after that incident, his father made a brief bleak appearance, and then disappeared forever. He had protested that it was too wet to go on the roof, but his colleagues had persuaded him as usual. They knew the alarm system, he did not, and they needed a look-out. He positioned himself carefully on the treacherous corrugated sheets, the edges of his feet catching the protruding roof bolts to prevent him slipping down, and to ensure his weight was carried on the steel purlins immediately below, instead of on the fragile sheets. He had a good view of the main road a hundred yards away, but he could not see the street below too well. A silent patrol car could crawl along the edge of the street and he would not see it. Tongue between his teeth, and keeping his balance with a fingertip touch on the roof sheets, he reached his left leg out towards the next bolt.

Whether it was just the darkness or an untoward shadow misleading him, or just bad luck, no-one will ever know, but he missed the bolt head. The edge of his foot pressed into the slimy asbestos surface and shot from under him. He crashed down face first onto the unsupported portion of the roof between the purlins and smashed straight through the ancient asbestos sheets. A second and a half later he hit the concrete floor of the warehouse at about thirty miles an hour, and died instantly. His partners in crime paid homage to his passing in the usual manner. They sacrificed the gain of the night to his memory by abandoning the safe they were trying to open, and fleeing.

The local business community was undismayed by the incident —in fact it was a source of mild amusement and satisfaction that summary justice had been visited upon one of the thieves that plagued the area so persistently. The more the merrier was the consensus.

However, there was no merriment in the Gwilier household. Neither Richard nor his mother were surprised when the police called the following day. She looked skyward when she saw them through the window, then donned the arrogant shell of indifference and contempt she wore for such occasions, as she walked to the door. But the normal routine was gone, and Richard knew it as he heard a strange cry from his mother. Abruptly she burst into the room. The shell had gone and Richard looked in stunned horror at his mother naked in her weakness and grief.

The next few hours were confused and bewildering. He was left with a comforting neighbour while his mother was whisked off gently but professionally to attend to various formalities. He knew he should be upset, but his father was rarely home, and the fact that he would never come home again left him unmoved. He had a sneaking feeling that from now on, things would probably get better.

And indeed they did. His mother had long since lost any great affection for her husband, as he had for her. Both had been feckless and foolish, and the marriage for the most part had degenerated into a quarrelsome and thankfully intermittent co-habitation. The black pall of grief thus soon slid away from the mother and she found a resource within herself she had never known before. She became a skilled reader of fine print, and a mistress of the social security system, the nett result of which was that more money came into the household than ever her husband had yielded.

Richard found a variety of ways of gaining access to this money. Nurturing the golden goose, he followed his mother's instructions to the letter whenever social workers visited, and he learned sufficient to be able to acquit himself capably if one called unexpectedly. For this he extracted payment, usually as a reward, but occasionally by implied blackmail. He preferred the former, but did not hesitate to use the latter if necessary. Also he noted that a casual and occasional exposure of his excellent fund of disadvantageous information had a beneficial effect on rewards anyway. His mother needed her partner in crime, and as he had the knack of pitching his demands only slightly above what she had in mind, and as he rarely made himself a nuisance, he was able to develop in her the habit of paying on request. Any small household tasks had a price. Keeping from under her feet had a price. Dealing with the occasional uncle she entertained could be extremely profitable, yielding payments from both parties if handled properly. He liked having money, and he had sufficient wit to realize that while he would always have to work for it in some way, there was work and there was work.

He enjoyed the acting and cajoling and thinking up new schemes, but the spark unwittingly struck by his father was beginning to flare up and he started looking beyond the small amounts he could acquire from his mother. It was difficult, however. He could wring more from his mother, but the costs of the wringing tended to be too high. He could win a little from his friends, but generally speaking they were poorer than he was, and nothing was to be gained by stealing from neighbours and local shopkeepers as the neighbourhood was too small and the risk of detection and local justice too high. The only prospect he had in sight was his forthcoming move to the senior school. Here, he reasoned, should be opportunity.

However, as he soon found out, such opportunity as existed

there was already being well abused by others. It was a large and very rough school. The teachers had to hold sway by main force and the children co-existed in a complex, vicious and ancient society of their own making that no adult might enter.

On his first day, Richard decided he liked the place. It had a good atmosphere for someone who was prepared to live by his wits. There was an aura of corruption and decadence that was like humus to a seedling, and he took root in it.

He was big and strong for his age—no mean brawler when provoked—and he had a small group of like-minded friends from the junior school who knew his worth as a leader, and who he knew could be relied on in emergencies. Because of this, he avoided the bullying that was methodically inflicted on most newcomers, but he took due note of it, and within a week of his arrival was receiving tribute from less fortunate souls for the protection he could offer against the rampages of the older boys. Most of the bullies were in the year ahead, venting, in time honoured tradition, the spleen of their own persecutions on their successors. Protection from them was fairly easy. The physical presence of Richard and the near presence of his friends deterred most would-be assailants, and for a short while life became profitable and calm, and he could turn his attention to analysing the effectiveness of the various battle weary teachers who had the task of imparting knowledge to him.

However, his enterprise did not go unnoticed, and one day while he and his friends were counting the weekly collection, he received a visit from a group of four fifth formers. Their leader was a sallow, rat-faced individual, and under his guidance the group practiced a very lucrative protection racket throughout the entire school. He was ill-disposed towards any suggestion of free enterprise by others, but occasionally he found it useful because he could put it down in such a way that it would reassert his position as sole owner of the monopoly. He was not given to subtlety. Placing one of his cohort on look-out duty by the door, he walked into the classroom with the other two, pushed Richard's friends out of the way roughly and took the money off the desk. Richard protested, but received a sharp smack across the face for his trouble. The rat faced youth seized him by the lapels, lifted him off his seat and held his face inches away from his own.

"Listen turd," he said. "When I want you to speak, I'll tell you."

Richard winced away from the youth's rancid breath, only to be jerked closer.

"We do the collecting round here, not smart little first year assholes, understand?" Richard nodded. Big though he was, his assailant was bigger and stronger, and more experienced in intimidation, and Richard was too frightened to speak.

"Good," said the youth, a little disappointed at the lack of resistance. "Don't give me any more trouble kid, or I'll really fix you."

He put a clenched fist against Richard's chin and pushed him back violently into his chair. Then he smacked him across the face again and banged his forehead on the desk. The last blow hurt Richard badly and he kept his head down on the desk and protected it with his hands while he tried not to cry. But rat-face had not quite finished.

"Cos of the trouble you've caused, the first year can start paying right away, and they can pay double for a few weeks. Just to make sure you've learnt your lesson."

Then he left, pausing only to nod permission to his colleagues to lay about them generally amongst Richard's watching friends.

There was a long silence, until eventually someone said, "You alright, Dick?"

Then another. "He can't do that can he?"

Richard looked up, his face red from the stinging blows he had received. His head hurt, but he had managed not to cry. The ambivalent expressions on his friend's faces abruptly turned his trembling fear into trembling rage. He would not lose everything he had gained.

"He's done it, hasn't he? But I'll fucking fix him, you see."

"You can't do anything, Dick, he's miles bigger than you."

"You heard me," said Richard, his bravado getting the better of his judgement. "I'll fix him. I'm not taking that off anyone."

He put his head in his hands for a moment and felt the rage and indignation pushing him to a crisis. He had to do something. No-one could be allowed to hurt him with impunity. Nor was he going to lose the money he was getting, especially if it also turned most of the first year against him—he needed them. What angered him as much as anything was the waste. If the suggestion had been made he would have been quite prepared to act as a collector for the fifth former—for a percentage.

Throughout the rest of the day the anger surged back and forth across his mind, bringing down on his head further summary punishment from his teachers for lack of concentration.

When the final bell went, he left the school quickly without lingering with his friends as he usually did. Crossing the road, he stationed himself behind a bus shelter so that he could watch the school disgorging its contents through the old-fashioned iron gates. Eventually the rat-faced youth came out, attended by his three friends. Richard moved after them, merging with the other children in the street, but keeping his eyes firmly fixed on his enemy. He had no idea what he was going to do. He felt the knife in his pocket, but dismissed that as being impractical. He did not really know how to use it, and the other boy was far too big for any kind of close combat. But he had to do something, he had to follow. His rage was choking him and making him tremble all over.

Gradually the crowd thinned out, making Richard feel more conspicuous, but rat-face soon parted from his friends, turning off into an alleyway.

Has he spotted me? thought Richard, and he crossed hastily to the other side of the road so that he could view the length of the alley without being too close to its entrance. Seeing rat-face disappear at the far end of the alley, Richard ran after him as quietly as he could, stopping just before the end. His heart racing, he peeped carefully round the corner, and was grabbed viciously by the hair.

"You must think I'm fucking blind, you stupid little nit," said rat-face breathing all over Richard's face again, and pushing him against the wall.

"Give me my money back," shouted Richard, surprising himself.

Rat-face started, and then gritting his teeth he gripped Richard's shirt collar, twisted it and forced his knuckles into Richard's throat. "Listen, turd. It wasn't your money then, and it isn't now. It's mine. And you're a real pain."

Then he released his grip and hit Richard in the stomach. Richard had never been hit so hard in his life. He felt all the air in his body leave him and all control with it. Then as he doubled over, the youth hit him in the face with his knee. Richard went sprawling in the alley, the only thoughts in his mind being pain and escape. He was dimly aware of his enemy approaching and he struggled to his knees and clasped the youth around the waist, partly to prevent him doing anything further, and partly to beg him to stop. Then he vomited. The youth gave a disgusted cry. In an attempt to avoid the acrid bounty being lavished on him, he struggled free from the unsought embrace, but lost his footing as he stepped back, and came crashing to the ground, banging his head on a concrete kerb.

Richard lurched back against the wall, gasping for breath, blood and vomit running down his chin and over his torn shirt and jacket. Suddenly his head was clear, as if the vomit had torn away all his fears and doubts. He looked at the bigger boy rolling on the floor, moaning and holding his head, and in a flash saw before him two ways. One of subservience and failure, of scorn and torment all his school days and probably after, of being the butt of other people's humours and fancies, and of bitterness and waste until he too would fall off a roof somewhere, sometime. And another way, of promise and success, one which he had momentarily been deflected from, one of wealth and independence, where people would do his bidding not he theirs. Let *them* fall off the roofs, he thought savagely.

Looking round at the jetsam littering the alley, his eye fell on a short length of timber. Quite calmly he picked it up and struck his fallen adversary with it repeatedly until he stopped moaning and moving. Then he went through his pockets, removed all the money, which was considerable, and walked quietly along the shadowy alley. No-one had seen anything and he knew it, and the money in his pocket felt exciting.

The rat faced youth spent a long time in hospital being repaired. Collar bone, shoulder blade and upper arm had been broken, he was massively concussed and for some time there was a suspected fracture of the skull. He was well known locally as a 'naughty boy' and the police, presuming that someone had at last caught up with him and given him his just desserts, were not over-assiduous in pursuing his attacker. When he eventually returned to school, he had no clear memory of the attack, and did not seem to have any great desire to restart his old activities, which had lapsed in his absence. Most of his followers had, subsequent to his attack, disclaimed any real friendship with him, being most concerned to avoid any vengeance that might be sought by the hitherto repressed schoolyard tribe.

Richard went from strength to strength. Without saying

201

anything, he made it quite clear to his immediate circle that he had done what he had promised, and that the matter was to be duly noted, but not spoken about.

As he moved up through the school the need to protect his peers from the depredations of seniors faded, and with it his income. After some consideration he transferred his main energies to running a lottery. He was pleased with the venture. It was easy to run, very profitable, carried little or no risk of parental interference and brought him a great deal of goodwill. And, if necessary, the profitability could be discreetly increased, for special occasions, by a little inconspicuous jiggery-pokery, such as arranging for one of his nominees to win. He was always careful to ensure that to outward appearances the lottery was honest and above board, and that he received only a nominal amount to compensate for his time and effort.

He was loath to lose the protection business totally, so he re-organized it more carefully. One group would terrorize the newcomers for a week or so, then another group, distressed at hearing of this plight, would offer protection for a fee. Richard himself never appeared in any of this day-to-day groundwork, and remained in the background, benign and distant. Again he pitched his premiums at a level to guarantee almost universal acceptance and minimum risk of exposure, and the premium was actuarially reduced as the pupils rose through the school. Nice touch that, he thought, keeps them in the habit of paying while they think they're getting something for nothing. When resistance was met he would examine the case in detail and decide whether the offender should be left uninsured and subsequently well and truly thumped, or whether he should be hired as a collector. He regarded the treatment of such cases as being one of the utmost delicacy.

Another sideline he found both interesting and enjoyable was pimping. But it was tricky and fraught with many unexpected hazards, not least the temperament of his young ladies. Although it left him with many pleasant memories, and made handsome profits, he was, all things considered, quite relieved when he left that particular venture behind him. The closed school community was ideal for protection and gambling, but girls...? There would be at least one furore per annum over some incident or other, and then the whole operation would have to close down, and he would have to use precious favours to preserve his anonymity. Still it was fun, and very profitable, especially with the blackmail business that built up around it. And Richard learned to use words and charm, as well as force, to implement his will. He found it personally distasteful to hit girls, and would only do it under fairly extreme circumstances.

Before he left school he tried dealing in drugs, but with no success. Having read in the papers of the profits to be made, he contacted a local pusher, an old friend of his father's, and inquired, discreetly, about the possibility of a franchise for the school. The man listened carefully to this serious and faintly sinister youth.

"There's no chance, Dick," he said. "If I sell to kids I'll end up in the river, no doubt about it."

"Well, just ask on my behalf. Call it a preliminary enquiry."

The man was very reluctant, but eventually agreed. When they met again he was puzzled. "It's only because of your dad I did this. Just asking could have been enough to get me put in hospital. I hope you realize that. But they wanted to know more about you."

So Richard told him about his operations at school, lying carefully about their size and profitability. A week later, the final message came.

"There's no chance selling at the school, Dick. No chance. But they said they'll remember you favourably."

"What's that mean?" asked Richard. The man shrugged.

"Oh," he said suddenly. "And they said, don't lie to them in future."

Richard sat stone faced. The man articulated the message again, carefully, then said, "Dick, it's good advice. Take it. If you've lied to them, don't do it again. Don't ever mess these people about. They frighten the people who frighten me, and worse."

The man's demeanour impressed Richard. He had never seen an adult frightened before, but a classic example was now sitting right in front of him. I wonder who 'they' are, he thought, and what kind of money they make? He considered enquiring further, but decided against it. He went to a great deal of trouble to preserve his anonymity—how much more would they go to? He had obviously used up a great many favours with this man, and would have to make some attempt at reparation in case he wanted future contact with 'them'.

"I'm very sorry if I've got you into any trouble with this," he said. "I didn't realize it meant you taking any risks."

"It's alright, Dick," came the reply. "Everyone understands. That's why I could ask for you. These people are businessmen, reasonable people, to a point. They're not interested in gratuitous violence. But they don't debate. You make your point, they listen, then you do as they say. No argument. Step off the straight and narrow, it'll be one warning, then..."

He drew his finger across his throat, evocatively.

"Even so," said Richard. "You stuck your neck out for me and I appreciate it." He thought for a moment. "I think I've got something you might be interested in, as a special thanks from me."

The man was indeed interested. It involved one of Richard's girls in a little extramural work, and he himself took a slight reduction in income that week, writing it off as a public relations expense.

In his last year at school he briefly considered the possibility of passing exams and moving on to the sixth form for a further two years of study. The income was, after all, quite considerable. However, after serious thought he concluded that the effort involved in passing exams could be better spent elsewhere, and that he had gained all the useful experience he could from school. It was time to move on.

His last coup was to persuade his 'managers' at the school to bank their income with him so that they could buy the business from him when he left. A couple demurred, saying they would probably let the business go when he left. Although this action really meant nothing to him financially, he resented being taken for a fool, and a week or so later he arranged for both of them to be found in possession of stolen goods—an offence involving immediate expulsion.

When he left, he left a great deal of potentially useful goodwill, and a school which collapsed back into normal childish disorder and anarchy within a term, as he had known full well it would. Also when he left, he was rich, by his own standards. The money he had earned, he had saved and invested, using this as an opportunity to develop a few aliases. Under the tutelage of his mother, these aliases were also used to supplement his social security payments. He was impressed by the fact that this yielded almost as much as his businesses at school and involved considerably less administration, so he slowly and cautiously expanded his range of identities. He was protected from detection by careful attention to detail, and by an equally careful control of his greed. He knew exactly when to say enough. He would manipulate the system, but never play it to its limit and draw attention to himself.

If luck went against him and he was found a job, he would attend punctually and show much willingness, but usually had to be regretfully dismissed within a few days because of his bumbling incompetence.

"Nice lad. I'd like to have kept him, but so clumsy, so careless, scatter-brained," would follow in his wake. The last thing Richard needed was employment obstructing his career. Such information as he gained from any employment about cash movement, alarm systems, valuable stock, and so on, he would sell to his growing number of street contacts.

On the whole, however, he became frustrated. He made a good income from various sources, but it was not the big time by any stretch of imagination. It would not buy expensive cars, a decent house, good clothes. It was not enough. But he faced the same problems as when he was young. Burglary was hardly worth the trouble. Anyone with anything valuable had it well secured, and then there was the problem of fencing the goods. Street robbery was messy and rarely yielded much.

Ironically, Richard had something approaching a conscience concerning wresting someone else's money from them by main force. It felt immoral to him. Anyway, these days, one was quite likely to come away from an attempted mugging feet first with a hole in the head, courtesy of some outraged and armed citizen. Computer fraud fascinated him, but he realized it was too far from the mainstream of his life at present to be a practical proposition. However, he noted it well for future reference.

Eventually, he turned his attention again to the lottery. It had been very lucrative at school and had built up considerable goodwill. It was worth a serious effort.

As he envisaged, it proved to be a lot less easy to set up away from the restricted confines of the school. But using the local pubs as his main bases, and by conspicuously demonstrating his honesty, he slowly got it started. Once he had established a round, he was able to hand it over to a collector, thereby taking a reduced income but freeing himself to start new rounds. He had little or no trouble with his collectors; he was meticulous in their selection and his open and pleasant manner tended to attract loyalty naturally. He was admittedly aided in this in the early days by an attack on one of his collectors.

A local gang of youths waylaid the man, robbed him and put him in hospital for a few days. The incident had been committed on the spur of the moment and the gang made no attempt to keep their identities secret, but it was the thin end of a wedge that Richard was not prepared to tolerate. He was a big man now, in every way—tall, muscular and fast—and, after visiting his collector in hospital, he went straight to the pub which the gang used as its headquarters. Marching quietly in, and without any preliminaries, he seized the two ringleaders, pushed their faces into the table and the pies they were eating, cracked their heads together with a thud that made the room shake, and then laid about the other four with brass knuckles and a blackjack, until he was satisfied they would spend longer in hospital than his collector. When he had finished, he took all the money they were carrying, paid the landlord for the damage, apologized most graciously to everyone and ordered drinks all round. It was a highly calculated piece of theatre. He knew that at that pub there was no serious risk of anyone reporting him to the police, and a conspicuous defence of his collector involving the meting out of summary justice to an unpopular group of hooligans would protect his other collectors and do his reputation no harm at all.

With the establishment of the lottery, Richard's income and status in the neighbourhood grew apace. He consolidated his position by putting money into two local shops, giving them an opportunity to brighten up their premises and take in more stock, while at the same time reducing the petty vandalism and theft that was endemic in the area. He was pleased with this legitimizing of part of his operation. It enabled him to draw an honest income and while he had to forego his personal social security payments, it did not affect those of his aliases. The shops were useful points of contact with the local people and were used discreetly to facilitate and simplify the running of the lottery. They were also a useful source of information about the financial standing of many of the locals, and enabled Richard to move into the money lending business. As time passed, he put money into most of the local businesses, purchased local properties and made a great deal of money manipulating the property improvement grant system. He became quite a rich and respected member of the community.

However, his disposition was such that he wanted the success of a venture purely as a stepping stone to the next one. He felt after a while that he had reached the limit of what was available in that district, and he did not know how to expand further. Bigger opportunities were available outside, he knew, but to seize them effectively he would need to have a great deal more commercial expertise and he would need policemen and local government officers in his pay. That would not be easy, and he did not really know where to start.

However, Richard's progress had not gone unmarked. One day he received an unusual letter. High quality paper and an expensive typeface, but no address, just a phone number. It was short and to the point.

Dear Mr. Gwilier, I have a business proposition I would like to discuss with you. I think it will be to your considerable advantage. Could we meet for lunch..." etc.

It was signed J. Smith, and the specified restaurant was both expensive and discreet. Richard stared at the letter for some time. It couldn't be a practical joke, and the venue and the whole tone of the note seemed to preclude anything sinister. Eventually, he picked up the phone and tapped out the number. An attractive voice at the other end of the line took the message that he would be delighted to accept Mr. Smith's invitation.

# Chapter 26

It was one of those increasingly rare, fine summer days when Richard Gwilier left his car in the multi-storey car park and made his way on foot through the few short streets to the appointed restaurant. It was lunch hour, and being the commercial area of the city, it was crowded. But the walk improved his appetite in more ways than one. Threading his way through the shirt-sleeved, summer-frocked and purposeful crowds, past jewellers and furriers and expensive car showrooms, and ridiculous but equally expensive fashion shops, reminded him that there were a great many people in the world with a great many desires, and a great deal of money, and precious little sense. It reaffirmed to him that if he kept his wits about him, he would find a place where his ambition could spread itself and lead him to a world which was permanently sunny. The sight of so many summer-clad girls also raised another appetite, but he reluctantly set it aside as being inappropriate at the moment.

He cut down a side street to shorten his journey and grimaced in distaste at the filth and rubbish littering the pavements. Looking instinctively upwards, he smiled as he saw the old brick walls of the buildings that presented their lavish fronts to the main streets. Old, disused loading bays with their iron doors, sometimes rusting, sometimes spruce with new paint, and tendrilled branches of ancient plumbing systems climbing hither and thither across the brickwork, impinged on his vision simultaneously. He knew some of the buildings would be almost two hundred years old, and would once have echoed to the voices of warehousemen and horse-drawn carts and the clatter of hoists loading and unloading heavy cargo.

Although he could not have said why, it gave him a companionable feeling to think of people working and striving in the past, and of people today using those same old buildings.

The restaurant was itself in a side street, and also housed in an old warehouse, albeit not as old as those which he had just passed. As the glass door closed behind him, he was momentarily disorientated. The noise of the street stopped abruptly, and his eyes took some time to adjust to the dim interior lighting.

"Can I help you, sir?" enquired a polite voice out of the gloom.

Gwilier's eyes slowly focused on a slightly built young man, immaculate in blazer and flannels. He cleared his throat.

"Yes, please. I'm meeting a Mr. Smith here for lunch..." He looked at his watch. "In about five minutes. Does he by any chance have a reservation, or should I wait by the bar?"

"Ah, you'll be Mr. Gwilier. Mr. Smith has just arrived. I'll take you to him."

Gwilier followed the man through double doors into the main dining room. It was not a restaurant that bowed to the grosser commercial necessities such as businessmen's lunches, and the room was comparatively empty—two expensively dressed old ladies, one nervous young man with a pretty girl, and various groups of earnest looking sales representatives wooing nonchalant clients. At a table in a corner, well away from the window and on the blind side of an exit door, Gwilier saw a smart looking man sitting alone and browsing through a menu.

"There's Mr. Smith sir, at the table in the corner," said his guide, stepping back to allow him to pass, and bowing slightly as he did so.

The man rose and held out his hand as Gwilier approached. His handshake was firm but gentle, and added immediately to Gwilier's initially favourable impression. He found hearty hand crushers immensely irritating, even though few could make any impression on his great fist. Superficially, the man was an average nondescript businessman, medium height, medium build, clean shaven, quite a lot older than Gwilier, but good looking, with straight dark brown hair, a square face and large brown eyes. After they had introduced themselves, he motioned Gwilier to sit down, and offered him the menu. Gwilier felt an ease and confidence in the man—in the way he moved—very relaxed. It made him feel gauche and clumsy and shabbily dressed. No-one had ever made him feel like that before, and he realized quite suddenly that this was the way he wanted to be, that this was a man to be watched and learned from, his own kind of man. He grinned and shrugged awkwardly as Smith looked up and smiled broadly as he caught Gwilier's penetrating gaze.

"You do right to have a good look at me, Mr. Gwilier. I must apologize for the unusual invitation, but my company is unorthodox in many ways."

"Your company being?"

A waiter appeared to take their orders before Smith could reply, and when he had gone, Smith seemed disposed to forget the question.

"You were about to tell me the name of your company," insisted Gwilier politely.

"The name wouldn't mean anything to you. We don't trade publicly in the normal sense of the word. We're a kind of... holding company."

"You're probably right," conceded Gwilier, following the cue. "I know nothing of high finance and... holding companies. So what can I do to help you?"

Smith leaned forward and spoke quietly. "My company is involved in a very wide range of activities. One of the things we do is keep our eyes open for individuals with special aptitudes. People with a flair for a certain style of business management. Flexible, practical people who know what they want and go straight for it, but without making waves. We're fairly certain you're just such a one, and we feel we may be able to come to a mutually advantageous arrangement if you're interested."

Gwilier allowed the wariness to show on his face. "I'm just a shopkeeper. I don't know anything about managing companies," he said hastily.

Smith interrupted him by reaching across the table and gently touching his arm. "Bear with me, Mr. Gwilier," he said. "I'm not wasting your time or my own. We've got a quiet hour or so to talk over a relaxed meal. I'll tell you about my company, and what I think you can do for it, and you can ask any questions you want, ok?"

"Fair enough," Gwilier replied. He appreciated the way Smith was handling him.

"But," continued Smith. "Just to prevent any misunderstanding and confusion. I should tell you..." The waiter appeared again, buzzed around a little and finally glided soup bowls in front of them before gliding off himself.

"As I was saying," said Smith, picking up his spoon. "We know about your enterprises at school, your lottery, the money lending, social security fraud, property grant fraud, and so on, and of course your legitimate fronts, your shopkeeping," he added as an after-thought. Then, before Gwilier could reply, he briefly quoted some figures, very accurate figures.

The whole of this was said in an offhand and open manner, devoid of any implications, and was concluded with another broad smile. Gwilier was frozen. Staring down at his soup spoon and try-ing to stop it shaking. His heart was racing, his temples throbbing, his throat felt dry and his mind was tumbling with probabilities and possibilities. He seemed to stay like that for an interminable time, then quite suddenly he relaxed and raised the spoon to his mouth. There was no way this man could be a police officer, his every instinct told him that, and anyone who knew so much about his operations must have the capacity for taking them over without consulting him. But they hadn't. They had quite simply handed him the hot brand of ambition and it was his decision—seize it or drop it. Smith had shouted 'open sesame' to the doors of his future and shown him a glimpse of another world. He laid his spoon down and looked into Smith's ingenuous brown eyes, nodding his head in ac-knowledgement.

"Phew," he said breathlessly. "You'll excuse me if I sound winded, but I like your style, Mr. Smith. Tell me a little bit more about this company of yours."

An hour and a half later, it was a very different Richard Gwilier who walked through the same sunny streets to his car. In reality he was walking along a fabulous road, a road paved with his un-fettered ambitions, a road peopled with others like himself. People who would think and talk and act, and who would brook no un-reasonable opposition, people who knew not only the benefits of being independent, but also those of looking after one another— his kind of people. He felt childishly excited.

Over the next few years he prospered. Slowly but surely he found himself placed in charge of most of the rackets in the city. He administered them as he had done his own. Always with a view to obtaining the most goodwill for the least friction, and he gained some self-knowledge when he compared himself with some of the organizers who fell within his demesne.

"Stupid, vicious and greedy," he said in some despair to Mr. Smith over one of their periodic working lunches. He was talking about a local pimp who had been withholding money and also blackmailing clients when he had been told not to.

"It's the waste that annoys me, Mr. Smith. My time and effort. Then I've got to find a replacement. And really, he's good at his job. It could all be avoided if only he'd listen and think."

Smith shrugged sympathetically. "I understand, Dick. It's both sad and frustrating, but..."

He left the sentence unfinished.

"As you say—but," said Gwilier.

"Do you want any outside help?" offered Smith.

"No thanks," said Gwilier, laying his napkin carefully by his plate. "His number two is an intelligent lad. I'll arrange for him to do the necessary, then put him in charge. He's not as experienced, but he'll listen and he'll learn. All in all, he'll be an improvement. And we can keep evidence of his..." he searched for a euphemism. "His entrance exam, just in case we need it later."

Smith nodded approvingly. "Sounds reasonable," he said. "Go ahead. But quietly, of course, and let me have the details first."

Gwilier considered his greatest achievement in his management of the city to be the successful bribing of two Customs and Excise officials, thereby greatly simplifying the then rather elaborate import procedures for drugs coming into the port.

"Nice balance of greed and fear, Dick. Very elegant and most impressive," commented Smith when he heard about it. "You're a credit to us. Well done."

But on the matter of drugs, he found the company very sensitive. He resurrected his old idea of selling drugs in the schools.

"They're nice, tight, closed communities, quite easy to organize and very easy to intimidate. It's all future custom, isn't it?"

They were walking in a small park in the middle of the city, and Smith motioned him to a bench by the edge of an ornamental pool.

"Dick, listen carefully. It's not often I have to give you guidance, but this is one occasion."

They sat down and Smith stared out across the pool. "Drugs are tricky. They're one of our largest enterprises internationally. They give us a complete captive seller's market with a massive built-in expansion factor as you know. User turns dealer to finance his own habit, and so on. Recruits turn recruiting sergeants. Fantastic, but..."

He turned and looked at Gwilier. "We know from experience that if we overdo it, we get a whole host of unpleasant and awkward social repercussions which in turn hit our other businesses, not least the legitimate ones, and if we don't keep distribution under absolute control, and I mean absolute," he emphasized. "Every idiot's in on the act making waves. And the profits are so high that the only way you can deal with them is..." He shrugged. "And that makes more problems. So, more than anything else we do, with drugs, you and me are soldiers—we do or die, not reason why, ok? We deal with local tactics. Other people have the information to consider and develop overall strategy. And part of that strategy is kids in the playground, no." He cut his hand down in a chopping action then stood up and put his hand on Gwilier's shoulder.

"I appreciate you're only thinking of the company, Dick. Everyone understands that. But that avenue is closed. For you and me it's literally a dead end."

Gwilier nodded. The phrase "Everyone understands that" jarred a little. He hoped he had not blotted his copybook. The way it had been said made it clear that his enthusiasm in this area was a worrying problem to his superiors.

"I'm sorry, Mr. Smith," he said at last. "I'm not usually that stupid. I should've worked it out for myself. It's just the remains of an old schoolboy idea. I get a little parochial at times." He looked up at Smith. "The matter's ended," he said.

Increasingly he found himself relieved of day-to-day administration and given special assignments. These took him all over the world and varied enormously. On more than one occasion he acted as Mr. Smith to some up-and-coming Richard Gwilier. He bribed trade officials behind the iron curtain. He beat out bush fires that had broken out between factions that did not even know they were working for the same organization. He discussed bona-fide export contracts with embassy officials and less than bona-fide export contracts with illicit arms dealers and smugglers generally. Then, more eccentrically, he had such assignments as flying to Melbourne to shoot a brothel keeper, a job which any local man could have handled. Even flying to New York and speaking a code word from a specific call box, then returning immediately. He never questioned such assignments, particularly the very strange ones. In his experience the company never did anything arbitrarily or whimsically. There was always calculation. He reasoned that all tasks he was given, and his efficient performance of them, would be important, and he completed them as meticulously as he could. He also reasoned that while he was being given a considerable overview of the company's activities, it would be only a fraction of its real size. The structure was basically cellular. Some big, some small, with very few people knowing how they were joined together.

Only on one occasion did he seriously consider levelling vitriolic criticism at his unseen employers, and that was when the two militant power workers were gunned down on the steps of the Magistrate's Court. From the company's contacts with terrorist groups he knew it was not one of them. It could possibly have been a group of irate amateurs—there was certainly enough public feeling against the men—but it was too well done for that. Then there was the use of the stolen police riot gun and smoke canisters, and their being left at the scene. Although the point had not been laboured by the media, everyone who needed to know, knew it was the unequivocal hallmark of one of the old gang leaders who had disappeared mysteriously years previously, in the days before the company had been formed and merged itself into legitimate society. Like the once and future king, thought Gwilier, sleeping until he's needed. It gave him a strange feeling. He had had no forewarning of the incident, and a great many waves were spreading. He was reluctantly deciding that he would have to speak to Smith, when Smith forestalled him.

Almost before Gwilier could speak, Smith said, "Don't say anything, Dick. Anything. When I look upwards, all I see are pale faces. Leave it. Mop up what you can. I'll do what I can here and come back to you."

Then he rang off. Gwilier's anger began to be leavened by alarm. What the devil was going on? The company could usually have its way by bribery or blackmail, and had the option of modest violence if those failed. Killings were usually matters of internal discipline

215

and were conducted very discreetly, such publicity as there was being directed exclusively at those for whom the object lesson had
been intended. Cautious and nervous queries were coming up
through his own organization, so he stamped out the embers before
the flames started.

"Leave it alone," he said. "It was a special problem and no-one
local was involved. Business as usual, keep your heads down and
your mouths shut."

Dismissing the matter as trivial and irrelevant to his underlings
was one thing, but convincing himself was another. Could it possibly be a power struggle going on somewhere above his head? He
could not believe that, or at least that such a conflict would be pursued in such a way. It ran contrary to everything he knew about the
company. It was as incongruous as knights in armour jousting. And
what earthly use was there in killing two ratty little militants. The
unions had always been the easiest of institutions to control. And
yet? Should he tighten up his own personal security, and that of his
organization? He decided that on balance he could not. Standard
company procedures were already very effective, and apart from
the occasional officer's parade to remove dust in the works there
was little that could be improved on. He would have to take his own
advice—business as usual. Perhaps Smith might find out what had
happened and be able to tell him, but perhaps not. He had to recon-
cile himself to the fact that he would probably never know why the
execution had been ordered. Even so, he resolved to be a little more
cautious than usual until he knew more or until it had all faded well
into the distance.

Some time later, while he was looking idly into a shop window,
his increased caution enabled him to spot the reflection of a dark car
pulling up behind him. Casually he put his hand in his coat pocket
and took hold of his revolver. The driver's window was wound down
and, heart racing, Gwilier peered into the vague reflection to see if
he could detect anything sinister in the car's interior. The driver's
face was turned towards him and it looked like Smith. Tightening
his grip on the revolver and carefully noting the passers-by so that
he could slip behind someone quickly if necessary, Gwilier slowly
turned round. It was indeed Smith at the wheel of the car. He smiled
and made a brief hand signal to indicate that everything was safe.
Gwilier returned the smile and moved forward, deliberately and

apologetically bumping into two people on the busy pavement as he did so. He saw the front passenger seat was empty, but he could not see clearly into the rear of the car. Smith's hands were conspicuously resting on the top of the steering wheel.

"Can you spare a few minutes, Dick?" he said. "There's someone who would like to have a word with you." He gestured over his shoulder.

Gwilier nodded and opened the rear door with his left hand, his right still in his pocket, holding the revolver. A stocky, black haired man was sitting on the side farthest away from the door. He smiled and, keeping both hands clearly visible, motioned Gwilier to step inside. Without taking his eyes off the man, Gwilier climbed into the car. It pulled away and joined the lunchtime traffic.

"I told you we'd have to be careful how we approached him, didn't I?" said Smith, inclining his head to address the passenger. "Dick's got eyes in the back of his head. He never misses a thing. A great watcher, Dick."

The black-haired man chuckled and spoke to Gwilier. "Yes indeed, Mr. Smith. You use the local cover well, Mr. Gwilier, but you can let go of your pistol now. We haven't reverted to the old days quite yet, and I must admit you're making me nervous."

He held out his right hand. "My name's Josephs, Mr Gwilier."

Gwilier's unease fell away at the man's tone and attitude—this was a company man. He released the revolver and shook the man's hand.

"I'm pleased to meet you, Mr. Josephs," he said. "What can I do for you?"

"Well, Mr. Gwilier, perhaps you can begin by accepting my apologies."

Gwilier's face showed surprise before he could control it.

"Mr. Josephs, we've never met. You owe me no apology that I know of," he said.

"Yes, I do," Josephs said. "I arranged for those two gentlemen to be dealt with. I had to do it quickly on orders from way up." He pointed upwards. "And I appreciate it will have caused you some disruption and personal alarm. So I've come to say sorry and to reassure you it was no reflection on you or your running of the city. It was a peculiarly unique situation. I'll finish the job by dealing with the police and media, and you can carry on with business as normal. I made the splash and I'll deal with the waves. If you could perhaps deal with the few remaining ripples, I'd be much obliged."

Gwilier sat stunned for a moment. Eventually he spoke. "I don't know what to say, Mr. Josephs. I accept your apology of course, but it wasn't really necessary. I realized it was something important and that the disruption would be temporary, but I must admit your assurance is welcome. The manner of the execution was so, er..." He searched for a word. "Public," he said eventually with a sense of anti-climax. Josephs nodded.

"Would it be an impertinence on my part to ask what it was all about?" Gwilier ventured.

"No, no," said Josephs. "No impertinence at all, you know we encourage intelligent enquiry. But I can't answer your question, or rather, I won't, because it's not in your best interests to know. Suffice it that those two trod very hard on a very big toe."

And that, Gwilier knew, was all he was going to get; but it would do. He raised his hand slightly to indicate his acceptance of this explanation and an ending of the matter. His vision of the company riven with internal strife evaporated totally. The mountain had come, unbidden, to Mohamed—what a firm.

"Would you like to look at some of the details of our operations, Mr. Josephs, while you're here?" he said, to set the conversation on a new, safer course.

"I would indeed, Mr. Gwilier, I would indeed."

So, for the rest of the afternoon they cruised around the city and its outskirts as Gwilier outlined his ideas for the future, breaking off occasionally to point out some item or other of particular interest.

Eventually they stopped outside his office.

"Mr Gwilier," said Josephs. "I've not been entirely honest with you about my visit today. It's true I had to apologize to you, but there was another reason why I wanted to meet you."

Gwilier looked at him cautiously.

"I've watched your progress carefully since you joined us," said Josephs. "And I've been very impressed. It's difficult to find good company men and we try to look after those we do find. So I've a proposition I'd like you to consider."

Gwilier sat very still. Josephs continued. "I'm reaching the age now to be thinking of retirement, and a replacement will be needed for me." He paused. "It should be some time away yet, but I think you can handle the job—with training of course—quite a lot of training. And I'd like to take you on as my assistant."

Gwilier felt as if a large weight had fallen on him. He stuttered his thanks.

"But I don't even know what you do," he said. "And what about Mr. Smith?"

Both men laughed.

"Mr Smith has his speciality, Mr. Gwilier, and you have yours. Fancy my job Smithy?" Josephs said loudly.

"Not in a million years," said Smith, still laughing. Gwilier's mind was still whirling. He did not understand this last exchange, but Josephs continued quietly.

"Don't worry about the details of the job. Believe me, you can handle them. You'll also make a lot more money of course. But mainly you'll be in a position to help with our broader planning and organisation. I think you'd enjoy that. You've got a lot to offer."

"But my..." Gwilier gesticulated vaguely and looked round.

"Your business here?" said Josephs. "There's no rush, Mr. Gwilier. Start thinking about who you want to promote where. We can have some heavy sessions later to go over details, and we've plenty of good people to look after any temporary gaps. It's not in our interests to let this operation stop. It's far too lucrative. And actually you won't be far away. You'll be able to keep an eye on things and give advice and guidance if necessary. Now!" He clapped his hands together. "Would you like to think about it?"

"I have," said Gwilier purposefully. "If you think I'm good enough, then that's good enough for me. I accept your offer, sight unseen. When do I start?"

Josephs smiled. "I'll be in touch in a day or two and we'll get started on the details."

Smith turned round awkwardly in the driver's seat and held out his hand. "Welcome to the pack, Dick," he said.

"Well," said Josephs. "If we're going to work together, I'll call you Dick if I may, Mr Gwilier."

Gwilier was opening the car door.

"That's fine, Mr Josephs," he replied. "In fact I'd prefer it. Being called mister makes me feel old."

Josephs smiled broadly. "Good," he said. "And you can call me Joey."

# Chapter 27

John and Freddy had two children—Phillip, after they had been married for four years, and Stephen two years later. Both were blonde with blue eyes, taking their colouring from their mother, much to Peter's amusement.

"It's time some of the offspring in this family showed a little sense," Peter pronounced.

John was as stunned at the birth of his children as his father had been at his and, solid in the love of his own upbringing, he spent time with them religiously, regardless of the requirements of the business.

He had watched his wife in amazement. Carrying Phillip, she became quiet and serene and full of ancient mystery, like a mystical, glowing symbol of fecundity, but with Stephen she seemed to be eight-foot-tall and full of thunderous energy.

"What's the matter?" asked Peter one day when he appeared in the office, wide-eyed and bewildered.

John slumped into a chair. "It's Freddy," he said, eyes wide.

"What about her?" asked Peter in some concern.

"I think I've been raped," continued John, oblivious.

Peter tried to keep his face straight. "You think?" he offered.

John reflected. "No, no. I'm certain. And she's very heavy, I can tell you."

"What happened?" asked Peter, slowly losing the battle with his face.

John took on a hurt and indignant look. "I'm not going into the details dad," he said haughtily.

"It may be just as well, on reflection," said his father.

John stared into space. "Crying out loud, dad. She growled at me."

Peter bent his head earnestly over his work. "Shut up and get on with your work," he said. "And don't let me hear about your knocking my second grandchild about with your unbridled depravity."

John made a strangled noise and delicately adjusted his posture in his chair.

The children were the opposite in character to their mother's pregnancies. Phillip was boisterous and adventurous and Stephen was quiet but alert and shrewd. They looked alike and got on very well together, their differing temperaments steering them away from sibling rivalry and towards co-operation.

After John's marriage, everyone had moved into the business's headquarters. Their own home being now far too large, Peter and Ann moved into the flat previously occupied by Peter's father, while John and Freddy moved into a large annex to the main building. Ironically, Peter felt more relaxed in the flat, immediately adjacent to the hub of his concerns, than he ever had at his old home. He did not pause to ponder the fact, but just accepted it with gratitude. It was a wrench to leave the old house, and Peter had spent a long time prowling round the empty shell muttering to himself, thanking the household gods for the happiness they had bestowed on him. As he closed the door for the last time and crunched across the snow to his car, he knew the very last remnants of his old life were gone. He was in the other world totally now, with only his wife to bind him to earth and sanity. Soon he would have to reach out and pull his son to his side. Between them they would be able to complete his task and rend some of the darkness from the business, reducing it to a less world-shadowing power.

He had found within himself a mounting desperation at the slowness with which he could proceed. The delicacy and intricacy of so many of the business's inter-connections made judgements profoundly difficult, and its innate tendency to expand spontaneously was almost unbelievable. He could not totally avoid the nagging doubt that it could not be reduced—perhaps only the balance could be shifted one way or the other. But he refused to accept this. It was made by men; it could be unmade by men. It was merely difficult, not impossible. He had to admit, however, that this was more hope than rational calculation.

Still, he would think to himself, just because I'm in a fog doesn't mean the road has no end. Then would come the desperation. It must have an end. His power was real, even if it was not what it appeared to be, not omnipotence. What would happen if it fell into the wrong hands? John would have to know the whole truth as soon as possible. He would have to help. Peter could not do as his own father had done, and as had been the tradition—hand down the sceptre at death.

John and Freddy in the annex were set fair for living happily ever after. Freddy, like Ann, did not want to know about the business. She knew it occupied that part of John which he kept separate and alone, and to enter that part would be to court the destruction of the good and true man that was the rest of him. Unlike Bluebeard's Judith, she knew that some doors are locked with good reason.

John learned more about the business daily, and it tended to occupy more and more of his time. Like his father before him he didn't like many of its facets, but accepted that they were effectively unavoidable. One day his father called him into his office.

"Sit down, John. I want to talk to you," he said quietly and very seriously.

John sat down and waited patiently. His father was sitting in the old high winged armchair, staring out of the window across the snow-covered gardens, and the room was warmed by a large blazing coal fire. Apart from the slight crackle of the fire, the room was silent. John looked at his father and seemed to see for the first time that the lines in his face were etched deeper than they used to be, and his whole posture radiated some great fatigue.

"Is there anything wrong, dad?" he asked after a while.

His father turned and smiled at him. "No. Nothing special. I was just thinking it's over twenty years since I joined the business. It's a long time to be in outer space." He paused and levered himself up out of the chair. "Still, we survive, don't we?" he said, going over to his desk. As soon as he sat down he started swinging from side to side. "You know this room has hardly changed in all that time."

"It's a still centre, dad," said John with a grin. "It doesn't move, but everything moves around it."

"Maybe," said his father ruefully. "I wish it were true. This particular bearing is beginning to feel the strain."

John looked concerned. "What's the matter, dad? You're not ill are you?"

"No, but I am burdened, and I'm going to give you part of that burden. We've got a lot to do and I can't handle it on my own, that's become abundantly clear. The time has come for you to join me in outer space."

A conflict of emotions rose up in John. Fear at what his father was going to do, and excitement.

"I don't know what you're talking about," he said. "But fire away."

His father stopped the movement of his chair. "What do you think of the business John?" he asked simply.

John was taken aback slightly. "Think about it?" he echoed. "That's a strange question. Why do you ask?"

"You first," said his father.

John shrugged and waved his hands vaguely. "Well, I suppose it's a curate's egg," he said flippantly. "A damn big one admittedly, but a curate's egg for all that."

"Good in parts, eh?"

"And bad in others," said John, a little more soberly. "Very bad in fact. By any definition we're a criminal organisation."

"Not by any definition John, but let that pass."

John seemed inclined to disagree—he started enumerating points with his fingers. "All manner of fraud—local, national and international. Smuggling currency, gold, drugs, arms. Corruption, buying officials and politicians. That's criminal. Then there's an almighty grey area. Legal and accountancy firms carving out loopholes in the law so that money from these ventures can be made legal." He paused.

"But?" suggested his father.

"But," continued John in a resigned tone. "We seem to have countless legitimate enterprises, from corner shops to multi-nationals, manufacturers, service industries, insurance, finance, agriculture, God knows what, and we're so big. Everything seems to depend on everything else. If we ditch the criminal activities they'll fall into other hands, things will run out of control, a large part of our legitimate side would disappear in the tumult, and the social consequences would be appalling."

"So what do you think of the business?"

John stood up and started pacing up and down. "I really don't know," he said. "I love it. It gives stability to large areas of commerce and industry. In some foreign areas it provides the only real law and order. It offers the most enlightened and sensitive management I could imagine. It's responsible for this whole country heading towards being self-sufficient in energy and food. Good grief, we can even start thinking of reaching a net zero consumption of resources, that's almost miraculous. And yet, the other side of it is frightful. All manner of civil servants and government employees are corrupted by us, businesses are ruined, drug addicts die because of us, women sell themselves for us. Anything that stands in our way is brushed aside with blackmail, violence, murder even, whatever's appropriate. I don't know what to think. It's a huge moral dilemma and I can't begin to resolve it. I'm in it, I don't think I want to leave it, I can live with it, cope with the paradox, but no, I can't resolve it or really clarify my own thoughts about its real worth."

Peter listened in silence to this summary of his own feelings.

"Sit down and listen, John," he said quietly. John leaned back in his chair. Peter leaned forward, his eyes bright.

"John, the business is far larger than you imagine. We have enough resources, contacts and expertise to expand indefinitely. This little room..." he waved his arm in an expansive gesture, "could be the centre of the richest and most powerful organization on the entire planet. We have the power to control every facet of national and international trade. We could abolish war, poverty, famine, all the great evils that plague mankind. Will you join me, John? Help bring the world into the light?"

John's eyes were wide in horror and disbelief. He shook his head as if to clear it.

"You're joking," he said, looking vainly for a sign of it in his father's face. But there was nothing. "Do that? With this organization?" Then, almost shouting. "Christ, half its life blood is drawn from those evils, or rather the evils that cause them—greed, malice, envy. If the business expands in its present form, they'll expand with it, and they'll expand a damn sight faster, because, by definition, they're the least controllable. There'll be no millennia started from here, only some grotesque dictatorship. And what happens when we die? Are Phillip and Stephen supposed to take over? And on and on? Some world-spanning dynasty?"

Peter stood up and slammed his hand on the desk. "John, we

need to expand—we've always expanded. It's essential. I'll need your help and I'll have it one way or another."

Inwardly John flinched under the impact of his father's massive authority, but he held firm and sent the wave hissing back. He looked up, his face set.

"Dad. I love you, but you're wrong. Part of me is tempted by what you say, but while I mightn't be able to resolve the moral dilemma of the business, I know it's wrong. It's got more potential for bad than good. I'm no match for you, but if you implement any expansion plans I'll fight you all the way, at whatever cost. You'll probably win, but it won't be cheap."

Then he turned his face away and clenched his teeth. "I can't believe I'm having this conversation. It's insane, dad, you know the business should be reduced not expanded. You must see it," he pleaded.

Peter sat down, grim faced. He glared balefully at his son. Then he slowly spun his chair right round. When he faced his son again, he was smiling.

"That's a relief," he said. "I see it perfectly well, John. I always have, and it's what I've been doing since your grandfather died. I'm happy you can see it for yourself. There's a dark streak in you, in all of us—me, your grandfather. If you'd gone for expansion I'd have had to slowly ease you away from the reins, and I don't think that would have been easy."

John took out a handkerchief and wiped his mouth and forehead. He breathed a long breath.

"You old... you frightened the life out of me," he said. "Why?"

"I just told you. To see which way you would go."

John grimaced. "But why now?"

"Because I think the time's right. Here." He pulled a crumpled manilla envelope out of his pocket and threw it carelessly across the desk. "There's a number in there. Your grandfather, with his usual sense of irony or paranoia, arranged for the Hand of God to deliver it to me on his death. By tradition I should be dead before you receive it, but times are changing." He looked out of the window. "Changing rapidly. And I need your help. Tap it into the computer. I haven't changed the master code, but all the details are up to date. I'll leave you alone. You'll need some time."

Two hours later he returned. John was sitting quietly in the high winged armchair, staring into the fire. His father sat opposite him. John spoke without looking up.

"I remember the day of grandfather's funeral. You were sitting in the dark in your office, with just a candle burning. You'd been through this, hadn't you?"

Peter nodded. "Similar," he said. "But it was a little worse. Your grandfather had set it up for a massive move forward. I've managed to trim it back quite a bit, but it's not been easy."

"I feel as if I'm in a dream," said John. "Or a nightmare. I can't believe it."

Peter's face screwed up in distress. "I'm sorry, John. I'd no alternative. It would've come to you sooner or later, and I need your help now. You'll get over the shock I promise you. You're the man for the job, there's no doubt about that. I'm just a caretaker really."

John pushed his finger under his eyepatch and massaged his dead eye.

"Is it troubling you?" asked his father.

John shook his head. "No. Not really. It itches sometimes. It wants to know why it can't see."

There was a long silence and John continued gazing into the fire. "What are we, dad? What on earth are we?" he said eventually. "How on earth did it all happen?"

Peter shrugged. "I suppose we're just the inheritors John. Your grandfather used to say, genes will out. Maybe he was right. I don't feel special but..." He shrugged again.

"But who created it all, dad? It's vast. Everything like I said before, but a hundredfold. An incredible international organization controlling all manner of both criminal and legitimate businesses all over the world. Adjectives don't exist to describe it. How did it come about?"

Peter smiled in spite of himself. "It's not really an area of scholarship in which meticulous records are kept, John. I suppose it just growed, like Topsy. Criminals have always looked for legitimate businesses to legalize their cash and personal status in society, and more than a few businessmen have turned criminal either accidently or deliberately, to avoid the rigours of taxation and bureaucracy."

John looked puzzled. "Accidentally?" he said.

Peter raised his eyebrows. "Come on, John, don't be naive. Man

227

needs cash, can't raise it from the bank, along comes your friendly moneylender and bingo, that's that. Or he's looking for a return on his skimmed cash and gets involved in money lending himself and finds his colleagues won't let him leave—in one piece that is."

John nodded. Peter leaned back and started to warm to his topic. "Then some lamebrained politician will boost trade with some ludicrous legislation that has very little public support. You've read about Prohibition haven't you?" He did not wait for an answer. "Fascinating era. That was probably the real big start. The money was big, the ambitions were big. Public opposition was nil. Incredibly fertile ground. Roots were sent down right into the fabric of legitimate society as the bright boys realized it was better business to buy and bribe your way than muscle it. And the more money you had, the better contacts you could buy in government and police. Turned gangsters into lawyers and accountants by the time it was over. Half in and half out of respectable society."

Peter fell silent for a moment as if ordering his thoughts. "Then I suppose the next big step was drugs," he said sombrely. "No public support here of course, but an incredible self-expanding captive market. And even more incredible profits, more corruption, more influence in high places—very high places," he said significantly. "There was so much money that diversification into all manner of legitimate businesses just boomed."

Peter leaned forward and stirred the fire with the poker. A shower of sparks rose up the chimney. He seemed to be talking to himself. "Not all smooth of course. Ruthless, greedy men would clash and quarrel. Matters would deteriorate occasionally. Three steps forward, two back—normal human progress in a good year. But, on the whole, the clever ones kept quiet, managed matters discreetly, sensibly, learned by other people's mistakes, co-operated and merged instead of fighting. Carried on buying people, buying influence, and so on and so on." He gave a sad little laugh. "And here we are. Sat around the fire. You and me. Sole proprietors. Probably the richest and most powerful people in the world, and nobody even knows about us. It's not without humour really. Now we've got to try and dismantle the whole thing. It's too big and too dangerous."

John had closed his eye. He spoke without opening it. "I'm not sure I can handle all this, dad. Blood's pounding in my ears. My head's spinning and I just want to stay in the dark and hide."

"You'll get used to it, John," said his father. "It won't take long, either. You knew most of it deep down. You've always known, haven't you?"

John was quiet for a long time, then he opened his eye. "If we get it wrong, this dismantling, the whole thing will fragment and run out of control and do more damage than if we left it alone." He closed his eye again. "Then each little operation we close may leave a vacuum and we'll have no control over who fills it, and we may be winding it down simply so that someone else can wind it up again."

"I know," said his father. "That risk will always be there. But we're not in that much of a hurry. We're talking about a life's work. Getting the legitimate to ease out the criminal by being better business. Making the criminal operations unprofitable. Maybe we're part of an endless cycle. Now we're peaking. In a few generations perhaps there'll be nothing and it will all start again. Who knows? Maybe we can do nothing about it really, but I think the greater risk is in leaving this organization intact to fall into wrong hands. Who knows what Phillip and Stephen could become?"

"I wouldn't wish it on them anyway," said John with feeling. "I'm with you if only for their sakes. It's got to go, no matter how difficult it's going to be."

# Chapter 28

There were several reasons for Peter introducing his son to the true extent of the business earlier than had been the way in the past. One was his own deep weariness. This sometimes felt unbearable, although looking back he remembered tell-tale signs that indicated his own father suffered similarly, so he reasoned that he should be able to cope with it if necessary. But mainly it was the success of John's heat storage discovery.

The prolonged series of increasingly bitter and lengthy winters coupled with poor chilly summers was presenting serious problems to agriculture and industry throughout the world, and the ability to store excess heat at one location and move it to another for controlled release made a substantial contribution to solving many of these problems. Ownership of the system appeared under many guises but was always ultimately vested in the business.

John made a special point of ensuring that Samuel Jenkins received due credit, and took great personal delight in visiting Miss Jenny to tell her a limited version of what had happened. She did not look any older, but she seemed to be a little slower and a little more frail. Tears started down her face as John told his tale, but at the end she smiled and clapped her hands in delight.

"How lovely," she said. "How lovely. Sammy would have been pleased. Mind you, he'd probably never have admitted it." And she laughed. Then, "But I'm awfully sorry about your eye. I did tell you to be careful. Oh, you poor boy."

Peter saw the massive revenue to be gained from the device as an opportunity to start reducing revenue from criminal sources and to begin replacing the bad with the good. And John agreed with him.

"I can't imagine us finding anything else likely to be remotely as successful," he said. "I'm glad you let me in now. It's going to be very interesting."

Slowly but surely, Peter allowed John to take more and more responsibility, while he moved gradually into the background. And slowly but surely John developed the skills and the attitude which showed him to be indeed the rightful successor to the business. The love and warmth of his marriage and the shrewd perceptiveness of his father tempered such tendencies as still remained towards impatience and harshness, and Hugh and Minna proved to be exceptionally able personal aides.

Highly capable observers and negotiators, they became John's eyes and ears, his special messengers. But their contribution had not been observed without contention. Peter found himself taking Joey's role.

"I'm not happy about it, John," he said. "What you're proposing for those two involves their knowing more about the real nature and extent of the business than anyone before except the man at the top. It's against our basic family security. Two pronged. No-one, but no-one, is permitted to know everything, and even though top men have to be bound by personal loyalty, we must also have personal means for their neutralisation if required. At your behest, we have nothing on these two to control them with, and precious chance of killing either if the need arose. Now you want to bring them further in? It doesn't feel right. Time and again it's been people like that who've turned traitor." John opened his mouth to speak, but Peter continued, becoming more and more agitated. "Christ John, even Joey doesn't know half of what you're proposing to tell them and we've all manner of ways of dealing with him. As far as he's concerned and as far as Hugh and Minna should be concerned, we're important officers in a very large international business, the full nature and extent of which is not their concern. It's always been done like that."

"Dad," said John, seizing the opportunity. "You don't know them like I do. They're special. And anyway, I'm not that stupid. There is no need for them to know everything, but they'll have to know more than we've allowed in the past if they're going to be effective on the ground. Times are changing."

"Times maybe, but people never," said Peter. "What if they turn on you?"

John paused. "Then I've no chance, have I?" he said. Both men sat looking at one another. "Trust me dad. Trust my judgement. Hugh and Minna are servants by choice. Even if they knew who I really was it wouldn't interest them in the slightest. They're too clear-sighted. They don't have that kind of ambition. Hell, *I* don't have that kind of ambition, nor you. We do this job because we've no alternative."

Peter nodded. "I'll trust you John. I always have. I've got to admit I've never understood either of them, not really. Go ahead, but be careful," he added reluctantly.

Peter was never wholly comfortable about Hugh and Minna's increasing involvement, but their contribution was substantial and he came near to admitting eventually that he might have worried unnecessarily.

By and large the contraction of the business went fairly smoothly, though part of it was bloody in the extreme. Both Peter and John were anxious to reduce the business's dependence on drugs for income, but this was a most entrenched and intractable sector, and the use of terror and force was inevitably widespread.

Overly recalcitrant traders were killed, as were various customs officers and other public officials who could not be persuaded to take a reduction in their "pensions". However, the killings, for the most part, were not arbitrary. Each was intended to make a specific point to a specific audience and, generally speaking, this proved to be the case. Such examples, plus the use of carefully garnered blackmail material, usually persuaded most "middle management" that early retirement was not too unattractive.

At the end of the trading chain, where the dealers were also customers, it was unavoidably unpleasant, and John became quite depressed at some of the tactics they were having to use.

"We've no alternative, John," said his father. "We always knew it would be bad. At that level, most of them are past all reason."

"But we seem to be catching innocent bystanders as well."

Peter sighed. "Not so innocent, John. If they're dying from our poisoned junk, they're junkies. If they're junkies then they're dead anyway. But while they're walking around they're infectious and spreading contamination. Using doctored junk is unfortunate and admittedly indiscriminate, but there's a limit to the number of people we can conspicuously kill directly. If we attract the wrong publicity, we'll have to slow down and then things will build up again, and even more will have to be dealt with."

John leaned his head back against his chair and closed his eye. "Yes I know," he said. "I'm sorry. I've got to talk about it sometimes or I'll imagine I'm morally justified."

Peter smiled sadly. "Well for what it's worth, as far as we can tell, it is for a greater good isn't it?" he said doubtfully.

"Yes," said John. "I hope so. One fig leaf of mitigation, however withered, is better than none, I suppose. What was it grandfather used to say to you? No ends, no means, only change? Well, we're certainly ending things for a few out there."

Then, the mood left him abruptly, like a cloud passing from the sun.

"Still," he said, standing up. "We don't begin to compare with the traffic statistics, do we? And no-one gives a fig about them."

Eventually all illegal sources of drugs began to dry up and the trading chains were broken beyond repair. Over the years there would be periodic resurgences as various entrepreneurs attempted to move into the gap, but a permanent watching brief was kept on the situation and such individuals usually found it more beneficial to trade in some other line instead.

Extensive and complicated ripples flowed from the hiatus. Addicts were driven in desperation to the usually inadequate legitimate sources of supply and caused such social problems that in many countries legislation had to be enacted to permit controlled supply. Ironically, the legalization and careful controlling of the drug supply sounded the death knell for the residue of the old illegal networks, with their inadequate and now suspect supplies. In less humane countries, addicts received cold turkey, some screaming in jail, some screaming in the streets. Some survived, some did not.

The business still held the manufacturing sources and used its influence to promote legislation which would permit controlled distribution to afflicted individuals, effectively retaining a reasonable proportion of its old customers.

A less publicly conspicuous ripple resulted from the large number of professional killers that the business had been obliged to use in the early stages. The logistics of the campaign had been enormously difficult, and John now had the age-old problem of what to do with a standing army in peacetime. Fortunately, the army did not know it was an army, and over time he was able to arrange that the more incompetent and unstable members be eliminated by the others, thus reducing the number to that more appropriate to the business's day to day needs.

While this went on, John watched his children grow strong and healthy. He spent a great deal of time with them, as did Peter, and ensured that they were quietly and surreptitiously trained, as he had been, against the day when they might have to take over the business.

Phillip was a strong advocate of justice and fair play and was invariably called on to sort out disputes at school, while Stephen would act as a special consultant, assisting when the arguments were finely balanced. Phillip was physically strong and agile but did not have his father's disdain for competitive sport. John frequently found himself stamping his feet fitfully at some school sporting occasion, unsuccessfully trying to find an ounce of enthusiasm in his heart, and though invariably failing, he always took delight in his son's delight.

Stephen was not as big or strong as his brother, although he was graceful and agile in his movements and had enormous stamina. He was totally uninterested in sport but took to aikido and pursued it with a determination far beyond his years. Minna trained with him, at his request, every day before and after school if she was available. At John's behest, she taught him much more than traditional aikido.

"He's remarkable, John," she said. "I don't know how someone his age could come to have such an understanding."

Certainly, Stephen had an uncanny grasp of the effects of avoidance, and not just in physical combat. On more than one occasion John found Phillip bubbling with rage and frustration after an argument with his younger brother.

"What's the matter now?" he asked.

"It's Stephen," gnashed Phillip. "Every time I argue with him, he's not there."

"What do you mean, not there?" laughed John.

"I don't know," Phillip cried desperately. "He's just... not there."

"Well," concluded John. "Seems to me that whether he was there or not, you lost the argument."

Phillip would then be allowed the luxury of jumping up and down on the spot.

Stephen also turned out to be musical. Not only did he inherit a love of music from his parents and his grandparents, but he acquired from somewhere an aptitude for performance. This was discovered by accident one day when he was quite young. Freddy was visiting a friend, and Stephen was left in the charge of the daughter of the house. She noticed the distant sound of childish piano playing, but gave it no thought until the daughter appeared, looking rather apprehensive.

"Mummy," she said. "I can't get Stephen off the piano."

A variety of bizarre images flashed through Freddy's mind as her friend replied: "What do you mean, dear?"

"He won't stop playing," said the girl.

"Stephen can't play the piano," said Freddy, mildly relieved that he was not standing on it, but concerned about his pounding it in the usual manner of children. "Is he making himself a nuisance?"

"No," said the girl. "I just can't get him to come away."

Action being the only recourse left, both the adults got up to go and examine this unexpected mutiny.

The winter sun was streaming through the windows, picking out specks of dust on the shiny black grand piano and falling half across Stephen sitting bolt upright at the keyboard. He was tapping out a television jingle with one finger. The scene took Freddy by surprise, and she was about to stride in and sweep him off the piano stool to return him to the social fold when her friend put a restraining hand on her arm.

"You don't have a piano do you Freddy?" she said quietly.

"No, why?" asked Freddy.

"Where did you learn to play that tune, Stephen?" said the woman, ignoring Freddy's query. Stephen turned and smiled, but did not stop his playing.

"I heard it on TV, you know," then he sang the words to his own accompaniment, a fluting clear voice free from embarrassment and ending in a laugh.

"That's very good," said the woman. "Do you know any more?"

He paused for a moment, then hesitantly started to tap out another tune. The woman went over and sat by him on the long duet stool.

"Try this," she said when Stephen had finished. "See? Shapes."

She played a simple three note arpeggio with her left hand, then the same with her right, an octave higher, then again with her left, yet another octave higher, and so on up the keyboard. Stephen's eyes lit up and he almost elbowed her out of the way to repeat the trick exactly.

The woman stood up and tiptoed back to Freddy. She gestured with her head and silently mouthed "Come on," and Freddy followed her out of the room in some bewilderment.

"What's the matter?" she asked when they reached the next room.

"It's remarkable," said her friend. "I know John and his father like music, but no-one in your house plays anything, do they?"

Freddy shook her head.

"Remarkable," repeated the woman. "Listen, Freddy. Stephen's got an unusual ability. He played those tunes absolutely accurately, note and rhythm, and he sang them correctly. I'm not sure but I think even the pitch may have been correct."

Freddy did not seem to be impressed; her face assumed a polite 'so what' expression. "They're only TV jingles," she said.

"You try playing them," replied her friend with vigour. Then she took up cudgels for Stephen. "More than that, he sat at that keyboard as if he'd been there all his life. Straight, relaxed." She took Freddy's hand. "His wrists and arms were relaxed, and his fingers curled so." She tapped on Freddy's hand in imitation. "Children just don't play like that. It takes ages to get them to do it anything like correctly. Ages, Freddy. It's not my business, but we've known one another long enough. I think you should have someone listen to him. He may have a great talent. I'll give you the name and address of my old teacher. She's very good. Very strict, but very nice with the children, and she'll give you a proper assessment."

Freddy was partly persuaded by her friend's enthusiasm, but Stephen tipped the balance. He was unremittingly excited for the rest of the day, singing and laughing and pestering to go visiting again, even though there was only 'a girl' to play with. John was met at the door and regaled with the whole saga before he reached the living room. He picked up his son and stared at him with exaggerated puzzlement.

"I think I've come to the wrong house. Who's this noisy brat?"

Phillip was torn between the utmost suspicion and giggling involvement by his brother's unexpected ebullience. John was intrigued by the incident when he received a calmer version from Freddy later that evening.

"There can't be any harm in it," he said. "And I've never seen Stephen so excited. He's obviously enjoyed himself enormously."

He took the piece of paper with the name of the piano teacher on it and went to his office. As he sat at his desk, Minna appeared in the doorway.

"Oh, you surprised me John," she said. "It's not like you to work late."

John looked up from the console and smiled. "No-one ever surprises you, Minna, least of all me. You were just frightened of missing something."

"And why not?" she said, moving round to see what he was doing. John swore as he miskeyed. "Here, fumblefingers," she said. "Let me do it."

"I can't get used to this new system of yours," he muttered in mitigation.

"Nonsense," she said tartly, fingers tapping away briskly. "You told me to keep us up to date, and this is it. More storage, quicker access, even better security. You've just got too many thumbs, that's all, you Neanderthal. Here you are."

She handed a paper to him. "Oh," he said in surprise as he read it. "She *is* good. Look at this. Pupils in all the best English music colleges and quite a few abroad. Very impressive. Well we'll see what she makes of Stephen."

So Stephen got his audition. The teacher's house was very ordinary, as was the woman herself, except that she seemed full of life and looked far younger than she really was. John went along as a matter of curiosity, and watched and listened as Stephen performed the little tests she set for him. He was not versed in the technicalities of music, but sitting in the faded armchair, he recognised a professional at work and became aware that this gentle little woman with her friendly, slightly fussy manner, a woman who could not hurt a soul to save her life, had only excellence for a standard, and was more ruthless in its attainment than even he in his own dire work.

"You must understand, Mr. Newman," she said afterwards. "Music is a hard life. Always demanding the highest standards. Very few make a living at it. Stephen has a remarkable aptitude. He's indisputably musical and talented, and whether he takes up music as a career or not, he'll always get great personal satisfaction from it. I'd be happy to take him on as a pupil."

And that was that. A piano was acquired by the household, and John prepared to adjust his son's regime to accommodate the extra work involved. Stephen, however, had other ideas. He got up two hours earlier, unasked and unaided, and applied himself with relish to whatever practice he had been set, plus a variety of other items he had not been set. John would lie in the warmth of his morning bed listening to the sound filtering through the floor. I don't know where *those* genes have come from, Stephen, but I envy you, he thought.

# Chapter 29

Although he was effectively in complete charge of the business, John sat to one side and let his father play the major role when Joey came in to discuss his retirement.

It was an emotional moment. Joey's loyalty was second to none. He had risen up through the ranks when life in the business was far from settled and had protected Peter's father's back on more than one desperate occasion. He had trained Peter and supported him when his father died and, with his vast experience in the business, had for a long time acted as a replacement for the old man while Peter adjusted to his new role. He had also played an important part in the training of John, not only in the selection of instructors, but setting their work in a broader context for the boy.

"I'm just starting to feel tired, Peter," he said. "I'm missing things. Details. Nothing important, but it's not good. We've got such a lot on with this drugs operation. One day I'll slip up badly and..."

"I understand how you feel, Joey," said Peter. "But you take things to heart too much. You set yourself high standards and, for what it's worth, I don't think you're capable of missing anything important, you're far too crafty. You've too many alarm bells built in, it's in your blood."

Joey nodded acknowledgement. "It's kind of you to say so, but I'm not so sure. In any case, it's time Dick got a chance to move up. He's a damn good man and they're hard to find these days. I'd like to recommend him as my replacement, formally."

Peter nodded. "Yes," he said. "I don't think there's any serious debate about that, is there, John? It's what we always intended for him... or, at least, hoped for."

"No problem," confirmed John. "He's like you all over again, Joey. We couldn't get anyone better."

The room became silent for a moment, the stillness broken only by a gentle clicking as Peter twisted his seat from side to side. Abruptly he laughed out loud.

"Jesus Christ," he said. "We're sitting here like a bunch of women at a wake. Joey, you know the rules, the old rules," he added with mock menace. "Nobody retires from the business. You're on indefinite leave on full pay. Dick will take your job and if anything special crops up we'll call you in as a consultant—ok?" Then, without waiting for an answer. "Where are you going to go?"

"Well, I'd like to stay in England," said Joey. "But..." He looked down and shook his head regretfully. "Everything seems to have changed. The place seems to be permanently in winter. Look at it."

He got up and walked to the window. Staring at his own reflection in the dark drizzling glass, he repeated himself. "Look at it. Rain and fog. We're getting miserable damp autumns every year, lousy summers, and we can guarantee snow, can't we? Guarantee it. I'm sure when I was a kid we rarely had a white Christmas. Now we have one every year, and sometimes even a white bloody Easter. I'm getting too old, Peter. The cold and the damp seem to be wearing me down. I'm no sun worshipper, but I'm no bloody Eskimo either. I'll probably go to Australia or South Africa, somewhere were there's a bit more sunshine and I don't have to walk around muffled up looking like a grizzly bear."

Peter nodded. "I don't know if there was more sun when I was young, but I certainly remember it that way."

"Dear me," came the mock plaint from John. "When you two old English gentlemen have finished your meteorological trip down memory lane, perhaps we can get down to details."

Both the older men looked at him indignantly, so he retaliated immediately, leaning back in his chair, puffing out his chest and putting his thumbs in imaginary braces.

"When I were a lad..." he began.

Peter looked for something to throw but contented himself with a dismissive wave.

"You've got no respect for your betters, my lad," he said. "Go and ask Dick to come in. The exercise will do you good."

Richard Gwilier's large frame always looked a little out of scale in the office, and he amply filled the armchair indicated by Peter. He looked a little uncomfortable, and was wondering whether he had slipped up on something important to be called to such a weighty gathering. Peter noted his agitation and went straight to the point.

"Relax, Dick, everything's fine. We just want your opinion on something."

Gwilier eased back into the chair a little more.

Peter continued: "Over the next few months, we'll be increasing your workload quite a bit."

Gwilier's face was impassive, but the news did not please him too much. He had plenty to do already.

"I appreciate you're heavily loaded at the moment, but this is important and I'd like you to think about who you'd recommend as an assistant, to take some of the daily routine work off you."

Gwilier began to look surprised. "Can I ask what all this is about? There are one or two people worth considering, but we're only going through a temporary busy phase. It's a bit hectic, but Joey and I can handle it without bringing someone else in. The way things are going we'll probably be a lot quieter in twelve months, and then we'll have an assistant we don't need."

"John." Peter turned to his son who got up and walked over to the fire. He stood with his back to it.

"Over the next few months, Dick, you'll be busy because Joey will be slowly easing all of his job onto you. He's retiring. Or more correctly, He's going on permanent leave." He smiled. "You're going up, Dick, and so's your income. You've earned the job and you're the only man fit for it."

He walked over to Gwilier and extended his hand. Gwilier stood up, visibly shaken. He took the offered hand and bowed slightly, as in fealty. John placed his other hand on Gwilier's and, large and powerful though he was, Gwilier knew he could not remove his hand from this gentle two-handed grip.

Feeling lightheaded and shaky, he whistled softly.

"I don't know what to say, Mr. Newman." He never could bring himself to call this powerful young man by his first name. "Joey retiring," he said. "I can't believe it."

He looked across at him.

"The ice age, Dick," said Joey, pointing a thumb over his shoulder in the direction of the window. "It's setting in my bones. I need sunnier climes. And old age too," he added. "I need more time to bang the bimbos these days."

"Joey," said John. "You've no sense of solemnity."

But Joey's levity helped Gwilier recover a little, though he was still a little heady.

"I don't know whether I can do the job, Mr. Newman. It's a big responsibility and I'm still learning new things every day."

"We all are," said Peter. "John's told you. You're the only man fit for the job. You're an asset to the business and you've a lot more you can give in the future. You'll do it, no problem, and no further debate."

A sterner note in Peter's final remark brought Gwilier quickly to earth.

"That's it, Dick," said John. "You and Joey can start discussing details. We've still got a business to run."

When the two men had gone, Peter stood up, spun his chair round idly and went and stood by the window to look out through his own image into the black autumn night.

"End of an era, John," he said. "Joey going. End of an era. A last link with the old wartime days even though most of it was really over when he joined us."

John did not speak, but watched his father.

"Still," continued Peter. "He wouldn't say anything, but he's been getting increasingly unhappy for a long time." Then, as if struck by a sudden thought, "I don't think he's ever fully accepted the balancing we do. He's really a fighter, a pusher, an expansionist."

John leaned forward, his face intent. Peter was talking largely to himself.

"He and my father climbed the last part, to the peak. They trampled over the other climbers who were still left and battled endlessly over hazard after hazard and made it to the top. But Joey couldn't see it. Then again, nobody ever told him. In fact, my father took great pains to make sure he never found out." He laughed a little. "As have we. So we can't move without going down, and Joey's always thought we were marking time, consolidating a new base camp as it were, prior to another ascent. One that never came."

John nodded. "Not a bad analogy dad, except that grandfather also helped build the mountain and told you to build it bigger, and now we're taking it down. We'll still be at the top, but the mountain will be smaller."

Peter laughed again and turned from the window. "Too many geological problems if we went up any higher, John," he said airily. "And it was spoiling the view for a lot of people."

Gwilier and Joey sat talking in Joey's office having finished their preliminary arrangements for the takeover. It had proved to be no great chore. Gwilier was already familiar with most of Joey's work, and their debate had concerned itself mainly with a replacement for himself. Their relationship had always been friendly and informal, but now it had changed subtly, and Gwilier felt he was being accepted as an equal, a real friend. Joey was relaxed and expansive.

"I don't know whether I'll miss this place or not when I go," he said, looking round at his modest office. "You couldn't find a better organization to work for, or better people. But the old days..." He pursed his lips and became reflective. "They had a bit of zing. You felt more alive. You could see things happening."

Gwilier raised his eyebrows. "Come on Joey. More alive? You're looking back with rose tinted spectacles. I know the kind of zing you mean. I've had to zing a few myself as you know. The only thing you see happening is blood and guts flying, and the only thing you feel is..." He held out his hand and trembled it significantly.

Joey grunted. "Even so," he said. "It's different these days. I don't seem to fit like I used to. A lot of things seem to have changed. Gradually, but quite definitely."

Gwilier shrugged. "Times change, Joey. Maybe you're right, maybe it is time for you to get off. Maybe I'll have this same conversation with someone in twenty-odd years' time."

Joey smiled. "I hope so, Dick. I hope you'll be here. I think you're going to find life very interesting. I don't know what's at the bottom of this drugs business, but I'm pretty certain young John's got some fancy stroke planned."

"Strategic planning," said Gwilier with a grin. "Ours just to do and die."

Joey laughed. "No Dick, we do, let the others die. Besides, you'll find you'll get more involved in planning from here on."

"What do you think it could be?" said Gwilier thoughtfully.

"No idea," said Joey. "None at all. I never told you of course, but this drugs business came out of the blue. I thought they'd gone bananas at first. The old man would never have done anything like that—he just wanted continual expansion, outward ever outward. But I've got to admit you can see some benefits already in certain areas—those where we were really deep. Incredible really, the planning. Less drugs, more social stability, bigger profits from our other activities. Less crime, less payments for the police..." His face was lit with admiration. "Very classy piece of work. Peter is quite a guy. Different from his dad. More sense of humour, more approachable, but a match for him I'd say when it came to the crunch."

"And John?" queried Gwilier, using his Christian name away from his presence.

Joey became thoughtful. "Yes. John," he said slowly. "I've watched him grow up. He's a throwback. I think he's probably a match for his father and grandfather put together, or he will be in a year or two. Give him everything you've got, Dick. You'll never regret it."

"And Hugh and Minna?" said Gwilier, anxious to glean what he could from this new relationship. Joey did not reply immediately. He shook his head very slowly.

"I don't know, Dick," he said. "The two of them have had some queer thing with John ever since they were at school, and more so since John fished Hugh off that mountain."

He paused, looking for something more helpful to say. "For what it's worth," he said eventually. "I'd say to trust both of them. That's my old-fashioned gut reaction. I can't understand either of them, but I'd trust them—with the business, and with John."

He banged the edge of his fist gently against his mouth as if to shake the words loose. "It's almost as if John was too big for one body, and somehow he's spread into theirs. They're like his eyes and ears, and..." He fell silent again, then quite abruptly his face creased into a smile. "In any case, what could you do if they turned nasty?"

Gwilier nodded in agreement with the implication. "What indeed?" he said. "I suppose I might just manage Hugh on a good day."

"A damn good day," interjected Joey.

"But Minna?" continued Gwilier, puffing out his cheeks and blowing noisily. "Never. I've never seen anyone so dangerous. And they never seem to sleep, either of them. Maybe they can do it with their eyes open."

"And two nicer people you couldn't hope to meet, right?" concluded Joey.

Gwilier raised his hands in acceptance of the point.

"I tell you, Dick. You'll never understand them. Not if you live forever. I don't think anyone will. But I'd still trust them."

# Chapter 30

It was not often that Peter involved himself in business matters any more. He clearly enjoyed his retirement and John was pleased to see him become more as he remembered him when he was a child. He was always a straight, erect man, but his straightness gained a greater lightness as the burden of the business fell from him, and he smiled a great deal more. Equally, John was saddened by the palpable signs of age etched in deep lines in his face, but he consoled himself with the fact that, on balance, Peter was happier now than he had been for many years, and that all of his predecessors had died in office. Peter was the first, if not to officially retire, at least to ease back. It was a hopeful sign.

He kept his father up to date on the state of the business, and weighed carefully any comments he made. But much of the work was routine now that the drugs trade had been reduced to a less corrosive level. Neither could see any opportunity for a major contraction which would not induce other equally serious problems, so John was resigning himself to a long careful pruning of the business.

In its modified form, the business presented far fewer serious problems. A large number of administrative irritations had disappeared with the drugs trade, mainly because there were fewer people to bribe and blackmail into co-operation, and less general social upheaval. This, coupled with the constantly improving computer network and the teamwork of Hugh and Minna, occasionally left John wondering whether he was needed at all. However, this was not too often, and John reflected that he seemed to spend a lot of his time floundering in the gap between power and control. The power could be used to control the big financial institutions, governments and bureaucracies without too much difficulty, because they were, for the most part, highly predictable and unimaginative.

"Governments are no problem," John said to Hugh. "Politicians generally tend to be gullible and vain, concerned more about their public image than the public good, and civil servants are so superbly arrogant. They always imagine that their department employs, or at least has access to, the finest brains in the country. Whereas, by definition, such brains wouldn't dream of working for governments. Their paucity of intellectual ability and vision has to be felt to be believed."

Commerce and industry presented more difficult problems. The larger companies could be manipulated like governments and for not too dissimilar reasons, but smaller ones were very difficult to control, showing an almost limitless ingenuity and cunning in dodging around obstacles intended to lead them in a direction they didn't really wish to follow.

"Don't worry about it. You'll always follow behind people like that," said Peter to John one day when a small British company had slithered from his grasp in patenting a new invention. "The best you'll be able to do is redirect them slightly, unless you go in really heavily, and then you'll risk losing most of the benefits you're after. Don't *you* make the mistake of thinking you employ all the cleverest people on God's earth."

John accepted the rebuke and never forgot it.

"John, I want to see you," came Peter's voice over the internal telephone. "We'll go for a walk. I'll meet you outside in ten minutes."

"A walk?" queried John.

"Yes, a walk. It's a beautiful spring day. I've something I want to discuss with you and I don't want to spend all day cooped up inside. Ten minutes."

He rang off without waiting for a reply. John thought for a moment. His father was up to something, that was obvious. He had been prowling round the office a lot more than usual recently, and Minna reported he had been using the computer to obtain data about their Middle East operations.

He stood up and rearranged some papers on this desk.

"Hugh, we'll have our progress meeting this afternoon if that's okay by you," he said.

Hugh looked up, a little surprised. "Sure. Whatever you want. There's nothing new anyway. Has something come up?"

John shook his head. "No. Dad wants to discuss something, and it looks as if he's intending to take some time over it. Either that or he just wants someone to go for a walk with."

"I doubt that," said Hugh. "He'd be out by now, holding your mother's hand, if that was what he wanted."

"True," replied John, putting on his jacket and looking out of the window. "Come to think of it though, it looks splendid out there. I don't think a walk around the grounds will go amiss."

The walk, however, was not around the grounds. It was over fields bright with spring flowers, and through woods burgeoning bright green with new growth. John had demurred when his father marched smartly out through the gates, crossed the road and clambered over a stile into the field opposite.

"Where on earth are you going, dad?" he asked.

"Are you tooled up?" asked his father sternly, ignoring the query.

"Of course," John replied impatiently.

"Good. Then come along, come along. It's a lovely day, everything's beginning again." And with that, he was marching ahead again.

John shook his head and smiled. "You'll ruin my shoes you know," he shouted after the retreating figure.

His father turned and scowled at seeing John so far behind. He waved an impatient arm. "Come on John. Shift yourself."

As the morning progressed, the two men walked leisurely side by side for many miles. Neither spoke much, but occasionally one would point to a bird or plant or some scurrying animal, and John realized he was walking over fields he had played in as a boy, and where his father had taken him for walks. Closing a gate behind him he looked over a common littered with dusty paths and rocky sandstone outcrops.

"Good lord," he said. "It's years since I've been here."

His father nodded. "Yes. It's a mistake to forget these things," he said.

Eventually they reached a local high spot and sat down on the rocks to gaze at the view. The sun shone bright on the river below, and on the distant sea, and birdsong seemed to fill the blue sky overhead.

"Here," said Peter, throwing an apple to his son. "You'd usually be pestering for something by now."

John caught the apple and stared at it. He'd been thinking exactly the same thing and he felt a tightening in his chest. He bit the apple noisily, it tasted as only an apple can after a long warm walk.

"What did you want to see me about, dad?" he said, with his mouth full.

"Oh yes," said his father. "I nearly forgot. I got so engrossed. Here..." he fished a newspaper out of his pocket and handed it to his son. "Read that."

He pointed vaguely at an article on the front page. John read it out loud. "Wolves escape from local zoo. Animal liberation campaigners today released a pack of wolves from..."

"No," said his father impatiently. He took the folded paper out of John's hand and turned it over. "That." He prodded with his finger.

The article announced that a General Haran had taken control as Head of the state of Tier d'Ynide, a small middle eastern country formed in the not too distant past by a rebel secessionist group. Its neighbour, Tier r'Vern had been formed similarly, and the two countries, initially because of the manner of their formation and then subsequently for other good and solid reasons, were largely ostracized by the rest of the international community.

Tier d'Ynide was a brutal military technocracy in which every conceivable technological device was used to control the population. Haran had been effective Head of State for several years, as right-hand man to the founder of the state who had slowly been sinking into senility. He it was who had perverted the founder's vision of bringing prosperity to his land and his people through the use of technology, and he it was who led it towards an Orwellian future. Part of Tier d'Ynide' s judicial calendar actually included Thoughtcrime in honour of this idea. His latest endeavours were rumoured to be the use of electrode implants for the control of prisoners, with a view subsequently to their being used on the entire population. But that was all that ever came out of d'Ynide—rumours.

Tier r'Vern was also a brutal police state, but a religious one, led by an obsessive leader known to his flock as the Great Father. No-one knew who the Great Father was or from where he came, his origins having been carefully mythed over. But his sway over his people was almost total, and any ripples of dissent were dealt with by his Holy Police Force, the Angels, who specialized in techniques similar to those of the Inquisition for purifying the souls of doubters.

All the major powers had dabbled with these countries in the early days, and all had been badly bitten in one way or another. The official consensus thus became to leave well alone, in the hope that eventually the two states would crack through their own rigidity. Unofficially, however, d'Ynide' s technical expertise and r'Vern's massive mineral wealth had ensured the development of a fairly vigorous network of black market traders who were known and used by most governments. Unfortunately, both countries also used these networks to export terrorism to deal with their 'enemies' in exile, and such terrorism in turn led to the growth of para-military opposition groups. In spite of the fairly frequent and bloody confrontations that occurred amongst these warring nationals in major foreign capitals, no serious action was taken by the international community to deal with the black marketeers. On the whole, it was felt, again unofficially, that their advantages outweighed their disadvantages.

The only thing that made strong men go pale in the corridors of power was the occasionally rumoured possibility that the two countries might come to some accord with one another. The combination of mineral wealth and technical expertise and two large fanatical and controlled populations, both possessed of the Great Truth and with a duty to proselytize, would dangerously destabilize the world's uneasy power structure, and the consequences would be incalculable. The spectre haunted many a government in its weaker hours, but consolation was twofold. The two people, though racially related, were culturally very different and were currently under orders to hate one another cordially. Then although they shared a short border, it was mountainous and difficult terrain and was divided by the turbulent Renviss Straits, a fifteen-mile-wide channel of thunderous, constricted melt waters from the mountains in the north. The Straits were almost unnavigable and because of the shortness of the border were easily accessible to the air defences of neighbouring countries. The imagined roar of the Renviss Straits had lulled to sleep more than one uneasy ministerial head.

John refolded the paper and looked at his father.

"So?" he said.

"What do you know about Tier d'Ynide and Tier r'Vern, John?" asked his father.

John shrugged. "Not a great deal. Hugh would know more—he drew the short straw for that area. They're two, newish, mad-dog middle eastern states. They're both dictatorships, but both seem to have a lot of support from their own people. And they specialize in exporting trouble."

His father nodded. John continued. "We get a lot of income from the illegal trading in the area, but it's expensive. Very high overheads. We have to pay people a lot to work there. The risks of 'accidental' death tend to be very high, even when we've some form of official protection. In many ways I'd prefer us to be out of there, but it's not really feasible."

Peter was slicing a blade of grass with his thumbnail. "Yes, I know," he said. "We've a lot of minor contacts, legal and illegal, who'd be left-high and dry and, as usual, plenty who'd move in after we left. But I've got some thoughts I'd like to discuss with you."

John leaned back on the sun warmed rock. "Floor's yours, dad. Fire away."

Peter laid the piece of grass down by his side and flicked it with his finger. "Ok. Let's agree some basic facts first."

John nodded sluggishly.

"Looking at the business as a whole, do you think we're making real progress towards reducing it and cleaning it up?"

John thought for a moment before answering. "We're making some progress, but it's certainly not spectacular. Heaven knows we've looked for another equivalent to the drugs business that we could hatchet but, as you know, there isn't anything comparable. We're victims of our own diversification."

"Hence the piecemeal careful reductions we agreed?"

"Exactly."

"But what do you think of the progress," repeated his father.

John sat up and sighed. "I've got to admit it's not good, dad. When you're messing about with small operations, new ones tend to spring up while you're cutting out the old ones. Really, we're too static, and to be honest it worries me quite a lot. I can see me footling around like this for the rest of my life and effectively nothing happening." He paused. "And there's always the risk it will all take off again."

"And the cause?" asked Peter. John looked at his father in puzzlement. "Bear with me, John. The cause?"

John leaned back again. "As I remember, we discussed this at some length the day you showed me the real size of the business, and reached no great conclusion."

Peter nodded. "Yes, I know, but take it further back," he said.

John blew out a long breath and looked thoughtful. "Well," he said. "I suppose if you go right back it's some kind of security thing."

Then he elaborated, jostled along occasionally by interjections from his father.

Groups of people learn to live with one another by having rules. Family rules, clan rules, and so on. Then the big clans turn these into laws as society becomes bigger, more complicated. That makes the smaller groups feel threatened again, insecure, so they start working to their own local family, clan rules again.

John nodded to himself. "The priority then becomes to obey the family's rules. Rules based on personal loyalties. Sod society's rules if necessary. But people are unconscionably fidgety apes, and vicious with it. They want security and resent authority both at the same time. A pack leader's life is difficult. Loyalties break down and change for all manner of reasons and you end up with endless manoeuvring and struggling for power and position. I suppose it's those who can both fight and talk who eventually take over."

"Very eloquent," mocked Peter gently.

John looked at him beadily. "Maybe," he said. "But we didn't come out here to play amateur sociologists, did we? What are you driving at?"

Peter looked at him purposefully. "So the problem we have is?"

John returned his gaze and then shrugged. "People, I suppose."

"People, of course," said his father definitively. "There's no point mincing words. Our grand plan is getting nowhere since the drugs trade was cut to size, and there's always a risk it'll start expanding again for exactly the reasons you've outlined. We've too many people. Too many clever, ruthless and ambitious people who know their trade and who breed their own kind. They're our root problem, they're the ones who have to be eliminated."

John grimaced. "I must admit, dad, I'd never thought of it in quite those terms, and you're probably right, but it doesn't seem to help the matter very much. I can't arrange an international Valentine's Day Massacre, can I? Or rather, I can, but the repercussions don't bear thinking about. We'd find ourselves oscillating back into the old days within weeks. You know that."

Peter raised his hand. "OK John. Don't get impatient. I'm not quite senile yet. I fully appreciate the problem. I'm just trying to make you look again at something you think you look at every day, but in fact don't. I want to give you the germ of an idea that I think might eventually give us the massacre we need without the bloodshed and without the repercussions."

John looked at the apple core he had been holding for some minutes. "I'm sorry, dad. I'm listening." He threw the core into some nearby bushes. "A gift to the mountain."

His father began. "Our main legitimate contact in both countries is Ralph Lowson, isn't it?"

Later that night Peter sat in his usual chair staring pensively into the fire. It had been an almost perfect day, full of sunlight, with life bursting out unhindered by the crushing winter. John had listened to his idea, and he knew it would germinate and come to fruition under his son's care in due course, and bring nearer the end of the furrow he had started to plough when he first took over the business.

"You alright, love?" said Ann, coming quietly into the room.

"Yes, fine," he said. "I was just thinking. It's been a good day. I enjoyed my walk and chat with John."

Ann smiled. "I thought you were worrying about something, sitting here in the dark."

"No," he said. "I like the dark. It's relaxing." He smiled. "And the fire will keep the wild animals away."

"Would you like a drink of coffee?"

"Lovely," he nodded. "Put Stephen's record on first if you would. The Debussy, L'isle Joyeuse."

Ann smiled again. Stephen had become a very able pianist. Not destined to become one of the world's greatest by any means, but a considerable musical talent for all that, and quite capable of sustaining a career as a concert pianist if he so chose. He had made a record at the behest of his father as an anniversary gift for his grandparents, and it was one of the few physical possessions that Peter cherished.

Ann put on the record and moved to the door. "He puts everything he's got into the end of this," said Peter. "It's terrific."

Ann paused in the doorway listening.

"Hey," said Peter. Ann cocked her head on one side. "I love you," he said. She smiled and winked as she closed the door.

Peter sat staring into the fire and closed his eyes slowly as the music soared to its conclusion.

A few minutes later, Ann returned carrying two mugs of coffee. The record had stopped automatically, and her husband was in the chair with his eyes still closed and a slight smile on his face. She put the mugs on the hearth and touched his arm gently.

"Peter. Your coffee," she said. He did not stir. She shook him a little harder. His head slumped forward. Like his father before him, he had picked his moment and died.

# Chapter 31

Ralph Lowson came to Peter's funeral at John's invitation. He was several years older than John, but had an equivocal ageless look about him, his greying hair belying his generally youthful demeanour, and his bright eyes and battery of smiling teeth illuminating what would otherwise have been a lean saturnine face.

"It's good of you to come, Mr. Lowson," said John, returning the handshake. "My father thought very highly of you and the work you do."

"You're very kind, Mr. Newman," replied Lowson. "I'm only sorry that we should meet for the first time under such sad circumstances."

John nodded and looked down. "Yes. It's because my father was talking about you the day he died that I asked you to come. I appreciate you're a busy man, but tomorrow I've some business ideas I'd like to discuss with you. I think you'll find them interesting."

Then, excusing himself, he moved away to greet other arrivals.

Lowson sat in an armchair and looked around at the assembled group. He knew Ann by sight and Gwilier quite well, but the others were strangers to him. From family likeness he identified Newman's grandsons—tall and well-built albeit not with his colouring. The genetic line persists, he thought. They were sitting attentively by their grandmother on a long couch while she was talking to someone. Gwilier's big frame was wedged in the far end of the room and Lowson looked at the couple he was talking to. As if aware of his gaze, the slender woman in a black suit turned and stared straight at him. There was nothing unpleasant in her face, indeed it was friendly and strikingly handsome, but Lowson felt the hairs on his neck rise, and his throat went dry. The man also turned to look at him, and under their combined gaze Lowson felt as if he were going to choke, until Gwilier passed between the couple and moved across to him.

"Ralph. Nice to see you." His great hand engulfed Lowson's. "You're looking a bit peaky. Long journey?"

"Bit rough," lied Lowson, standing up, hoping to shake the fear out of himself. To his amazement he found his knees were shaking.

"Come and meet Hugh and Minna. They'll be interested to meet you."

Introductions made, Lowson began to feel a little more at ease, but he made a powerful mental note to avoid dealing with this strange couple unless it was absolutely necessary.

"Well, well," said Hugh. "So you're Lowson Construction. It's a pleasure to meet you. You're our strong arm in the wild and woolly east. I really don't know how you manage out there."

Lowson smiled and winked. "Local knowledge," he said. "These people always want something building, and they've always plenty money and plenty cheap labour, and precious few regulations regarding their welfare."

"Sounds rather harsh," said Minna.

"It is, Miss Adrin," replied Lowson, just managing to keep his voice from trembling. "It's difficult to imagine what it's like especially if you're born and brought up in a country like England. They're a harsh people with a harsh history, living in a harsh terrain, and if my firm didn't do their work, someone else would."

Minna smiled and bowed slightly, but offered no comment.

After a few minutes' cursory conversation, Lowson beat as dignified a retreat as he could, excusing himself and moving over to offer his condolences to Ann. He held her hand gently. "It might not mean much to you, Mrs. Newman, but if it hadn't been for your husband, my company wouldn't exist now. It's a sad day for us all."

During the short ceremony, Lowson pondered his first real contact with the Newman family. Lowson Construction was a large multi-national organisation, but he knew that the Newman's financial interests could buy it twice over and not miss the money. And yet they looked such a prosaic English family, living over the shop in their old English house. He himself lived the way he felt rich people ought to live, his lifestyle conspicuous and extravagant. His many houses in many countries were large and lavish, and his various appetites matched them. He had never been able to tempt Peter Newman into any form of excess on the few occasions when Peter had visited him abroad, and his privileged position in Tier r'Vern and Tier d'Ynide gave him a very wide range of excesses to offer. Peter had just smiled, thanked him and bowed out, and so had Gwilier, although, he suspected, a touch more reluctantly.

The ordinariness of the Newmans disturbed him. Faithful marriages, loving children. Somehow it was wrong. He had noticed, however, that the house was a discreet fortress, with probably a great deal more out of sight, and some of the people there made him feel distinctly vulnerable. He found himself shuddering unexpectedly at the thought of Minna Adrin. Whatever she was, she struck a terrifying chord deeper within him than his mind was prepared to go. He looked across the aisle of the chapel to where she was standing, a few rows in front of him. As he looked, she turned her head slightly as if listening, and he dropped his head and fumbled with the prayer book with unsteady hands.

And yet for all this feeling of submerged power, here he was, standing surrounded by genuine grief. There was nothing he could feel that was typical of the undercurrents that usually flowed on such occasions. He was with an ordinary family that had just lost a beloved father figure, while the death of a powerful magnate usually brought out old tensions and rivalries, plus barely disguised relief and shufflings for position, with lawyers waiting in the wings sharpening their knives for the carving of the estate. Question mark followed question mark.

The day after the funeral, Lowson and John met to discuss the idea that John had mentioned. John hadn't slept at all and it showed. Freddy had done what she could to ease his burden, but in the end he got up and prowled around the house and grounds in an attempt to quieten his seething brain. Neither the cool night air nor the effort had worked, and his face looked uncharacteristically grey and drawn in the morning light.

"You'll forgive me if I'm a little terse, Ralph. I may call you Ralph?"

Lowson nodded.

"To be absolutely honest I'd much rather be elsewhere, but we're both busy men with others dependent on us and we can't afford the luxury of such preferences, can we? Regrettably, business must carry on as usual."

Lowson nodded again. "Yes, it's not easy, sometimes," he said.

John stood up and started pacing to and fro as if to shake off his mood.

"You're a rich and powerful man, Ralph," he said. "And like most rich and powerful men, your main ambition is to become richer and more powerful. Is that a fair observation?" He stopped walking and looked at Lowson.

"It's blunter than I'm used to and perhaps a bit over-simplified, but it'll do for a summary," replied Lowson, a little winded by the abrupt approach.

John began pacing again. "Thanks to your ability to capitalize on the head start my father gave you, you're one of the few people who has anything approaching direct access to, and to some extent the confidence of, the leaders of Tier r'Vern and Tier d'Ynide."

He paused, and Lowson watched him.

"I've reasonably direct access to Haran," he said. "But only the Guardian Angels have access to the Great Father. As for confidence, well I..." He shrugged.

"But you're nearer to the Great Father than any other foreigner?" John pressed.

Lowson nodded. "Yes, I suppose so," he said reluctantly.

Suddenly John spun his chair round, sat down in it and turned to face Lowson directly. "If these two countries, with their respective resources and large populations, could co-operate with one another, they would form a very rich and powerful alliance, teeming with opportunities for people such as ourselves. Especially if we had helped bring this alliance about. Wouldn't that be so?"

Lowson smiled nervously. "Possibly. But your 'if' says everything that can be said about the idea," he replied.

John looked at him intently for a few seconds and then grinned as if he had just seen something surprising.

"No, it doesn't," he said. "You've had this same idea yourself if I'm any judge, and the only thing that's stopped you is lack of funds and back-up."

Lowson's mouth dropped open momentarily and then he too grinned. "Only pipe dreams, Mr. Newman," he said. "Only pipe dreams. I've never really seriously considered it."

"Then do so now," said John. "Very seriously."

Lowson leaned back and crossed his legs as he prepared to take charge of the proceedings in his capacity as local and technical expert.

"Mr. Newman," he began. "It's quite possible that Haran could be persuaded of the value of such an arrangement, he's a cynical and highly pragmatic bastard. I suspect the Great Father also could be similarly persuaded, although he's a much less stable character, and a very oblique approach would be needed. Given that, it'd probably not be a massive effort by either to persuade their respective followers to see the new light. But..." He paused and lifted his hands for emphasis. "The proposition simply isn't practical. There's not even a simple road between them. You know about the Renviss Straits?"

John nodded. "In general terms," he said. "Go on."

"Well, that's it," continued Lowson. "Simple, routine daily travel isn't available and without that, any kind of major co-operation isn't an option." Then he leaned forward, more confidentially. "And even if it were, their neighbours wouldn't sit still for an alliance like that. They'd be the first to get the chop and they know it. They watch the Straits like hawks as it is, and if things got rough they'd be able to destroy any transport crossing over."

He sat back and waited for an acknowledgement of his contribution.

"That's broadly my own assessment," said John. "The problem of mass communication, transport, is paramount. Planes and ships are too small and too vulnerable."

Lowson nodded.

"So we'll build a road."

Lowson started. "You're joking," he said half derisively. "Across the Straits?"

John nodded.

"It can't be done," said Lowson definitively, slumping back in his chair. John also leaned back.

"Ralph. Don't give me all that 'can't be done' nonsense," he said, conscious of his father's shade at his elbow. "Of course it can. All it needs is money and expertise. I can arrange the first, you can provide the second."

Lowson closed his eyes and endeavoured to collect his rapidly scattering thoughts.

"But you've no idea what such a venture would cost. Neither country can possibly afford it," he said at last.

"Not on their own, no, I agree with you," John said. "But when they've joined together, and with the appropriate advice, they'll be more than able to afford it. We'll get our money back and more, and a massive stake in both countries."

Lowson shook his head. "You're forgetting international opinion. They'll screw anyone who touches a venture like that, and... and..." He stuttered. "And a road would still be vulnerable to attack."

John opened the drawer of his desk and pulled out a file. "Valid points Ralph, quite valid. International opinion is tricky, I grant you, but I think it can be handled. Defence is no problem. Our little causeway, our viaduct, may be static but in being static it can be used as a base for defensive weapons systems, an aspect that will bring in some enthusiasm from one or two people I know in the arms trade."

He flicked through the file casually. "I haven't really given you a fair idea of our proposals. But I needed to see your immediate reactions. Have a look at this before you go."

He handed the file to Lowson. "I appreciate this has all been rather sudden, but my father spoke highly of you and judging from your record, I think you're the man for the job."

Lowson looked at the file.

"It's only outline, of course," said John. "But it goes into the matter in greater detail than we've been able to discuss in these few minutes. I know I can rely absolutely on your confidence. Just let me know yes or no when you leave. If it's no, give me your assessment of why. If it's yes, give me any thoughts that come immediately to mind, and we'll set things in motion for working out the details."

Later that morning Lowson asked to be excused from lunch with John and Freddy.

"Perhaps he's still recovering from the travelling," said Freddy.

John smiled. "No. He's fit as a flea. He's just reading a business proposition I put to him this morning."

"Hm," grunted Freddy. "It's either very long or very gripping. You're a hard taskmaster, John, making him work at your father's funeral."

John's face became thoughtful. "Yes. I'm afraid I'd no real control over the timing. Ironically, it's dad's idea he's looking at. I've been working on it solidly since we came back from that walk."

He fell silent. Freddy looked at him, then put a hand on his shoulder.

"It's kept my mind occupied," he said. "And dad wanted me to get on with it quickly. It's important."

"What's Lowson got to do with it?" asked Freddy.

John's face cleared. "Oh. It's the biggest opportunity he's ever had. If you listen carefully, you'll probably hear him laughing hysterically. I expect he's read it about ten times in sheer disbelief."

Freddy smiled to see John's spirts returning.

"What is it?" she asked, pushing him to one side as she started to lay the table.

John waved his hands vaguely. "Just a rather heavy construction job abroad," he said. "But very lucrative, and just up his street."

"He mightn't want it," said Freddy. "He might say no."

John laughed outright. "Not in a million years, Freddy, not in a million years."

And, of course, he was right. Lowson, having studied the report, saw vistas open before him that in spite of his ambition he had never imagined existed. The risks in the scheme were not small, but the returns were sufficiently large to make them irrelevant, or at least acceptable, and the whole was helped by the official isolation of the two countries, so assiduously maintained by the rest of the world.

"You'll understand, of course," said John as he walked with him across the tarmac to his private plane. "That I'm not alone in this venture. No one organization could possibly fund such an operation," he lied. "But from now on, security is everything. All contact between us will be by courier and encrypted message. You needn't concern yourself with the aliases and dummy companies that will be used to distance us from the deed, but be assured they will be extensive."

He took Lowson's arm. "I've breached security already in contacting you personally, but my father said you were to be trusted and he persuaded the others that it would be safe. I felt your part was so important that you were entitled to know the whole picture, bar the names of the backers of course. But then, even I don't know all of them."

He was interrupted by a large jet flying low overhead and filling the air with its monstrous din. He grimaced. "I've got to emphasize what it says in the report, Ralph. If any public mention is made of the scheme at this stage, it'll vanish instantly. And if my name's mentioned, so will I."

Lowson nodded. "I understand perfectly," he said. "And if you vanish then my company vanishes too. You still own most of it."

John smiled and placed an arm around Lowson's shoulder. "I'd forgotten that," he said. "But that's not what I meant. You're the last of my worries. It's the security awareness of our future clients I'm uncertain about."

Lowson shook his head vigorously. "Forget it," he said. "You've no problem there at all. I'll deal with everything personally, naturally, but it doesn't really matter. You need to understand these people. Both Haran and the Great Father are paranoid and they maintain power by inducing paranoia in everyone else. Nobody dare trust anybody, because everyone, and I mean *everyone*, is likely to be an informer. Once a thing is marked with an official seal, especially the leader's seal, people won't even admit to having seen it."

"Good," said John. "It doesn't sound very pleasant, but it's certainly reassuring."

He held out his hand and Lowson took it. "Do nothing for now Ralph. I'll be in touch within the next few weeks."

When Lowson had embarked with one last acknowledging wave from the doorway, John turned and walked towards his car without looking back.

That night he sat alone in his darkened office, the absence of his father dominating his thoughts. The darkness of the office mirrored his own inner darkness. *You picked a hell of a time to go, dad,* he thought resentfully, then he wrinkled his face in self-deprecation. *Still, you went in style. Quietly, but in style. I hope I go as neatly.* His thoughts about his father clattered to and fro without release or relief. Repeatedly he crammed them into a corner and turned his mind to his father's grand design, but they flooded back every time, until eventually he closed his eyes and leaned back in his chair and waited alone in the darkness until they had all run their course.

After a while, they settled into a sad steady rumble and he tried to turn his mind to the new project again, but it was too hard. He sighed.

"Too tired," he said out loud. The sound of his own voice seemed odd and startled him back to normal. He stood up and looked around the office. *I can see why you brought me into the business dad,* he thought, *and for what it's worth I forgive you. I've little or no love for it, but I wouldn't be elsewhere. Some destiny, eh? I'll pull your last scheme through. It's a good one. I doubt I'd have ever thought of it. Even if it finishes me it'll leave things clear for Phillip and Stephen.*

He closed the office door gently behind him and walked softly back to his home.

In the shade along the corridor, Minna wiped a tear from her eye as she watched him go.

# Chapter 32

The next day, John called Hugh, Minna and Gwilier to his office and told them to keep the rest of the day free. After he had outlined part of his father's idea, and told them of his meeting with Lowson, he invited comments. Minna had been fidgeting for some time.

"Christ, John," she burst out, unusually profane. "You shouldn't have been so direct with Lowson. He's not family. I'm not happy about this. It exposes you and puts you right on top when it all comes out. And why on earth do we want to get so involved with these two lunatic countries? It's bad enough dealing with them on the fringes."

The others expressed agreement. Minna had summarized their misgivings succinctly and accurately. John avoided answering the main thrust of her concern.

"What makes you unhappy about Lowson, Minna? He's just your average multi-millionaire chief executive of an international company. A public face and a private one. The public one is honest and confident enough, if rather brash." Minna snorted quietly. "While the private one gets on with all the corruption, blackmail, general hatchet work and so on, that are a necessary part of international commercial life."

"Brash is putting it very mildly," said Minna with distaste. "For our purposes, he's grotesquely ostentatious. Far too many people know him, and far too many know what he's really like. He's a weak link John. He's too vulnerable. You must see it."

John looked at the others, raising his eyebrows.

"I think Minna's right," said Gwilier. "He lives like a potentate when he's out there—an incredible lifestyle. And when he's back in the west he gets as near as he can to it by playing the playboy. Getting himself photographed everywhere and screwing everything in sight."

"Your main concern then is what?" asked John. "That he's well known, or that he's promiscuous? These don't affect his value as our agent."

Hugh's face wrinkled in puzzlement. "John, you're not usually so obtuse," he said. "What are you up to? You know perfectly well what concerns us. Lowson's whole lifestyle indicates instability. His whole record shows that he doesn't know what he wants but is boundlessly ambitious. He's exactly the kind of person that the business has spent years weeding out. He's quite capable of working out some cock-eyed, half-baked scheme for his own ends that will screw up everything. And because you've approached him directly, you'll go too. Even a hint of a link between you and him in a venture like this and you'd be the centre of all manner of publicity and probably legal investigation."

John smiled. "Yes, Hugh. I agree with everything you've said. All of you in fact. Unfortunately, Lowson's a key man in this scheme. He's the only one with the necessary contacts and I wanted to check we were all of the same opinion. We can work out details later, but I'm working on the principle that a weak link ceases to be a weak link once it's known about."

"John," said Minna wearily. "This is all irrelevant. You haven't answered my question. What is the point of this scheme? It hinges, at least initially, on Lowson, who is arguably not prime material. It's massively public. It'll bring the world's media far too close, and if it succeeds, what then? The gains are debatable. We'll get more from Tier r'Vern and Tier d'Ynide admittedly, but the trouble they'll cause in the rest of the world will make endless problems for us. We'll go out of balance, John. We'll be making an expensive rod for our own backs. Why, John? It just doesn't make sense."

John rattled a pen between his teeth and started twisting his chair from side to side.

"Hugh, Dick. What do you think?" he said.

"I agree with Minna," said Hugh. "I know it's your father's scheme John, his last idea, but it's wrong."

"I've been out there," said Gwilier. "I think it can be managed, but I can't see the point. Haran and the Great Father are dangerous people, and vicious beyond belief. If they ever get together they'll wreak havoc, and a lot of our other interests will suffer as a result. Places like that are only of any value to us when everywhere else is basically stable."

John rattled his pen again and looked at the three of them. Their responses had been as he had anticipated and he was pleased with their criticism so far. He smiled broadly.

"Well?" he said. "Finish it off."

Hugh and Minna read the sign in their old friend and relaxed. Gwilier felt the change of mood and realized he was suddenly on his own, and something was expected of him. *Give him everything you've got*, came back to him. He took a risk.

"I don't think this is your father's scheme. It's too stupid." He paused thoughtfully and then raised a qualifying finger. "Unless it's part of some other, bigger scheme. Something very big, like when we cut the drugs trade down to size." He snapped his fingers softly. "That's it. It's something to short circuit all this small-time pruning we've been doing."

John looked at him for a long time in silence, and Gwilier wondered if he had overstepped some mark.

"Good," said John eventually. "Very good. Joey did well when he found you, Dick." He looked extremely pleased. Then he stood up. "But I'm afraid I'm going to have to ask you to keep that as your guiding light for a long time. It's not in your interests to know any more at this stage except that what's afoot is for everyone's greater good and it's going to require our best endeavours to make it work —our very best. And in spite of the extra work that will be involved, everything else must carry on as normal."

When Gwilier had left the room, John returned to his seat.

"Dick's still too much of a gangster for the whole truth yet, but he'll be alright in the end," he said. Then, leaning back, he looked at his two friends. "Now I'll tell you what it's really about."

When he had finished, the room was silent. His listeners sat still and assessed the magnitude of the venture he had described. He had outlined the need, which was indisputable, and he had outlined the various alternatives, all of which would be too slow. It was a scheme that fitted the size of the business and would be for its greater good indeed. Hugh and Minna said nothing, but they were patently excited.

"I don't want to discuss any details now," said John. "Just spend the next few days getting used to the idea. It's going to take a long time to implement, but we can do it, and we can do it well. In fact, we've got to."

Minna could not contain herself any longer. She let out a great laugh and clapped her hands. "It's terrific, John, magnificent. Like a Wagnerian opera. When do we start?"

John raised his hands as if to ward off this enthusiasm. "We'll start preliminary planning next week, Minna. Let it stew for a day or two."

When he was alone, John stood up and walked over to the window. He loosened his tie as the warmth of the Spring sun fell on him. His dark mood of the previous evening had disappeared under the day's work, but it returned now, though with much less intensity. He knew it would become fainter and fainter, but it would never leave him—nor did he particularly want it to.

Opening the window, he leaned out and breathed in the scents of the garden. He felt very relaxed. All the simple pleasures he valued were a monument to his father, and he honoured it. A faint sound rose up from below, a mixture of piano playing and voices. He could not make out what was happening, but he recognised both Stephen's playing and his mother's voice.

Stephen had been particularly distressed by the circumstances of Peter's death and Ann had taken him under her wing after the funeral. Although unable to grieve outwardly himself, John understood his son's pain, but had difficulty in offering solace, and he was content to leave his mother to occupy herself thus. He could not, however, forebear a wry observation that his mother's wing was not always the downy bed one might expect.

"Your ma's a tough old bird," Peter would say, whenever he was obliged to retreat in disarray from the hearth for some misdemeanour, and John had always found it to be an apt description.

Stephen also found this out fairly quickly. His grandmother gave him comfort and support through his first adult tears and his first glimpse of the moving gown of mortality, but she prevented grief turning to self-indulgence with impeccable timing.

"I'll never be able to play that piece again," said Stephen mournfully.

"Yes, you will" said Ann flatly. "Go and play it right now—right now! We've both got to get used to it."

Reluctantly Stephen moved to the piano and began to play. It was a lifeless performance, and towards the end he stopped with tears streaming down his face.

"I'm sorry, gran," he said, wiping his eyes and then blowing his nose. "I can't do it."

Ann was breathing deeply to control her own tears. She narrowed her eyes theatrically.

"I should think you should be sorry," she said brusquely. "I've never heard you play so badly."

The change in tone startled Stephen and his face assumed a hurt look.

"Gran. I can't do it," he said, plaintively. "It's too upsetting."

Without a word Ann marched over to the piano and, leaning on it, looked squarely into her grandson's face.

"Stephen. You're a professional musician, or you pretend to be. Don't give me that 'can't'. You play and you play well, no matter what you feel like, no matter what the circumstances. Did your grandfather teach you nothing? Now get on with it."

She picked up the piano score and stood behind him so that he would not see her tears.

"I'm not going to have a splendid piece of music spoilt just because your grandfather happened to be listening to it when he died. If it's good enough for him to die to, it's good enough for you and me to live to. Play!"

It was a masterclass such as he had never had, but by the end, both could begin to face the memories that the piece brought to them.

It was the shadows of this exchange that drifted up to John as he leaned on the windowsill. He did not know what was happening, but judged from his mother's tone that Stephen was being lifted well clear of the Slough of Despond, hosed down and dumped on dry land.

He left the window open and returned to his desk. Picking up a pen, he doodled "Lowson" on the pad in front of him. He doubted that Lowson was going to be a weak link in the early stages, his greed and ambition would ensure his silence very effectively. Anyone who survived over there, especially one who knew both sides, had to know when to keep his mouth shut. But at the end? He doodled question marks around the name. That really would have to be worked out in great detail. A light gust of wind from the window curled up the edge of the paper he was working on and brought with it the sound of Stephen's playing again. Almost certainly the details would be different from those envisaged now. Plans change, especially long-term ones. Anything might happen. One of the beloved leaders might be assassinated or overthrown in a coup, or their zeal in encouraging international terrorism might provoke an international response.

"Or there might be an earthquake," he said out loud scornfully, throwing his pen lightly onto the desk and leaning back. As soon as he had said it he remembered that it was indeed an earthquake area, and he smiled at his inadequate irony. He dismissed the conjectures from his mind. Whatever happened, the end object of the scheme would remain in view and would be achieved. The business was big enough, flexible enough and had sufficient resources and talent to ensure it.

Stephen's distant playing filled the room and turned John's mind to consideration of his children. Both had been surreptitiously and rigorously trained as he himself had been, and while he had to admit he did not have his father's touch, he had been able to retain their friendship and affection as they had grown up and gone their separate ways.

Phillip was very much like himself, and already working on the fringes of the business. He would ultimately take over as its head. But Stephen was more of a puzzle. Competent, even adept in all the same skills as his father and brother, he seemed to do them with a sense of willing duty rather than interest or enthusiasm but, apart from the initial selection of his tutors and ensuring he was approached by the right agent, he had carved his own way as a professional pianist. John found his youngest son enigmatic. He could not sense what was deep down inside him. Could he take charge of the business if necessary? Would he want to? Would he quarrel with his brother and wreck the business with an internecine power struggle as had happened in the past?

John shrugged impatiently. Details, details, he thought. The kid was sound enough. The world of the professional musician was no more all sweetness and light than the world of any average businessman, and Stephen would invariably discuss his tactics and plans with his father for ensuring he was heard by the right people at the right time, and given the right kind of exposure in the press and television. John helped him with advice when he could, but some instinct prevented him using the business to artificially promote his son, and while he could never really get used to the bloody-handed sword-wielding that occurred in the music business, he could see that Stephen was more than able to look after himself. Genes will out, he mused, and new ones will sneak in.

He went to the window and shut it gently, blotting out Stephen's quiet intrusion. Returning to his desk, he tapped instructions into his computer. Lowson's history appeared on the screen and John stared at it for some time, wondering if he had missed anything the first time he had studied it.

Ralph Lowson had had a fair battering in his time. His father had built up the family business from nothing into a large international construction company. Against all advice he had overextended it during a boom period only to have it collapse when the boom ended. A wild ranting individual possessed of a fair streak of megalomania, he could not face the fact that he had so wilfully steered his precious craft onto the rocks so he killed his wife and himself with a shotgun, leaving Ralph to discover the bodies and a long rambling note generally distributing blame to everyone except himself.

Ralph, in the midst of this horror, had found himself set to preside over the final dissolution of his father's empire when Peter Newman, in his guise as a banker, moved in and took over the company, giving a large portion back to Ralph and discreetly providing him with opportunities to get the company back on its feet again. Although Peter had wanted a building company in connection with various schemes the business had in mind, the collapse of Lowson Construction was none of his doing, and his subsequent purchase of it had been a routine exercise in bargain hunting and diversification. His generous treatment of Lowson was inspired, and the Company had never looked back.

Peter's, and now John's, involvement with Lowson Construction was as a director of the bank that had purchased the company. The business owned the bank of course, but as usual that was through a tangled web of proxies and dummy companies that could never be exposed, even if anyone had had the wit to suspect it was there.

Ralph had done well. He had, as Hugh and Minna had pointed out, several of his father's traits. He was greedy, ambitious for both wealth and power, and totally unscrupulous. But he was not stupid, nor did he have his father's megalomania. He knew he was capable of making mistakes and he could admit them to himself. He just made sure that someone else took the blame whenever they happened. And, of course, he was charm itself.

John tapped in a password that would give him more personal information. He could not help smiling at his father's distinctive prose style amongst the psychological profiles and personality analyses.

*Take no notice of this crap, John. I think Lowson is a reasonable risk, but he'll need to be watched. I don't think he will betray the venture because there is nothing in it for him if he does, but he may well try playing some little game of his own at some stage which could prove awkward. He is complicated, as you might gather from the saga with his father's business. What is not on the main record, and what makes him even more complicated, is the fact that when he found his parents he had just received a message from his wife that she had had twins. Not the good news you might think. Anika Gruber she was called, Nicky for short, and a prize cow by any definition. If she was gang-banged it would be the gang who sued for assault. And she was a sadist. She specialised in humiliating Ralph in public, and I shudder to think what she did in private. As far as I can find out, when she discovered she was pregnant, she left Ralph. Just disappeared. He tried to find her but could not, especially as he was frantically working with his father to try and save the company. Ralph got the letter at the office. Something like "Congratulations daddy. One baby boy, one baby girl, mother very well, babies as well as can be expected." Couldn't resist, you see. "We'll let you know when we want money, Love Nicky. PS boy to be called Oran, girl, Helen. Surname Fiddes, after my latest." Then he went to his father's house, in some state as you might imagine, and found both parents splattered all over the bedroom.*

John screwed up his face at his father's turn of phrase.

*Apparently he went berserk. Actually had to be restrained for a time. Strait jacket padded cell etc. Nasty. Then along comes wife number two (to be) in the shape of Sigrun. Scandinavian, tall, blond, beautiful. A real stunner, John. Lays on soothing hands and lo and behold, a miracle. Ralph is up and about and ready for action in no time flat. Why he treats her the way he does I do not know. Some insecurity thing I suppose. He still needs her I think, deep down. She steadied him in some way. Tail piece— Mr. Fiddes was not only Nicky's latest, he was her last. He had nursed her through a rather unpleasant pregnancy in the hope that her vile temperament was a temporary chemical aberration and that happy-ever-afters would follow. What followed was a string of step-husbands, shall we say, and the realization that Nicky's temperament was permanent and typical. Eventually he strangled her with her latest beau's trousers, he having made an excuse and left with some alacrity when Fiddes returned unexpectedly. Fiddes was jugged for twenty-five years or so, in spite of Ralph paying his defence lawyers, and Ralph got his kids back. They're about two years older than Phillip, I think. Oran works with his father, and Helen (don't laugh) is a trainee in a large American undertaking firm. Showing great promise apparently. Leading executive material, they say. Ralph let them keep their temporary stepfather's surname by way of honouring the man's contribution to the general welfare of society."*

John pondered his father's comments for some time. Instability, Hugh had said. It was Lowson's instability that gave him the insight to deal with Haran and the Great Father, but he would indeed have to be watched carefully. He pressed the intercom.

"Minna?"

"Yes."

"Put Lowson under full observation will you?"

"I've already done it. But it's not easy. I can tap his computers and put in alarms so that we get a call if he's doing anything unusual, but he travels a lot. Reliable access to his mail and phone calls is almost impossible."

"I understand," said John. "Just do what you can. No expense spared. It's part of our reinforcement around the weak link."

# Chapter 33

In addition to reinforcing his weak link, John took extra steps to dissociate the bank from the business. If anything went wrong at this stage, he and the bank might suffer, but nothing would lead an investigation in the direction of the business. He was not satisfied with the arrangement—he did not relish risking a jail sentence, even as a fairly remote possibility—but with Lowson as his best way in to Haran and the Great Father, he had no alternative but to deal with him personally and run that risk. Hugh and Minna and Gwilier would act as his main agents, but it would be an easy matter to keep their status obscure as far as Lowson was concerned, and, at John's request, Minna arranged a series of false identities they could bolt into at the flick of a switch if necessary, without relinquishing their positions in the business proper. Later on, when the scheme got under way, a far more elaborate fog of companies and aliases would be generated to obscure the source entirely and to leave investigators stranded in the middle of nowhere. He looked forward to the day.

They christened this fog the labyrinth.

The weaving of this first safety net had been facilitated by recent developments in computer technology. John's grandfather had set the tone.

"Whatever else happens, we must retain complete control of the electronics industry. We must know at all times who is developing what, and we must always, always, have the very latest equipment. We cannot afford the luxury of anyone playing with these toys without our knowing about it, least of all governments and military establishments."

His greatest contribution to the business had been the final achievement of that goal. Peter had agreed with the policy and consolidated it, and so had John in his turn. He had some small reservations, though. Modern computers were unbelievably powerful and versatile, and the business had the most powerful and versatile of them all. The engineers who had devised it were under the impression they had been working for the U.S. Government and had not protested too strongly at having to work in isolated groups under high security, accepting, albeit reluctantly, that no one person should have a view of the whole. High salaries helped, of course. In the end the project had apparently been cancelled through lack of funding and the teams dispersed under the usual oaths of secrecy, back to their old jobs—the more ingenious among them being kept routinely under observation.

In reality they had completed the task and their results were brought together under Minna's supervision by experts more directly involved in the business. As the original teams had consisted of the best designers in the world, and as the funds available had been more than adequate, the net result was a system years beyond anything else available then or now. There was no other computer it could not gain access to and no encryption it could not break, and with the business owning most of the industry, there was no chance of its being accidently surpassed. They also maintained a substantial interest in the many consultancies that specialized in exposing computer fraud and installing security systems. It frequently saved them a lot of time accessing confidential data.

With its advent, many aspects of the business's affairs had become easier to manage. Information from their vast network of contacts could be checked and confirmed. Financial deals could be better anticipated. The last of the computer fraudsters were eliminated except such as were necessary to keep the consultancies in business and to keep an area of enterprise available for the growth of interesting new talent. Blackmail became much easier—all else failing, a complete and obnoxious criminal record could be inserted into the past of some possibly blameless official who was in the way of a project. It was usually fixed in such a way that he could disentangle it, given time, but the implications were usually sufficient to make him realize the error of his ways.

It was this latter aspect that most concerned John. The capacity of the machine to re-write history was terrifying. It was an instrument for dictatorship such as never before existed. He kept his thoughts to himself, but he had to face the fact that he did not know how to deal with the problem. Pruning the business, rationalizing it, excising its cancerous elements, generally reducing it, was the right thing to do, but letting go of the power was another matter. Without the power, he could not do what he had to do, but while it existed, it could fall into hands that would abuse it and rebuild what he was dismantling, making it more powerful than ever. On his busy days he could retreat into his warm snow cave. The dismantling is enough for one lifetime, he would tell himself. But in his quieter moments he knew that sooner or later he, or worse, someone else, would have to go out and face the blizzard of this unresolved dilemma.

Over the months following Lowson's visit, work began on the details of the scheme.

"There's a lot of loose ends," was Hugh's predominant comment.

"There's no problem while we can see them," John would reply.

Minna's main concern was for John's public exposure.

"Minna, I'm as anxious as you to ease myself and the bank away from this, but we can't do it properly until the scheme gets under way. Lowson won't do anything foolish and he's the only one who could injure me. For now he knows he's onto a good thing, and he thinks he's got the possibility of blackmailing me if he needs to. It'll make him feel more secure. Later on we can channel everything into the labyrinth and cut it adrift, and everyone, him included will be safe."

Minna accepted the conclusion but muttered a little. John had no serious doubts about Lowson's loyalty—any problems there would come much later. His immediate concern was the pivotal role that Lowson had to play in the initial negotiations with Haran and the Great Father. Still, he decided, there was nothing he could do except trust his own judgement and his father's. Then he fell back on his deep optimism. Even if Lowson cocks it up, he'll get part way in and we'll be able to follow. There's nothing we can't do if we set our minds to it.

It was a crisp wintry day when John gave Gwilier the documents containing the opening moves for the venture, and sent a bland coded message to Lowson's New York office advising him where and when to take delivery. As he pressed send on the console, he leaned back with a sigh of relief.

"We're off," he said to Minna and Hugh. Then, banging the arms of his chair as he stood up, "And so am I. There's nothing we can do now but wait and watch, and I'm going for a walk with my wife." He turned as he reached the door. "When I come back. I'm going to take you two down to the gym and paste you. You've both been forgetting the company rules, and you're looking pretty stodgy to me. A work-out will do you good."

Hugh looked at him disdainfully and pointing a finger at him with his thumb raised said, "We'll be waiting for you bub." Minna looked at him innocently, then she took hold of her left forefinger with her right hand and pulled it until a resounding crack resonated round the room.

"You're quite disgustingly cheerful today," said Freddy, looking up at him as they crunched through the snow. John put his arm around her and gave her a squeeze.

"I am indeed," he said. "It's a great day to be alive and you're a lovely woman to be with." He kissed the top of her head.

"If I didn't know you better, I'd say you'd been drinking," said Freddy.

"Ah, no. It's just that you're too intoxicating by far," he replied. "Come on." He seized her hand and pulled her across the hard snow-packed road through a gate and into the fields.

John generally shed the tensions of his work when he came home, but Freddy had noted the darkness slowly growing in her husband over the last few months and she had known instinctively the best way she could help was not to try to help—it had been almost unbearably difficult at times. Now this darkness had gone—every vestige blown away. Obviously some difficult decision had been considered and made—no words were necessary. She put her arm around him and the two marched across the fields leaving green striped footprints in the shallow snow to show their passing. The snow had come early and would probably melt in a few days in a damp penetrating thaw wind, but today was sunny, cold and dry. Their breath steamed in the air and the cold pinched their noses red.

Reaching the top of a hill, they leaned back against a stone wall and surveyed the view. The countryside had a patchwork, slightly surprised look, as if the snow had caught it unawares. It had not been heavy enough to cover the trees and hedges and they stood stark and aloof as if drawing up their skirts against the encroachment of the snowy fields. A line of tracks caught John's eye. He walked over and crouched down to examine them. Freddy was unimpressed by this display of curiosity.

"Well, Mr. Holmes, and what do you deduce?" she said.

John ignored the whimsy and looked puzzled.

"I don't know, Freddy," he said. "They look like dog tracks, but more than one dog, running in single file. How peculiar."

He stood up and looked in the direction the tracks went. "Come on," he said impulsively, and strode off after them.

Freddy started to follow him, but he began a long-legged loping trot and she began to fall behind. Coming to the top of a slope which led down into a wood in a small valley, he stopped and raised his binoculars. Freddy caught up with him, puffing, and inclined to be indignant.

"Listen, Nanook," she growled. "We're supposed to be out for a walk, not training for the Winter Olympics."

He put his arm around her. "Look," he said excitedly, pointing down to the edge of the wood. "Just to the right of where the tracks go into the trees."

Freddy screwed up her eyes and peered intently at where he had pointed.

"I can't see anything," she said.

"Here," he said, handing her the binoculars. "Down by that little cluster of bushes."

Freddy clicked her tongue irritably and swore as she fiddled with the binoculars.

"Why you have to meddle with the left focus I don't know," she said.

"Hurry up. They'll be gone," said John impatiently.

Freddy scanned from left to right along the edge of the trees, then stopped.

"Oh I see," she said, indifferently. "A couple of dogs. Alsatians, I think."

"Look again," said John in a low voice.

Freddy screwed her face up as if she could increase the magnification of the binoculars.

"I think there's another one, or perhaps two, in the bushes," she said eventually. "Who'd let nice dogs like that roam about free?" she continued, handing the binoculars back to John. He almost snatched them. She looked at him. He was fiddling with the left focus and bobbing up and down with excitement.

"They're not dogs, Freddy. They're wolves. Magnificent grey wolves. They must be that pack that was released just before dad died. Oh, what a pity he can't see them. He'd have been so excited."

He took his wife's arm and handed her the binoculars. "Look at them Freddy. Aren't they splendid? Wolves. Back in England. Welcome home, welcome home," he whispered across the fields. Freddy looked through the binoculars and then lowered them. She showed none of her husband's excitement, her face was a little drawn and her voice uncertain.

"Wolves, John. They're dangerous."

John was too enthralled to notice her concern. "No," he said absently. "Not at all."

He took the binoculars from his wife and peered again at one remaining figure standing at the edge of the trees. The wolf was looking straight at him, its ears raised and its tail wagging uncertainly. John held his breath for fear of disturbing it. Another, smaller wolf came out into view, and brushed lightly against the first one. Abruptly the larger one turned and the two disappeared into the undergrowth, quickly but unhurriedly. John noticed the exchange of expressions between the two animals, and sensed the nuance and complexity of their communication. Briefly, but very vividly, as he had on that Welsh mountain, he felt the spirit of the animal he was watching. The certainty that he was being observed by something—something just outside the range of his vision, something that was possibly, but not immediately, dangerous. He felt the scents and sound of the trees and the rest of the pack behind him rustling in the undergrowth and waiting, and the past urgency of the exposed trot across the open snow. He felt the hierarchy of the pack under him and the difference in him that made him the leader—benign, yet totally intolerant of any who would defy that difference.

"John."

Freddy's quiet voice and her hand on his arm brought John's mind back.

284

"Alpha," he whispered, almost reverently.

"What?" said Freddy.

"Alpha," he repeated. "That's what they call them. Alpha wolves, the pack leaders. That was him. Looking after his family."

He was talking to himself.

"John," said Freddy again. "Shouldn't we tell someone?"

John straightened up and looked thoughtfully at the spot where the wolf had disappeared.

"Tell them what, Freddy?" he said in his normal voice.

"Well. Wolves," she said uncomfortably. "They're dangerous, aren't they? They'll kill someone."

John shook his head. "No, they won't. Not if they're left alone. They'll pinch the odd piece of livestock, maybe a straying pet, but they'll not tackle anything big unless they're really hungry."

He put his arm around her and they turned to walk back home. Freddy was fretting and continually looking over her shoulder.

"What's the matter with you," said John after a while, knowing full well what her concern was.

"Nothing," she said resolutely, staring rigidly forward again.

"Yes there is," he teased. "You're frightened of the big bad wolf coming up behind you and grabbing you aren't you?"

He stepped quickly behind her and seized her waist with both hands, digging his fingers in. She squealed, spun round and pushed him in the chest. The blow caught him off balance on the slippery surface, and he sat down incongruously in the snow. Seeing her spouse thus downed, Freddy, in the time-honoured manner of wo-mankind, stooped for a moment and then hurled a snowball at him. Then several more as he staggered to his feet. He was laughing uncontrollably and holding his stomach.

"Peace," he gasped when he had recovered sufficient breath. "Peace. I surrender. I'm no match for your indefatigable treachery. It'd be a rare hungry wolf that would tackle you. Oh, weren't they beautiful?"

His face became rapturous again. Freddy grudgingly admitted that they were rather handsome creatures, but niggled on about their ferocity as they walked.

"And since when do you know anything about wolves, Jack London?"

"I'm just infinitely wise," said John. "It's a gift."

"You know what I mean," she said more seriously.

"Yes, I do," he replied soberly. "Take my word for it, they'll hurt no-one unless they're provoked or desperate. They've just had a bad press. You can read about them for yourself when we get home. They're intelligent, shy, affectionate creatures with an enormously sophisticated social life. They're meat-eating predators I'll grant you, but aren't we all? At least they hunt their own."

Then, abstractedly, following his last thought: "There's only one really dangerous animal on this planet. We both married one, and bred two."

Later that day he told Hugh of the sighting and instructed him to ensure that the wolves would be left alone.

"Get one of our insurance companies and a conservation group together and cobble something up guaranteeing payment for any livestock they kill. And get them made a protected species."

"You seem unusually concerned, John," said Hugh. "I didn't think you were that much of an animal lover."

John pursed his lips thoughtfully. "I'm a freedom lover, Hugh. And it's something else. Intuition, Hugh. They belong here. More than we do. They fit. And they're beautiful. Somehow they're what it's all about. They're not for some psychotic ape to use as target practice. I can't explain it Hugh, but believe me, if I hadn't felt *your* dog's feelings on that mountain, I wouldn't have known you were still alive. We both owe them something. It's a personal debt."

Hugh looked at hm. "I don't really understand, but I'll do what you say and gladly."

As he was leaving the room, John called him back and looked straight at him.

"Don't misunderstand, Hugh," he said grimly. "Put the word out very clearly that if anyone injures them it'll be their head that ends up on a shield."

Hugh nodded. Something deep had stirred in John's nature; he could feel it himself as he looked at the stern figure behind the desk. Woe betide anyone who harmed those wolves in any way. You're some mean ape, John, he thought.

# Chapter 34

Lowson's negotiations with Haran and the Great Father or, more correctly, his Guardian Angels, took a long time but were not as difficult as he had envisaged. In so far as anyone knew the two leaders, he knew them fairly well, and in so far as anyone knew Ralph Lowson, they knew him fairly well. They did not, of course, trust him, nor he they, but he was an important and influential foreigner and one of the few who was prepared to work for them. The fact that he was without any local political ambition, and the fact that one of the conditions of his assistance was secrecy about certain aspects of the work, gave the two leaders a good measure of the extent to which they could rely on him.

Officially, and for presentation to the rest of the world, Lowson Construction built hospitals and schools, effluent treatment works, dams for irrigation and power schemes, and other such worthy public works. When cornered, Lowson sometimes had to act as apologist for the two regimes.

"Yes, I appreciate that from time to time, human rights are being denied in these countries. But some of the reports in the western press are greatly exaggerated and seem to be based on guesswork rather than on solid information. You must understand that these countries are pulling themselves out of the middle ages, and such a road can never be easy. There are years of brutal tribal tradition to be swept away, and then there'll be the slow gradual process of re-education. I'm satisfied that General Haran and the Great Father are attempting to lead their peoples toward some form of democratic government, and in due course both countries will be accepted back into the family of nations. I think if you study the history of these countries, you'll find that even with these occasional, admittedly regrettable, aberrations on the part of the authorities, life for the ordinary person is much less severe than it used to be under previous regimes."

There was enough truth in such statements to prevent an outright condemnation of his work with the regimes, especially as his sincerity was so patently obvious especially when he could add: "Of course, all the work we do is worthwhile and beneficial to the ordinary people and offers employment and a standard of living hitherto unknown."

Some thought he was genuine but naive, others suspected such protestations deeply, but access to Tier r'Vern and Tier d'Ynide being what it was, no-one could seriously argue with him, and no-one was going to condemn him for building hospitals and schools and the like.

In reality, Lowson Construction also built police barracks and prisons and all manner of military establishments including airfields and missile bases, and indulged the rich elite of both countries in their private mansions and other extravaganzas. Although the local employment his schemes offered conferred a standard of living hitherto unknown to the luckless inhabitants—it was effectively slave labour.

Ironically, the standard of the construction work was very high. Both countries were blessed with severe and extreme climates and not infrequently suffered severe earthquakes. There was no room for amateurs in the building industry in either. The high-ranking patronage that Lowson enjoyed was not so robust that if could withstand the consequences of some of his buildings collapsing or even beginning to deteriorate rapidly, and so he built accordingly. He instilled a similar reverence for good practice into his designers and supervisors.

"If you're incompetent on a building site in England, then, depending where you start from, you may be sacked or promoted. Here they'll cut off your head—eventually."

Phrases such as 'industrial relations' tended to lose a lot in translation into the local languages. It was only the need for high standards that gave the local labour any protection from being worked, literally, to death. Hours of work were restricted because excessive fatigue threatened the quality of work. Scaffolding, cranes and plant were secured and maintained because apart from being expensive, breakdowns and collapses could do damage, and could impair work where continuity was essential. Labour, however, was plentiful, and men falling off, into or under things, being crushed in trenches or by ill-driven equipment, being choked in dust and fumes, was of no great import.

The labour force did not protest too much. In Tier d'Ynide, individuals were brought up to be subservient to the state. In Tier r'Vern, they were similarly educated to be subservient to the will of God, as promulgated by his prophet and son, the Great Father. Any individuals showing any marked tendency to be less than totally subservient soon attracted the attention of the respective corrective agencies: Horan's Kithrile Poliz, and the Great Father's Angels.

Both dictators knew that whatever else he might be, Lowson was neither stupid nor foolhardy, and would not approach them with a scheme intended to defraud them, or one that would not be worthy of serious thought. Nonetheless, the scale of the proposal silenced both of them for some time. When the silence ended, their reactions were peculiarly similar, and had it not been for the considerable physical differences between the two men, Lowson, in his constant shuttling to and fro, would have had difficulty in remembering which country he was in.

The Great Father was shapeless and huge, with a round flushed and shiny face surrounding sharp, deeply buried eyes. In public, his shape was shrouded in flowing gowns, giving him the appearance of great solidity and permanence. His voice was deep and rich and his flowing oratory resonated with the hearts of most of his people. Those who noted that the emperor was naked were usually sufficiently astute to keep their observations to themselves. In private, he leaned on body slaves when he was not sprawled over couches or holding court from his massive bed and his booming voice was turned down almost to a whisper. He would frequently hesitate and gesticulate his fat bejewelled hands as if trying to catch words from the air.

Haran, by contrast, was tall and lean. His gaunt, high cheekboned face and tight mouth were decorated with a thin moustache and a goatee beard. His posture was ramrod straight and he moved as if his joints were incapable of bending. His rooms and office were large, but obsessively simple and clean, and he too knew the hearts of his people, or at least the dark side of their hearts. He could stir them with his oratory, but his voice was harsh and his presentation clipped and staccato in private and in public. He always wore a black military uniform, and never socialized, nor sought solace in the embrace of man or woman.

But the two men were, in essence, identical. They lusted for power and knew no restraint in their efforts to obtain it. Both governed by inducing mass paranoia, and calculated though it was, it was still only a reflection of their own characters. Lowson watched each in turn balancing advantages and disadvantages, probabilities and improbabilities, under the magnifying glass of their own suspicion and ambition.

Each had reservations about working with the other, but these reservations were confined almost exclusively to considering how the necessary changes in attitude could be presented to their respective populations.

In the end, both decided that this was no serious problem. The hostility between the two peoples was largely artificial, having been induced in the early days of the revolutions when the people needed an enemy to focus on. Now, the whole world was their enemy and the need to hate their neighbour correspondingly reduced. Through control of the media and education systems the mutual abuse could be stopped, gradual reference could be made to the common racial heritage of the two peoples, then, in true Orwellian fashion, Haran would announce that Tier r'Vern was, and always had been, a friend and ally, while the Great Father would have yet another vision, revealing God's will that the two peoples unite. If necessary, the priesthood could be purged of those who had so striven to deceive the people, and the Great Father would once again have saved his people from the insidious machinations of the Evil One and his earthly agents, the barbarous dictatorships of the USA and Eastern Bloc.

Uppermost in the two men's minds was the nature of Lowson's backers and the price they would exact for their assistance in the venture.

"They are men such as yourselves, men of ability and power, men who are choked by the restraints of democracy and so-called freedom, men who are weighed down by the whims of the incompetent masses. They are men who would join hands in fealty to you and be the barbs on the spearhead of your world revolution," spieled Lowson over many meetings.

Their price?

"No more than the privilege of establishing special trading links with you so that they could better prepare the beachheads for the battle to come."

Then the silence descended again.

"What's the matter, Ralph?" asked John over a crackling line.

"I don't know," came the reply. "I don't think it's anything serious. I think they're both chewing everything over. It's decision time— they have all the information I can give them. They'll be taking a breath before they take the plunge."

Lowson was nearly right, but he had not given them quite everything they wanted. Back in John's office he explained the remaining problem.

"I think both of them need a token of some kind. An earnest of your ability to deliver the goods."

"What do they want?" asked John easily.

"It's rather difficult," replied Lowson. "They're both being a bit coy, and it's only an impression I'm getting. Something I can take back and drop into the scales to give them that last tilt, a little push in the right direction."

"If you've nothing positive, Ralph, speculate," said John.

"I have been," said Lowson. "Haran's not too bad. Probably a couple of million in his Swiss bank and a new identity for him to move into in case things get rough, might do it. But the Great Father's a different kettle of fish."

"In what way?"

"Well, I don't know him as well. I've to deal quite a lot with two of his Guardian Angels even when he's there. Haran calculates everything and stands aloof. The Great Father believes more of his own propaganda, he gets more involved, he really does think he's his people's saviour."

"A thug and a loony," muttered Hugh from his chair by the window.

John smiled and Ralph breathed out noisily. "It's a bit more complicated than that, Hugh," he said. "But it'll do for now, and I don't know what to do next."

John pursed his lips and frowned a little. "Awkward," he said.

"We'll have to keep waiting. Ralph, I'll give you carte blanche. Plus or minus a few million is neither here nor there. Put it as straight to Haran as you think you can. Drop hints around the Great Father then play it by ear. We'll see if we can tempt him down to earth." Then, as an afterthought. "Belay that a moment, Ralph. When you've found out what they want, as near as you can, check back with me, don't agree it immediately. I'm sure we'll be able to improve on whatever it is they want. It'll pay dividends later."

It was several weeks before Lowson surfaced again. Haran had, as envisaged, presented no serious problem, accepting a substantial sum and some impressive software, although Minna had reservations about that.

"He can open a personal file on every single inhabitant with that machine, John. Do you think it's such a good idea to encourage his 1984 vision quite so much?"

"Yes and no, Minna," John replied. "No, because he's vicious and cruel and will abuse the power of the computer in every conceivable repressive manner. Yes, because he'll need our people to handle the thing. All his information will become ours and we can analyze it better than he can. Also we can put our own information in if we need to manipulate him or protect ourselves."

Minna was still uncertain.

"Minna, don't worry. If the worst comes to the worst we can bomb the whole system at the flick of a switch. You'd enjoy that, wouldn't you? Leaving him legless."

The Great Father, however, was more difficult. Lowson laid out bait as instructed, but only one ripple appeared on the surface.

"I'm sorry John," said Lowson. "He says he wants to see you. He says he needs to feel what you're like, to see if you have the word of the Lord with you, to use his words."

John sat silent for some time until Lowson's voice crackled out of the phone again.

"John?"

"Yes. I'm here, go on."

"I've done my bit as oily rag, now he needs to see the engineer."

John made a quiet clicking noise with his tongue and looked out at the grey wintry sky visible through his office window.

"I wouldn't mind a bit of sun at the moment, Ralph," he said casually. Hugh and Minna signalled acquiescence. "Set it up Ralph. But right in the middle of his own palace. No bland neutral territory. Do you understand?"

"Not entirely, John, but I'll do what you say."

"And Ralph. I'll leave the diplomatic niceties to you, but make it quite clear that it's *their* engineer I'm coming to see, not his oily rags."

Lowson was silent for a moment, and his voice was doubtful when he spoke again.

"John, he's a difficult and dangerous man. I'll have to brief you carefully before you meet. And the middle of his palace doesn't sound like a good idea."

"Don't worry, Ralph. I'll listen carefully to you, when the time comes. But the venue is my choosing, and his palace is essential."

Lowson offered no further comment and rang off with a simple acknowledgement.

John looked up at Hugh and Minna grinning at him. "You are a sod, John," said Minna. "If you're going to beard a lion..."

"It's got to be in his own den," Hugh finished the observation.

"Exactly," said John. "But it isn't going to be easy. There's a lot of ifs, and a lot hinging on too few people. Still, I don't see we've any alternative, unfortunately."

To visit one country without visiting the other would be to destroy the results of Lowson's protracted negotiations, so it was arranged that John would visit the two heads of state and the sites proposed for the approach roads to the crossing. Tier r'Vern being the easier to reach, he would visit there first and then fly on to Tier d'Ynide.

"That shouldn't tread on anyone's toes," concluded Lowson as he finalized the arrangements.

"Do you really have to go?" asked Freddy, trying not to sound like a clinging wife. "You read such terrible things about those places."

John took her face in his hands. "It's only for a few days, love. I have to see the people who want Ralph for this particular job. It's very big and they need personal reassurance about his funding. It's only the locals who get maltreated; Ralph's safe as houses, so we'll be ok. In any case, I'll have Hugh and Minna with me."

Freddy embraced her husband and then let the matter drop.

John did not do a great deal of travelling and she knew he didn't particularly relish it. She smiled.

"For an international wheeler dealer, you're certainly a stay-at-home, aren't you?"

John looked sanctimonious. "If the good Lord had wanted me to be a gadabout, he wouldn't have made you for me, would he?"

Freddy screwed her eyes up dangerously.

"Hm," he said. "That was pretty good. I must remember it for the future."

Both were a little uneasy walking the borders between family and business, and one of the reasons John disliked foreign travel was that it intruded one onto the other and sometimes necessitated his lying to Freddy, or at least not telling her the whole truth. Freddy disliked his leaving for similar reasons. She couldn't avoid asking, and she knew his answers could be untrue. John's affairs in the business were whatever they were, and she was prepared to leave them unquestioned. Her pre-marriage vow to herself was sustained by a deep, old and fearful instinct that no idle curiosity could disturb.

# Chapter 35

The journey to Tier r'Vern was made in Lowson's private plane with everyone except Lowson using assumed names. Such few people as were interested in the flight assumed it was another of Lowson's famous, or infamous, junkets, and it caused no stir.

Phillip had been left in charge of the office for the few days they would be away, with Gwilier discreetly but tightly holding the reins. That was another reason why John did not like travelling—he was fairly suspicious of random chance. *I'll have to be careful I don't change into a potty old recluse,* he thought as the plane broke through the clouds into the dazzling winter sunshine.

As far as he could see there were white clouds below, smothering the country in what seemed to be a huge cotton wool blanket. Even though it was only a few minutes away, it was difficult to imagine that this impressive expanse of pristine whiteness was grey, dark and cold underneath. He felt the sun through the window, warm on his face. *I wonder if we could use helium balloons to float our heat stores up in glass boxes to catch this winter heat,* he thought idly as he rested back into the luxurious upholstery.

Lowson's hedonistic and extravagant lifestyle was the very opposite of John's, and held no attraction for him, but he was a first-class host and travelling companion, and when they had discussed such business matters as needed to be discussed, he eased the length of the journey for the others with a steady stream of anecdotes and conversation. However, he assiduously avoided the use of his considerable repertoire of erotic sagas in deference to what he considered to be his guest's rather staid, if not puritanical, views on such matters.

John hoped they might have been able to make a low pass over the Straits where the crossing was proposed, but Lowson denied the request. The area was far too dangerous. Every state guarded its borders with hair triggers, and with such a short border between the two countries, a slight miscalculation could take them over the wrong country and into a great deal of trouble. Even without miscalculation, there was always the risk of misinterpretation by neighbouring states which could have the same effect.

"The rule here is shoot first and apologize afterwards. Life is very cheap," said Lowson.

John accepted the reasoning. He had had the jet fitted with long range detection equipment and some anti-missile protection, but he had no desire to see it used just for the sake of a whim on his part.

"So we fly very straight, very slowly and very noisily, do we?" he said.

"Precisely," said Lowson.

When they arrived at the Great Father's private airport in Tier r'Vern, any vestiges of the recent winter cold lingering in their memories was evaporated as the heat of the concrete surface bounced into their faces. Lowson seemed to come more alive in this alien brightness, as he moved jauntily down the plane's steps to greet a slightly obsequious waiting official. No introductions were made, and the party moved down an avenue formed by two ranks of white uniformed guards to a large car. The car also was white and bore the same winged insignia as the guards.

"Who're the troops?" asked Minna as they settled into the air conditioned cool of the limousine.

"Those are the army, police, citizen's militia, secret police, everything. Those are the Great Fathers' Angels," said Lowson.

"All in white," mused Minna. "With golden wings for a badge. And did I really see gold plated SMGs back there?"

"You did," said Lowson. "The Great Father's theology is very junior Sunday school. All his angels are clad in white and all their implements are gold. Well, gold coloured anyway."

Hugh gazed out at the dust cloud they were trailing behind them. Turning to John he whispered, "Do you think we should move in on the laundry concessions around here?"

John smiled. "I think we should keep the smart-alec remarks to ourselves until we're home." he said. Then, more seriously, "Everything here seems to indicate the need to keep our wits about us."

"How does he control his Angels, Ralph?" asked Minna.

"Same way he controls everything else," replied Lowson. "He has a highly efficient terror machine which he uses on anyone without scruple and which he lubricates with chronic paranoia."

"What do you mean?" she pressed.

Lowson was still nervous of Minna, but he turned round a little, and leaning his arm on the back of his seat, tried to look at her. "Everyone informs on everyone else. Periodically, people are publicly denounced by the Angels and no-one knows who they can turn to for support. Anyone who has been near to the victim usually finds it advisable to dash forward and admit their involvement and claim it was only because they suspected him or her of blasphemous ideas, which they then fabricate to save their own necks. It's profoundly unpleasant, but it's far from being a new idea. And it's a very effective way of controlling people."

"And then he does it personally to the odd Angel now and then?" said Minna.

Lowson nodded. Minna leaned back and stared out of the window, and there was silence in the car as it careened along the glaring road.

"Where's the weak link in his power structure, Ralph?" asked John after a while.

Lowson looked thoughtful. "It's hard to say. It's not the kind of matter you can get information about, and it's very unhealthy to ask anything about the Angels. One of the reasons I'm accepted here is that I'm conspicuously indifferent to local politics and social conditions."

"Speculate," said John. Lowson pondered briefly. "His power base is definitely his Angels. But as I said, they're subject to the same induced paranoia as everyone else. The difference between them and the ordinary people is that they're treated exceptionally well. Good money, food, board, clothes, all provided, exemption from certain of the restrictions on sexual matters, and great status. Status is very important out here, as you know. Everything tends to reinforce the system, they've a lot to lose if they slip up, and they've got denouncement quotas to meet or they go the same way."

297

"All his old partners are dead, aren't they?" said Hugh.

"Oh, yes," said Lowson. "They all went ages ago."

"He's really got the place sewn up," said Minna. "He's going to be quite a handful."

"Yes," agreed Lowson. "A lot of people have tried to find a weakness, but he's too well entrenched. He's spent a good deal of time and effort consolidating his position and he's virtually unassailable. Even his elite personal guard, his praetorian guard if you like, his Archangels, are kept on the move. Every now and then one of them bites the dust, *pour encourager les autre*. The only way he'll go out is when someone smothers him on his deathbed."

The remainder of the short journey was spent in silence. John noted the excellence of the road over which they were travelling, and also that the driver didn't concern himself about other road users. Quite a few cyclists and pedestrians had to dive for their lives as the car sped through the dry open country, and he was disposed to knock on the separating partition and remonstrate with the driver when they entered a more populous suburb. Abruptly, however, the car turned off the road and passed through a wide arched gateway set in a tall stone wall. Glancing over his shoulder John saw two large gates sealing the entrance. The car moved briefly along the edge of what appeared to be a lavish ornamental park, then passed through another gate and began a steady climb up a winding road cut into the side of a cliff. Again John noted the high quality of the work, both in the road itself, and the retaining walls and the occasional short tunnels. The driver seemed to know only one speed—fast. And the car surged forward effortlessly up the hill. The final stretch was dead straight and led up to the Great Father's palace.

It was obviously a modern building, glistening white in the hot sun, but it was bedecked with minarets and domes and high narrow arches, giving it a Moorish look.

"Unusual," said John.

Lowson just grunted, a slight tension in his face.

John looked at him. "Ah," he said. "I see. The Great Father did a Captain Flint on you, did he?"

"Sorry?" said Lowson.

"Buried the diggers along with the treasure," amplified John.

"Yes," said Lowson sourly. "I lost good men building this place.

They all had unfortunate accidents, just to protect his secret hide-aways and exits."

His tone was uncharacteristically bitter. John sympathized, but the fact that accidents had been arranged gave him some indication of the esteem in which Lowson was held. Normal routine would probably be disappearance. Certainly those who had arranged the accidents would have disappeared by now and quite probably those who arranged their disappearances would have gone also. The Great Father would be a man who covered his tracks very well.

The car pulled smoothly to a stop, precluding any further discussion, and the door was opened by a large, stone faced Angel. The sudden blast of heat made John want to hold his breath for fear of his lungs being seared. The Angel spoke to Lowson in the local language, and Lowson replied similarly. Turning to John he said, "This gentleman is Michael, one of the Great Father's most high-ranking Archangels—his personal bodyguard, in fact. The Great Father has commanded him to take us to our rooms where we can rest and compose ourselves before we enter his Holy Presence."

John looked at the man carefully, ensuring that his own attitude and expression were completely neutral. He was massive, and John felt the power and arrogance that radiated from him. Deducing from Lowson's speech that Michael quite probably understood English, John spoke directly to him but addressed his remarks to Lowson.

"Ralph, would you ask Michael to thank the Great Father for his consideration and generosity? A brief rest would be most welcome."

Lowson dutifully translated, and Michael nodded a curt acknowledgement. The formalities over, John smiled and slowly extended his right hand. A brief uncertainty came into the big man's eyes. He was used to people reacting to his presence, but this strange dark suited individual with the covered eye gave away nothing. No fear, no threat, nothing. A sudden light flickered in the single eye, and almost without realizing it, Michael felt himself reach out and grasp the offered hand. John bowed slightly and Michael returned the bow. Somehow he felt he was out of control. The man's grip was not strong, but Michael knew he could not withdraw his hand until it was released. Then Lowson introduced him to Hugh and Minna. They also gave nothing away. Strange black clad creatures with bright eyes, hovering around their master. Michael felt slightly light-headed as though he were stretching up high on his toes prior to crashing forward from a great height.

As Minna's gaze turned away from him, the feeling passed and he recovered most of his inner composure. A brutal and savage man, cross-grained with deep layers of cunning and cruelty, who had pounded his way to where he was quite literally over the broken bodies of thousands of victims, he felt like a wild animal that had heard a distant sound, a significant sound, but not clear enough to be identified as hunter or hunted. He shrugged off the last of his unease, consoling himself with the fact that he could obviously deal with these three singlehandedly, and rationalizing that it was probably their unusual appearance that had momentarily disturbed him. Three black stains in the welter of snow-blinding whiteness that normally surrounded him.

"What's the matter?" John asked Hugh and Minna as Michael closed the door behind them. Hugh gestured towards Minna. Her face was set as she flopped down in a chair and rested her chin on her hand.

"Minna?" enquired John.

She looked straight ahead and said nothing for a moment. Then, "He's a torturer," she said quietly.

"Who is?" asked John.

"That big bastard, Michael," she replied.

Lowson started and gesticulated silence, touching his ear with his finger and mouthing "bugs".

"It's alright, Ralph," said John, lifting what appeared to be a pen from his pocket. "We're jamming everything. Discreetly. Just enough to make it sound like a speaker fault."

He returned his attention to Minna. "Go on," he said.

Her face wrinkled in distaste. "I can smell blood on him and hear screams."

"Be careful Minna," said John. "We're vulnerable here, and there'll be lots of people like that in this place."

Minna shook her head. "No," she said. "Not like him. He's something special." She turned and looked at Lowson. He was sitting uneasily, trying to understand this odd conversation. "He is special, isn't he, Ralph?"

Lowson cleared his throat nervously. "Well," he began. "Yes. I suppose he is." He paused. "Michael served his apprenticeship in the executive branch of the Judiciary."

John cocked his head on one side slightly.

"A torturer in their Inquisition?" asked Minna.

Lowson nodded. "He became one of their top men. He's a very creative thinker in his own way, they say."

John puffed out his cheeks and blew a long breath. He glanced at Hugh and Minna.

"If opportunity presents, he's yours," he said.

Lowson felt disorientated, just as Michael had before.

"What are you talking about?" he hissed in alarm.

John smiled reassuringly and raised a placating hand. "I'm sorry Ralph. Just a little in-house briefing, nothing to get upset about." Then, matter-of-factly: "Now, tell me again about the courtesies I must show to our would-be client."

The decor and furnishings of the palace were lavish and ornate but monotonously gold and white. The only colour was the occasional glimpse of the blue sky, and the bronze scars made by the faces of the white clad attendants they encountered. The quartet was guided by Michael through winding corridors and stairways towards the Great Father's inner sanctum. Generally, the journey was downwards. Radar and rockets up top to praise the heavens, while you keep your holy backside well down in the rock, thought John. At least I haven't come to that yet.

They arrived at a circular anteroom, occupied by an official seated at a desk and flanked by two Angels. Smiling, the man stood up, rubbing his hands together as he walked to meet them. Bowing low, he introduced himself as secretary to the Great Father.

"Greatness," he said apologetically to John. "I crave your indulgence. I've been told of your traditions, but I must ask that your weapons be left here. Objects of violence must be kept from the Great Father. He feels the cruelty of the world deeply. The very presence of such objects causes him great pain and anguish."

John, forewarned, nodded his acknowledgement and without speaking took out his revolver and laid it quietly on the desk. Hugh and Minna did likewise with their innocuous looking .22 automatics. The secretary's face showed relief and some triumph as he reached forward to pick up the guns. Gently, John bent forward and rested his forefinger on the back of the man's hand, lowering it onto the white desk top. The man looked up and met a smiling face and a baleful glare from a single black irised eye. His hand was not being pressed onto the desk with any force, but he could not move it.

John spoke to him very quietly. "Out of respect for your holy master I've accepted you as his agent, and didn't have you killed outright for the request you've just made. But these are precious relics with a value far beyond their immediate seeming, and no power can protect you if you dishonour them with your touch."

He released the hand and stood up. "I leave them in your charge. It is a sacred trust."

The secretary's head seemed to sink into his shoulders and he bowed, almost touching the desk with his forehead.

"Greatness," he said hoarsely.

A low bell-like sound resonated through the chamber. The secretary scrambled from behind the desk with a mixture of relief and trepidation.

"His Holiness commands... er... requests, your attendance," he said, the whites of his eyes showing as he avoided looking directly at any of the group.

*Don't raise your head above his, speak before you're spoken to, or let your shadow fall on him. And for pity's sake don't touch him.* Ralph's brief litany of protocol ran through John's mind as they prepared to enter the Great Father's chamber. *And don't forget he's a psychotic,* he added for his own benefit, *we're too vulnerable here.* Two large, gold-ornamented doors opened smoothly and apparently of their own accord, and Lowson led the group forward.

At first John could not see clearly because of the intense illumination, but after a few seconds his eye adjusted and the details of the room began to appear. The room was not particularly large, but the ceiling was high and domed and covered in elaborate patterning, picked out, inevitably, in gold. On a raised dais opposite the door, the Great Father was sprawled across a huge couch and accoutred in flowing robes which made it difficult to discern where he finished and the decor began. He was flanked, at the foot of the stairs to the dais, by Michael and another, similarly huge, Archangel. Around the room, standing motionless, were a dozen or so Angels carrying gold plated machine guns. Non-violent ones, presumably, thought John wryly, thinking about their own pistols lying outside.

Theatrically, the brilliant lighting was arranged so that the Great Father dominated the whole room and appeared to be the source of the illumination. John took it as a positive sign that the problems of height, shadow and touch had been effectively eliminated by the Great Father's grandiose stage management.

Lowson led the group forward and stopped at the foot of the dais. John considered his host and wondered what it was like to be trapped in such a grotesque body, and what kind of a mind would such chronic helplessness breed?

The Great Father raised his hand in benediction.

"Raff," he whispered. "It is pleasant to see you again. Bring our guests forward and present them."

Lowson did as he was ordered, and when the Great Father had indicated that they might sit, he retired discreetly to one side.

The Great Father addressed John. "Raff tells me you are a man of great importance and wealth, a man who wields great power, a man of vision and courage."

John decided to make no verbal reply until he could feel out the character of the man a little more. He nodded his head slowly, as if in gracious acceptance of a simple truth, but said nothing.

"In my simple way," continued the Great Father, "I too wield a little authority. Authority granted to me by the Lord above." He rolled his eyes upwards and brought his hands together in an attitude of prayer. "Granted to me so that I might bring light and hope to my people and lead them to their true inheritance on earth. It is a thorny path."

"Indeed, Great Father," ventured John solemnly. "We both bear the grievous responsibilities that accompany such authority."

The Great Father nodded in turn, then abruptly changed direction. His whisper became a little less subdued, and his elaborate gestures and pauses faded slightly.

"Your scheme," he said. "Is indeed visionary. Our neighbours across the Straits have long been considered our enemies. Agents of the Devil. But I have prayed and looked into my heart, and heard the voice of the Lord speak clearly. Scales have fallen from my eyes. They are not the Devil's agents, but his unwitting victims. It is our duty, and the Lord's will, that we lead them back to the paths of righteousness."

John had never envisaged any serious theological or ideological problems arising to bedevil the scheme once its value had been seen, so he took this as another positive sign. He nodded again and gestured with his hands to indicate that he was unworthy to make such profound discoveries.

"And your scheme had such a visionary quality that it could only have come from the Lord." He raised a finger. "This bore heavily on my meditations."

"The ways of the Lord are not ours to judge," said John. The Great Father raised a ponderous hand in acquiescence.

The discussion wandered around in an aimless fashion for some considerable time after that, a vague mixture of overall policy and pettifogging detail wholly inappropriate at this stage. Whatever else he might be, the Great Father was not an incisive chairman. John began to wonder what it was all about. Minna's hands were moving in genteel nervousness. He was hesitant to ask outright why the Great Father had asked to see him, but the present discussion seemed to have no end in sight. Or was he missing something? Once or twice he thought he felt an unease in the Great Father, a faint tension in the room, as if he was waiting for something, but he dismissed this as being tension and over-anxiety on his own part.

Minna shifted slightly in her seat and the nervous hands signalled their imperceptible code.

"Trouble," they said. "Be alert."

*I am,* thought John, but still he felt nothing positive. *Let's shake things up a little.* "I'm unfamiliar with the details of your process of government, Great Father," he said. "I'd be interested to know if any of your advisers have a view of our proposal which could perhaps expand its scope."

The Great Father hesitated. "I am the Lord's chosen. I cannot allow myself to be tossed and torn by the winds of democracy. I cannot have my clear vision of the Lord's will blurred and muddied by the narrow, tainted sight of the untutored multitude."

Briefly his eyes flickered to his two Archangels, standing massive and still at the foot of the dais. John missed it, but Hugh and Minna did not.

She signalled again. "Trouble at t'mill."

John smiled inwardly. So that was it—employees cutting up rough. It figured.

"But I must have compassion," continued the Great Father. "The

Lord's true vision is too bright for most. They must be led to it gently, lest the too sudden sight of it should strike them low. My Archangels here, Michael and Gabriel," and he opened his arms in an expansive gesture, "are my earthly hands. They guide my priests and followers in the understanding of my will, the Lord's will, and I listen to them in matters of earthly counsel."

John took a chance, and spoke directly to the two men, as at an ordinary business meeting.

"Please speak freely, gentlemen," he said authoritatively. "We may be following a divine intention, but the crossing of the Strait is a very earthbound matter, and your opinions could be very pertinent."

The Great Father looked casually away from him as he spoke, and John noted that the two men glanced at one another, not at their leader, before relaxing their formal stances. It was only a small thing, but it changed the atmosphere of the meeting as if a switch had been thrown. *Oh dear,* thought John, *it looks like the courtesies are over. I wonder who's really in charge here?*

Had the praetorian guard taken over? Was the Great Father really a frightened puppet retained because of his ability to move the masses, or was he a cunning old devil who was paying out enough rope for these two to hang themselves with? On balance, he was inclined to think the latter. The Great Father had been there a long time, and Michaels and Gabriels must have come and gone in the past. Then again, he could be wrong. And who was going to be the hangman?

Michael spoke first, in heavily accented but accurate English.

"You ask too high a price for this venture." He sneered and made a contemptuous gesture when he said venture. The Great Father did not react, but Lowson went white.

*It would appear the gloves are coming off,* thought John. "What price is this?" he asked quietly.

Michael screwed up his mouth as if speaking English were distasteful.

"The foreigners who will infect our country, bringing their decadence and filth to destroy our people as they destroy their own, and expecting immunity from our laws."

"Without the aid of these people, the crossing cannot be built. Your nation will not receive the technical aid it needs to develop and strengthen itself from any nation other than Tier d'Ynide, your cousins in the wilderness," said John, still quietly. "Your country will fade and die without it. The price, as you call it, is negligible. A few minor concessions out of respect for the different cultural ways of those who will have helped you. People of courage and vision."

Michael clenched his fists. "No," he said. "No-one must be beyond our laws. They are truth and must pervade the whole world in time."

There was a fraught silence. The Great Father did not move. Minna sat fidgeting her hands slightly, watching the two Archangels towering over her. Lowson's racing pulse could be seen in his temples, while Hugh casually took a coin from his pocket and started turning it over nervously between his thumb and forefinger. John looked at the Great Father, but no response came. The man was overseeing the whole scene as if in complete indifference.

*You fat sod,* thought John, *you've got us here to precipitate a crisis just so you can clear up some domestic nonsense.* He kept his voice quiet and reasonable.

"Michael, you must accept my guidance. You have little or no experience of the ways of the rest of the world. The few who will eventually come here will pose no threat to your country and your law. They'll be its friends. They'll give you contacts with many sources of trade and commerce throughout the world, to enable you to spread your great truth. No-one else will help you."

Michael was just about to reply when Gabriel spoke. His voice was deep and cultured, but John did not need to see Minna's signal. Very dangerous. It emanated from the man like a living thing. "Now that we have seen you, and spoken to you, and have your measure, we are happy that we will be able to obtain this aid you speak of without this elaborate, expensive and time-consuming escapade, with its consequent involvement with our neighbour and dubious friends," he said.

John smiled at him broadly. "Please elucidate," he said. "I appreciate initiative and new ideas."

"Ah," said Gabriel regretfully. "It is alas not a new idea, but a very old one. You are a rich and powerful man. We shall simply offer you our continued hospitality until your friends provide us with the aid we need."

John affected a look of disappointment. "I'm afraid your scheme may have the elegance of simplicity, but it shows a lack of detailed consideration. Only my employers would be likely to pay for my return and at best they could only provide you with a few computers and some... training. At worst, and if they abide by their normal policy, they'll give you nothing but bad publicity, and you'll be left with me, a humble administrator with no technical expertise whatsoever. Now, Tier d'Ynide, on the other hand, could give you extensive aid in return for materials. Machines and training that could modify every facet of your government administration, your industry, agriculture, your armed forces."

Gabriel sat down by John and looked at him closely. For all his calm manner and cultured voice, a madness glinted in his eyes that John knew could not be assuaged by any amount of reason.

"There will be no publicity," he said. "You came here secretly. Your employers do not wish it known you are here. Even we do not know who you are. Ralph will handle the matter for us very discreetly. I'm sure that while your employers may throw their lesser employees to the lions of moral righteousness, they will not throw such as you. We can keep you for as long as we need, until we are satisfied with what we have received. Years, if necessary. Such details about your company as we need and that Ralph doesn't know, we can obtain from your assistant and your secretary here. Michael is quite a specialist in such matters."

John put his head in his hands and sighed. Then he turned and looked at Lowson.

"Surely you're not a party to this, Ralph?" he said. It was perfectly obvious from Lowson's face that he was not. He seemed to be struggling to say something. Gabriel spared him the effort.

"No, no, my dear sir," he said. "I doubt he would have been agreeable to such a scheme, but he is..." He searched for a word. "He is a pragmatist. He stands in great awe of you, which is why you are here, but he knows where his best interests lie. We have many ties on Ralph."

He sat back and smiled. "Now," he said. "Is this not a far simpler, more effective scheme than yours?"

John rubbed his top lip thoughtfully with the side of his curled forefinger.

"Yes," he conceded. "It has a certain crude charm to it, but it can't work, and it's not in your best long-term interests. It's more fraught with hazard than you've realized. Even in international relations, honour and trust count for something."

"Tut, tut," said Gabriel with a sinister chuckle. "Now it is you who are being naive. You must surely know there are no rules in life."

John smiled to himself and looked up at the ceiling, his thoughts suddenly full of his father and his grandfather. He returned his gaze to Gabriel and looked straight into his eyes.

"Nonetheless," he said. "As I just said to Michael, you're not experienced in the ways of the outside world. You've been isolated for too long. I've come to you as a friend, and everyone needs friends. Trust me. Accept my guidance. Your scheme will lead only to death and sadness for you."

Gabriel felt the threat in the single black eye, even though the face was smiling and the manner gentle. He moved his head back a little, puzzled.

"Who can hurt us here? No-one knows you're here. You've taken pains to ensure that yourself. You are quite a big man, but you are as a child compared to me and unskilled in physical combat. Your assistant is a simple office worker, and your secretary, while strikingly beautiful, is hardly likely to wreak much havoc here, is she?"

Minna looked at him nervously.

"And Ralph," he continued. "Poor Ralph can't help you for many reasons. Come now, let us end this charade and talk seriously about how we can put this revised project into practice. A great deal of unpleasantness will be saved by a little co-operation."

John slumped slightly. He looked up at the Great Father to see what could be read there.

"Great Father. I appeal to you. This is infamous work. If you allow this to happen you will set your country on an ill course. No good can come of such treachery. No-one will ever trust you again."

The Great Father did not speak. His face was passive, but his eyes glinted momentarily with fear and, more significantly, helplessness. *Well now,* thought John. *You let these two get too close, didn't you? At least we know who's in charge now, don't we? Time indeed to end this charade.*

The knot of fear that had been growing in him rolled over in his stomach. Too vulnerable. But this he had known from the start, and accepted it. A brief vision came to him of the end of this great project, his father's last great idea, an extinguishing of hope, of exile among these lunatics whose asinine schemes would not put them in even the lowest echelons of the business. And then the mayhem that would occur as the business lurched out of control in the absence of himself and his aides. It was wrong that such consequences should pivot on such a fragile fulcrum, but there had been no other alternative. That, if anything, defined the essential wrongness of the business.

That momentary overview of his position gave him what he needed. Genes will out. His temperament and training took the ball of fear and squeezed it into a hard glistening sphere of cold anger. It would not be easy. He knew Minna and Hugh could handle Michael and start on the guards, but he was a little less certain about his own ability to deal with Gabriel. He was a formidable man.

Then the anger diffused through and out of him and he relaxed completely. Movement was his to control absolutely—his body predicted nothing.

"I don't know what to say," he said helplessly.

Minna had not moved. She sat on the edge of her chair, apparently resigned, while Hugh sat similarly, still fiddling with the coin in his right hand. They were sitting to his left, and he turned towards them, bringing his right hand across himself and extending both hands to them in a gesture of helplessness. He made the tiny signal the couple had been waiting for, then with both his hands still stretching out to his left, he turned his head to the right as if in a last appeal to Gabriel. Gabriel gazed into the solitary, unreadable eye and did not see John's right hand whipping round until it was too late. The edge struck him above his top lip and a massive concussion filled his head. He was dead before the heel of John's left hand followed through and caught him under the chin, breaking his neck.

As soon as John had signalled, and before his right hand started to move, Hugh cried out in a sing song voice, "Yoo-ee, Michael, catch," and flicked the coin in a high glittering silver arc. Michael's eyes followed it involuntarily. He could not stop them even though he realized it was his last mistake, as out of the corner of his eye he saw Minna surge out of her chair. There was no debate now about hunter and hunted. Michael knew nothing except a hideous certainty when he saw Minna's movement. She was not a woman, but something out of his most terrible dreams—she was his destiny. In those bright, fast-approaching eyes was the fear of a thousand of his victims turned into hate and vengeance. His mind turned into a fleeting, terrible scream of fear before she reached him and drove a pitiless fist into his extended throat, but all the world heard of his dying was a brief, rather inhuman, hissing and croaking.

While he was still falling, Minna seized his pistol from its holster, as did John from Gabriel's, and in a roaring burst of fire they dealt with those attendant Angels that Hugh had not finished off. So fast had been the action that few had had chance even to bring their weapons to bear, and none had fired.

Suddenly, the room was filled with silence except for the roll of a single empty cartridge case across the floor. Gunsmoke drifted faintly in the bright lights, and its acrid smell caught in John's nostrils. He noted absently that the white walls were red spattered in a few places, making a surrealistic pattern. Minna caught his gaze.

"Soft lead hollow points probably," she said.

John nodded.

"Collect the guns, Hugh, and keep one on the door," he said, moving Gabriel's body and reaching into his pockets. He pulled out a loaded magazine and some loose cartridges—soft lead hollow pointed bullets as Minna had said. He dropped the part spent magazine from the gun into his left hand, inserted the new magazine and checked there was a round in the breech. Then he reloaded the first magazine and put it in his pocket.

Minna was muttering to herself as she reloaded Michael's big automatic.

"Sledgehammer," she said in distaste. "We'd have finished in half the time with my .22. And less mess. I'd to take two body shots for sighters."

John let her spit out her self-reproach. Minna was what she was because of her ruthless self-criticism—criticism that should not be hindered.

When she had finished he told her to help Lowson. "I'll have a word with his holiness," he said.

Lowson had taken a headlong dive as soon as he realized what was happening. He was picking himself up shakily when Minna offered him her hand.

"You OK?" she asked in a concerned voice. Lowson did not dare look at her.

"Yes, fine," he said. "No... yes... just... shaky."

He sat down in a chair and buried his face in his hands.

"It'll pass," said Minna.

The Great Father sat motionless as John approached him up the steps of the dais.

"God's will, your Holiness," said John, without any hint of irony. "The Devil comes in many guises, does he not?"

The Great Father opened his mouth, but no sound came out. John stood behind him and laid an affectionate hand on his shoulder. The bright lights threw his shadow across the Great Father and across the floor to dominate the room.

"I think," he said, "that you're in a position to announce that through divine intervention you've been saved from the agents of the Devil. Agents who came in the form of your most trusted servants. You can exhort your citizens to even greater vigilance, and any further aspirants to the position of Archangels will almost certainly be hesitant about indulging in any excess of personal authority, don't you think?"

"Yes," said the Great Father, with some difficulty. "Agents of the Devil. Yes. He blinded me to their true nature until the Lord intervened and the scales fell from my eyes."

*Again,* thought John. "As your humble protector, may I trust the safety of my agents and employees to your hands in the future?"

The Great Father nodded earnestly. "Of course. They'll all be most honoured guests."

The Great Father was stunned as much by the sudden and unexpected return of his power as by the whirlwind violence that had returned it. The head of the serpent having been lopped off, the body would be no trouble, but he realized it was essential he maintained the friendship of this lethal one-eyed man and his awesome servants.

As if reading his thought, John emphasized the point. "You must understand, Great Father, that I am not too happy about this type of conduct. It disturbs my routine, and puts too many more important matters on the wheel of chance. However, it's not uncommon, and had Michael and Gabriel detained us a mere day longer than we envisaged, then a far greater vengeance would have been wrought on this palace and yourself. I'm the respected servant of powerful men who'll not tolerate my being abused. They'll deal honourably with anyone, but we're always prepared for every treachery. Accept my guidance, give your blessing to this project. It will yield you a treasure chest, where Michael and Gabriel would have brought you a coffin."

The Great Father nodded his agreement. John patted his shoulder and stepped away from him, his shadow vanishing as he moved from the light. From the foot of the dais he looked up. "Perhaps later we can visit the site of the city that will guard the crossing, and you can bless it. It'll be an affirmation of the new beginning for your people."

"John."

Hugh's voice brought John's attention to the mounting hubbub outside the door.

"The natives are getting restless," said Minna.

John looked up at the Great Father and nodded his permission. "Speak to your people."

The Great Father pressed a switch on the arm of his couch.

"My people," boomed his stentorian voice throughout the palace. "Today a great evil has arisen and a great and wondrous miracle has been wrought..."

# Chapter 36

The blessing of the site of the city which was to be the guardian of one end of the crossing was a comparatively modest affair. The Great Father was still shaken at the sudden and violent change in his fortunes, and the demise of his Archangels did give rise to some minor administrative problems. Also, the site was only a rough-hewn plateau made suitable for the reception of small aircraft by men who had reached it only after a long and difficult journey through harsh mountain terrain. Its inaccessibility precluded any joyous crowds other than those who could quickly be squeezed into the Great Father's fleet of light planes, so these would be added afterwards to the films which were to be taken by the official news crew.

Minna and Hugh discreetly ensured that neither they, Lowson nor John accidentally appeared in these films.

After the brief ceremony, Lowson took John up onto a nearby crag that overlooked the Straits. The view was impressive. Cliffs and rocky slopes tumbled away from them, down into the shoreless edge of the Straits, and some fifteen miles away, but seeming much closer, was the equally harsh coastline of Tier d'Ynide. Between lay the treacherous Renviss Straits. Even from this height, John could see the water surface was scrofulous with foam and turbulence glinting in the sun. To their right on the far shore, one black mountain could be seen in the distance, dominating its local group.

"Mount t'Innged," said Lowson in reply to John's query. "They don't normally name mountains round here, but that one's special."

"In what way?" asked John, staring thoughtfully at the brooding peak.

Although there were no eavesdroppers, Lowson instinctively lowered his voice.

"Well. Before himself took over," he jerked his head discreetly towards the huge white clad figure below, currently being positioned by his camera crew, "the natives used to worship that mountain as the home of the giant god t'Innged. One day, they said, when he is old, he will seize the mountain and hurl it down upon them and destroy the world for its sinfulness."

John smiled. "That's a little unusual," he said. "Disasters like that are often associated with the loss of some spectacular balanced rock, but I've never heard of one involving a whole mountain falling down."

"Don't forget, John," said Lowson. "This landscape is geologically quite young—it's unstable. That's why the Straits are so turbulent and so fast. These people are used to earthquakes, in so far as you can ever be. Big rockfalls are routine. Their mythology's not completely... mythic."

John nodded. "Point taken. And it's a splendid mountain."

"Yes," agreed Lowson. "Not exactly world class for height but, as you say, quite splendid—very impressive."

The party made its farewells to the Great Father at the now holy site, and then flew by helicopter directly to Tier d'Ynide.

Conversation was not easy over the noise of the machine.

"Assessment," shouted John to Hugh and Minna.

"Too close for comfort for my taste," said Hugh. "But the good guys won in the end."

"Yes," John agreed. "But we'd no alternative, had we, given the cards we were dealt? I'll confess to some doubts about dealing with Gabriel, but..."

"Yes, I noticed," said Minna. "But it was lovely timing that. I barely picked it up myself. Your relaxation's improving." She paused briefly. "But you still need to loosen up your hips." She twisted in her seat by way of demonstration.

John laughed. "You're probably right, Minna, but that's all behind us now. What about the Great Father?"

"No need to ask," said Minna. "He'll be alright now. Quite trustworthy in his way, oddly enough. And he won't let his personal guards get such an upper hand again in future. There'll be some rare old purging over the next few weeks I'll wager."

"Resentment?" queried John.

"Maybe a little," said Minna. "But mainly relief. He picked up your cues fast enough and he's far from being stupid. He's seen what we can do on a small scale on the spur of the moment, and given he's paranoid he'll exaggerate wildly about what we can do on a larger scale. I think he knows he got off lightly and isn't being blamed. He knows he's still needed and that it's in our interests to help and sustain him. It's a good balance. I think we did very well considering how it could have come out."

"I agree," said John. "Very well indeed."

Then he turned to Lowson.

"Ralph," he said. "What the hell happened?"

Lowson went pale as the memory of the massacre returned.

"I don't expect miracles, Ralph, and I know you have to keep your nose right out of certain matters in these places, but didn't you have any idea what those two lunatics were going to do?" In deference to Lowson's patent distress, John pitched his query in gentle tones.

Lowson shook his head desperately. "None at all, John. None at all. Whenever I've dealt directly with the Great Father, they've always been there, and a lot of the detailed negotiations were with them and a few lesser officials." He put his hand to his chest. "If I'd had the faintest inkling of anything like that I wouldn't have walked *me* into it, let alone you, for pity's sake."

John patted his arm. "I understand, Ralph. No-one's blaming you."

He dismissed any lingering doubts. At worst, Lowson was a very unwilling party to the would-be abduction, and, like the Great Father, if he had had any intention of playing some game on his own it would be well and truly dead by now.

"There's no question in any of our minds about your loyalty," continued John. "But I want you to think very carefully now." He looked earnestly into Lowson's face. "Is there any chance we could be walking into something similar in d'Ynide?"

Lowson answered immediately with a shake of his head. "No. I've been thinking about nothing else since..." He did not finish the comment. "Haran's a much more, how shall I say, Western dictator, if you like. Logical and sophisticated. And I've had much more personal contact with him from when he was the power behind the throne. He spent years manipulating the old man. He knows all the tricks. No-one will get anywhere near as close to him as those two Archangels did, and live. He oversees a lot of administrative work personally, and never lets anyone else get anything approaching an overall view."

John sat back thoughtfully. Lowson's comments coincided with other information he had gathered about Haran. And he had taken the straight bribe and the contingency rescue route.

His reverie was interrupted as the helicopter bucked and jerked suddenly. Hugh looked out of the window.

"Coastline," he said. John turned, and saw through his window the bulk of Mount t'Innged in the distance, looking black even in the bright sunlight. He wondered what walking through these mountains would be like. No marked paths here, no civilization within a few hours walk, pitiless heat and cold—not a terrain for idle leisure. But living in it, a man would find new depths within himself. *Still*, he thought, as he thought almost every day, *you don't have to come this far to die on a mountain.*

Then his thoughts returned to the matter in hand.

He yawned. "It's been a busy couple of days," he said. "I don't think we'll have any more trouble, but stay loose."

Haran's headquarters were rectangular, functional and spartan, with stainless steel and black predominating. It was peopled with unsmiling and regimented souls. As John had envisaged, there were no problems. Haran gave his guests every courtesy and was quite straightforward, if stiff and humourless, in his dealings. He was much closer to John in character than the Great Father, and clearly differentiated between his private and public personas. He thanked John for the arrangements that he had made for him, assured him that in due course he would work for the best interests of the two countries when they were eventually joined, and generally seemed anxious that the scheme should begin in earnest as soon as possible.

He had obviously caught wind of the attempted palace coup in Tier r'Vern, and he asked about it quite directly, a brief smile threatening to crack his thin mouth. He accepted John's non-committal reply with a similar smile.

"A little domestic problem, I think, General. Fortunately, we weren't involved, but the Great Father seems to have everything under control. In fact he seems to have reinforced his position. So our scheme can go ahead unhindered."

Only one thing scarred the visit to d'Ynide. The four of them were sitting in a guest room until Lowson's plane was ready for take-off. John was beginning to feel a little fretful. He really did not like being away from his family and the heart of the business, although he had to concede that the visits had been most successful. He was running over the events again. The problem at Tier r'Vern had been unexpected, but those two clowns had forced the issue and would have done it in some other way sooner or later, especially if he had not agreed to make the visit.

The business's well-tried policy of personal defence, his own ability to make rapid assessments, and the special skills and teamwork of Hugh and Minna had combined to deal with the problem but he did not like it. It was a single node in his plan on which all could have foundered and, looking back, it seemed to have been far riskier and more dangerous than it had seemed at the time. Then again it had been unforeseeable.

He stretched his legs out. Just reaction, he thought. No harm in it. You've done all the analyzing you can, just let the thoughts come and go—let them wander freely then they won't fester. He closed his eyes and settled back in his chair. Then suddenly he thought, *thanks dad. If I never thanked you before, then I do so now, you'd have been pleased as punch at the three of us.*

Abruptly he opened his eyes. The murmur of his friends had stopped. Minna was sitting up in her chair, her hand raised slightly, stilled in the gesture she had used to cut short the conversation, and her head turned slightly to one side, listening intently. John moved a little in his chair so that he could better draw his gun if necessary.

"What's the matter?" he asked softly.

Minna's hand beckoned silence. "There's something queer outside the door," she said after a moment.

"Queer?"

Before Minna could reply, the door swung open and revealed a figure in an olive green overall. For a moment it stood in the doorway, and then hesitantly and awkwardly walked forward a few paces before stopping again. Lowson swore under his breath. The figure seemed to offer no menace, but made John feel uncomfortable. Minna's reaction was startling.

She spun round to Lowson.

"What is it?" she hissed, eyes gleaming.

Lowson turned his face away from her baleful gaze, without any pretence of politeness, fear radiating from him.

"Minna," admonished John gently. "What on earth's the matter?"

"He knows," she said without moving, still keeping Lowson transfixed. John reached forward and touched her arm.

"Easy, Minna," he whispered. "Let him go."

Then, turning to the figure, he said, "Can I help you?"

The figure swayed slightly and stared fixedly ahead, its face devoid of response and its eyes glazed.

"Probably doesn't speak English," volunteered Hugh.

"He can't answer you," said Lowson, taking out a handkerchief and wiping his forehead.

"Can't?" queried John. "Why not? What do you mean?"

Lowson was taking deep breaths, trying unsuccessfully to calm himself. John made a note to keep him further away from Minna in future. He seemed abnormally sensitive to her.

"He's the remains of one of Haran's experiments, probably," said Lowson finally.

John looked at the vacant figure. He felt a chill pervade him, belying utterly the hot sun pouring through the windows.

"What kind of experiment?" he asked.

"Behaviour control experiments," said Lowson. "Using electronic implants in the brain."

"Jesus Christ," said Hugh softly. "I thought they were all newspaper nonsense."

"Explain," said John.

Lowson was reluctant. "I don't know much about it. A lot of it's just rumour. It's something they developed from their interrogation techniques. They're hoping to use it for prisoner control, in the jails. In its simplest form it's an aerial and amplifier which causes pain. Prisoner walks past a certain point, through a control beam and wham—intense pain and the activation of an alarm. They say it'll make prison conditions more humane."

John could not take his eyes off the swaying figure.

"And this one? This man?" he asked.

"He's probably... a mistake... on the operating table," said Lowson. "A slight mistake." He swallowed and continued. "The big mistakes

318

usually die. It's not a society for looking after its helpless. Those you see wandering about in green overalls, as far as I know, are near misses. They're virtually catatonic. They do various menial jobs about the place."

He mopped his forehead again.

"Brave new world," said John to himself, standing up. He felt that Lowson knew more than he was admitting, and as if in confirmation Minna spoke urgently.

"John. He's no mindless catatonic. There's a man screaming inside him."

John felt his eyes widen in horror and the hairs on his neck and arms crawl upright. He was about to speak when two white coated officials bustled in through the open door. Their coats bore the bracketed trident emblem of the Kithrile Poliz.

"Ah," said the smaller of the two jovially. "Here we are. I hope our friend's not disturbed you." Then, confidentially, reassuringly. "He's one of the cleaning staff, sad case. Brain damaged at birth. Quite harmless, but apt to wander at times. I do hope he didn't startle you."

"No, no," stammered John, unthinkingly polite.

"Good, good, good," said the busy little man. He took a device from his pocket and tapped its keys fussily. "Come along," he said playfully. The figure turned round and walked out of the room. The busy little man closed the door behind him with a friendly wave to the silent group. John felt Hugh and Minna about to speak and he cut them off with a sharp gesture. *We'll discuss this later,* he thought. *The sooner we get our computers in here, the better. There's too much we don't know.*

He sat down wearily. "Ralph," he said. "Be so kind as to find out how much longer your plane is going to be, would you?"

Stepping out of the plane into the English winter, John shivered and fastened his coat up to the neck.

"Good to be back," he said, taking a deep cold breath. "Good to be back."

Lowson had stayed on in Tier d'Ynide to continue with details of the negotiations and to launch his design teams on the monumental task ahead. John, Hugh and Minna had spent most of their return journey in an uneasy silence. The figure in the green overalls

319

haunted them all. There would be plenty of time to talk later, and they all needed to rest and assimilate what they had seen and heard.

John looked at his car, waiting on the tarmac and lit by lights shining from the airport terminal. It was flanked by heaped rows of freshly cleared snow. Gwilier's comforting bulk was at the wheel, and Freddy's smile reached out to greet him and pull him back to earth.

# Chapter 37

Lowson's expulsion from Tier r'Vern and Tier d'Ynide was public and spectacular. Arriving at the airport he was greeted by reporters from the press, television and radio, none of whom would normally go out of their way to greet a civil engineering contractor expelled from some totalitarian state. But Lowson was different. He might be the head of a large multi-national company, but he was accessible and he could almost always he guaranteed to say or do something controversial. His lifestyle was flamboyant and well away from muddy boots and hard hats, and his long links with two of the world's most detested regimes made him attractive game for the media.

"Gentlemen, gentlemen," he said smilingly, lifting his arms as if he was trying to beat the jostling group flat. "Oh, and ladies" he added apologetically, affectionately squeezing the hand of a particularly strident female who had succeeded in making her way through to him by the very effective use of her otherwise unseasonal stiletto heels on the feet of her colleagues. The hubbub fell slightly.

"Gentlemen. For the time being I've got to say 'no comment' to you all. I'm sorry about that, you all know how I love to talk, but I've had a very hectic two weeks, which did not end as satisfactorily as I had hoped. Also I've a large number of employees still over in r'Vern and d'Ynide, and their safety is paramount."

Various cries of dismay rose from the reporters.

"Come on, Ralph, give us something, off the record."

"Off the record," repeated Lowson with studied thoughtfulness. He looked from side to side and then bent forward conspiratorially. "Off the record," he said. "It's going to be a long hard winter."

This brought further protests as he strode off towards the lounge. The group babbled after him until he stopped abruptly and flopped down wearily on a nearby couch, his long face taking on a tired and weary look. The reporters circled him and waited.

"Give me some time, folks," he said. "You know I don't want to mess you about. But it's been rough, and unexpected and I'm bushed. I do have a lot of staff out there and I don't want any off-the-cuff remarks of mine to put them in jeopardy. Let me see my directors and shareholders first, then the foreign office people, and I promise you a proper press conference as soon as I can. OK?" His demeanour as much as his words seemed to mollify his besiegers, and after taking a few photographs and filming some apologetic "no comments" the group gradually dispersed.

When they had gone, a man approached Lowson quietly and sat next to him.

"Anything for me, Ralph?" It was a reporter from one of the more respected trade papers, a reliable and trustworthy man. Lowson smiled and shook the man's hand.

"Nice to see you, Derek," he said. "I noticed you avoiding the circus."

The reporter smiled in return. "Discretion is the better part of valour, Ralph. I think that harridan from the Daily Whatsit has maimed three for life, and those TV people with their long mikes..."

Lowson could not forbear laughing at this, coming as it did from such a staid individual. "Oh well. We can't all be respectable can we Derek?" he said. "I've seen you tread on a few toes before now."

"Rarely," replied the man, with dignity. "And usually only in self-defence."

Lowson's smile faded and he sagged back into the couch. "I'm sorry Derek. I've nothing for you, on or off the record. What I said was straight up."

"Are you sure about off the record?"

Lowson screwed up his mouth pensively and looked at the man.

"Off the record. Right off it, Derek, understand?" The man nodded. "I'm out, Derek. And someone else is in."

The reporter whistled. "Who, for heaven's sake?"

Lowson shrugged. "I haven't a clue, not a clue," he said.

"But you've been there for years, you've got unparalleled local knowledge. Who on earth can equal that?"

Lowson shrugged again. "I told you, Derek, I haven't a clue." Then, more earnestly, "But they've got all my records and most of my key staff, and they'll just have to do as they're told, independent of any hoohah in the world's press and the UN."

The reporter nodded. "And what are you going to do?" he asked.

"What I said. Shareholders, directors, foreign office, and then I'm taking a long rest. Somewhere quiet and away from this ice age."

"Your blood's getting thin, Ralph," said the reporter standing up.

"Thanks for the information. I'll keep it under wraps." They shook hands again. The reporter looked at him. "You're looking tired Ralph, take it easy," he said.

Lowson raised a hand in acknowledgement and the reporter moved away into the airport crowds.

Lowson made some front page news and appeared briefly in most of the TV news programmes. The weightier editorials and one of the TV magazine programmes pursued the matter in a little more depth, speculating on the cause of Lowson's expulsion after so many years of faithful if controversial service, and on the probable future of his company. On that, Lowson was his old self.

"It's never nice to lose a good client," he assured his interviewer. "But the company has world-wide interests and a good solid trading base. It's a minor setback, not a death blow by any means."

On the matter of why he had been expelled, he continued to plead the safety of his workers still over there, and on the matter of who would replace him to complete the various, not insubstantial schemes already under way, he shrugged.

"I wish I knew," he said. "It'll probably come to light eventually. But it needn't be one of the bigger concerns. Don't forget I've a great many key designers and engineers over there. It's not going to be in their interests to do poor work so almost anyone could organize them."

John clicked off the television set and nodded contentedly. Freddy caught the gesture.

"What are you looking so pleased about?" she asked. "Isn't the bank one of Lowson's main backers?"

John did not want to lie too much. "Yes," he said. "It is."

"Is this business going to give you any problems?"

John pulled a face. "Financially it'll be a bit of a blow, but we're big enough to ride it out without too much trouble. In a way I'm glad Ralph is out of there. They were always a hot potato."

"Is that what you went over for? To try and keep that contact?" asked Freddy.

"Partly," John replied. "But they're grotesque places. No information about what's happening, skulduggery on skulduggery, gunpowder treason and plot par excellence. It's dreadful. Ralph seems to thrive on it, but it's not my style at all."

Freddy raised her eyebrows to crown a look of disbelief. "Huh," she said. "I wouldn't say you were the epitome of openness and clarity when it came to business."

John gave her a wry look but chose not to pursue the remark.

He leaned back and watched her through his half-closed eye. So far so good, he thought. Very shortly, Lowson's value as a headline would be almost nothing and he would be able to slip into the background, ostensibly taking a long holiday to recover from the strain of recent events, details unpublished, which led to his leaving Tier r'Vern and Tier d'Ynide. Foreign Office officials would potter about making vain efforts to recover his staff, but their inevitable bureaucratic ineptitude together with occasional snippets of leaked information that Lowson's employees, while unequivocally hostages, were being treated well and were in no immediate danger, would ensure that the matter would be kept well to the rear of general public interest.

The whole matter had been carefully arranged between all the interested parties, so that when construction eventually became visible to the rest of the world, Lowson would be able to stand up in public and claim no knowledge or involvement. A series of identities had been prepared for Ralph to ensure he could pass through neighbouring countries to gain access to Tier r'Vern and Tier d'Ynide at any time if he was needed but in fact, there should be no great need for his frequent presence on site. The "hostages" were key people who had been carefully selected, not only for their skills, but also for their willingness to go along with the scheme. Individual motives were as varied as the number chosen. Some wanted the money, some wanted to tackle the monumental challenge, some had personal loyalties to Lowson, others dared not show their faces in most other parts of the world. All would be able, in the future, to say they had been forced to work, and John ensured that the two conditions for security would be met. They would all be very well paid and receive handsome pensions. Enough compromising evidence would be gathered, or manufactured, against each, for blackmail, should the need arise.

The less capable, the more scrupulous, those with relatives at home who could become a nuisance, were "expelled" along with Lowson as a tribute to his skill as a negotiator under difficult conditions. The selection of the key people had been the next largest hurdle to be cleared after gaining the acceptance of Haran and the Great Father, and it had gone fairly smoothly.

"That's an old man's trick," Freddy's voice cut across his self-congratulation.

He opened his eye and scowled at her. "What is?" he demanded.

"Nodding off in the chair," she said.

"I did not nod off," he said indignantly. "I was thinking over a business problem."

Freddy blew a raspberry. "Go on," she said disparagingly. "You were snoring like a grampus."

John grunted. "If it's not too much to ask, may I enquire the reason for this quite unprovoked attack and that vicious calumny about my breath control?"

Freddy folded her newspaper and dropped it by the side of her chair. "No, you may not," she said, standing up. "But you may take me for a walk."

John's eye widened. "It's freezing out there, Freddy," he said.

"Good," she replied. "It'll sharpen you up a bit. Make you stop bringing your work home and nodding off with it in front of the fire."

"Oh," he said, in mock contrition. But he realized she was right. Since his father's death he had become increasingly preoccupied with the Renviss project. Not without reason—it was massive and important—but he had started to break his own rules, the business's rules. What could be done would be done, he knew that, and then it should be left behind when he closed his own door. It was a long-term project and he could not afford to fret over its details incessantly or he would lose his edge, and start to make mistakes. What subconscious process had led Freddy to make her bantering stand he had no idea, but he was thankful for it. Not for the first time, the ties of love and affection for his family had pulled him back to earth, as they had his father before him.

325

Outside, the landscape was bright with moonlit snow, and patchworked with inky shadows. The unlit roads in the immediate vicinity of the house could be negotiated without the aid of a torch, and Freddy set John a brisk pace for the best part of an hour, although she slowed down a little when they moved off the road and took a short cut through a small copse, the stark branches dark enough to be silhouetted against the black sky.

"Wooooh," he hooted suddenly in her ear, seizing her round the waist.

"Don't do that," she snapped as she slapped his hands away. Then she put both her arms through his and leaned on him as they walked. Leaving the copse, they were walking across a field back towards the road when John stopped abruptly and held his finger to his mouth for silence.

"What is it?" Freddy whispered.

"Sh... sh..." he said urgently. They stood for what seemed a very long time, he listening intently, she listening suspiciously.

"There. Listen," he whispered. "Very faint."

Then she heard it, a long way away, a distant, plaintive howl, perhaps a chorus, coming and going on the imperceptible night breeze. John stood absolutely still, holding his breath. Then a car passed on the nearby road, and as its harsh headlights destroyed the delicate winter scenery, so its noise swept away the distant message of the wolves. John's face was aglow.

"Did you hear it?" he said, putting his arm around his wife and moving off towards the road.

She nodded, but did not speak.

"What a sound," he said. "They're a long way away. I hope they come closer."

"Well I don't," said Freddy. "I've no desire to be chased by wolves every time I go for a walk."

John chuckled. "I told you when we saw them by the wood, they're not dangerous. They'll have to be desperately hungry before they'll have a go at a wild ape. We might think this is a bad winter, but it's nothing to them. They'll find enough to eat, don't mither."

Freddy's expression remained unchanged. He stopped and turned to face her.

"Freddy, I'm serious. They're sophisticated social animals. Don't confuse them with people. They kill to eat, to feed themselves and their young. They've got most of our civilized traits and few of our more murderous ones. Don't worry. Just listen to that song, and feel a little envy."

She smiled. "John. You're a screwball. For a business tycoon you're still a schoolboy. I love you but I don't think I'll ever understand you."

"Don't worry love," he replied. "Neither will I."

Later that night John lay awake and reviewed his recent conduct. It left a lot to be desired. The rules that governed the business were the distillation of the wisdom and bloody experience of many generations and were put aside only at terrible risk. Having broken one rule, how many others had he neglected? How much carelessness had he injected into the running of the business, just because the Renviss project needed such special attention? He found himself staring at the obvious. If the business started to slide, then Renviss would become irrelevant, or worse. He nodded to himself and made a stern resolve. As far as he could see, no great harm had been done, but it could have been. He had been on the verge of a serious misjudgement. He turned on his side and kissed his sleeping wife's forehead.

"Thanks," he said.

# Chapter 38

The crossing of the Renviss Straits presented Ralph Lowson's team with design and construction problems well above the average. Extremes of temperature, most unzephyr-like breezes, fast and turbulent currents and the need to have the structure protected against missile and other attacks, plus the occasional earthquake to stir things up, came to an impressive total.

The crossing was to be almost a mile wide, narrowing only towards the centre where a great bridge would arch across the deep channel which was the path of the original river. Seeing a model of the scheme, the Great Father's eyes had glinted when they lit on the bridge.

"Ah," he said, breathlessly. "It will be a covenant to my people for generations in perpetuity as they spread the Lord's message across the face of the earth."

Lowson was less than pleased at this. The model had been made in the early stages of the scheme, primarily as a focus for initial ideas from the design team, and the Great Father had spotted it almost by accident. Subsequent surveys showed the central channel to be much wider than indicated by the old records they had to use for preliminary work, and some form of suspension bridge would have been a far more economical choice. However, out of all the grandeur of the scheme, the Great Father seized on the bridge. His bridge. His covenant. And Lowson thought it wisest to let the matter lie, even though it presented some hair-raisingly difficult technical problems. John agreed with him.

"The extra cost is unfortunate but not really critical, Ralph, compared with the rest of the job and what we're all going to make of it.

If it keeps himself quiet it'll probably stop him fiddling with other parts of the scheme. Let your lads enjoy it. There must be some satisfaction for an engineer to build the biggest ever."

Twenty traffic lanes and ten rail lines shared two separate levels down the centre of the crossing, an umbilical duct between the two countries. At the sides, extending to the edges of the crossing, would be huge building complexes. The Renviss crossing was to be no ordinary river crossing—a slender road on stilts. It was to be an elongated city. More correctly, an elongated fortress, a great steel and concrete shackle binding the two countries together. Mounted along each side, but well hidden, would be missile launching areas to protect the bridge from air attack. Its defences, however, would be twofold. When news of the scheme eventually spread abroad, with it would go the information that the building complexes which formed its greater part were to be used not only for industrial and military purposes, but also to house thousands of civilians. An attack on the crossing would thus become an attack on these innocents. Such a detail would not ultimately deter an attack if hostilities broke out, but it would defer it for a long time.

At each end of the crossing would be a great city, tiered into the sides of the coastal ranges, and from each of these would spread road and rail links, soaring over valleys and twisting and tunnelling through the mountains, to serve the heartlands of the two countries.

Accessibility being such a difficult problem from the point of view both of bringing materials into the country and then transporting them to the crossing sites, it was decided that the scheme should start in Tier r'Vern and move across to Tier d'Ynide. The most important road and rail links would be built up to and through the mountains, providing access for the materials for their own building, and subsequently for the building of the crossing.

The irritating grain around which would grow the pearl that the Great Father had christened his Celestial City would be a huge construction camp serving the crossing.

For contending with international opinion, everyone would have preferred to start at both ends and to meet in the middle. But that option was not practical.

"It'll be a long time before anyone finds out what's happening and even longer before they'll try to do anything," said John in reassurance. "Don't forget that this crossing will be equipped with defences as it is being built."

The decision had in fact come as a relief to him. It eased his cash problems, and in extending the project it gave him greater flexibility for his long-term plans.

As the months went by, the scheme slowly got under way. Security was phenomenal. Even John's closest advisers knew nothing of the true purpose of the various financial transactions they were manipulating. Only John, Hugh and Minna had overall view and they ensured that all cash movement was routed through a myriad untraceable manoeuvres that were the genesis of the labyrinth. Head Office staff was discreetly reshuffled from time to time, but this had always been a standard routine, and caused no special problems or concern. By definition, people who rose high in the ranks of the business knew very well which side their bread was buttered and understood the need for and the implementation of the business's security arrangements. They advised and commented freely when asked, and even when not, but all knew that ultimately, theirs was to do or die, not reason why.

John used Hugh and Minna to deal with the finances while Gwilier acted as his main liaison with Lowson and the two heads of state. To everyone's surprise, not least his own, Gwilier became interested in the technicalities of the scheme. In fact, the birth of his interest came like a revelation to him when he was with Lowson on one of his periodic visits to the site.

Lowson was occupied with a phone conversation, and Gwilier found himself looking idly over some drawings. To his innocent eye, they were minor works of art, with their neat clean lines and immaculate printing. They had a precision and elegance which appealed to some aesthetic sense within him. Quite abruptly he realized that what he was looking at on paper was something he had actually seen only a few minutes earlier. Without a word he picked up the drawing and ran out of the office into the dazzling r'Vern sun and the dust of the busy site. Keeping a careful ear open for the approach of the death-dealing dumper trucks that the local labourers drove with such abandon, he wandered over a section of newly laid road in search of his vision. There it was. Nothing spectacular, just a large rectangular culvert passing underneath the road to carry floodwater from the few severe summer storms that occurred every year. Gwilier looked at the drawing and at the culvert and the road over it. The reality did not have the clarity and elegance of the drawing, but it was unmistakeable.

He gazed at it like a child. Lowson came up to him, puffing slightly, and peered anxiously around his arm at the drawing.

"What's the matter, Dick?" he asked.

Gwilier shook his head and felt rather foolish. "Nothing Ralph," he said. "I've only just realized that this is that."

He tapped the drawing and pointed to the culvert. Lowson's long face lit up in a friendly laugh as he looked at the expression on the face of this huge, sophisticated and normally enigmatic aide of John Newman.

"Oh, Dick," he said. "You take me back years. You just reminded me of what it's like when you see your first drawing actually being built. It's a very strange feeling—very scary."

He shook his head in delight, then his face became sad and pensive as if he was passing again the darker portions of his life that had signposted the journey from that exciting loss of his draughtsman's virginity to the present.

"Come on," he said impulsively. "I'll show you some more."

And the rest of the day was spent poring over drawings with Lowson, pencil in hand, explaining and sketching, and Gwilier finding himself more and more enthralled with the splendid scheme he was party to. John could not forbear a little teasing whenever Gwilier's accumulating technical knowledge accidently slipped out in conversation.

"You're like a grandparent with its grandchild, Dick, you and this scheme. All the fun and none of the responsibility."

"Yes," said Dick unashamedly. "And why not? It's great."

Hugh and Minna never visited the site again, nor did John. They were his subtle messengers, charged with the task of implementing the main thrust of his plan. The personnel involved in the scheme were selected very carefully. Slowly, cautiously, Hugh and Minna laid out bait to attract these people, the business's more unsavoury servants, and slowly they were drawn in. Some, for the most part crime leaders from across the world, became involved directly. Information was rumoured to them via sources they considered reliable, or on whom they depended, that an offshore scheme was afoot that would develop into one of the biggest gambling and leisure complexes in the world, in a location which would not have extradition treaties with anyone. It would be a project whose sponsors could look to have special protection in the international troubles that would arise when the scheme was finished, as finished it surely would be. Just rumours of course, at first. Then Hugh and Minna would use their other political and law enforcement contacts to apply a squeeze here, a little pressure there, just to remind these big wheels that there are bumps in every road, no matter how well padded you are, and to cast the mirage of this El Dorado in an even more favourable light than could be done by appealing to greed alone.

"They're sweet really," said Minna, in a mood of heavy irony. "All they want in life is a little security."

Eventually all the chosen were to be seen jostling and clamouring at the trough. A similar ploy was used to suck in those captains of industry and their political allies whose enterprises and attitudes stood in the way of John's plans for the business, but the emphasis here was mainly in the especially discreet banking and company law facilities that would be available in this new venture, particularly for those who helped in the early stages. For the smaller fry, corrupt officials and lesser politicians and the like, a net of a different mesh was laid, and they were lured into backing some of the hundreds of companies who were unwittingly acting as sub-contractors to the scheme.

John took it as a point of honour, and as a salute to his father's early days, that as far as was possible or appropriate such companies would be found to be innocent of malice in the event of an expose, while their backers would be flushed down the toilet.

Little bubbles of news appeared occasionally in the papers, where some minor leak had sprung in the security, or where a rumour had been misdirected, but all served to shore up the credibility of the project to its investors. As a rule, John did not like to tamper too much with the press and the broadcasting media. "Too many people jealously guarding their right to say what they like regardless of anyone else," he would say. "And a damn sight too many people holding the steering wheel for my taste. All of them arguing about where they've been, and no-one looking where they're going." Useful for mass murder, he concluded, but no good as a rule for the more precise social engineering he required.

Altogether it was some four years before John could confirm with Hugh and Minna that everyone who was to be involved, was involved. The situation would be kept under constant review. Some might be eased out, others might be brought in, but for most, the die had been cast. Coincidently, at about the same time, the first road and rail links had completed their tortuous journey through the mountains and had arrived at the coast of Tier r'Vern. Hitherto, the technology of Tier d'Ynide had been used to confuse and distort satellite observation, but now the burgeoning site camp and the beginning of the work on the crossing was visible from other shores and from distant aircraft.

John smiled as he read the first flurry of alarmed headlines.

"Good," he said. "Excellent. Now the ordure's starting to hit the fan, our investors won't even try to look back."

The carrot of greed, and the stick of fear of discovery, urged them on in one direction only. Some of the direct investors were already borrowing, unwittingly from other business sources, to solve the cash problems caused by their over enthusiasm. It would be only a comparatively short time before they realized that they could only go forward, because to back out would, amongst other things, involve massive financial losses. The press stories heightened the excitement and helped to ensure continuing support. A slight tremor passed through those investors from legitimate business, but they were easily quietened by the same "old boy" assurances that had drawn them in in the first place.

"Into the penultimate phase," said John. "We've nothing to do now but keep our eye on things and weather the political storms that will blow."

And blow they did. Great howling gales, mighty gusts of oratory, swirling clouds of political analyses. Anxiety from Europe, stern resolve from the USA, clenched terseness from the Eastern Bloc, bravura and panache from Latin America, some very ambivalent wind watching from the kite fliers of China, and varying degrees of confusion from everyone else. Lowson was tracked down, ostensibly on holiday again.

"I've told you gentlemen. Even now I still have no idea who is building this thing, or how it's being funded. It was never even discussed with me."

"But Mr. Lowson, it must be your people who're doing it."

Lowson rounded on the unfortunate questioner. "I know damn well they're my people. I've been shouting about it for long enough, ever since I was expelled. What am I supposed to do about them, hitchhike out there and bring them back in a rowing boat down the Straits? And what are *they* supposed to do? Risk being shot, or worse, because our politicians haven't the wits to get something worked out for them? And don't quote me on that last bit," he snarled as an afterthought.

The UN nearly passed a resolution banning all trade with the two countries until the British Ambassador delicately pointed out that they had passed one many years previously. It was taken out, dusted and reaffirmed, and most countries tightened up their own "no-trade" legislation. National security agencies started ferreting around to find out where the resources and money were coming from, but the business's track-covering was of a high order, and Minna's computer system was used both to spot trouble coming, and to insert red herrings into official records if anyone appeared to be getting too close.

The crossing, however, moved inexorably forward and life in the office for John and his two messengers became comparatively calm.

# Chapter 39

At home, John's life was not quite so calm. He didn't have his father's exceptional sensitivity in dealing with his children and, while no serious friction arose, he found it difficult to guide Phillip in exactly the way he wanted him to go.

"He's too damned honest. Too much sense of fair play. Life's a game, play it by the rules," he confided to Hugh. "I ask you, where did he get an idea like that from? He's not enough of a controlled schizophrenic for this business. But I've got to bring him further in, Hugh, one way or another. He's got all the makings if I can just straighten him out. God, I wish my dad was here."

Hugh was less concerned. "You're too close John. He's OK. I know the lad's in his twenties, but he adores you and he listens, John, he listens—the family trait. He'll be alright when it comes to the crunch."

John looked at him almost plaintively.

"To be honest," continued Hugh. "I've a feeling that Stephen's the one who'll surprise us. They may end up in tandem yet."

John shrugged off the mood. There was nothing insoluble in the problem of his sons if he bent his mind to it, but Hugh's remark about Stephen did make him ponder.

Stephen had, and could continue to have, a moderately successful career as a concert pianist but on his last visit home he had been strangely subdued. Eventually Ann prised it out of him. For some obscure reason, she cultivated the image of a frail and foolish old lady, while in reality she was sharper and more alert than she had ever been, making Freddy laugh with her acid observations, and deflating John when he aspired to pomposity.

She inveigled Stephen into playing for her, and when he had finished she sat there in silence. Stephen looked at her suspiciously.

"Well?" he said, bracing himself for impact.

There was a long silence, then she said, very gently, "What's the matter Stephen?" The suddenness of the question and the sensitivity in the voice brushed aside Stephen's reserve and any fumbling excuses he might have sought.

"Is it that obvious?" he asked.

"To me," replied Ann. "Come and sit down and talk to your old gran."

So they talked for a long time. Stephen loved his music; it was a deep and integral part of him. He loved playing it, and most of the people he played with, but he found the life of a touring concert pianist less and less to his taste. The need to play to order, the endless fatuity of critics, the political backbiting in orchestras, petty jealousies between conductors, the ceaseless round of airport lounges and identical hotel rooms, all conspired to weigh leaden on his soul. He spoke quietly and purposefully, his voice devoid of wingeing self-pity or reproach, and Ann was reminded of Peter as she sat and listened to his quiet analysis of his inner distress.

"Somewhere, gran, somehow, I'm on the wrong track. What I'm doing is not what I want to do. Something's awry and I can't spot it. I don't think I'm just tired, and I don't think I'm being naive or petulant, but something's wrong. What do you think?"

Ann looked at him for some time. "I don't know Stephen," she said eventually. "But I'd trust my own judgement if I were you. I've heard more joy in your scales at 5.30 in the morning when you were little, than I heard in what you just played. It would be a tragedy if your will to make music was destroyed by the constraints of being a professional pianist."

She smiled. "I think maybe there's too much family in you. A streak of impatience. You like to do things your way, because not only is it right, it's the best. And you won't suffer fools gladly. Your father's the same and so was your grandfather. And there are many fools out there. Am I right?"

"It's an interesting thought," said Stephen noncommittally.

"Good, then think about it a little," said Ann. "See what conclusions you reach."

In the end, Stephen decided to take a year off. A year away from the concert circuit to recharge himself or reassess himself, he knew not what, but certainly to await conclusions. He would follow his fancy, play what he felt like, when he felt like it. John listened to his mother and then to Stephen, and gave him his head.

"Don't worry about the money, Stephen. That's one burden we've never had to carry."

A few weeks into his temporary retirement, however, saw Stephen prowling round the house at a loss for something to do.

"Get him out from under my feet, John," came the instruction from Freddy as they sat down to dinner one evening. "I refuse to run this house as a refuge for bewildered musicians."

Stephen's mouth dropped open and Phillip burst out laughing.

"What have I done?" protested Stephen.

"Where would you like me to begin, Stephen?" said Freddy. "I married one caged lion." She waved a spoon airily towards John. "But I'd hoped to breed something a little more civilized. Now I've got you wandering about the house like something out of Edgar Allan Poe. And you can be quiet, Phillip, you're not much better. I'm sure you could both do a lot more to help your father if you tried."

John raised a hand to stop the banter before it became acrimonious.

"You're too soft, John," continued Freddy, ignoring him. She flicked a thumb at Phillip. "This one could do more," and then at Stephen. "And give this one something to do while he's sorting himself out."

Both her sons seemed inclined to dispute, but she shushed them sharply, rapping her spoon on a plate. "Eat your meals this instant."

Later in the evening, John had a long talk with Stephen, as a result of which the young man took the first steps into the business, following the trail of his older brother. To John's considerable surprise he took to it with enthusiasm. Hugh just nodded. Whether Freddy's half humorous remarks had hit a nerve in Phillip, or whether the thought of his brother close behind alarmed him, or he had simply missed the unconscious support of his sibling, Phillip's attitude changed from that time and he began to take a much more serious and realistic interest in the business and its many facets, much to John's relief.

At the same time, John was reminded of the basic fragility of the business. Would Phillip and Stephen always be able to work together as joint heads of the enterprise? Or would they quarrel and initiate some horrific split? And what if they married and had children? He had been lucky in his wife and children, as far as he knew, but would they be? The succession could become an appalling problem. Two brothers might manage it together, but three or four? He could not shrug this problem off, but he relegated it to a quiet place in his mind, to be reconsidered from time to time.

Meanwhile, the Renviss crossing continued its slow but relentless progress out into the Straits. Gwilier spent a great deal of time on site, watching the massive caissons being made and floated out and sunk to form the innumerable supports to the huge structure, barges and tugs struggling in the swirling water to maintain the positions dictated by laser guidance beacons.

"Why so accurate, Ralph?" he asked. "Surely it's not that important."

Lowson agreed. "Not with the caissons true, but it doesn't take much more effort to put them in right than to put them in wrong, and some of the decking work has to be very accurate. We learned a long time ago, Dick, or rather other contractors before us did, that these are inhospitable countries for foreigners who make mistakes. I set the standard, a professional standard. Everything's got to be spot on. It gets everyone in the right frame of mind. And it can save a lot of time later on. You watch."

Gwilier did watch. He was good at watching, and he missed very little, his large frame becoming familiar throughout the whole site, and his increasingly critical eye becoming a useful extra contribution to Lowson's already stringent quality control regime.

He remembered Lowson's comments later when he saw great steel beams and plates being lifted into position and bolted as if they were part of a child's construction kit. He remarked on the precision of the workmanship to a foreman. The man patted the massive beam he had indicated, then looked up at the crane supporting it, towering high into the sky, and then down into the foaming turbulence below.

"With one of these swinging in the breeze," he said. "And all that down there, this is neither the time nor the place to be messing about reaming out holes or drilling new ones just because some prat in his cosy workshop hasn't done his job properly."

Gwilier said he thought the comment was fair.

"In fact," continued the man, by way of amplification. "If I have to ream out any holes, then I'll personally ream out the arse of the said prat with the same drill."

Gwilier nodded but thought better of making any further observations. These people had their own man-management systems.

Internationally, the storm rumbled on. Publicly, at the UN and in the parliaments of almost every country on the globe, and privately in the various intelligence agencies of the same countries. At the calm eye of the storm were one or two statesmen and officials who accepted that the operation was being superlatively organized. There was a fair amount of accusation and counter-accusation, angry sabre rattling and indignant denial, but the reality was that not a vestige of a clue could be found that linked anyone definitely with the scheme.

It was obvious that the finance for the scheme was being arranged through the coarser meshes of the international banking network, but any attempt to deal with them trod on far too many toes, and provoked as many responses as there were interested parties. John found that he could rely almost totally on international inertia and cupidity to protect that flank.

John yawned conspicuously every time the matter appeared on the TV, went for long damp walks, held his wife a lot, read books, listened to music, and generally entered a quiet and peaceful phase of his life. On very quiet nights he would go into the garden or out into the fields, and occasionally he would hear the wolves howling in the distance.

# Chapter 40

The Northern Hemisphere suffered three vicious winters, crackling under ice and snow in places and at times that had not felt ice and snow in known history. White peaks were to be seen all year in Scotland and Wales. The sea froze and coastal dwellers normally immune to the exigencies of a snow-covered landscape had to learn what their inland cousins had been contending with for years, while those same cousins sat still and muffled under an appalling white blanket. Animals and birds died, people died, buildings collapsed under unprecedented loads, and the world seemed to be holding its frosted breath.

The British found an old, long-dormant spirit of camaraderie in the face of this common adversity, and restocked their racial memory for subsequent nostalgia. Energy conservation preserved most from the excesses of the climate, and self-help groups formed to look after the elderly and the sick, to feed animals and to clear roads and paths. The sledge and the skate became commonplace, and one or two enterprising towns held fairs on their frozen rivers.

In the meagre summers that separated these winters, emergency agricultural plans turned all fertile areas into food growing land and did much to move forward John Newman's plans for the country's total self-sufficiency in food.

"There's even snow on t'Innged," said Gwilier, his voice distant over the telephone. "And they say the great lake at its foot is frozen over. I can believe it. We're getting occasional small ice floes drifting down the Straits. It's an incredible sight."

John expressed his surprise. "Are the Straits any quieter with the colder weather upstream?" he asked.

"No," came the reply. "Not so that you'd notice. We lost two men yesterday working without a guard rail. They never stood a chance in the current."

John drummed his fingers on the desk and could not keep the concern from his voice.

"You keep your eye on Phillip, Dick. I sent him out there to get a bit of experience, not to end up as an accident statistic."

"Don't worry, Mr Newman," said Gwilier. "Phillip can look after himself, eyes in the back of his head. Then I look after him as well —without him knowing, of course. In any case, Ralph takes special care of his key staff and guests. It's the locals who get the rough end of the stick."

"Yes, I know. I didn't mean to come across as the anxious father."

The project was half finished. Its massive bulk of roads, railways and buildings thrust out from Tier r'Vern and culminated in midstream with the Great Father's huge arch bridge, a soaring tribute to its designers and builders, and a memorial to the hundred or so workers that had died during its construction.

"Did you design this for Iceberg impact," said Gwilier ironically to Lowson as they watched an ice floe bounce from caisson to caisson on its way downstream. Lowson shook his head and smiled.

"No, Dick," he said. "You've got me there. I must admit negligence. What a sight. It's as incongruous as a sandstorm in Alaska."

"Will they actually do any damage?" asked Gwilier more seriously.

"No. A little impact damage maybe, at worst, but that's all, nothing of any consequence."

"You can feel the vibration when they hit," said Gwilier. Lowson looked at him and then stamped his foot on the metal deck.

"Yes," he said. "But it's no worse than that is it?" Gwilier felt the vibrations generated by the blow and grudgingly admitted that he supposed not. Lowson smiled and took him by the arm.

"Sorry, Dick," he said. "That's an old professional's trick for dealing with distraught householders who think our machines are shaking their homes to pieces. Don't worry about the ice. This lot's designed to take full traffic, which is considerable, plus a fair-sized earthquake before anything starts to pop. A few outsize ice lollies won't shift it."

They walked along the deck a little way.

"Don't worry about the vibration either," continued Lowson. "Your body's very sensitive to vibration. Believe me, you'll be out of a vibrating building in mortal terror long before it reaches the stage of being structurally damaged. Out and running."

"I'll take your word for it, Ralph," said Gwilier, leaning on the guard rail and peering across the Straits to the distant snow covered peak of t'Innged.

He changed the subject. "That's really quite an eerie sight don't you think?" he said. "You know what the locals are saying about it?"

Lowson looked at him askance. "They don't talk when I'm around," he said.

"That's true," said Gwilier. "I'd forgotten you were the official establishment, as well as not being here officially. Well, they say that t'Innged's hair has gone white because he is growing old, and soon he will rise up and destroy the world as prophesied."

Lowson nodded. "That's the advantage of local knowledge, Dick. Good weather reports. I wonder if he'll be immune to ground to air missiles?" he said, looking at the ports along the side of the deck.

Gwilier laughed. "Yes," he said. "I think if the old giants had known what we were going to turn into, they'd have made a bigger effort to get rid of us when they had the chance. Jack the Giant Killer equipped with heat seeking and laser guided missiles doesn't seem right somehow."

A car horn and a cry interrupted their conversation. Turning round, Gwilier saw Phillip Newman getting out of a battered site Landover. With him was another young man about the same height but with a willowy build. He had narrow eyes, made more so by being screwed up in the bright sunlight, but the long face indisputably reminiscent of Ralph Lowson.

"Oran," shouted Lowson, running forward to meet the two men. He embraced his son affectionately. "I didn't expect you so soon."

"Well, it's not exactly scheduled airlines you've got here is it?" said Oran Fiddes, in a soft, rather sibilant voice. "I arrived early, but I'm more jet-lagged by Phillip's driving than by the flight."

Phillip laughed. "Well, I knew your father was looking forward to seeing you so I thought you wouldn't mind the risk. I can assure you I'm infinitely superior to some stone-faced chauffer from the Angel barracks. They always drive as if the Good Lord was keeping them on the road."

"That's true," said Lowson. "Thank you, Phillip, that was very kind of you."

He introduced his son to Gwilier and then excused himself and wandered off with his arm around his son's shoulders, talking excitedly.

Oran Fiddes was only a little older than Phillip but he was already an experienced and capable engineer. His father had brought him to site to begin teaching him about what he called the more unconventional aspects of the construction business, and it looked as if lessons had begun immediately.

Gwilier leaned back on the guard rail and looked at Phillip.

"That seems to be your good deed for the day, Phillip. I didn't expect you until tomorrow. Have you fixed him up at the camp?"

Phillip nodded. "Yes, in his dad's suite for the time being."

"What did you make of him?" continued Gwilier.

"I don't know really," said Phillip. "I've met him briefly once or twice before. He's friendly enough. Quite the raconteur, like his father, a real charming yarn spinner. Why do you ask?"

Gwilier shrugged and turned round to look over the Straits towards t'Innged. "No special reason," he said, but the slender young man disturbed him in some way, especially when he saw him with his father. *You're getting old,* he thought, *like t'Innged, a giant frightened by the little people.*

In the bleak heart of the third and most terrible winter, John Newman called Hugh, Minna and Gwilier together for a long discussion.

"In my opinion we're ready for our last move," he said. "Dick, I'm bringing you right in on this now, because you've earned it, and I think you're ready for it."

*And the risk of your knowing doesn't compare with the risk of what you might do by accident if you didn't know,* he thought.

Then, to the group, "Rules as usual, folks. I'll lay out the case. You'll act as Devil's Advocates and blast it to smithereens."

Minna smiled and cracked her fingers.

Peter's scheme had been quite simple. The business had to be reduced in size. It had grown predominantly from the weak, fearful and envious side of human nature, implementing its will through violence and terror and corruption. Only over the last few generations had the increasing prosperity of the world and its own success forced it into more humane and civilized endeavours. But its potential for evil was still too great and it had to be reduced before that potential asserted itself, as inevitably it would as the quality of its leadership diminished, as inevitably *it* would. The drugs trade had helped expand and consolidate the business, and its timely removal, bloody though it had been, had directed it towards a more helpful future. But it had not been enough. A further purging was required, but no single remaining aspect of the business carried the same concentration of undesirable elements, so Peter and John had reluctantly been obliged to embark on a long, slow, piecemeal pruning.

In his retirement, Peter had seen the basic futility of this more clearly than when he had been directly involved in it. He saw his son pushing through his life with growing weariness, against a mounting pressure which would overcome him in the end and almost certainly overwhelm everyone else. It came to him that if no single feature existed in the business which was suitable for excision, then one must be created into which all the unwanted elements of the business could be channelled, and then the whole jettisoned.

Once he had clarified his thoughts into the form of a problem, he considered the matter of looking for a solution to be routine, although possibly arduous. And while John came to know that he was far better equipped to run the business than his father, he would admit that he would probably never have such an insight as drew Peter to the concept of the Renviss crossing. It was like Hereward's last blow, epic and fit for legend.

The discussion was nearly finished. It had been long and thorough, and John was summing up, enumerating points on his fingers.

"Everyone's in. Right over their heads."

When the balloon went up, organizations and individuals all over the world would be exposed, bankrupted, discredited, jailed, and one way and another removed from the business.

"We're clear."

Minna's computer skills had been used to tangle the labyrinth of the financial dealings beyond any possibility of unravelling. Any line of enquiry would eventually turn back on itself. Nothing could be traced back to the business. For anyone who got that far, the labyrinth had a false centre which would leave the impression that Tier r'Vern and Tier d'Ynide had initiated the scheme and approached the many disparate groups directly. If Haran or the Great Father survived the consequences of the exposure and the abandonment of the project, they would be in no position to contradict this impression, other than to make vague references to a trio of people they had seen only once, many years ago. Their words were unlikely to be given any credence, but contingency plans were available for their assassination by dissidents if necessary.

"Lowson's clear."

His secret visits to the site could be presented as attempted negotiations for his men and, at worst, he could plead that he was obliged to help organize site work for the same reason. He could publicly regret the Faustian bargain he had made with Tier r'Vern and Tier d'Ynide in his younger days that had led him to such captivity. Lowson's men knew nothing of the true nature of the scheme. All presumed it was simply some massive money-making scheme by an employer who generally looked after them very well. They could all claim they were obeying orders for fear of their lives, and none were likely to jeopardize their bonus payments and pensions by conjecturing otherwise. It would also be explained, discreetly, that their continued co-operation could be achieved in other ways if necessary.

Lowson would be the most resentful victim, not without justification, but he would be very well looked after, and he would be unlikely to attempt to expose John as that would destroy both himself and his company, and in the absence of proof would yield nothing. However, he was still the weakest link, and Minna had a special watching brief on him so that he could be dealt with summarily if he became too restive.

"The good guys are ready."

This had been the hardest part—one of the main reasons why the project had continued for so long. All Peter's and John's experience told them that it was pointless to arbitrarily remove unwanted personnel. Others of a similar calibre invariably moved into the vacated space. So great pains had been taken to ensure that for each space that would be made, a more benign organization or individual could move in. It was far from being clear cut, but the group agreed it was as good as they were likely to get, and that while the turbulence and ripples flowing from the coup could not really be calculated, there would be the major nett benefit they needed.

"Well Dick?" John turned and faced Gwilier.

The older man looked up at the ceiling for a while then spoke quietly. "Joey once told me to give you everything I've got. He said you'd be a match for your father and your grandfather and that I'd never regret it. Well," He slapped his knees softly. "You are, and I haven't. I never thought I'd say this, but as I've grown older I've come to see parts of the business in a different light. Especially since being really involved over there. They're foul places, out of control. And the business has places just as foul in it, places that could easily get out of control."

He stood up and extended his hand. "I'm with you through to the end. There's enough darkness in the world without us creating more."

John stood up and took the offered hand in both of his. Minna leaned back in her chair.

"That's that then," said John briskly. "Minna, Hugh, start the wheels in motion so that the good guys will be in the right places at the right times. We'll blow the whistle as soon as I can get Phillip and Dick out there."

Phillip was to play the chief part in the next act of the drama. At his father's instructions he had already established contact and arranged a meeting with a journalist who was one of the group that hovered more or less continuously around the border of Tier r'Vern. Ostensibly Phillip was part of a small dissident group living in the mountains near the border, one which had infiltrated the work force on the crossing and was committing small acts of sabotage. At this meeting, Phillip would arrive late, and in haste, looking battered and unrecognizable and would hand over a similarly battered computer print-out. This would contain full details of all the expendable parties involved in the scheme, and the extent of their involvement. A brief tale of heroism and sacrifice by members of the group would be gasped out and then Phillip would disappear into the rocks. Gwilier would accompany Phillip across country to the desolate meeting point, and depending on circumstances would put a few rifle shots over the reporter's head, as from a pursuing patrol, to further emphasize the value of his acquisition.

"I can't tell you what's in this, Phil," said John, handing him a waterproof wallet. "But it's very important, to say the least, as you may have gathered. Keep it on you all the time, and destroy it if anything goes wrong. Give the envelope inside to the reporter, say your piece, and then get the hell out of there quickly. Don't forget, ask him for two clear days before he publishes, as your group will be in danger. That should guarantee you at least one day, and you'll be well clear by then."

He turned to Gwilier. "You know what you've got to do, Dick?" Gwilier nodded. "Best of luck then. The operation's already started. Send me the signal as soon as you've completed your part successfully and are clear."

As the two left the room, John pressed a switch on his desk and extinguished all the lights. Then he moved over to the high winged armchair and sat for a long time gazing into the glowing embers of the dying coal fire.

# Chapter 41

Gwilier checked his pack for the last time and threw it on the bed, then he paced once again across the room and stood staring out of the window. They were in the residential quarters of the site camp, ostensibly for a single day's hunting the next day. The great arch of the bridge was clearly visible in the Straits.

"What's the matter Dick?" asked Phillip. "You're wearing the carpet out. It's not dangerous what we're doing, is it?"

Gwilier half turned towards him. "No," he said offhandedly. "Nothing we can't handle. The travelling will be the hard bit. I was just having a last look at the bridge."

Then he swore inwardly.

"A last look," said Phillip, catching the slip immediately. "What the hell's in that envelope, Dick?"

Gwilier looked at him. "If your father had wanted you to know, he'd have told you. If he hasn't told you, then it's not in your interests to know. You know that."

"Doesn't he trust me?" asked Phillip.

Gwilier smiled. "Completely. You're the only person he'd trust to do this job. But the contents of the envelope aren't relevant. All you're to be concerned with is the efficient execution of the job in hand."

"Do as you're told and shut up, eh?"

Gwilier laughed in spite of himself. "I don't think your father would have phrased it quite like that, but yes. Trust him. You'll not be doing anything you'd be ashamed of, and I guarantee you'll know what was in the letter within the month."

"But we'll not be coming back to Tier r'Vern will we?"

Gwilier shook his head, but did not reply. Phillip watched him as he looked again to the window.

"Come on, Dick," he said, standing up. "Let's go down and have a last prowl round the site. Walk up the arch and say cheerio properly before our 'hunting trip' tomorrow. Oops..."

The cry was at the rumbling tremor which passed through the building. Phillip sat down abruptly and Gwilier steadied himself against the window frame.

"Earth tremor," he said before Phillip could speak. "Bigger than usual, I'd judge—could be a bad one wherever the epicentre is. Fortunately, everything round here's designed for fairly severe earthquakes so we're safe enough if there are any aftershocks. You OK?"

Phillip was wide eyed and shaking his head. "Yes I think so," he said. "Just a little dizzy, disorientated. Just give me a moment."

He took a few deep breaths. "Wow," he said softly.

A few minutes later they were driving down the winding road which led to the crossing. The sky was clouding over and the arch of the bridge loomed ahead of them, looking black and sinister against the darkening sky.

"Of all the days we pick to look at the view, it has to be cloudy," said Gwilier regretfully. "I suppose the moon will be blue tonight."

"Come on, Dick," said Phillip. "Cheer up. In this light it'll probably be very dramatic."

It was possible to walk inside any of the arches, but the experience tended to be claustrophobic and was not helped by the presence of missiles at regular intervals along the journey. They opted to walk along the top of one of the outer arches. A little way up, Gwilier turned and noted two site workers entering the same arch. It was the two who had been travelling behind them on the road from the site camp.

The journey to the top was made at a steady pace, and in silence, but both men conceded that they were out of breath when they arrived.

"I won't tell your father how out of condition you are, if you don't tell him how out of condition I am," said Gwilier, laughing.

"It's a deal," puffed Phillip. "Jesus, that's one hell of a hill."

Gwilier stood very straight and gazed around. "You were right Phil," he said. "Look at that view."

The Straits below were grey, dark and ominous, reflecting the lowering sky above. In the distance the coastal ranges stood out like black teeth. Even the snow on the higher peaks looked black. Very faintly in the far distance, a light red glow on the horizon indicated the setting sun was hitting higher, whiter peaks. Gwilier stepped proprietorially into a partly completed look-out post. It was one of his own small contributions to the scheme.

"You've all this fancy radar and detection equipment here," he said. "But put a man up there, an old-fashioned look-out, you can see nine countries. He'll see what your radar will miss."

And his idea had been accepted.

His foot caught on something and there was a clatter and an oath.

"What's the matter?" said Phillip.

"Nothing," said Gwilier. "Some painter's left his stuff here, all over the floor. Still, I don't imagine he was expecting visitors tonight."

He was just about to bend down and right the scattered paint tins when another sound rang out. It was one of the hatches to the interior of the arch clanging open. Two figures rose wraith-like in the gloom and stood for a moment with their back to Gwilier and Phillip.

They were dressed in the site uniform of Lowson's men. Gwilier was about to speak when they both turned round, bringing to bear two twelve bore pump action riot guns. Gwilier froze, not so much intimidated by the maws of the two guns as stunned by the faces of the assailants.

"Ralph. Oran. What the hell are you doing?" he shouted.

"Don't move, Dick," said Lowson. "Or you, Phil. Not a muscle. I've seen the way you people can move. That's why we've got these."

He flicked the muzzle of his gun upwards. He was out of breath and obviously agitated.

Gwilier winced involuntarily at the gesture.

"I'm not moving, Ralph," he said, managing to keep his voice steady. "Neither of us are. Let's all stay calm and you tell us what's going on."

Years of defensive living had rapidly dispelled his immediate sense of shock and disbelief, but he was trying to push from his mind the endless ramifications of what he was seeing. Fortunately for now, he noted, Phillip was still immobile, paralysed by Fiddes' unblinking narrow eyes.

"What's going on, Dick, is a change in the power structure, and you, or to be exact, Phillip, is the key."

Lowson's urbane and charming manner had disappeared entirely, his face had become vicious and frightened. He looked dangerous.

*Only just in control,* thought Gwilier, *be careful.*

"What do you mean, power structure?"

"The power structure in the new joint state, Dick. A place in the sun for me and for Oran."

Gwilier shook his head as if he could not hear properly.

"Ralph, I don't understand," he said, vainly searching for some opening which would give him a chance to move and use his own gun. "When this job's finished, you'll have a massive stake in the joint state, you know that. And in all the firms that move in."

Lowson sneered. "No Dick. This job isn't going to finish. I don't know what's going to happen, but something will, and I'll probably be expendable."

Gwilier's heart lurched. It was inconceivable that the plan had escaped Minna's security... but...

He seemed to feel the bridge falling away from under him.

"What on earth makes you think that, Ralph. It's crazy. Why shouldn't it finish?"

Lowson thrust the riot gun out at arm's length and Gwilier flinched again.

"I've known John Newman too long. He's totally incapable of allowing these two countries to unite—they'd create havoc in the world and he knows it. He couldn't do it."

"But..."

"But nothing, Dick. It's only come to me recently, but it's as clear as crystal now. He's up to something. I don't know what it is, but I'm not in on it, nor Oran."

He glanced briefly at his son. "We're just cannon fodder."

His voice rose and Gwilier quailed inwardly at the intensity of his unhinged passion. That was it. No-one had told him anything, he realized. They did not need to. He had listened to his instinct, the instinct that had made him what he was, his feral animal instinct. And it was right. John had let him get too close and he had smelt the truth even though he did not know what it was. Now, years of festering resentment had burst in the man like a great boil.

Oddly, this reassured Gwilier. It was just a miscalculation, and it was his job to attend to such matters when they arose.

"Ralph, you're wrong," he said. "Newman's absolutely straight. God almighty, he and his father both bailed you out. Helped you become what you are."

*True enough,* he thought ironically. *We fed a psychotic on unbridled fantasy and here he is.*

Lowson pointed the gun at Gwilier's face again, like an admonishing finger.

"I'm not wrong," he said. "Something's going to happen, and soon. I can feel it."

His voice rose again. "And I'm not debating it up on this bloody bridge. This isn't how we planned it, but you're away again tomorrow for God knows how long, so we've had to take the chance you've given us. Newman doesn't have a monopoly on flexible planning. Start moving. Down the other side."

He was breathing heavily again. "My boat's there, then over to Tier d'Ynide."

Gwilier's restraint almost broke. "You blistering lunatic, Ralph. You don't know what you're doing."

"I know exactly, Dick, exactly. When Phillip is fitted with one of Haran's electrodes, John Newman will do anything I tell him. I'll call all the shots."

Gwilier's eyes opened in horror. "You're insane," he said, his throat dry. "Make Phillip into one of those automated zombies? Have you no idea what kind of a man you're dealing with?"

"Don't worry, Dick. I've seen him operate. He won't get within arm's reach of me or any of mine."

Gwilier put his clenched fists to his forehead in frustration.

"Ralph," he said quietly. "You're my age, for God's sake. What can you possibly get that you don't already have. This is an incredible folly. Newman has resources you can't begin to imagine. Nowhere in the world will be safe for you."

He paused as a thought struck him. "Great God," he said, real concern in his voice. "Minna will come after you, man."

Lowson faltered at the mention of Minna. Then he tightened his grip on the gun.

"While we have his son, Newman will do as he's told and so will Minna Adrin. Now move."

He gestured with the gun. Phillip turned round slowly. Gwilier noticed that the shock had gone from his face, and he too was just waiting. He stepped gingerly out of the look-out post and flicked a brief hand signal to Phillip.

Stay calm and wait.

It was a long journey down the arch and across to Tier d'Ynide. Somewhere along the line, Lowson would slip up and Gwilier would be able to end the matter. All he had to do was wait and watch. Frustration boiled in him such as he had not known in years. It was incredible, a man of Lowson's ability, thinking he could pull off a ludicrous stunt like this, a street hijack. It was pathetic, what a waste. The man must be cracked right through.

He cut his rambling thoughts short.

He hasn't killed me—which would have been a wiser thing to do. Just wait—be patient.

But patience was not necessary. Larger forces than he or Lowson or John Newman were at work. He suddenly felt giddy. The edge of the look-out post moved towards him and he caught it to recover his balance. He tried to focus on the coastline, but everything seemed to be moving. There was a cry and a clatter. Looking round he saw Phillip hanging on to the guard rail while Lowson was on his knees, clutching at an upstand for balance. He was still holding his gun, but Fiddes had dropped his and was struggling to recover it as it jiggled along the deck and went over the edge.

It was another earth tremor.

Then the air was filled with a terrible rumbling. A rumbling which seemed to shake loose the marrow of his bones. The bridge bucked, a dreadful jarring jolt that lifted all four into the air. The wind went out of Gwilier as he landed and he felt vomit form in his mouth as the bridge swayed again, and nothing he touched or looked at seemed to be fixed or solid.

"Hang on, Phillip," he shouted needlessly.

Lowson was still clinging onto his gun. His face was green with terror, but he was still too dangerous to tackle recklessly. The bridge surged again and Gwilier staggered across the look-out post. Lashing out to get his balance, his great fist smashed into the alarm button that was intended to announce the sighting of an attack. Immediately, the immense roar of the warning horns on the bridge and in the camp filled the Straits and supplemented the rumbling of the earthquake, their sound oscillating with the doppler effect of the moving bridge. They had been another of Gwilier's contributions and they sounded a dirge for him now.

He did not hear the shot that hit him. He thought the bridge had bucked again when a blow knocked him to the floor. Only when he looked down and saw red exit holes on his chest did he realise he was dying. He turned and saw Lowson, his face now livid, struggling to use the pump on the gun with one hand, while clinging onto a rail with the other. He felt very calm and peaceful, his balance seemed to have come back and Phillip seemed to be shouting something, but he could not hear what it was. Then Phillip was wrestling with Lowson and Gwilier saw Fiddes struggling across the rippling deck towards them. Gwilier knew what his obligations were.

Give him everything you've got.

Mr Newman would shake his head ruefully and admit the miscalculation and thank him for dealing with it, he always did. He walked unsteadily across to the fighting men and, casually hurling Fiddes to one side, he lifted Phillip gently off Lowson, and took Lowson up in a mighty bear hug. He felt an impact on his leg and knew that Lowson's pinned arm had fired the gun again, destroying his left leg. Holding Lowson in his terrible embrace, he swayed gently with the bridge, his eyes on the horizon. Suddenly a great red gash like a huge sword cut appeared in the clouds, and the setting sun streamed through.

"Look, Ralph," he whispered softly, as if to a child. "Sunset."

But Lowson was past all hearing and hung limp like a broken toy in his grip. Gwilier sank to his knees and slowly fell face down over Lowson's body. The swaying of the bridge eased a little and the rumbling seemed to subside, but Gwilier's horns thundered on.

Phillip scrambled to his feet and lurched across the deck to the look-out post. His mind was awash with terrible fears, but he knew he had to deal with Fiddes for the havoc that had been wrought on his friend, and then he had to do his father's will, alone now. Fiddes was grovelling around on the floor of the look-out post and Phillip was about to take hold of him when another jolt pushed him upright, his eyes staring at the horizon.

It had changed.

In spite of himself he cried out in amazement to his one-time friend.

"Oran. It's gone. It's gone. The mountain. T'Innged. It's gone."

Then, in the distant upper reaches of the Straits a strange boiling appeared, red in the setting sun. He did not know what it was, but he felt a chill. It was a great ice-laden wave, ripping its way down the Straits at the behest of the old god t'Innged. Great ice blocks and huge boulders grinding and screaming like malevolent teeth carried in millions of tons of displaced water. The Great Father's covenant would be as matchwood to it.

But Phillip did not see this. Fiddes blinded him. Struggling on the floor while his former captive stood paralysed, gazing into the distance, Fiddes hand let on an open paint tin. He clambered to his feet and dashed the contents into Phillip's eyes. Phillip let out a terrible cry and lurched forward seizing Oran in his agony. They tumbled to the floor, Fiddes trying to extricate himself, Phillip seeking some way to end his pain. His flailing hand connected with a hard shaft and he seized it and swung a mighty blow at his dark enshrouded tormentor. Then he was free. The hammer had struck Fiddes on the temple and killed him instantly.

Sobbing in pain and terror, Phillip struggled to his feet, still clutching the hammer. The bridge bucked again as a fresh tremor struck. He staggered back nine paces and fell over the edge of the bridge into the abyss below, as t'Innged's icy teeth struck the bridge. To the roar of ice and earth and Gwilier's booming music was added the shriek of steel and concrete torn past the limits of their strength as caissons were torn up from the tortured rock below, and the great arches buckled, twisted and floundered into the red-lit foaming torrent.

The next day, crowds gathered on the beaches downstream to watch the remains of the crossing float by with an escorting flotilla of icebergs. Some of these washed up on the shore, a source of great excitement to the local children, but unhappier things came ashore also, for the wave had torn up many coastal villages and most of the site camp.

Among the crowd were reporters and cameramen preserving the horror for posterity.

*Greater love hath no man than that he lay down his life for a thirty second slot on the television news,* thought one of the reporters bitterly as he watched.

He was a bulky red-haired man and his face was creased with distress and conflict as he waded into the sea and pulled yet another body ashore. It was a blond-haired young man, a European. Gently the reporter brushed aside some seaweed lying across the man's eyes, and his already sad face trembled as he gazed at that of the dead man. The features had hardly been damaged by his travail and struck chord's in the reporter's memory.

"Oh no," he whispered. "Oh, God, no, no."

He reached into the dead man's pockets in search of some form of identity that he did not need.

He retrieved a waterproof plastic wallet.

# Chapter 42

Freddy called to say she was stranded at her friend's house. John told her not to make any attempt to try and come home as a blizzard was blowing up.

"It looks as if it'll be a bad one," he said. "Give me a ring tomorrow. Lots of love."

He was actually glad of the opportunity to be alone. There was no reason why anything should go wrong, but he could not help feeling a little fretful, just waiting.

Hugh and Minna were across the world fulfilling their tasks and Phillip and Dick would do theirs faithfully, he knew. The next few months were going to be very interesting, but whatever happened, life for himself and his two sons was going to be much more hopeful and free.

The phone startled him out of his reverie.

"John?" said a strange voice.

"Yes," he replied hesitantly.

"John Newman?"

"Yes. Who is this?"

"It's Thomas, John. Thomas. Thomas-not-Tom."

John's face lit up and a bright corridor opened across his life to more innocent days.

"Good God, Thomas. I haven't seen you in years. How are you? And the family?"

Then, realizing what he was doing, he sobered.

"How did you get this number, Thomas?"

"John... I'm so sorry..."

\* \* \*

John laid the phone down gently.

The silence of the room seemed to close in around him, and deep inside he felt the coiled threads that were his hold on life begin to snap, one by one. The bright corridor that Thomas' name opened had closed as quickly, and a great burden of years and responsibility weighed down on him.

He sat for a long time without moving or thinking. Then slowly he began to function again.

Phillip dead, Dick presumably dead.

All the people on the site gone.

The bridge as well.

The Straits would be as if nothing had ever happened. But his plan survived. He rubbed his dead eye. Not quite the plan he had intended. His print-out was public property and it would do its job just the same. But it was inexorably linked to him through his own son. The blazing gaze of the world would fall on him, not on some vague confused multifaceted conspiracy. The examination of him would expose the business no matter what he did, and the consequences of that would be worse by far than if the whole thing had been left alone.

Occam's razor scythed away John's alternatives in ruthless seconds.

He went to the computer, tapped in a coded message and sent it to Hugh and Minna: "Imperative the plan must, repeat must, proceed as arranged. Special instructions on your return."

Then he typed his confession for public view, placing himself conclusively at the centre of the vague conspiracy, far far away from his life as a respected banker. He gave his reasons as base power and greed. His friends, family and business colleagues would be seen to be blameless and deserving of sympathy, and the world's vengeance would spend itself on the other conspirators as intended.

Then he typed a message to Hugh and Minna.

"I love you both, my friends and messengers. Have no regrets. The plan was good—is good. One of the ripples has drowned me by accident, it could not be helped. Stephen will be the head of the business now. He can handle it. Show him his cage—but gently. It is bigger than mine. Instruct him well and cherish him as you have cherished me. Tell my mother and Freddy and Stephen I am sorry for the pain I must cause them, but it is to avoid a far greater pain

362

for a far greater number. Tell them to ignore the abuse that has to fall on my head—who steals my good name steals trash. I shall be beyond all hurt. Ask their forgiveness for me and thank them for the endless light they have poured into my life."

Then, as an afterthought. "Minna, I leave you the dilemma of your terrible computer. Perhaps it will be Stephen's destiny to resolve it."

Outside, the blizzard was screaming—the very spirit of this third and most terrible winter. He left the house lights on, illuminating the swirling snow and, closing the door gently, he walked out into the storm.

He walked endlessly, feeling the wind snatching away his body's heat. He had done everything he could, but something was missing. He was only a little way from his death, but real peace eluded him.

As his faculties faded, the wind turned into the voices of a million demons cackling and jeering at his back, and he wanted to run. Large areas of time disappeared. He found himself lying down, then on all fours, then raging out loud like Lear, until finally he collapsed on his knees in the snow.

"Sit up straight," boomed a voice out of the past.

He obeyed, and tried to say "Hai, sensei." But nothing happened.

Then suddenly the wind was gone, but he could not remember its passing. He was kneeling on a high rock overlooking the river and the valley, with the sea in the distance. It was where he had sat in the sun with his father on the day of his death, and the birth of the Renviss scheme. The moon was dazzlingly bright and everywhere was crystal still and white, unbelievably fragile and beautiful.

There was a vestigial shivering within him, but he could not feel the cold although he could feel it cracking the rocks.

*You will not freeze my soul while I can see sights like this,* he thought, and he watched and watched.

Then a movement caught his eye, and a loping figure approached him slowly, its eyes green in the moonlight. It was a great grey wolf, viewing him cautiously, its ears slightly back and its tail wagging low and hesitantly. It was a majestic animal, but he could see it was battle-scarred and old.

He could not move.

Did not want to move.

There was no fear.

Briefly their eyes met and John was suffused with the spirit of the animal. He felt its tired loneliness. He felt it yield in defeat to a younger wolf. He felt the sadness of living at the edge of the pack, receiving only the offhand companionship of those lower than him, that he had once led. He felt distant memories and scents of a warm mother, and rolling and romping in the sunlit grass before the spirit of his greatness unwound and brought him to the head of his family. But underneath it all was something he could not identify, a resignation, an acceptance.

Then the wolf was gone.

Don't go, his mind cried, stay with me.

He felt it sitting by his side.

He felt its head point upwards

Then it began to howl.

A long vibrant soaring cry that filled his universe from the ground to the sky with its ancient song.

It sang of his life and its beauty and warmth and love, and it sang forgiveness for its horror.

It sang of burdens borne and laid down.

It sang of a greener, kinder world that he had helped to make.

John felt the last warmth leave his body as tears ran down his cheeks from both his eyes.

Tears of grief for his father and the untimely death of his son and for the pain he must leave behind for others.

Then tears of gratitude for the great gift of life and for the solace of the wolf's song.

Then it sang of the flowing of the new into the old and took his spirit high above and released it into the moonlight.

# About the author

Roger Taylor was born in Heywood, Lancashire, England and now lives in the Wirral. He is a chartered civil and structural engineer, a pistol, rifle and shotgun shooter, an instructor/student in a highly personalised form of aikido (heavily influenced by tai chi and systema) and, not least, an enthusiastic and loud but bone-jarringly inaccurate piano player.

Ostensibly fantasy, his major work—the twelve books of the 'Chronicles of Hawklan'—is much more than it seems and has been called 'subtly subversive'. He has also written *Aikido – More Than a Martial Art*, the fantasy novel *The Keep*, and *Travellers* which is science fiction.

# About the author

Roger Taylor was born in Heywood, Lancashire, England and now lives in the Wirral. He is a chartered civil and structural engineer, a pistol, rifle and shotgun shooter, an instructor/student in a highly personalised form of aikido (heavily influenced by tai chi and systema) and, not least, an enthusiastic and loud but bone-jarringly inaccurate piano player.

Ostensibly fantasy, his major work—the twelve books of the 'Chronicles of Hawklan'—is much more than it seems and has been called 'subtly subversive'. He has also written *Aikido – More Than a Martial Art*, the fantasy novel *The Keep*, and *Travellers* which is science fiction.